NUTCRACKER

JOURNEY TO CANDYLAND

TONY BERTAUSKI

Copyright © 2023 by Tony Bertauski

All rights reserved.

No part of this book may be reproduced in any form or by any electronic or mechanical means, including information storage and retrieval systems, without written permission from the author, except for the use of brief quotations in a book review.

For Ben.

1

The building looked like a toy left out in the rain.

It was on the corner. The paint peeling from gray wooden slats. The gray of dead fish. Weeds grew from cracks in the foundation. A stop sign leaned away from it. Even it didn't want to be near it. It was one of those buildings people forgot. Even when they were looking right at it.

Marie stared from the back seat of the car. *This can't be the place. We're lost.* Then again, she'd felt lost for a while now.

Aunt Rinks was in the front seat, scrolling on her phone, chewing on a stick of black licorice like a dog gnawing on a rubber bone. She emerged from a social media black hole and said, "This it, Vern?"

"This is it."

"Why didn't you tell me we were here?" She whacked him on the chest, then snapped a photo through the windshield. Tapping her phone, she muttered while typing, "So... much... potential!" Her phone whooshed it into the social media stratosphere.

She opened the car door and heaved herself out. The foam flip-flops crusted with fake jewels popped on her feet. She pulled her I HEART CRABCAKES T-shirt (a real deal at the gas station; changed into it in the bathroom) over the flesh roll squeezing out of her jean shorts. When she lifted her phone, the shirt crept back up and revealed the tattoo. It used to be the name of an ex-boyfriend, but that was covered with the queen of hearts from a poker card. Only this queen had been left out in the sun too long.

Flip-flops snapping, she went to the front of the building. Sheets of weathered plywood covered what, at one time, were wide storefront windows. She peeked through a knothole.

Uncle Vernon picked at his teeth. He found a small glob that was soft and white. It was wedged into his dirty fingernail. He inspected it. Marie looked away. She didn't want to see what came next.

Aunt Rinks turned her phone on herself, the building behind her, and adjusted her headscarf. She smiled for a selfie; then it was fish lips. Then two fingers and a thumb. She repeated the sequence from another angle, swiped through the photos, and tapped the phone.

Whoosh.

"Vern, come on. Get out here."

Uncle Vernon crawled out from behind the steering wheel. He dropped the keys in his front pocket and scurried around the car. His button-down shirt looked like a thin sheet wrapped around a stick figure, like laundry hung to dry. His ribs would protrude when the wind blew it against him.

"Over there," she said. "From the corner."

He took her phone. He knew what to do. Aunt Rinks with her hand on her hip, knee bent. Aunt Rinks with pinky to the corner of her mouth. Aunt Rinks surprised. Uncle Vernon bored.

"You all right?" Marie asked.

Her little brother, sitting next to her in the back seat, nodded.

His ball cap was pulled down to his eyes. He didn't need to watch the Aunt Rinks Show to know what was going on. Marie took his hand, and he let her. The car smelled like expensive cheese stuffed in a laundry bag. She didn't know what bothered her more, the smell or that she'd gotten used to it.

She cracked the door. The air was humid and crisp. Not cold enough for a sweater. Long sleeves maybe. It was a bit salty, but she knew they weren't near enough to the coast to smell the ocean. Her senses had been corrupted by the odors baked into the car's interior.

A block behind them, Christmas lights were wrapped around palm trees. *OPEN* signs lit store windows. They had passed a coffee shop on the way. There had been mechanical elves in the window, slowly swinging mallets and pulling saws. It felt normal back there.

"That's the building Mom told us about," Marie said. Fritz frowned. He pulled his hand away from her.

Uncle Vernon was trying to open the front door on the building. Aunt Rinks pushed him away, and he watched with his hands on his bony hips. He tried again while she barked at him like a dogsled driver, her hacksaw voice cutting across the street. People down the street were looking.

Their aunt and uncle gave up on the front door and walked around the corner.

Marie and Fritz sat quietly in the cheesemobile. She hoped no one would come down to talk to them before they aired the smell out of their clothes. Still, she was hoping maybe this was the wrong place.

"I thought it would be nicer," Marie said. Fritz nodded.

"Bring the bags!" Aunt Rinks waved her arms like she was landing a plane.

Marie waved back so she would stop. Fritz got out on his side. He pulled his hat over his eyebrows, not because strangers were looking. He wore it like that. The strap on the back was adjusted to the smallest setting. It had been red once, now sun-bleached rose with a briny stain around the band. Aunt Rinks had tried to throw it away once. Marie wouldn't let her.

The hatchback was covered in stickers, most of them faded and curling. *I Stop for Selfies* was above the license plate. That was right below the newest sticker, a clear one with white letters across the window that read *@RINKSRULES*. Uncle Vernon complained he couldn't see out the window, but driver safety took second to likes.

There were three suitcases, a footlocker, and two trash bags full of clothes. And a cooler. Marie's stuff was in a duffel bag. Fritz searched through the pile of stuff. Marie handed his backpack to him. He kept searching, agitated.

"What's wrong?" Marie asked.

He typed something on his phone, showed it to her. She helped him look through the trash bags. The rest of their belongings were in a storage locker a thousand miles away. Not enough room in the car, Aunt Rinks had said. They'd go back for it one day.

Fritz kicked a soda can around the corner. The building was long. The plywood spray-painted with big loopy letters. Fliers were stapled to it, some rotted from the rain. The soda can slammed off the brick foundation each time he kicked it. Marie picked it up and put her arm over his shoulders. He let her.

A chain-link fence enclosed an area behind the building. Branches reached through the rusted wires. The gate was stuck open, the bottom dug in the dirt. A brick sidewalk, lumpy from tree roots, led to concrete steps and Uncle Vernon and Aunt Rinks.

"It's the right key," he insisted. "The lock is rusted. See?"

"Use both hands," Aunt Rinks said.

"And break the key? Just... back up a step. I can smell your breath."

She stood like he'd coughed on her. "No, you can't."

"I need some WD or oil. Something to lube it up."

"Can't you just spit on it?"

He shook his head. Then, on second thought, he yanked it out of the lock and dropped a bubbly glob of saliva on the key, rubbed it around with his finger and tried again. Apparently, spit did not cut through rust.

The windows were normal sized on the back of the building. The windows were fogged with algae. The brick sidewalk led deeper into the trees. Marie stepped closer, saw what looked like a patio and firepit. A couple of chairs overtaken by vines.

"Where's his skateboard?" Marie said.

"What?" Aunt Rinks said.

"Fritz's skateboard. We packed it in the car."

"Darlin', the skateboard didn't make it."

"That's his skateboard. He wanted it here."

"Well, we can't get everythin' we want, can we? And to be honest, he's goin' to get hurt on it and then what, mmm? Break a bone or twist his foot, and I ain't takin' him to the doctor because he wants to roll around. Makes no sense. And it's not like I threw it away, so wipe off that look. Now where's the rest of the bags? Go," she said to Marie and Fritz, shooing them like flies. Then handed a tube to Uncle Vernon. "Try that."

"What am I supposed to do with Chapstick?"

"Squeeze it in there," she said.

"It don't have dry lips, Rinks."

"It don't hurt to try. Always negative."

Marie dropped her duffel bag and helped Fritz take off the backpack. Should've known her aunt was going to do something like that. The skateboard meant more to Fritz than *rolling around*. Nothing Marie could do about it now.

They walked back to the car. She paused at the curb and closed her eyes. Christmas music was coming from somewhere down the street. She imagined a fireplace and cocoa, the smell of an evergreen tree with presents underneath it. A warm feeling around her, like a blanket made of smiles.

Fritz tugged on her sleeve.

Sometimes she lost track of time when she closed her eyes. Time traveling, her therapist had called it. Sometimes that was good. Just don't get lost. *Be here, now.* Marie blew her hair from her eyes. She needed a cut months ago. Now she was in the habit of blowing it out of the way. They grabbed the rest of the bags.

The back door was open when they got back. The Chapstick must've worked. Aunt Rinks was laughing that laugh that cut their uncle at the knees. She was right every now and then. And nobody ever forgot it.

"Come on," Marie said. "We can't stay out here."

Fritz didn't want to go. There was a grim look under the bill of his cap. This didn't feel like Christmas. They pulled the luggage behind them, thumping up the steps.

"Hey, hey, hey." Aunt Rinks pulled the door open, the rusted hinges screaming. "That better not be scratched. Respect other people's property, Fizzy."

"Fritz," Marie said.

"I'm sorry?"

"He doesn't like Fizzy," Marie said, for the thousandth time.

"Murry, darlin'," Aunt Rinks said with a big red-lipstick smile. "You don't get to choose your nickname. That's how it works. Now put that over there and bring the rest." She peeked under Fritz's bill. "Pick it up now, all right?"

She didn't look away until he nodded. They went back down the steps for the remaining suitcases. Marie kicked the footlocker when they got to the car, put a dent in the bottom of it. They carried the rest of the luggage up the steps, put them inside the doorway.

It was dark inside.

Aunt Rinks was using the light on her phone. There was a long table to the left. It was darker to the right, but Marie could see the outline of a couch.

"Why aren't the lights workin'?" Aunt Rinks flipped a switch. "Did you call the power company?"

"I called them," Uncle Vernon said.

"Then why ain't they workin'?"

He growled somewhere in the dark. Something fell on the floor. He let out a curse word and felt his way into another room. Marie and Fritz went back to the car for the trash bags of clothing. Down the street, a group of kids were coming out of a video game store. They huddled around someone's phone. Marie and Fritz stood there and watched. She put a hand on her little brother's shoulder.

"It'll be all right," she said. She said for both of them to hear.

UNCLE VERNON FOUND the circuit panel. Marie liked the dark better.

There was a kitchen table inside the back door. Twenty years of dust was inside a teacup. A small kitchen was to the left of that, a small stove and a small refrigerator that was knocking. To the right, a couch with faded floral patterns, the side of it used as a scratching post.

The floor was covered with dirt. Little clods of dirt.

"Vern? Can you get some of these boards off? We need some sunlight."

"There ain't no windows, Rinks. That's why they got boards."

"We need fresh air, Vern. We're in the South, now. We can put them back up."

"Rinks, can we get settled first?"

"Hey, did you get the Wi-Fi?" she said. "I'm gettin' two bars."

She held her phone up, swung it around. Then took a selfie with pouty lips. Uncle Vernon tripped on something in another room and launched another curse word.

"We're not staying here, are we?" Marie said.

"Your room's over there." She pointed. "Somethin' wrong?"

"Aunt Rinks, this place is…"

"It's what, princess?"

"I didn't think we were sleeping here."

"Do you have money for a hotel room?" She put the phone down and waited for an answer. Marie didn't have any money. She was seventeen. Hadn't worked a job since summer. What money she had was controlled by her aunt.

"Murry? Answer me. Do you have money?"

"My name's not Murry."

"Well, do you have money, whoever you are?"

"No."

"No, what?"

Marie tried not to roll her eyes. "No, Aunt Rinks."

"How about you, Fizzy? Do you have money for a hotel room?"

"Stop it, Aunt Rinks," Marie said.

"He can shake his head."

"We don't have money. Do you really want to sleep here?"

She wiped the corner of her mouth where lipstick was smudged. "You think you're too good? There's a roof overhead. Lights, water. I buy the food. I pay your phones. What else do you want, Murry?"

To not sleep on mouse turds. Marie almost said it.

"Here's what we're goin' to do. You're goin' to take your things in there. I brought a... Vern? Where's the blow-up mattress?"

"It's in the thing," he called.

"Well, once we find it, you fill it up with air." She held up her hand. "Don't ask for a pump. That air in your lungs is free. Once you get that, there's a broom over there to sweep up all this dirt. We're going to make this place nice and tidy before it gets dark." She clicked her tongue and winked. "You bet on it. Now get over here. I want a picture with my children."

Marie cringed and held her tongue. Aunt Rinks was too dumb to know that wasn't dirt on the floor and the table and counters. She squatted between Marie and Fritz for five selfies. She turned her head so the thin scar on her left cheek was hidden.

Whoosh.

THERE WAS A CRACKING SOUND.

A sheet of plywood peeled off the front of the building. Uncle Vernon, his fingers hooked over the top of it, went crashing down with it. He barked like a sea lion, rolling on the sidewalk and holding his ribs.

Marie stood under a flickering fluorescent light—the only one working in the front room of the building—with a broom in her hand. This part had been used for something other than living. There were empty shelves and a small stage in the corner, a place where a local musician might strum an acoustic guitar and sing cover songs. There was a counter with an antique register that still worked when Marie had pecked the keys.

The sunlight coming through the uncapped window lit up a network of cobwebs on the ceiling. A dust storm hovered in the room.

It caked the inside of Marie's nostrils. A moldy taste was in the back of her throat. It wasn't just dust she was eating. She'd swept several piles around the room, and most of it was dried little torpedoes.

"What happened?" Aunt Rinks threw open the door from the living area in the back part of the building. "Did you break somethin'? Vernon!"

She ran down one of the empty aisles—those two-inch foam flip-flops snapping her feet—scattering piles of mouse poop like a spilled bag of rice. She stopped at the big plate of glass Uncle Vernon had exposed, the surface hazy with grime and dirt. She put her hand on it and looked down at the sidewalk.

"I told you there were windows!" She turned around, said to Marie, "I told him." Then came the laugh. She got two rights in one day. "Where's your brother? He should be helpin'."

"He's working on the mattress."

"Fizzy! Come out. I know he ain't deaf. We need this all swept up by tonight. We'll open more windows and get some fresh air in here. Buildings are like people: they need to breathe." She inhaled deeply, then broke into a coughing fit. "Hey—don't break it!"

Uncle Vernon was pulling on the front door, which was frozen in the swollen frame. Mount Vernon had erupted. All it took was uncapped rage and a busted finger to get the door open. A gust of air sent more dust up Marie's nose. She pulled her shirt over her face.

"I told you about that window, didn't I?" Aunt Rinks said. "Now get the other boards down, and this place will shine."

"Look." He held up his finger. The fingernail was already purple.

"You need a Band-Aid?"

"No. But I ain't got the tools to rip all that down right now. Can't we just relax a second, Rinks? We just got here." He put his finger in his mouth. "When's supper?"

"What'd you say?"

"I'm sayin' I ain't ate since breakfast."

"You get those other boards off, and I'll have somethin' for you to eat." She grabbed his hand and kissed the finger. "I'll make somethin' special."

That cheered him up and depressed Marie. She knew exactly what *somethin' special* was. They ate *somethin' special* four times a week since Marie and Fritz had moved in with their aunt and uncle.

"Fizzy!" Aunt Rinks shouted like a dog barking in the middle of the night. "Come up front! Vernon, the faster you get them boards down, the faster I'll cook. It'll be hot and ready and waitin'." She batted long, fake eyelashes. "There's the man of the house. Come on in here, Fizzy. We were just talkin' about you."

Fritz zigzagged his way around the piles Marie had swept into an obstacle course. Hat pulled down, eyes on his shoes. He stopped in a dusty sunbeam. The flickering fluorescent turned his hat different colors.

"Where's your broom, son?" Aunt Rinks said. Marie cringed when she called him that, but kept her mouth shut. "Where's his broom, Murry? There's still sweepin' needin' done in the house part, and this whole store is a long ways from clean." She tilted her head and squinted. "What you got there?"

His left hand moved behind his back. Marie didn't see what it was. Aunt Rinks had an eye for things like that. Things like secrets. Things she wanted because someone else had them. Fritz wasn't moving.

"Come on. Let me see it. Ain't no secrets in this house." She held out her hand. "Fritz, come on. I just want to see what you got." She wiggled her fingers. "We're wastin' time here."

He held it against his stomach with both hands. The wooden figure wasn't more than a foot tall. It had black boots that looked painted onto its legs and a red jacket with white loops fastened to buttons. A tall hat with a looping chain was above bushy eyebrows. A mustache that curled above a square mouth. The eyes... they were spooky. Like green gemstones nestled beneath bushy brows. When you looked at them directly, they looked back.

"Where'd you get that?" Aunt Rinks moved forward. Her hand rising as if it were possessed. The impulse to take was a spirit that possessed her.

Fritz took a step back.

"Marie, where'd he get that?"

"I don't know."

"Well, he got it somewhere. It wasn't in his backpack, I can tell you that."

Of course she knew that. She went through their things all the time. Marie would be missing lip balm or hair bands, small things that didn't cost a dollar. Aunt Rinks would swear she didn't know how they'd gone missing. A week later, she'd be smearing her lips with lip balm she said she found.

"You find that in the house? Bring that closer, so I can see. It's dark, and I just want a peek at—"

She swiped for it. Fritz saw it coming, put it behind his back. Marie stepped between her brother and her aunt.

"It's his," Marie said.

"He found it here is what he did. This is *my* house. That makes it *my* toy."

"This place belongs to *us*."

Aunt Rinks laughed like a chainsaw. "You don't own anythin', darlin'."

"My mother inherited this building. Not you."

"Yeah, well, your mother ain't here—"

"Rinks," Uncle Vernon said. Uncle Bag of Bones wilted with shame for his wife's behavior.

Aunt Rinks cleared her throat. Every bit of fake happiness slid off her face like a hot candle. She'd crossed a line. Marie hoped she felt bad for it. Although Aunt Rinks never felt anything real. But it was there, somewhere deep inside her. An emotional decay that made her say things like that.

Marie was shaking. Her fingers had curled into her palms. She pulled Fritz behind her.

"I'm sorry," Aunt Rinks said. It was hollow. But points for the effort. "I just want to see it, that's all. Not too much to ask."

"You already saw it," Marie said.

"Just let the boy have it, Rinks," Uncle Vernon groaned. "Does everythin' have to be a fight?"

Something boiled inside her. A chasm of endless hunger, an emotional pit she filled with shiny things and photos and likes. No matter how much she shoveled into that black hole, there was always room for more. Why would she want a toy? *Because Fritz had it and she didn't.*

"Go do the windows, Vern."

Pop-pop-pop went the flip-flops. Marie shielded her brother. A minute later, a broom was tossed on the floor. The door to the back of the house closed. Marie picked it up and started sweeping. Fritz helped her make little piles. He held the broom in one hand.

The nutcracker in the other.

2

Forgot the dish soap.

If Rinks didn't set a reminder, she didn't remember. Her phone was her second brain (almost tied for first). Her phone was her life. *How did people survive without them?*

She rinsed a pot in the sink. The water had a murky look at first, sort of like tea, but cleared after a minute. It was cold, though. She thought it would be warmer. This was the South, where winters were spring, and spring was summer. Here it was Christmas, and Vern was walking around in a tank top.

She put the pot on the electric burner, turned it up. She ripped open packages, stacked squares of dry noodles, and wiped a scatter of dirt balls off the stove. They were everywhere. That happened when a building sat empty for twenty years. Dirt turned into dirt balls. It was science. Dirt attracted dirt and—boom—dirt balls.

Deep down in her brain, though—in her gut—she knew exactly what those things were. And where they came from.

It was better not to know. She hid that knowledge from herself. That was called *compartmentalization*. She'd heard that word on a podcast. It was the ability to lock up knowledge. To focus without distraction. Elite performers mastered compartmentalization. How else could they get on a stage in front of thousands of people and not freak out?

Rinks could compartmentalize. She was a performer. One day, she'd be elite at it.

The storefront rumbled. Another board came off the windows. The last one, she hoped. In the morning, the storefront would be sunshine. Those people down the street would come looking. They'd see her in there, bringing life back to this cracker box. They'd be gathered around coffee cups, talking about what was happening, who the lady was with the fashionable headscarf.

She thumbed her social feed.

Her posts had hundreds of likes. Those little hearts warmed her, stirred something sweet in her belly. Felt good. She held the phone up, snapped five selfies with the pot of water behind her. She picked one, ran it through half a dozen filters till she was tanned and glowing. Angel-like. The scar on her cheek erased. The line that haunted her. A few inches higher, she would have lost an eye, doctors said.

"Getting... hot... in... here," she typed. "#rinksrules." *Whoosh.*

She opened another app. This one added likes to the post. She paid for those; they weren't real. *Momentum building*, the app called it. People got behind things when they looked popular. For an extra bump, she could add positive comments.

Looking good, Rinks!

Love the headscarf.

You are beautiful.

Water still not boiling. She scrolled the feed to avoid emotions that sometimes escaped those little boxes she stuffed them in. Inky nasty little things she didn't want to feel or think about. Toxic fumy things. It was better to keep a tight seal on those. What she said to Marie and Fritz in the storefront, when he was hiding that toy from her, the thing about their mom not being there—*my sister*—had poked a hole in her emotional footlocker. Because what she said was mean and ugly. She didn't mean it (but she did). The only reason she said it was to get them back. To poke them. They poked first, though, not letting her see what he had and all.

This is my building.

They weren't old enough to inherit it. Marie would be eighteen in a month or two weeks or something like that. Marie didn't know any lawyers to advise her. Rinks didn't, either; eighteen sounded like the right age to get an inheritance. Best not to talk about all that.

Besides, they were too young to see the building's potential. They would just sell it, and it wasn't worth a nickel like this. It needed to be loved and nurtured. Rinks never had kids, but if she did, she would be a great mother. She had instincts. It wasn't fair to judge her mother skills on how Marie and Fritz acted. They were like rescue dogs. They came with habits. You couldn't blame that on her.

The building, though, it had good bones. She wasn't sure what that meant, heard it on TV once, and it sounded right. The building could be a studio, she was thinking. Like a place for photos or plays. Culture. Towns like this were about culture. She hadn't worked out the details, but she would make culture happen in this dump. She deserved this building, not her sister. Awful what had happened to her, though. Just awful. Still, she didn't deserve to inherit the building from their aunt. That wasn't mean. Just facts.

"Supper ready?" Vern was covered in dust and dirt balls.

"Not like that, it ain't. You go on and shower first."

"Hot water fixed?"

"Not 'less you fixed it. I'm cookin', not plumbin'."

He slid his hands under his sweaty pits. "The water's cold, then?"

"It's just water, princess."

"Rinks, I ain't takin' a cold shower with the heat not workin'."

"Well, then put on a coat. Besides, cold water is good for you. I heard someone talk about it. Makes adrenaline and hormones and, uh, dopey."

"Dopamine?"

"See there? It's already makin' you smart. Now go on."

He looked across the room, over that disgusting couch, toward the bedroom where they would sleep. The bathroom was between their room and where the kids would be sleeping. It had an old-fashioned bathtub (the kind with claws) with a showerhead. But no shower curtain.

"Make those kids take one, too," she said. "They smell like rescue dogs."

Then she scrolled her social feed. Already two hundred likes.

A CANDLE WAS on the table. Brand new. She'd found it under the sink.

There were four bowls of noodles. One had a double stack. That was for Vern. Season packets were next to each bowl along with plastic forks. Supper looked fancy tonight.

Vern came out wearing the same jeans he worked in (said he couldn't find clean ones, but then he couldn't find a booger in his own nose), but had a new sweatshirt on. It was Rinks's sweatshirt, a gray one. Looked like a blanket on him. His hair was damp, and he was chattering. He speed-walked past the couch and nearly skidded into the table. He started ripping open a packet.

"Manners," Rinks said.

"Just gettin' ready, is all. Any cheese?"

She frisbeed a slice of yellow. It slapped on the table. He peeled off the wrapping and stirred it into the noodles along with a packet of chicken-flavored seasoning. He licked his lips. Rinks noticed he'd shaved. That was awful nice of him.

The kids came out next, wearing the same clothes they'd had on all day, dusty and wrinkled. No respect, those two. Rinks stood at one end of the table. Marie and Fritz stared at the bowls like they were fishing worms.

"You all shower?" Rinks asked.

"We did," Marie said.

"Then why ain't your hairs wet?"

"No shampoo."

"Right. No shampoo. And you ain't cold or shivering."

Marie shrugged. "Water wasn't that cold. Was it, Fritz."

He shook his head. His old hat was over his eyes. That thing had been around too long. The lucky hat. *The not-so-lucky hat.* A cruel smile cracked her lips. She packed away the mean feeling that came with it.

"You need a haircut," Rinks said. Marie pushed it out of her eyes. It just fell back down. "Fizzy, no toys at the table. And take your hat off. That ain't polite."

He had put that wooden toy next to his bowl, and the big eyes stared at Rinks, taunting her. Fritz put it on his lap. She was going to make him take it to his room, but that wasn't a fight she wanted to fight. Not right now.

"We goin' to do a prayer," Rinks said.

Ready with his fork, Vern said, "Prayer?"

"That's right. Everyone, bow your heads." Several seconds of silence passed, broken only by Vern swallowing the saliva in his mouth. "I just want to say thank you for this place with all its potential. We're here safe. We got food and electricity. We got each other. And, you know, just thank you for that. Okay."

"Amen."

"Now everyone say a gratitude before we eat," she said. Vern groaned, and she ignored it. "Just somethin' about what you're grateful for. I think it's a good way to start."

"I'm grateful for this food," Vern said.

"Me too," Marie said.

"No. Can't do that. Vern already said it, and so did I. Come up with somethin' else."

Her lips tightened. "I'm grateful to be here with Fritz."

That stung a little. "Uh-huh. What about me and Vern? You grateful for us?"

"Yep."

Rinks let it go. "And you, Fizzy?"

"Aunt Rinks," Marie said with those sassy, narrow eyes.

"He can write out what he's grateful for. Here." She dug a scrap piece of paper out of her handbag and a tiny pencil she took from a golf course. "Make it short, but mean it."

He wrote one word in neat letters. *Marie.*

"Me and Vern?" Rinks said.

He nodded. Rinks let that go, too. She was kind that way. Someone had to be the adult in the room.

"Great," Vern said. "Can we eat before my stomach shrink-wraps?"

He didn't wait for an answer, shoveled a forkful of noodles that would choke a mule. Broth went flying from his lips as he sucked it in. The next shovel went in before he was done chewing. A thin string of yellow cheese dangled from his chin. He looked like an animal, all hunched over and shivering. Fritz ate almost as fast, smaller bites, though. He held the toy on his lap like it would run off if he didn't.

Rinks tapped her cup with the plastic fork. It thudded instead of rang, but they looked up. She cleared her throat. Then decided to stand up.

"I would like to apologize. I said somethin' earlier today that was not very nice. About your mom. *My* sister. It's been almost two years since they, well... you know. There's not a day that goes by that I don't think about them." Deep sigh. She pried open a box of emotions that really were inside her, let them come up and mist her eyes for effect. It worked. "They were just so special to me and to you, too. I know you miss them as much as I do. They're here with us today, at this table. I can feel them."

She raised her cup to Marie. This wasn't a toast, but she did it anyway. Fritz didn't pay no mind. Marie was stabbing the noodles like they were trying to escape.

"Do you accept my apology?"

Marie nodded. So did Fritz. The apology didn't have the impact Rinks was shooting for. It looked like she'd just given them homework.

"Do you have somethin' to say to me?" Rinks said. Marie and Fritz looked at each other. "Maybe you have an apology, too. I'm just sayin', you wouldn't let me see what Fizzy found. I was just askin' to see it." She looked down her nose. She waited.

No apology.

"I'll be honest, it hurt my feelings a little bit, what you did. It was selfish."

Marie shook her head. Rinks was truly getting upset. What she said wasn't true. It didn't hurt her feelings that they were being selfish. It made her mad. This, though... after that heartfelt apology about their mom (*her* sister) and they couldn't admit their own selfishness?

"I don't think this is fair." Rinks put her cup down. "I'm only askin—"

"Enough." Vern slapped the table. The bowls rattled, and Rinks jumped a little. "What is it you want from them, Rinksy? It's a toy! Let it go already. My god."

The edge on his voice was hard and sharp. Rinks put her hand to her chest.

"You want to see it?" he said. "Fritz, come on. Hand it over." He beckoned with impatience. Slowly, Fritz lifted the toy from his lap and passed it to Vern. "Look, Rinks. A toy. A silly, wooden toy with a weird mouth and a sword and all that. Here, feel it. Then give it back to the boy, all right? He found it, it's his, who cares."

Vern shoved it at her. She took it with a helping of guilt and a touch of shame. Vern had that way about him. She always said he had different people inside him. Like, seven of them. They were his internal family system. (She'd learned that in a psychology class she took at community college, where she attended one semester.) Most of the time, he was meek little Vernon, whom Rinks liked the most. But there were other Verns, like when he was hungry or tired or concentrating. Seven Verns altogether. She counted.

This was Stern Vern. And Stern Vern cut through the hogwash. She liked that one, too, even when he stood up to her. Because he was usually right. The toy was stupid.

She slid her bowl to him.

"What's this?" he said.

"You been workin' all day. I'm not hungry."

"You ain't eatin'?"

"It's all right. I had a few snacks. Go on."

She'd eaten all the chocolate protein bars and granola trail mix they'd packed before leaving that morning. The wrappers were stuffed behind the refrigerator. She'd eaten so much black licorice she'd brushed her teeth three times that day.

Vern scooped the noodles out with his fork. He cut the mess with his pocketknife, which he wiped on his sweatshirt (her sweatshirt), and twirled half of them on his fork. He held it up and looked at Fritz. Then that sweetheart reached across the table for Fritz's bowl, which had been drained of noodles and broth, and slapped the extra helping in it. Rinks covered her heart with both hands.

That was Sweet Vern.

"I'm just curious," Rinks said. "Where'd you find that toy?"

She just couldn't let it go. She told herself it was just curiosity talking. But she knew. Somewhere locked away, a part of her was whispering to find out more. *We want the toy,* it said. And she did, she wanted the toy. Even if it was stupid.

"It was on the shelf," Marie said.

"What shelf, exactly?" Rinks said supersweetly.

"In the storefront."

"The store, huh. Which shelf?"

Marie shrugged. She didn't know. Or she was lying. Rinks never bet on anything. But if she did, she'd bet a bucket full of gold it was the second thing.

"Funny. There was nothin' on those shelves that I saw. Vern, you see anythin'?"

"Who knows, Rinks." He scooped the last noodle out. "Does it matter?"

"I just thought it was strange. You know, the only toy in the buildin'. I mean, it's in such good shape. It don't make sense. Maybe it means somethin'."

"It don't mean anythin'," he said. "It's a toy. Right, Fritz?"

He winked at the boy. She didn't like that. Ole Sweet Vern was becoming Sneaky Vern. She could feel it. Even after she gave him all those noodles. Team Vern was her favorite. That was the Vern who had her back. Now she was alone and aching to get her hands on that toy again.

We want, the part of her said.

"I was thinking we could get a Christmas tree," Marie said. "We could put it on that little stage with lights. Now that Uncle Vernon has all the boards off the windows, people will see it. They might start coming down this way. It'd be a good way to get some attention. It would brighten up the place."

"That's a great idea." Rinks rested her chin on her hands. "We got to buy food, though, hon. Fix that hot water heater so you don't have to keep takin' cold showers. And we need to get Wi-Fi runnin'. Your uncle Vern has to work, you know."

Vern sat back, nodding. She could feel his support on this one. He sucked his teeth and then said, "We can probably cut one of the trees out back, you know. One of those small magnolias would make a good one."

"Magnolia? How do you know what a magnolia is?"

He shrugged. "I can find some lights to put on it."

"Where you goin' to find lights?"

He picked up the bowl and slurped the last of the broth. "Somewhere."

Yeah, somewhere. She knew what somewhere meant. Vern had a way of *finding* things. Rinks looked the other way when it came to that.

"Oooor," he said, "maybe Godfather can help."

Marie frowned. "Who?"

Vern started laughing. Laughed so hard and long he ran out of breath. Rinks smiled at first, then felt troubled by what was so funny. She clearly wasn't in on the joke. He wiped his eyes, giggled some more. Then pushed away from the table.

"You all are in for a treat."

He found a toothpick in his front pocket and slid it in the gap between his front teeth. Making a loud sucking sound, he went to the bedroom. Marie asked what that meant. Rinks shrugged like she didn't know.

"Ah-ah-ah." Rinks held up her hand when Marie pushed her chair back.

"May we be excused?" Marie said through a locked jaw.

"Yes, you may." Rinks smiled. "You and Fizzy can wash the dishes in the sink. I made supper. Your uncle Vernon is tired."

"Only if you stop calling him that."

Rinks smiled and winked. That cheered her up. She sat at the table while they cleared the dishes. Chores were good for children. They needed structure. Maybe there wasn't enough of that, the way they talked to her. The way *Marie* talked. Fritz didn't ever talk. A blessing in disguise.

Rinks went to the storefront and walked around with the lights off. She studied the shelves. There was nothing on them. Never was, either. She could tell by the dust. She stared at the lights down the street where people were gathered. Marie did have a good idea, though. A Christmas tree would make people curious.

Rinks decided she'd suggest it tomorrow. Like it was her idea.

3

Their room was a small workshop with an air mattress. Marie's breath came out in thin, white wisps beneath a flickering fluorescent lamp. A gouged and scuffed workbench was against the wall. There were shelves on the back of it, against the wall. No tools in the drawers, but a few jars contained screws and washers. Nails.

No mouse turds. Not one. Even if Fritz had swept the room when she was in the storefront, a few would've been left behind.

Fritz put on one of Marie's sweatshirts.

"You going to wear that to bed?" She flicked the bill of his cap. "Probably a good idea. Brush your teeth?"

He nodded. She didn't feel like checking to see if his toothbrush was wet.

The sleeves bunched on his arms. He pushed them up, and they fell back down, gathering around the toy he was holding. Marie could hear Aunt Rinks and Uncle Vernon talking in the other room. She couldn't believe they were going to sleep on that mattress. It had to be thirty years old with twenty pounds of dust mites.

"Where'd you find that?" She poked the toy.

He pointed at the large opening in the workbench shelves. The wall behind it was covered with thin squares cut from a four-by-four post, each of them sanded and lacquered and tacked into place. The grain formed a patchwork of irregular bullseyes. Marie had no idea where he'd found it.

"Can I see him?"

Fritz handed him over. The soldier was a foot tall. Sturdy and stiff. The jointed legs and arms flexed easily when handled. The hat was black and tall, the boots shiny. The red uniform starched. A thin black strap was around the waist with a metal scabbard attached. A long patch of white whiskers was attached to the blocky chin. The mustache was painted in the shape of two teardrops.

"Does he have a name?"

Fritz took out his phone. It had been over a year since she last heard him speak. Marie had taught herself sign language watching videos, but Fritz refused to learn. He typed his answers on his phone.

"Nussknacker?" She pulled the lever on the back of the toy. The square mouth slowly opened. "You sure it's not Crack-a-tooth?"

Fritz barked laughter and shook his head. She gave the toy back to him. He clutched it under his arm and typed some more.

"Yeah. I'm hungry, too," she said. "I can't eat any more noodles, though."

Fritz opened the door. Aunt Rinks and Uncle Vernon were still in their bedroom. He closed the door quietly, then went to his backpack, reached to the bottom, and pulled out two protein bars. Chocolate peanut butter.

Marie snatched one. "Where'd you get these?"

She knew where. Aunt Rinks always kept a secret stash of black licorice and protein bars. The licorice she didn't need to hide, but the protein bars were basically candy.

They scrambled under the blankets—which were wool moving blankets—and threw them over their heads. They took the wrappers off slowly to keep from making noise. Aunt Rinks could hear a candy wrapper from across the street. Marie shoved the wrappers under the air mattress.

"Oh my." She closed her eyes. The chocolate melted on her

tongue. She tried to chew slowly, but it tasted so good. And they came from Aunt Rinks's secret stash. She was done in two bites, licking her fingers.

They stayed under the blankets. It was an old technique their dad had taught them. *Breath blanket,* he called it. When it's cold, keep your head covered. At some point, though, you had to come out for air.

They didn't have pillows. She gathered what clothes they weren't wearing and balled them up, gave a stuffed pair of sweatpants to Fritz (who was still under the breath blanket). She rolled up a towel and placed it along the gap of the door. It wasn't to keep the cold air out.

"Listen," she said, "there's a good chance a mouse or something will move around at some point. Don't freak out. They're small and harmless, just looking for something to eat."

Then she thought of the wrappers under the bed and moved them to a drawer in the workbench. When she turned around, Fritz was pointing at the shelf on the checkered wall. There was a clock up there, half covered by a dirty rag. She pulled it off.

It was nothing she'd ever seen before. And not pretty.

The clock was embedded in the belly of an owl. The wings spread out twenty-four inches on both sides, the molded feathers brown with flecks of gold. The round eyes were globes of white with black, slitted pupils. The beak hooked over the number twelve.

Fritz held up his phone.

"*Nussknacker says that will keep them out,*" she read. "Okay. He tell you anything else?"

He typed again.

Her hands sank in the air mattress as she leaned over to read it. "*We're going to Godfather's tomorrow night.* How do you know that?"

He typed an answer.

"When did you hear Aunt Rinks on the phone?" she said.

He pulled the nutcracker out from under the blankets. So he was using the toy to express his thoughts. She was fine with that. It was a therapy toy.

"Did Nussknacker say who Godfather is?" she asked.

She read what he typed. According to Fritz (via Nussknacker), their dad had worked for him. Their dad had worked in technology. Marie couldn't recall a Godfather, though.

"Does he have a name?"

Fritz didn't hesitate. *Herr Drosselmeier.* That gave her a small chill, how fast he came up with that name. It wouldn't be the last time she felt chills. He'd probably overheard Aunt Rinks say the name. Her phone voice could be heard across the room during a concert.

He held up the phone one more time. It was an answer to a question she was about to ask.

"He's *our* godfather? Great. Can't wait to meet him. You ready for bed?"

She pulled the string on the fluorescent light. Without windows, the room was pitch black. She used her phone to find her way to bed. It was already losing air. Fritz bobbed like a buoy when she climbed on. They pulled the covers over their heads.

The nutcracker was kicking her in the side.

THERE WAS NO TRAFFIC OUTSIDE. Aunt Rinks and Uncle Vernon had lived (before they drove cross-country) next to an interstate. Long-haul truckers made noise all night long, jake-braking onto the nearest off-ramp. In the workshop where they were sleeping, it was dead quiet. If a mouse passed gas, they would hear it.

"You want to do a memory?" She felt him nod.

This was a game Marie's therapist wanted her to play. Teri was her therapist. She had short hair that was always in a clip. She crossed her legs like they were made of rubber, and spoke with soothing tones that irritated Marie, at first. She was engaging, though. When Marie talked, Teri listened like Marie was the only person in the world.

Teri had asked Marie to visualize a box. It could be any size, any color. The box symbolized a container that held her emotions. That was the problem, her emotions. Marie had locked them away to avoid feeling them. Teri had never come out and said it like that. She didn't need to. Marie knew she didn't feel anything. *Don't let anyone tell you how to grieve,* their neighbor had told her before she and Fritz moved in with Aunt Rinks and Uncle Vernon. Marie had cried, of course she did. But when Fritz stopped talking, she dried those tears up.

So there was a box of emotions inside her. No matter what color Marie tried to make it, it always ended up black. A black box Marie had put a lock on.

Recalling your favorite memories will open it.

Marie didn't want to open it. She didn't want to forget her parents, but she didn't want to remember everything. There were feelings locked in that box for a reason. They could stay in there until forever. Wither up like winter leaves.

Even though Marie didn't see Teri anymore (she was a thousand miles away now; thank you, Aunt Rinks), she still played the game. *You don't need that therapist,* Aunt Rinks had said when they were ready to move. *You know why she wants you comin' back, right? She runs a business, Murry. She makes money off people sick in the head. You ain't sick. You just need to do it on your own like the rest of us. We're just fine.*

Whether they were fine was debatable.

Marie always played the game when she couldn't sleep. She'd close her eyes and whisper it to herself like a story. She would stop when the shudders began. Her chest would flutter. She'd cut it off before her eyes were wet. *Baby steps,* was what she told herself.

She'd started playing the game with Fritz when neither of them could sleep. They'd had two single beds in one room at Aunt Rinks and Uncle Vernon's house. Marie would tell a story from one bed. He would listen in the other. If the memory game would help her, maybe it would help him. And when she focused on Fritz getting better, the shudders didn't come as easily.

That was really why she played it.

She didn't think Fritz would remember this memory. He was three years old. Marie was thirteen. It snowed that Christmas. Nothing new where they grew up, but that was a record year. It snowed on Christmas and the day after that. Cars were buried, and people had to dig their way out of their houses.

On the third day, the sky was blue, and the air was crisp. Dad stood in the front yard, wearing a T-shirt and snow pants. He thumped his chest and howled. Marie and Fritz watched from the window.

"Challenge!" he called through his hands. "I call a challenge!"

No one answered because no one was outside. That didn't stop him. He went door-to-door with a shovel. When he came back, he was powder white and rosy cheeked.

"We got ourselves a challenge, kids," he had exclaimed. "Get ready."

Dad had made up the rules. Twelve families were ready. They could only use the snow in their front yard. At five o'clock, Mr. and Mrs. Podelini—the old couple who gave Chex mix to everyone at Christmas—would be the judges.

At noon, Dad rang a cow bell. The digging began.

Snow shovels and snow blowers, buckets and wheelbarrows. The Kellys backed up their truck and pushed three feet of snow out of the back. The Simpsons brought out ladders. Eric Stuzzy was on stilts (he got them for Christmas).

Fat snowmen and skinny ones and families of all sizes. The Pedersons made snowdragons. The Harrelsons made an igloo. The Farrells made a one-hole golf course (Leo was a state champ golfer). The local news came out in a four-wheel-drive truck. A man in a puffy jacket interviewed Dad. He was on the late news.

Marie and Fritz's family built one giant snowman with a super fat bottom with a turret for a head. Dad named it Tank. He climbed out a second-story window onto the porch roof to put a plastic football helmet on it and two charcoal briquettes for eyes. Nearly fell off when he slipped on the shingles. Mom wasn't happy with that.

They dug a shallow tunnel in Tank's belly just big enough for Marie and Fritz. Mom was worried Tank would collapse on them. Dad made sure it didn't. They used a trash lid for a door. Marie and Fritz huddled in the cold dark, waiting for Mr. and Mrs. Podelini to come by. They jumped out to surprise them. Mom and Dad shouted, "Twins! Oh my God, Tank had twins!"

Mr. Podelini wiped his eyes laughing. Mrs. Podelini didn't think it was so funny. They should have won, but the judges voted for Jacob Chopon's castle with a drawbridge and a plastic-lined moat. Dad presented them with the honorary broomstick as winners of the first (and only) Snow Build Classic. He spray-painted the handle silver and the bristles red.

In March, Marie saw the silver handle poking out of their garbage can. She took it home.

Fritz was snoring when she finished. Marie stared at the ceiling. It felt like Tank was standing on her chest. Pressure billowed the sides of the emotion box like a boiler shooting steam. Traces of that memory smelled like Mom's cookies. She squeezed her eyes shut to seal the black box closed before the shudders came.

She pulled the cover over Fritz's shoulder. The room was cold.

SOMETHING MOVED.

Marie sat up in the dark. Her bottom was on the floor. The air mattress had deflated. Her heart sprinted laps inside her chest when something touched her leg.

She scrambled for her phone, felt around on the floor. Her fingers hit something hard and plastic. She touched the screen, flashed it around the room. Fritz was curled up and facing away from her, his head resting on a pair of sweatpants. She stood up, pulled back the covers, passed the light around the walls and into the corners. Nothing moved. Not even a mouse.

Her breath steamed into the phone's light. The owl's predatory stare looked down from the shelf. She was about to climb back in the deflated bed when she saw the nutcracker on the bench. He was standing at attention in front of the checkered wall, right where Fritz said he found him. Fritz must have gone to the bathroom and put him back. Maybe that little sword had poked him awake. *Good,* she thought. It had been poking her all night.

It was hours before she fell back asleep.

IN THE MORNING, Fritz was at the kitchen table, hunched over a bowl. His hat pulled over his eyes, spooning globs of instant oatmeal into his mouth. The nutcracker stood in the middle of the table, stiffly at attention. Guarding the bowl of oatmeal, should anyone try to take it from Fritz.

The kitchen didn't look as bad as it had the day before. There were still cobwebs on the ceiling and random *dirt balls* on the floor. It was sort of like camping. *It's all about your attitude,* Mom used to say. *It doesn't* have *to bother you.*

Mom would never have slept here, though. Marie was sure of it.

"Morning," Marie said.

Fritz waved. Oatmeal dripped from his chin.

"What's Uncle Vernon doing?" she said. He was cussing from somewhere in the building. Fritz shrugged. "Where's Aunt Rinks?"

He pointed at the door.

Marie stepped out back. It was brisk, the air filtered clean. She'd been in that dustbin too long. The morning chill felt good on her face. She smelled her sweatshirt, hoping it hadn't absorbed the mustiness. She was going to have to shower eventually. Cold water or not. But that wouldn't matter much if her clothes smelled like a bag of dead bugs.

Aunt Rinks was pulling vines off the decaying Adirondack chairs. Weeds were growing in the firepit. She was wearing a coat and gloves. Also shorts and spongy flip-flops. Marie watched from the top step. Red lines crisscrossed Aunt Rinks's legs where thorns had grabbed her. *Not a good look for selfies,* Marie thought.

"Good morning," Marie said.

"'Bout time." Aunt Rinks looked up with a handful of hairy vines. Marie hoped it was poison ivy. "Daylight burnin', young lady. You need to wake up when we do."

"I didn't sleep much last night. I heard mice."

"Don't put that thought in my head. Uh-uh."

"You heard them?"

She held up a stop sign. "Don't talk about it. I mean it. That was just the building settlin' last night. Nothing runnin' around."

Another curse word came from inside the building. "What's Uncle Vernon doing?"

"Fixin' the heater. We goin' to clean up this sittin' area today, build a fire tonight. Be a nice photo, don't you think?"

"I thought we were going to Godfather's."

Aunt Rinks looked like someone pinched her. "Where'd you hear that?"

"That's what Uncle Vernon said last night at supper."

"I don't believe he said we were goin' there." She knocked dirt off the gloves and eyed Marie. "You eavesdroppin' on my phone callin'? That's bad manners, Murry. I don't go snoopin' through your phone, do I?"

Yes, you do. Marie had changed her passcode twice, but Aunt Rinks would somehow catch her typing it in. Sometimes her phone would be in a different spot if she left it out.

"Are we going to Godfather's, then?" Marie asked.

"Don't worry about that. Right now, I need you and Fizzy to run down the street. Vern needs his coffee, and the machine ain't workin'."

"Do you have money?"

"I got money, don't worry about that." She dug a wad of bills out of her pocket. "Don't spend none on anythin' else. Just coffee. And take this."

She climbed out of the weeds. A vine lassoed her ankle and nearly took her down like a rodeo calf. She lost a flip-flop and had to fish it out of a green tangle of weeds. She limped toward a cardboard box, cussing without apology, and dug through it. She came up with a half-filled jug of milk. She popped the lid off and sniffed. Her eyes teared up. She emptied the contents in the bushes, white chunks falling on leaves.

"Take this." She handed the jug to Marie. "Go on and rinse it out in the sink real good, till it don't stink."

Marie held it at arm's length. "And then what?"

"Have them fill it up with coffee. Don't let them overcharge you. That's, like, a pot of coffee, no more."

Drinking coffee from a sour jug was one thing. Asking someone to pour hot coffee into an opening the size of a quarter was another.

"Don't give me that look. It's just a container. Make sure you rinse it at least three times. Oh, and grab all the packets of sugar and creamer while you're there."

"All?"

"All. Those things are free to payin' customers. No limit, either. Vern loves his sugar and creamer. Now go on before he throws a pipe through the wall. He didn't sleep much last night either. Don't drag your feet."

Marie rinsed the milk jug in the kitchen sink like her aunt wanted. The water had a rusty tinge. Smelled a bit like burnt match. The coffee was going to smell like curdled acid when Uncle Vernon poured a cup from it. This was going to be embarrassing. At least it got her out of the building.

"Come on," she said. Fritz pointed at the jug. "You'll never guess."

ONLY HALF A BLOCK from the building, the street was festive. Lights wrapped around palm trees, decorations strung between buildings. There were flowers in pots and wreaths on the doors. Stores were just beginning to open, and people were already shopping. It had a local feel to it, no big chain stores. There was a karate school, a yoga center, an art gallery, and a boutique. A used bookstore where you could trade books. A shoe and luggage repair shop (Marie didn't know places like that still existed). And a video game store.

The café was next to the video game store. *The Coffee Place* was printed on the window. The paint was peeling from the letters. Inside the big window, three mechanical elves were slowly moving in a bed of cotton. One had a wooden mallet, another was pulling a saw, and the third one was supervising. Their green clothing was dusty, like they'd just been pulled out of storage and put on display.

Fritz stood in front of the video game window. He and the nutcracker were watching a group of kids playing a game.

"You want to wait out here?" Marie asked.

He nodded, so she went in alone. A little bell rang when she opened the door. Old music came out of the café, the kind with an accordion. A fog of sweets and coffee grinds lured her in. A few people sat at tables with tall paper cups and laptops. An old woman was wiping down a small table with a rag. She turned her head like her neck was stiff and wished Marie a merry Christmas.

Marie got behind a man wearing a bike helmet and skintight shorts. She held the milk jug behind her with an awful turn of embarrassment in her stomach. At least there were only a few people to witness this crazy request. And if they didn't do it—if the woman behind the counter didn't fill up that sour milk jug with coffee—Aunt Rinks would drag Marie down there and throw a nuclear fit. And film it for social media.

Please fill this up.

Bicycle Helmet had a big order that required a cardboard tray. Marie distracted her nervous stomach with the pastries inside the glass counter. Homemade danishes and donuts and muffins and cookies. Dollops of strawberry jam and swirls of icing. Her mouth began to water. She looked at the wadded bills in her hand. She could buy a slice of banana bread for a dollar. They could eat it before they left the store. Aunt Rinks wouldn't have a clue. It wasn't like there was a standard price for a milk jug of coffee.

"Merry Christmas, young lady," the woman behind the counter said with a jolly accent from another country. She was as round as the woman wiping down the tables. Her hair was thick and white. Red suspenders strung over her round shoulders held up a baggy pair of red trousers. "What can I get you this morning?"

"I know this'll sound strange," she whispered. "But can you fill this up with coffee?"

She looked at the milk jug on the counter. Thick, white brows shaded her eyes. She scratched her doughy chin (where several curly sprigs of whiskers had sprouted) with stout fingers, then twisted off the lid.

"Don't smell it," Marie said. "It's for my aunt. She wanted me to bring it down here. Their coffee machine is broken. They like coffee. Lots of it. I don't think they care what it tastes like, as long as it has caffeine."

"I have better idea."

She took the jug with her. Marie felt relief it was no longer in sight. How she was going to carry a jug of thin plastic full of hot coffee back to the building, she hadn't figured out. She looked around for the condiments table. There were bowls of sugar packets and little plastic cups of creamer. She was going to take a handful, that was it. Tell Aunt Rinks that was all they had. Throw in a couple of wooden sticks to make her happy.

A group of kids were outside on the sidewalk. One of them was Fritz.

Marie's first thought was he was making friends. They were the ones from inside the video game store Fritz had been watching. They were about his age. There were three of them. She smiled, imagining him sitting in a circle with them, playing video games. He'd had friends when he was younger, but not since they had to move in with Aunt Rinks and Uncle Vernon.

Maybe, she thought, *this move will be good for him.*

That fantasy vanished just as soon as she thought it. The boy with a neon green stocking cap snatched the nutcracker from Fritz's hands. Fritz tried to take it back.

Marie bolted away from the counter. She was across the store before she realized what she was doing, throwing open the door—the little bell clanging like a church bell—and onto the sidewalk. She appeared so quickly that the boys jumped.

"What are you doing?" she said.

Stocking Cap Boy nearly dropped the nutcracker. In an instant, the boys ran. Marie lunged at the one who had taken the nutcracker from Fritz. She caught the pocket on his jacket, heard the seam rip. She jerked him back like a roped calf, pulled the nutcracker from his hand.

"This isn't yours," she said. "Why would you take it from him?"

"You're going to pay for this jacket."

"Apologize to my brother," she said.

He tried to shimmy out of his jacket. She grabbed him by the T-shirt. It was too much, what she was doing. She was scaring him, but she couldn't stop herself any more than a mama bear could let someone pet her cubs. Instinct had a firmer grip on her than she had on the boy. And he wasn't going anywhere.

"Let me go."

He swung at her. She reached back to make sure Fritz was behind her. She let go, and Stocking Cap Boy stumbled off the curb and nearly fell.

The boys who ran away were coming back. They came out of the video store with another boy. This one was about Marie's age, maybe a year or two younger. He was a foot taller and as skinny as a cinnamon stick, wearing high-top shoes that weren't tied and gray sweatpants cut off at the knees. Polka dots of acne on his chin.

Marie pulled Fritz behind her and widened her stance.

"She ripped my jacket." Stocking Cap Boy showed Acne Boy his pocket.

He strode at Marie. "What's your problem?"

"He took something from my brother."

Acne Boy's grin chiseled into his cheeks. He looked down at what Marie was holding. He seemed relaxed, but she sensed tension in his posture. She was ready for what he was about to do, but he was faster than she expected. He plucked the nutcracker from her hand before she could turn away.

With an ugly grin, he held it over his head. "A doll?"

This got a laugh from the boys. The instinct that had sent Marie running across the café filled her once again. She was possessed, focused. Cold as the sidewalk under her shoes.

"Give it back," she said.

Acne Boy thought that was funny, the way she said it. It had an *or else* sound to it.

Marie's mom had taught her to fight.

Her dad hadn't been much of a fighter. Her mom had been scrappy. At least, that was what her dad said. They wouldn't share stories, though. Marie'd been to wrestling camp every summer, learned jujitsu one year, and even tried out for the boys' wrestling team. She was a decent grappler, but not good enough to make the team. But against someone who'd never wrestled? That was why her mom had taught her.

It had been a while since she'd been on the mat—not since they moved in with their aunt and uncle—but she could tell Acne Boy wasn't a fighter. He could swing a fist like any testosterone-fueled teenager, but he didn't *know* how to fight. It was the way he was standing, no center of gravity. No base. She could shoot his legs before he knew what hit him. *A brawler can't fight on the ground,* her mom used to say.

Acne Boy raised the nutcracker higher. He was going to smash it on the concrete. If she took out his legs, he'd hit his head on the sidewalk. She didn't want to do that. If he took a swing at her, that was different. She made sure Fritz was still behind her. She was about to say something, bait him into coming at the girl who didn't look afraid, when—

"Ahhh!" Acne Boy cried.

He grabbed his finger. The nutcracker fell from his hand. Somehow, it caught on the string holding up his sweatpants. There was a sharp *ping*. The sweatpants fell halfway down, exposing red boxers. A pink line appeared on the soft flesh above his waistband. He grabbed his pants before they fell to his knees. The string dangled loosely.

Fritz grabbed the nutcracker off the sidewalk.

"Enough!" The old woman came out of the café. The rag over her shoulder. "That is no way to behave on street, Bobby. You too, Sean. You know better, all of you. These are new children. Go. Go home. All of you, before I call your mothers and fathers."

Bobby's finger was red and swollen. The nutcracker had somehow clamped onto it, and by random chance, the sword attached had cut the boy's sweatpants. They backed away from the old woman, her hands planted on her waist like an old country warrior. They wandered toward the video game store, muttering to each other. Bobby held up his sweatpants with one hand.

"Santa bring you coal next time," the old woman hollered. She turned to Marie and Fritz. "Come inside, children. Ms. Clara have something for you."

❄

"Have seat."

Ms. Clara pulled chairs out from a table in the corner, then shouted at the woman behind the counter in another language.

"Let me see." She turned Fritz's head, examined both cheeks. Squeezed his shoulders. "Strong like bull, you are. You don't scare easy, no? And I call their mother next time. Their father don't care, like the boys, but mother will make them care. How about you, young lady?"

"I'm fine," Marie said.

Ms. Clara sat down with them. "Of course. You run to your brother. I see you. Very brave."

Marie shook her head, slightly embarrassed. The line between bravery and stupidity was thin. She should've grabbed the nutcracker and left it at that. There was no reason to grab the boy and demand he apologize. That was stupid. Someone could've gotten hurt. Fritz or her or one of them, all because she wanted to teach him a lesson for messing with her brother.

The woman from the counter slid a tray onto the table. One of her suspenders dangled at her hip. She wiped her hands on her red trousers, strung the suspender over her shoulder, and bowed with a twinkle in her eye.

"Thank you, dear. Enough," Ms. Clara said. She shook her head and gave an impatient cough. "My sister, Trutchen. Always with the show, she does."

There was a resemblance between the two women. Both soft and sweet, like yeast rolls. Both with smiles in their eyes. Ms. Trutchen was endearing if not jolly. The way she bounced with each step to a song only she was hearing. The little bell rang, and she greeted the new customers with a boisterous merry Christmas. Ms. Clara rolled her eyes.

"This for you."

She put mugs in front of Marie and Fritz. It was hot chocolate with a heavy dose of whipped cream. Also, there were two pastries with flaky crust and blobs of jelly on top.

Marie stopped Fritz before he inhaled one. "We can't afford these."

"Nonsense. It is Christmas. This boy needs to eat." She tapped the bill of his cap.

Fritz had the pastry in his mouth before Marie could say thank you. He took two bites before swallowing, then sipped the hot chocolate.

"Thank you," she said. "My brother, Fritz, says thank you, also."

"I see."

He was nodding with a foamy mustache on his lip.

"He doesn't talk," Marie said.

"Is that right? Why is that, Fritz?" the old woman said.

He did what he always did when someone asked that question. Pretended like he didn't hear it. Maybe he didn't know why. The doctor said there was nothing physically wrong with him. A therapist worked with him. They mostly drew pictures. The therapist said he would talk when he was ready.

It'd been almost two years.

"Well, Mr. Fritz, there is no need to talk in here. Only be good listener. Huh?"

Fritz smiled bashfully. Ms. Clara squeezed his shoulder. Marie had the urge to weep. The kindness toward her brother was so genuine.

"Sooo... this cause all the trouble, huh?" Ms. Clara reached for the toy and stopped. "May I?"

Fritz handed it to her.

"Nutcracker." She studied the front and back, ran her finger along the painted teeth that, somehow, had clamped down on Bobby the Acne Boy's finger. (Must have been the way he was holding it.) Ms. Clara suffered no misfire. "This toy come from my country, you know. We put the Nussknacker on front step at night. He protect the house from bad wishes and such."

Marie felt a chill. "How'd you know that was his name?"

"Nussknacker? Everyone call him that, from my country. Here, it is nutcracker. Even though he never crack nuts." She gave the toy back to Fritz, who was already on his last bite. "Where did you get him?"

"Our building down the street." Marie pointed in that direction. "It's on the corner. Our uncle took the boards off the windows yesterday."

Ms. Clara frowned. "The toy store?"

"It was a store, I think. There's, like, living quarters in the back. That's where we're staying."

"I don't understand."

"Like, sleeping. We don't have enough money for a hotel. Well, I mean, we probably do, but Aunt Rinks doesn't want to spend it." Ms. Clara was nodding along but still not understanding. "My mother had inherited it from her family, like, a long time ago. We never came to see it, though. My great-aunt owned it. She was my grandmother's sister."

"Mrs. Corker?"

"You knew her?"

Ms. Clara slapped her knee, then shouted in her native tongue to Ms. Trutchen, who was reaching for a muffin in the glass case. She listened to what her sister said, then raised a pair of silver tongs.

She shouted: "Merry, merry!"

They shared a laugh. Marie was lost, took a sip of hot chocolate that was rich and tasty. She pushed her plate toward Fritz. He took the pastry with a smile bigger than the one before. The urge to weep was in her throat again.

"You are Marie Corker, then?"

"Stahlbaum. My great-aunt was on my mother's side."

"Ah. Your great-aunt was legend." Ms. Clara leaned over the table. The weight of her elbows tipped the table toward her. "Every Saturday, starting November, there would be line around corner. Store would fill with children and parents. She would sit on rocking chair with purple blanket and cup of tea in both hands. Like this."

She demonstrated with Fritz's mug. It was already empty.

"At noon, children and mothers and fathers gather around her. She would tell stories... great, great stories. They get lost in them, like, what is word... *hypnotize*! No one speak or move when she tell stories of Santa Claus and reindeer and snowman and elf. My sister and I, we were younger then, not children, but we go sometimes to hear. It was hypnotize. We would feel it, you know, like energy. Like *magic*."

She sighed.

"And Mr. Corker, he was toymaker. He was one who fill all the shelves with toys. He make them in back of store. Children love them. Look!" She shouted in her native tongue. Ms. Trutchen disappeared around the corner, came back to hold up what looked like an orange octopus. "He make those. And also elves, you see in window there. He make those, too. They work now over twenty years. He was master toymaker."

The mechanical elves didn't look like the work of mastery. But for two free pastries, she didn't disagree.

"Elves not so good, huh?" Ms. Clara said.

"No! No, I think the elves look great. Very, uh, very old school, you know. Authentic."

The old woman leaned back in the chair to share something with her sister, who gave a smile and a thumbs-up. "They are not so good," Ms. Clara said. "They are special, though. Mr. Corker, your great-uncle, he was very nice man. Became quite good game maker before they close. He make games, make up rules and pieces. Very complicated, sometimes. Not like today's games where everything all *pew-pew*, you know. Thinking games, he make. Not always fun, but challenging. People play them and learn. Children play them here with us. Beat us."

Ms. Trutchen must have heard her and scoffed.

"What happened to the store?" Marie asked. "Why did it close?"

"Oh, children get older. They get phones and things, I think. Mr. and Mrs. Corker get older, and one day they close. But no one make toys like that today. Or tell stories." She squinted through her round spectacles, lifting her chin to see through the bifocals. "You look a little like her, I think. The eyes."

She shouted at Ms. Trutchen and pointed at Marie. Marie didn't understand the answer.

"She say shape of your face like hers. But she wrong. It is the eyes."

Marie laughed. She'd never seen a photo of her great-aunt. Marie looked like her mother. When they'd compared pictures of each other at the same age, it was hard to tell the difference.

Ms. Clara called another order to her sister. A minute later, she brought a plate, this one with four slices of banana bread. Fritz didn't ask for permission. He started eating. Marie took a bite of one. It was magnificent.

"So, your mother and father will open store?"

Marie shook her head. "My parents passed away." After all that time, it still hurt to say it out loud. Especially in front of Fritz.

"I'm so sorry, dear."

"We live with our aunt and uncle now."

"They are here?"

"We're living in the store. I don't know how long, though. There's a lot to fix, though. The heater isn't working, or maybe it is now. The coffee machine didn't work. My aunt sent me to fill up the milk jug. It's kind of gross."

Ms. Clara listened with kind eyes. Marie had the urge to tell her everything, from the time of her parents' accident, to moving out of the house they grew up in, and how different Aunt Rinks and Uncle Vernon were from their parents. Maybe she would have said all those things if Fritz wasn't there.

She put her hand on Marie's hand. "I am very happy you are here."

The urge to weep came closer.

Ms. Clara excused herself. "Enjoy bread. I will be back."

※

MARIE FINISHED the piece she'd started, then broke the last one in half and gave it to Fritz. She savored the last sip of hot chocolate, scooping the cream out of the bottom of the mug with her finger and licking it off. Fritz was laughing at the whipped cream on her nose. She wiped it off and tried to put it on his nose.

"This for you." Ms. Clara came back with a cardboard container. A bladder of coffee was inside it. "Much better than milk jug."

There was a bag full of sugar packets and creamers. It was too generous. If Ms. Clara only knew Aunt Rinks wanted Marie to steal all of it. There were also two blueberry muffins the size of small cakes. Marie and Fritz would eat them on the way back and hide the wrappers.

"Come back tonight for food, if you like. We have chicken salad and borsht and pelmeni. Very good for you. Ms. Trutchen is good cook, but don't tell her so. Head too big already."

"Thank you so much. You're too kind, really. I think we're going to our godfather's for dinner tonight. He lives here, somewhere. But maybe tomorrow we'll come."

"Oh, that is nice. Who is your godfather?"

Marie couldn't remember. She looked at Fritz. He paused, then typed the godfather's name on his phone. Ms. Clara looked through the bottom of her glasses. She shouted at Ms. Trutchen. She gave a thumbs-up.

"Do you know him?" Marie asked.

"Everyone know him, dear."

Marie and Fritz took their time walking back to the old toy store. He was too full to eat the muffin, so they hid what was left in their pockets for later. Uncle Vernon was thrilled with the coffee. Aunt Rinks was even happier they took all the sugar and creamer.

4

A headache started behind Rinks's eyes and skimmed across her forehead. She looked through the plastic bags piled on the kitchen counter for a protein bar. All that was left was packages of instant noodles and slices of yellow cheese.

Vern was in the next room, talking on the phone. She pulled the wrappers from the protein bars out of hiding and counted them. Only ten. She'd packed twelve. She kept searching.

"Yeah, I'll hold." Vern came out of the back room.

Rinks shoved the wrappers in one of the plastic bags. "What're you doin'?"

"Cable company. Where's the coffee?"

"Ain't you supposed to be fixin' the heater?"

"I can't work without Wi-Fi, Rinks. And it ain't that cold in here. Ain't you got somethin' you can put on, like long pants or—hello? Yeah, I'm here. Uh-huh. I just told the lady…"

He went back to the bedroom, where he'd walk circles. He couldn't talk on the phone without pacing and waving his hand, pointing like the person on the other end of the call was standing in front of him. It made her anxious.

Rinks needed a shower and clean clothes. She felt dirty. Not pretty. She adjusted her headscarf, grabbed a sponge, and started wiping the counter. She held up her phone. This would be called *mornin' chores.* She took twenty selfies. Each one was awful, even with filters. She scanned through photos taken yesterday. She needed to post. Had to keep her stream flowing.

Being a social media queen was hard work.

People had no idea what it took. Finding something original was exhausting. Her feed was good and active. Lots of comments. She read some of them, which people told her not to do. How else was she going to know what her fans were thinking?

Love the headscarf!

Beautiful!

I wish I were you!

That warm, fuzzy feeling grew in her like a seedling feeling the first rays of morning. Didn't matter if those comments were real ones or the fake ones she bought, she ate them up like glazed donuts and felt the headache fade. She should have stopped reading after three good ones.

Scarface with eye shadow.

A shot to the ribcage. The scar on her cheek was showing in the photo, and that comment went at it like a haymaker. There was no way to punch back. She wanted to delete the post, but then all those luscious comments would go away. *Why do people have to be so mean?*

The door opened. The kids came inside carrying a box.

"Where you been?" Rinks said. "I could have crawled down there myself faster than you."

"Almost got in a fight," Marie said.

"Coffee!" Vern came speed-walking out of the bedroom with the phone against his ear. He grabbed a mug from the counter, blew inside it, then turned it upside down. One of those dirt balls fell out. He filled it from the plastic spout on the fancy box and slurped it black. "Ahhh. You got in a fight?"

"Almost," Marie said. "Someone was picking on Fritz."

"You pop him?" His teeth were pickets stuck in a gummy smile.

"No. He took the nutcracker. I made him give it back."

Rinks shook her head. *That toy*. Might be for the boy's own good to take it away, the problems it was causing.

"The kid's older brother tried to break it. One of the owners of the café, her name's Ms. Clara, broke it up. Made them leave. She was real nice, sat down and talked to Fritz and me. Our place was a toy store. Did you know that?"

"Yeah. I knew that." Rinks didn't know that. "The shelves and everythin', Murry. Ain't it obvious. Fizzy got that toy, which I should take away, the trouble it's makin'."

"Those boys were bullies," Marie said. "It had nothing to do with the nutcracker."

"It had somethin' to do with it. You almost got to fightin' over it. Give it here."

Rinks stuck out her hand. Fritz got behind his sister, who didn't move when Rinks stepped toward them. Rinks was going to grab the boy—

"Leave him alone, Rinks," Vern said.

"Don't talk to me like that! I'm all scratched up from workin' all morning while these two been tellin' stories, and I ain't had a shower in two days."

"Well, take a shower, then."

"I ain't had time!"

"Hello? Yeah." Vern headed back to the bedroom. "I been on hold fifteen minutes now."

Rinks didn't need this aggravation. All she wanted was coffee and a shower. And a protein bar. "Hold up." The kids were trying to escape to the tiny room where they were sleeping. That was when she noticed a bulge in their pockets. "Come here. You can keep the stupid toy," she said when Fritz hesitated.

She urged them closer. There were crumbs on his shirt, just below the collar. She plucked off a big one.

"What's this?"

Marie dug a half-eaten muffin from her front pocket. She elbowed Fritz, and he did the same. Blueberry stains were on his fingers.

Marie put a wad of money on the table. It looked pretty much like the money Rinks had given her.

"Ms. Clara gave us the muffins," Marie said.

"She just gave them to you."

"She felt bad about the boys, I think. You can count the money. It's all there. She gave us the coffee for free, too, in that travel box."

"Fancy," Rinks said. "Where's the milk jug?" Marie shrugged. Rinks was agitated, which didn't make a lick of sense. Free coffee in a fancy tote was exactly what she wanted. Why should she feel like a scumbag? "You makin' friends already?"

"She's a nice lady. You should go talk to her. She knew my great-aunt—your aunt—who owned this place. Said she was a good story-teller; kids would line up to hear her stories. Maybe we could do that, too. You know? We could make this a toy store again."

Rinks looked in the plastic bag Marie had put on the table. It was filled with sugar packets and little creamers. "This all of it?"

"I didn't steal it. She gave it to me."

"You expect me to believe that?"

"She was just being nice."

"That what you think? Listen, no one just gives things away. She's expectin' somethin' back for this. You ever think of that? She's fillin' your head with ideas; what's in it for her, huh? Maybe she was makin' money from all those kids listenin' to your auntie's stories. You think Vern can just quit his job and start makin' toys? He don't know how to tie his shoes let alone how to stitch up a teddy bear. And who's gonna tell the stories that make all them kids line up?"

"You can."

"Don't sass me, young lady."

"You could stream it on your social post."

Rinks was taken off guard. Because that wasn't a bad idea. Good, even. Imagine posting a bunch of little kids sitting around her. It would be content. But suspicion undercut the intrigue. What was Marie getting at?

"What are you hidin' from me?" Rinks said.

Marie sighed. "We got coffee and the sugars and creamers, just like you asked. What else do you want?"

"You were hidin' those muffins. What else you hidin'?"

"She gave us some hot chocolate and a pastry, but we ate those when we were there."

"I knew it." She pursed her lips.

"She was being nice, that's all. She knows our godfather, too. Said everyone around here knows him, like he's famous or something."

"Cable's comin' tomorrow." Vern snatched the half-eaten muffin off the table and stuffed the whole thing in his mouth while filling up his mug with coffee. "We'll have internet. Probably need to have someone come fix the heater."

"We ain't goin' to see Godfather tonight," Rinks announced. "Call him, Vern. Tell him we'll do it another time."

"What?" Crumbs shot from his mouth. "Why?"

"You want to spoil these kids? We got a lot of work to do around this place. There ain't time to go drivin' around havin' supper with someone we hardly know."

"Rinks," he said, chewing slowly, "we can't just cancel like that. It ain't polite. He invited us. And, you know, the heater needs fixin'. He might want to help with that when he sees the young ones."

He shrugged those boney shoulders. Like that was that. Rinks wanted to go, sure. She knew all about Godfather, even more than what Vern told her. Man was generous, and when he saw these two little needy kids with the sad story, he just might fix the heater and who knew what else. They could go see him without the kids, just to teach them a lesson, but that'd be hard to explain why they left them behind.

They were hiding something, though. The little brats. They'd only been living with her a couple of years, but already Rinks had developed X-ray vision. She knew when they were up to something. She knew because that was what she had been doing at that age. And Marie and Fritz's mom—Rinks's sister—she wasn't an angel.

"Gimme your phone," Rinks said.

"Why?" Vern said.

She took it from him and turned away, scrolled through his contacts, and found it listed as *Godfather*. When he started to throw a fit, she held up a stiff finger and put the phone to her ear. It was ringing. Then someone answered.

"Hello?"

"Is this the, uh..." Rinks forgot Godfather's name. "Is this Godfather?"

"He is not available. How may I help you?"

"Well, we're comin' to supper tonight. He invited us."

"Ms. Rinks. Oh, yes. We are very much looking forward to your visit."

"Great. Well, we can't do it tonight. Somethin' came up, and we just need to come over in, like..." She looked at Marie and Fritz standing there with their mouths open. "Three days. How about that?"

"I am sorry to hear that. Are the children feeling well?" the voice said.

"They're fine," she whined. "Misbehavin' is all."

"I am afraid we will not be able to reschedule the visit. He is very busy at this time of year. He was anticipating your arrival tonight. I do hope you can come. He has something very special to give you."

"Like what?" Rinks said.

"Gifts, of course."

Gifts? "Who'm I talkin' to?"

"I am the Counselor."

"Counselor?" Rinks said. Vern's eyes lit up when she said that, for whatever reason. "Like a camp counselor?"

The voice laughed. "No, Ms. Rinks. I am a caretaker. Shall I cancel your visit tonight?"

Rinks was in a corner. The kids needed a lesson for whatever they were up to. Postponing the visit would be a good one. Make them wait. But it felt a little like she was punishing herself if she cancelled. *There are gifts.*

"No," she said through her teeth. "We'll be comin'."

"Great! We will see you tonight."

She threw the phone on the table. She felt worse than she had before the brats got back with the coffee.

"Well?" Vern said.

"We're goin', all right. But not before this place gets cleaned. Floors need mopped and the windows shined. I don't want to see one dirt ball anywhere, or I swear I'll call back. Understand? And Vern, you need to get workin' on that heater. Just cause it's Christmas don't mean presents are free."

Marie and Fritz looked just the right amount of sad to satisfy Rinks. Fritz showed his phone to Marie. She shook her head.

"What'd he say?" Rinks said. She grabbed the phone and read what he'd typed. *Doesn't Santa bring presents free?*

It sounded full of sass, the way Rinks read it. A real smart mouth. Rinks thought about it, because Fritz looked like he was waiting for an answer. Like he'd really asked the question. Like he wanted an answer. Rinks had an answer for him. She gave the phone back. She bent over and put her hands on his shoulders.

"Fizzy," she said gently, "Santa ain't real."

Fritz looked confused. So did Vern. Marie grabbed her brother from Rinks, gritting her teeth to hold back a stream of bad words. Rinks wanted one of those sass words to leak out, just one, and she would teach her a real hard lesson. A seventeen-year-old princess wasn't too old for a spanking.

They left Rinks alone, though. All of them walked away. She was in the kitchen by herself, alone with her victory. She'd won the imaginary battle of wills.

And felt worse than ever.

❄

I want your eyes. *So chocolate!*

Favorite comment of the day. Rinks always thought her eyes were a rich chocolate brown with spokes of toffee. That was how she described them. It was nice someone noticed.

"Slow down, will you?" Rinks said. "Or I'll puke in your lap."

"You can't look at your phone, Rinks," Vern said. "Makes you carsick."

"Phone ain't got nothing to do with it, Vern. You even know where you're going?"

"Following GPS." When Rinks picked up her phone, he added: "Seriously, put your phone down."

"You put your phone down."

He laughed. Maybe it was her stupid comeback. What was he so happy about? He'd been humming Christmas songs, and when he knew the words (which was rare), he'd look at her until she looked away. Then suck his teeth.

"You should have shaved," she said.

He explained how carsickness worked, how the brain couldn't make sense out of moving if she was focused on her phone. He was wrong because it was the winding road that made her sick. Not her phone.

She turned up the radio. It was mostly static. Radio stations didn't broadcast this far in the country. They were barely going to have enough gas to get back home. She found country music, which was better than Vern's Christmas Fun Time.

Anxiety nibbled at her mind like little sharp-toothed guppies. She didn't know this Counselor she'd spoken to on the phone. If he was a counselor, then he was going to judge her. She had enough people doing that already.

Plus, she'd never met Godfather before, either. The closest she'd ever come was when Fritz had been born. Marie had been ten years old. It had been her birthday. They'd invited all these people for a cookout. Rinks and Vern had gone. Godfather was supposed to be there. *The great gift giver*, they called him. But then he didn't show. A present arrived later, though. It was a stack of books, ones Rinks had never heard of.

It better not be books tonight. She wasn't going to suffer this trip for a bunch of dumb stories.

"How much longer?" she asked.

"Not much."

"We got enough gas?"

Vern adjusted the rearview mirror. "Marie? Ask your aunt Rinks a question to take her mind off this trip."

"I don't need distractin'."

He patted her arm with his clammy hand. He should be way more nervous than she was. Fact, he should be ashamed, going to see Godfather after what he did. Vern wasn't a good emotional compartmentalizer. He might talk dumb, but he was smart. And somehow naïve.

"Fritz wants to know what a godfather is," Marie said.

Rinks turned to look back. "You don't know?"

"Is he related to us?"

"He ain't." Kids were dumb. But Rinks didn't exactly know what a godfather was, either.

"What is he, then?" Marie pressed.

"It's just a title, like missus or mister. It don't mean nothin'. Like you know people who get a degree and get called doctor, but they ain't a doctor."

"You mean a researcher," Marie said.

Rinks flinched because she couldn't think of that word. "Like that. He ain't family or anythin', so don't get any ideas." What ideas she meant, she didn't know. "He's just someone you know. Well, not you. Your parents. Your dad, I mean. His boss."

"You worked for him, Uncle Vernon," Marie said.

"He did," Rinks answered. "He quit, though. Didn't like workin' for the man."

"Why?"

"He was judgy," Rinks said. "Full of himself. Thought he was better than others. Some people are like that." She patted her husband's knee. He didn't agree with her but appreciated the support. "Vern ain't like that."

Rinks felt good about her answer. She was itching to slide her thumb up the glass of her phone, take a quick peek at her last post (Vern had taken a picture of her in front of the toy store with clean windows: *new place looking good!)*. She heard a phone tapping in the back seat. Fritz showed his phone to Marie.

"What'd he say?" Rinks said.

"Nothing."

"Marie? What'd he say?"

She paused to think up a lie. Rinks was about to grab the phone when she said: "Can we live with him?"

"No, you can't live with him. He ain't family." That felt like a sharp stick. "How many times I got to tell you?"

"He meant all of us," Marie said. "Like, can we all live with him?"

"Instead of the place we got, is that what you're sayin'?"

"He just means, like, hot showers and beds."

Rinks had a long answer for a question like this. An answer she'd delivered many o' times. It was a sermon on gratitude. Sometimes she pounded a table like a preacher delivering the hard truth to a spoiled congregation. Now was a good time to fire it up.

"We're here," Vern said.

The country road was narrow and dark. No streetlights. Just pine trees and dead grass in the ditches. "I don't see anything," Rinks said.

He held his phone while almost coming to a stop in the middle of the road. There was a dirt road on the left. He looked around before deciding to pull in. This wasn't what Rinks was expecting. They were soon in a tunnel of oak trees and spooky darkness. If this was a dead end, they were going to have to back all the way out.

"Vern, if this is wrong, we could be in trouble." Rinks knew how country folk were about unexpected visitors. They didn't greet them with cookies.

"It's the directions."

"Well, what's that, then?"

There was a broken-down trailer buried in the trees. A rusted truck with flat tires and small trees growing in the bed of it. Bottles and buckets on the front steps lit by a moth-riddled porch light. Algae-caked walls. Darkened windows dimly glowing with yellow light, the kind of light that comes from lamps with lampshades, with old-fashioned bulbs that get hot.

"That ain't it," Vern said.

"You need to back up."

"Hang on a sec. Let me just—"

"Vern. Now."

"All right, all right, all right."

He shook his head, like Rinks was being paranoid. She was the only level head in the car. Billionaire Godfather, or whatever he was (trillionaire?), didn't have a trailer within a country mile of his property. He didn't live in one, for sure.

Things were about to get weird.

Vern put the car in reverse. They didn't move. Then everything went quiet. The radio was silent, the headlights went out, and the engine turned off. They were looking at a dark and sinister thicket of sticker bushes.

"What are you doin', Vern?"

"I didn't do anythin'." He turned the key. His foot thumped on the accelerator. "It just turned off."

"Well, turn harder!"

"I'm tryin'!"

Rinks leaned over the steering wheel like maybe there was a button he hadn't pushed, like he'd forgotten how a car works. He fought her off. The car was getting hot. It felt like coils in a toaster were glowing underneath them.

"What's that?" Marie pointed.

There was a light in the sticker bushes. A red light that lasered out of the branches. *Well, this is it,* Rinks thought. *Vern done made someone mad enough to melt us like candles.*

It disappeared like a flickering lightning bug. The bushes began to shake.

The lights in the trailer turned off.

❄

THE TREES SHIMMERED like asphalt on a summer day. The oak trees were coming to life. Rinks would blink, and they were right back where they were. The leaves were quivering, though. Wind blew through the branches.

She grabbed Vern's hand. He squeezed back. Rinks reached into the back seat and found Marie's arm without looking for her. She was about to crawl back there with them, wrap them up in her arms and duck so they didn't have to see what came next. Like a bear with laser eyes was going to attack. Or little green aliens coming out of the trailer with cans of beer or whatever they drank after a hard day of kidnapping humans for experimentation.

The bushes began to roll back like twiggy curtains. They opened to a dirt road. A corridor of oaks reached over it, their branches twining together like gnarled fingers draped in curly strands of moss.

And lights. Thousands and thousands of tiny lights were strung in the trees like itty-bitty stars as far as they could see. Enough lights to take a crew of a hundred people all year long to wind around the trunks and branches. They hung in long strands.

The radio came on loud and clear. They jumped at the sound of it. Rinks screamed just a little and nearly crushed the bones in Vern's hand. It wasn't country music blaring from the speakers.

It was Christmas music.

The car started on its own. Vern turned the music down, asked everyone if they were all right. Rinks shook her head up and down and side to side. She didn't know the answer to that question.

"I think this is it," he said.

"What?" Rinks said.

He put the car in gear. "It's exactly what he'd do."

Rinks couldn't argue. If she had all the money ever made in the world, she'd have a secret entrance, too. Add a water slide, maybe a trapdoor. Not a broken-down trailer, though. Rich people were weird.

Vern eased onto the dirt road that didn't have any tracks, just dead grass like no one ever drove on it. Rinks looked back at the kids, who were staring out the window. She felt a twinge of resentment and jealousy at the look of wonder on their faces. They were too young to know things like this could go sideways. Then she felt trapped when the sticker bushes rolled closed behind them. The lights in the trailer turned back on.

The road turned this way and that, curving through a forest dense with trees and blackness between them. Branches scratched the sides of the car and windows. Rinks was as tight as a spring. She pressed her face to the window to see if anything was out there. Her breath fogged the glass.

"Look at that," Marie said.

"What is it?" Rinks blurted.

"Look." She pointed out the window. Rinks didn't see anything. "It was a deer, I think."

"You think? What'd you mean *you think*?"

"It had antlers."

Lots of things had antlers. Moose had antlers. Elk had antlers. Rinks couldn't think of anything else. Unicorns, maybe. Monsters, for sure. What if Godfather was a crazy scientist? Vern hadn't talked to him in twenty years. Out of the blue, he'd sent Vern an invitation for dinner. Like somehow he knew they were coming. A man like that knew things. He knew they were the rightful owners of the toy store. She hadn't thought much beyond that.

Rinks wasn't much of a planner.

The road straightened out, and they drove up an incline; the engine changed gears as they neared the top. Over the front of the car, they saw the trees open. Vern stopped. The headlights shone through brushy saplings and a titanic oak tree with branches the size of tree trunks. Beyond it, tucked under a loose canopy of mossy limbs, was a cobblestone house.

It was a cottage. Smoke puffed from a stone chimney. This had to be where the grounds manager lived, but the road ended. There was nowhere to go besides back. They hadn't missed any turns. Not that she saw.

"This can't be it," she muttered. "I mean, he's rich. Right?"

"Yup," Vern said.

The cedar shingles were mossy. The walls of the cottage were boulders the size of truck tires. Candles flickered warmly in the inset windows. It was less threatening than the trailer—whatever that was about—with a harmless country feel. The kind of place you'd see on a screen saver where people would want to spend retirement away from the hustle and the bustle. All it was missing were bright fairies floating around it.

"Maybe it's his vacation home," Marie said.

"One way to find out," Vern said, and pulled the handle on his door.

Rinks grabbed his shirt. "That's your plan? What if this is the wrong place?"

"You think the gate would have opened if it was?"

"What gate?" Rinks looked at the kids. "You see a gate? I didn't see a gate."

"Those bushes was a gate. That red light was some sort of identifier that let us in."

That tracked. The way those bushes rolled opened, the car mysteriously turning off and back on again. Weirdest gate she'd ever seen.

"And look. See that?" He pointed at the door.

She squinted to see what the headlights illuminated. The front door was thick and dark, curved at the top. A wreath with a red ribbon was on it. She didn't get what was so revealing.

"Inside the wreath," he said.

She squinted harder. It was dark green. Pear-shaped. Then she put it together. It was the logo of the multitrillion-dollar tech company Godfather had run for the last however many decades.

An avocado.

❄

Rinks corralled the kids in her arms, with Vern leading the way. She felt better with them clamped against her. Like teddy bears. It looked like she was protecting them, even if she had them in front of her.

A short walk paved with round stones was surrounded by ferns and moss-covered rocks. Plastic-wrapped candy canes were stuck in the ground like winter flowers. A small sculpture watched them approach. It was a fat man with a round face and small eyes. The arms were strangely short. It was carved from granite. The belly had been worn smooth for luck. Long locks of hair cascaded over the shoulders, the details finely chiseled.

They bunched together at the front door. "Must be the doorbell," Vern said.

He reached for a strap of silver bells nailed to a board and shook it. It made a pleasant melody. Rinks stepped back and dragged the kids with her. Vern stood front and center. There was nothing at first. He was about to shake the bells again when they heard a voice from inside.

"Coming!"

The door started to open, letting out a warm breath of cinnamon and nutmeg and roasted things. *Chestnuts?* Rinks thought. *Nobody roasts chestnuts.* It did smell nutty.

A tall figure stepped out wearing a bright red, sleeveless robe of sorts that trailed down to the ground. Rinks squeezed the kids. Even Vern jumped back as the person or whatever it was threw its arms out.

It announced: "Merry Christmas!"

Rinks felt the fuzzy edges of shock hum in her head. Vern had described what Godfather had looked like the last time he'd seen him. This was not him. In fact, this was nothing like anything Rinks had ever seen in her life. The gray thing on the doorstep was not a person.

"Welcome. Please, come inside. It is a bit chilly. I am sure you must be feeling the nip of winter." The thing stepped aside to make room. "There is a fire to warm yourselves."

It waved a gray arm that was muscular and toned. Arms to die for that were dull gray and smooth as a newborn.

"What is that?" Rinks said. "Vern?"

Vern's mouth hung open: shock dashed with fascination. Warm colors passed on the host's face, if that was what you wanted to call it.

There was no eyes or nose or mouth or ears. A colorful plate where a face would be.

Marie said the obvious. "It's a robot."

"That ain't no robot," Rinks blurted.

"My apologies." The thing put a hand to its chest, as gray as the rest of it. "I understand your surprise. Perhaps I should have prepared you. I had assumed Mr. Vernon knew what to expect."

"Did you know, Vern?" Rinks said. "Did you know about this?"

It had a head and shoulders, arms and legs. It did not have a face. Just a bump where a nose would be (a small one at that) and the hint of a brow. It wasn't a man or a woman. A thing that spoke softly. Slightly masculine.

"I am a robot, I suppose. Although that is a crude description." Colors cascaded down the faceplate as it spoke. "More accurately, I am embodied artificial intelligence."

"A Counselor 5000," Vern muttered.

"Precisely!" It clapped. "Although that was the prototype. I am simply Counselor."

"I knew it," Vern said. "I knew when she called you on the phone! I worked on the sensory pads, helped design the fingertips." Vern took the Counselor's hand, traced the smooth palms that had no creases. *Creepy*. Ran his hand up the muscled forearm in a way that made Rinks jealous. "The project was a failure."

"As you can see, I am a success. There is still testing to complete before I am made public."

"Testing?" Rinks said. "Like you might freak out on us?"

"I am a caretaker, Ms. Rinks. I am here to help." It removed its arm from Vern's caressing curiosity, held out its hand. Rinks regarded it like a plate of worms.

"Go on, Rinks," Vern said. "Don't be rude."

Rude? It was a machine. Just because the thing talked didn't make it any different than a bicycle. They were all waiting for her to do something. So she shook its hand, wincing as if it might crush her bones. If Vern worked on it, there would be glitches. For sure. But her hand didn't break. The Counselor's grip was comforting. Warm and soft. Like the smooth part of a puppy's tummy. Rinks suddenly felt at ease.

"It is a pleasure to meet you, Ms. Rinks," it said. "And you must be Mr. Fritz. A pleasure to meet you, sir."

Fritz shook its hand, clutching the toy in his other arm.

"And what have you there? Is that a nutcracker?" The Counselor bent down, eye to eye with the boy. "That is a very special toy. You must be a very special boy if it chose to protect you."

Rinks snorted, then covered her mouth. Just because the block of wood carried a sword didn't make it walk and talk and choose who got to keep it. It couldn't protect a flea.

"I am happy you are here." The Counselor's faceplate bloomed yellows and oranges. "And you must be Ms. Marie. An honor to meet you, ma'am."

It shook her hand, too. It was a little over the top, like the thing was greeting celebrities. The colors grew brighter and more intricate. All Rinks had gotten was a smattering of greens and coarse gray when it shook her hand. She held onto the kids just in case the thing blew a sprocket.

"Let us go inside." It stood up to its full height of six feet. "Herr Drosselmeier is occupied at the moment. He will join you after dinner."

"Wait, he's not here?" Rinks said.

"He will be," the Counselor said. "He is very busy at this time of year."

"It's fine, Rinks," Vern said. "He never shows up."

"What do you mean he never shows up? Why'd we come all the way out here?"

"He does a telecommute thing. I never seen the man in real life."

Rinks backed up a step. "This is a trap. He's not here because he fired you, and this is a trap."

They were a bit confused by this. What trap would Godfather set for a former employee who worked for him twenty years ago? And why? Rinks just felt a little off balance. All the dumb colors Rinks had gotten when the Counselor shook her hand; then the toy had picked

Fritz to protect instead of her. She didn't feel appreciated. A little respect was in order.

"I wasn't fired," Vern said. "It was downsizin'. You know, company payroll and redundancies, things like that. No big deal."

"Mr. Vernon was on the naughty list," the Counselor said with a splash of brown.

"No, I'm—what?" Vern said.

"You took company material."

"I did not. I *borrowed* it. Just some extra parts we weren't usin'. It was a misunderstandin' and an overreaction, but it's all good. Look, it was twenty years ago. Do we have to talk about this now?"

"Was Godfather mad at you?" Marie asked.

"No. No, no, no… is he?" Vern asked the Counselor.

"If he is," Rinks said, "then this is a trap."

"I assure you, Herr Drosselmeier does not harbor ill will toward Mr. Vernon. He cares for all, naughty and nice. Now, if you are ready."

The Counselor held the door open. The kids walked inside. Rinks grabbed Vern.

"What'd you mean you never seen the man? Don't you think I'd want to know that before comin' all the way out to the middle of nowhere if that man wasn't here?"

"Rinks." He patted her arm and smiled. Charming Vern had a way of relaxing her. "Nobody ever sees him in person. This is normal. I'm sorry, I shoulda told you."

She took a deep breath. Normal was a planet far, far away from here. A dumb cabin with a robot butler? How many people could say they'd done that? If this was a trap, there was nothing they could do about it now. Rinks pulled out her phone.

May as well get some likes.

5

The cabin was plain. An unfinished dinner table. A wood-burning stove. A simple Christmas tree with homemade ornaments in the corner. Not something you'd expect when a robot answered the door.

The Counselor entered with a flourish, the sleeveless red robe swishing around his smooth gray legs. It was impossible not to smile. He oozed magnetic goodwill like a blast furnace. His hand melted around her hand when he shook it and warmed her like a heat lamp. He was someone she wanted to be around. She wanted to hug him.

"Nice," Aunt Rinks said flatly. Then snapped a selfie.

"I am sorry, Ms. Rinks, no photos are allowed. I hope you understand."

"Sure." She tucked the phone in her waistband. "So is this it?"

"My humble abode." He turned in a circle. Bowed. "Welcome."

"I think it's lovely," Marie said. "It's authentic. Warm. Fritz thinks so, too."

"Thank you, Ms. Marie. What about you, Mr. Vernon?"

"Oh, yeah. It's, uh, very real. Woodsy. Smells old. When was it built?"

The Counselor put a slender finger to the lower half of his featureless face. Where lips would be. "Company secret, I am afraid."

"This is a secret?" Rinks snorted. "Where's the fireplace?"

"There is a wood-burning stove in the kitchenette to keep us cozy. I have prepared dinner, which I hope you will enjoy." He gestured to the rough-cut table. "Please have a seat."

There were six chairs but only four table settings. The plates were fine china; the silverware gleamed real silver. They pulled the chairs from the table, the legs scratching the wood planked floor, and sat down. There was no couch or recliner. No television. Just a sad tree in the corner, which was better than no tree at all.

The Counselor returned from the other side of the cabin, wearing an apron (*I Cook Better Than I Look*), and lit two candles on the table, wagging the matchstick to extinguish it. He went back to the kitchenette, his footsteps treading as lightly as a cat's.

"I understand you are vegetarians." The Counselor chuckled, turning his head. His face glowed pink. "That is a joke. There is bread on the table. Please help yourselves."

Uncle Vernon unfolded the napkin in a basket. He was the first to grab a breadstick; the first to eat one. They were lightly toasted, coated with olive oil. Marie took a bite that melted on her tongue. It was warm and salty. The Counselor filled their glasses. Uncle Vernon got sweet tea. Aunt Rinks a soda. Marie and Fritz lemonade.

Aunt Rinks took a photo, shook her head at Marie to keep her mouth shut.

"I cannot express just how nice it is to have company at Christmas. I have been so looking forward to your visit. Tell me all about yourselves. I am eager to know you."

Only chewing sounds. Then Aunt Rinks went: "I'm a social media expert. An influencer. You know what that means?"

"I do. Do you promote a brand?"

"Yeah, me." She stuck her finger in her mouth to dig a clump of bread from her cheek. "I have about ten thousand followers, hit a thousand likes daily. Headscarves are my thing. I make them, mostly tie-dyed. Do some silk painting. Probably start sellin' them once we get the store open. Vern works for an insurance company, does it remotely. So, you know, he can do it anywhere. That's why we're movin' down here. Our building used to sell toys."

"You are in the old toy store?" the Counselor said. "How exciting. Will you reopen it?"

Aunt Rinks snorted. "We don't know anything about toys. Thinkin' 'bout a studio with different sets. You know, a place where people want different backgrounds."

"You are a photographer?"

"I won't lie, I'm pretty good. But it won't be like that. More like a selfie store. Haven't worked out the details."

"Interesting. You sound like you know quite a bit."

"I do pretty good." She grabbed a second breadstick. Uncle Vernon was on his third.

❄

THE COUNSELOR BROUGHT dinner to the table. Each plate was something different. Uncle Vernon had a pile of homemade noodles with chunks of chicken. Aunt Rinks had fried chicken and a sweet roll. Fritz got a plate of tater tots and a hamburger. And Marie was served her favorite: spaghetti and meatballs.

For someone who didn't know much about them, the Counselor got his dinners right. No one seemed to notice. Except Marie.

"Do you have a predinner ritual before you eat?" the Counselor asked.

"No," Uncle Vernon said, chewing the last of his breadstick. "We pretty much eat."

"Very well, then. Let us eat," the Counselor said. Although he wasn't eating. Do robots eat? *Not if they don't have a mouth.*

He topped off their glasses. The room was filled with chewing and slurping, finger-licking and moaning. Uncle Vernon hovered over his plate like a commercial vacuum. Aunt Rinks pulled her sweet roll apart, eating it a piece at a time.

The Counselor sat at the table. "Marie, tell me about you."

Marie had been thinking how to answer that question. She wiped her mouth with a linen napkin and decided to keep it brief. "I like to read and draw. I miss my friends. I like to fish, too."

"That sounds exciting." The Counselor leaned on the table. Listening with full attention. "What did you catch?"

"My dad would take us out on his boat in the mornings before the sun came up. We would go to the middle of the lake when the water was smooth. Some mornings there would be fog over it. It would be so quiet. Just the sound of bugs and mourning doves. Or fish jumping. We didn't catch much, but we still did it."

"That sounds lovely," the Counselor said.

"In the winter, the lake would freeze. Mom taught us to ice-skate. We would go in circles. Fritz was learning with hockey skates. He was even starting to skate backwards. I liked the figure skates. Mom taught me to spin."

"Oh my. I will bet you were good at it."

Marie blushed. "Not really. My mom was really good."

"She wasn't that good," Aunt Rinks said.

"Yes, she was." Marie felt her face flush. "She won awards."

"Your mom was an okay skater who got lucky, that's what she was."

"You're wrong." Marie held her fork like a stick. "She was really good."

"It's my opinion, sweety," Aunt Rinks said supersweetly. "You can't correct an opinion."

Marie stared at her spaghetti. Her appetite had excused itself from the table.

"It sounds like you have wonderful parents." The Counselor didn't follow up on that. He knew far more than he was letting on. He turned to Fritz and said: "What about you, Mr. Fritz?"

"My brother doesn't talk," Marie said.

"He can talk," Aunt Rinks said, slurping her soda. "He just don't want to."

Marie held her tongue. Aunt Rinks was baiting a fight. If they were back home (or at that mouse-infested toy store), Marie would have left the table. Would have gone to bed without eating, and given her aunt an earful on the way. Fritz was breaking his tater tots apart and dropping them on the plate. The bill of his cap shielded his face.

"Mr. Fritz," the Counselor said, "may I touch your shoulder?"

The Counselor didn't move until Fritz nodded. The Counselor gently placed his hand on Fritz's shoulder. His words came out softly. "You do not have to talk until you are ready."

The Counselor kept his hand there, his faceplate a myriad of greens and yellows. Marie held her breath, afraid a sob might slip out that she'd regret. Fritz held the nutcracker on his lap, staring down at it. For a moment, Marie felt something she hadn't felt in many months. Something that had failed her over and over. She couldn't help it, though, with the Counselor's gesture and Fritz's silence.

She imagined what her brother sounded like. Each day the memory of his laughter, his rapid-fire laughter, the way he talked in one long sentence when he was excited—when he caught a fish, when he skated backwards—was getting harder to remember. Marie tried not to hope that would change.

Because hope was a liar.

❋

"STAY WHERE YOU ARE." The Counselor began clearing the table. "I hope you enjoyed the food."

Uncle Vernon held his stomach and burped. Then gave a thumbs-up. At least he didn't fart.

"It was wonderful," Marie said. "Fritz loved it."

She and her brother didn't finish their meals. Not because it wasn't good.

"The duck was a li'l greasy," Aunt Rinks said.

The Counselor took her plate of bones. It looked like scavengers had picked apart a carcass. "It was chicken."

"Coulda fooled me. Is the Godfather comin'? It's gettin' late; the kids are tir'd from a long day of cleanin' the building. We need to get goin' soon."

"Herr Drosselmeier will be here soon. We have a few minutes before he arrives." The Counselor returned to wipe the crumbs off the table. "In the meantime, I would like to present my gift to you. I have been working on it all day."

Aunt Rinks looked at the sad tree in the corner. No Christmas presents were beneath the scrawny limbs. "We, uh, didn't bring anythin', just so you know. Didn't expect a..." She gestured at the Counselor, didn't finish her thought. *A robot.* Was it customary to bring a robot a gift?

Marie would have. Maybe a new apron. *World's Best Robot Cook.*

"I think my gift is quite fitting for the owners of a toy store and descendants of a storyteller."

"It's not a toy store," Aunt Rinks said. "*Was* a toy store."

The Counselor stacked the dishes in the sink and removed his apron. He stood in the middle of the small cabin, fiddled with the sleeveless robe. "I have a story."

Aunt Rinks looked at Uncle Vernon, who shrugged. "Stories count as gifts?" Aunt Rinks raised her eyebrows with a smirk. Marie had a feeling what she and Fritz would be getting for Christmas. They scootched their chairs around to face the tall and muscular android, who was fidgeting in place.

"This is for all of you," he said. "Are you ready?"

"Yes," Marie said. Fritz nodded.

"Fire away." Uncle Vernon leaned back in his chair, fingers laced over his bloated belly. Looked like he swallowed a balloon.

"Okay." The Counselor simulated a deep breath, chest expanding and deflating. He shook his hands. "I feel nervous, I think. You are my first audience." His faceplate flushed pinks and reds. "Everyone is looking at me."

Marie giggled. Fritz smiled.

"Well, go on," Aunt Rinks said. "It's just us."

"Right. We are friends." Then he muttered to himself: "Just like I practiced."

This brought more giggles from one side of the table. Uncle Vernon, too. Aunt Rinks rolled her eyes. The Counselor put a fist to his faceplate and made the sound of one clearing their throat. Even without a face, it was easy to forget he wasn't human.

He began. "Once upon a time there was a king and a queen who lived in a castle as sweet as their rulers. It was a land of tasty treats and perfumed air, where the Orange Brook trickled, the Molasses River flowed, and the Lemonade River ran. It welcomed all travelers through the Almond and Raisin Gate to the Candy Meadow. The Christmas Wood, with its delicious, candied ornaments, sprang forth the temperamental Chocolate River that sometimes overflowed its banks with frothy currents.

"If weary travelers were strong and steely, they would pass through the lovely villages of Bonbon Town and Paper Land, through Sweetmeat Grove, where the fruits were large and honeyed, and onward to Confectionville, where the market of all that is fair and scrumptious is made and traded. There they would find our happy rulers in the Marchpane Castle.

"They were happily married and ruled the rivers and woods and villages in between. Those who lived in the kingdom loved the royal couple, and that is why on a special day they cried huzzah!—to celebrate the birth of their daughter. A festival in her honor that lasted thirty and one days." He cupped his hands to his face. "*Huzzah, Princess Pirlipat! Huzzah!*"

"Pirlipat?" Aunt Rinks snorted.

"Shhh," Marie said.

"The princess never cried. She slept through her very first night. She began crawling before she was three months old. The king and queen loved her very much, as did the people. Everyone cheered her name. Everyone except for the Mousequeen.

"The Mousequeen ruled over Mousalia, but she lived in the cellar of the castle with jarred preserves and pickled vegetables and hanging meats. She did not like the attention given to the princess. Before she was born, the royal staff would allow her and her hundred children to make bedding with straw. They would bid them good morning and evening. And, most importantly, they would leave table scraps in the cellar for the Mousequeen and her hundred children. The king and queen, it was said, had forbidden them to enter the kitchen, where it was warm, when the seven-headed Mouseking tried to steal food from the cupboard. They were chased off with brooms and banished from the castle."

"Seven heads?" Aunt Rinks said. "The Mouseking has seven heads?"

"And a crown for each one. The Mousequeen vowed revenge for starving her children and exiling the Mouseking. She swore to take away the very thing the king and queen loved and hurt them like they hurt her. The king and queen had posted many guards, but that did not stop her. On a cloudless night, she snuck into the princess's room when the guards were sleeping and cursed the child.

"The king and queen awoke in the morning to find their perfect child crying. They recoiled at what they saw. The princess was unrecognizable. Her head was enormous, and a tufted beard had sprouted on her chin. She grinned when she cried in an unnatural way that made the servants cringe when they saw it. No amount of cuddling and rocking could soothe her. The queen was distraught and wept. The king sent his guards in search of the Mousequeen.

"They did not have to go far. The Mousequeen appeared before the royal court, smug in appearance. She demanded the Mouseking be returned to the castle. The king granted her wish. But this did not change the princess. The Mousequeen had tricked him. She did not say she would remove the curse."

The Counselor stuck out his belly and said with a bassoon voice, "'What do you want, then, to bring back my daughter as I know her?'

"The Mousequeen paused for a very long time. It satisfied her to see the king in distress. The queen had not left her room in weeks, wailing through the night. She did not want this to end so quickly and had not thought about what it was she wanted. She made up something quite impossible."

He wiggled his fingers near his face and spoke with a gravelly voice. "'It is quite simple, dear king. Princess Pirlipat must eat a crackatook.'"

Marie looked at Fritz. He was so absorbed by the story that he did not seem surprised by what the Counselor had just said. *Crackatook?*

"'The crackatook is the hardest nut in all the land,'" the Counselor said in the voice of the king.

"'Yes,'" the Counselor said in the voice of the Mousequeen. "'It must be cracked by one who has never shaved or worn boots their entire life. Then they must hand it to her without opening their eyes.'"

"'Very well!' the king replied. 'Send my men on the fastest horses—'"

"'Aaannnd,'" the Counselor interrupted himself as the Mousequeen, "'they must take seven steps backwards.'"

The Counselor held up one greedy finger.

"'Without stumbling.'"

There was a long pause. Everyone waited for what came next. Even Aunt Rinks listened with her mouth open.

The Counselor continued: "The king's men searched on their fastest horses, going to all corners of the land to find a crackatook. Months went by and then a year. The queen was dying of a broken heart. The king did not sleep. A dark cloud had fallen over the kingdom, and the sun no longer appeared. All hope was lost.

"But then one drizzly morning, they returned to the gates with a young man. He was barefoot with a long, pointed beard on his chin and curls of whiskers on his upper lip. The royal staff rushed him to Princess Pirlipat's room. They did not delay. The young man put the crackatook between his teeth to break it open. With the nut in hand, he closed his eyes and handed it to the princess.

"The king and queen hugged each other in the corner of the room, their faces wet with tears. The child ate the nut. Her head shrank, and the tufted beard vanished. Their precious child returned. They counted out loud as the young man, their savior, with his eyes closed, began stepping backwards.

"One! Two! Three! Four! Five! Six!"

The Counselor held up six fingers and paused, looking at the expectant faces around the table.

"On the seventh step, there was a great squeal. The Mousequeen had slipped under the young man's foot. Before he finished lifting the curse, he stumbled backwards. 'Ooooo' was the collective gasp. The king and queen clutched each other. They stared at the crib where their child lay, holding their breath, waiting for her deformity to return. It was the young man, however, who had taken the curse upon himself.

"His arms and legs grew stiff. His jaw became square, his teeth big and white. The once strapping young man transformed into the nutcracker."

He gestured to Fritz's toy standing on the table.

"The seven-headed Mouseking, at that very moment, attacked the nutcracker. The king and queen grabbed their child. The royal staff ushered them to safety and bolted the doors closed. They waited outside as the battle ensued. Night came, and in the morning, they still heard the clash of weapons and objects crashing. It went on for six nights; each morning the battle grew louder.

"On the seventh morning, the door opened. The victor emerged. Standing tall in a bright uniform, with his weapon sheathed in his belt, the nutcracker was victorious."

The Counselor locked his hands and shook them over his head. Then he took a deep bow. Several seconds passed.

"Is that it?" Aunt Rinks said.

"Yes," the Counselor said.

"What kinda ending is that? What happened to all the other people, Princess Pitter-patter and the rest?"

"I do not know how the story ends," the Counselor said.

"What'd you mean? It's your story. You can't tell a story without an end. That's not a story."

"It doesn't matter," Marie said. "I loved it."

It wasn't just a story. There was something about it he was trying to say, but Marie couldn't quite see it.

"Let me ask you somethin'," Aunt Rinks said. "Was that supposed to be a Christmas story?"

The Counselor looked at the ceiling. At first, it looked like he was in thought or trying to remember something. Then his face shone like a star. They shielded their eyes from the glare.

"He is here," the Counselor said.

6

The door on the back wall of the cabin was different than the front door, like it was made from heavy slabs of oak or cypress, but the hinges were bulky plates of iron. The Counselor put his hand on the L-shaped handle. Mechanisms shifted inside the lock, clicked and popped. The handle released downward. The door swung like a vault door. An icy draft escaped the dim opening.

"Watch your step," the Counselor said. "There are banisters on both sides."

"Where we goin'?" Aunt Rinks asked.

"Herr Drosselmeier is waiting."

The Counselor held the door open. Uncle Vernon didn't hesitate. Marie and Fritz followed him through the door and down a short flight of steps. The banister was polished platinum, cold and smooth, and slid under Marie's hand. Fritz was behind her. With each step, holiday music grew louder.

Aunt Rinks was the kid left behind when all her friends went into the haunted house without her. "Wait!"

The steps led to a wide balcony. Uncle Vernon was already at the railing. It arched outward in a half circle that overlooked a larger room. Marie's and Fritz's senses were filled with the aroma of nutmeg and spices.

"Look at that," Uncle Vernon muttered.

The far wall was two stories tall. It was a giant pane of glass bisected by a stone chimney with a roaring fireplace at the bottom. Marie expected to see oak trees and lights on the other side of the glass wall, the kind they'd seen when they drove in. It was nothing of the sort. Nothing like it at all.

Snow.

As far as she could see, all the way to a flat horizon, was snow and ice. The sky was a black sheet speckled with stars. Ribbons of color danced across it.

"That looks like the North Pole," Marie said.

Uncle Vernon offered a blocky-toothed smile. "That ain't a window, darlin'. That's just a projection, like a TV. Can't tell the difference, though. Can you?"

Aunt Rinks joined them. With one hand on the railing, she snapped a photo. "What is this, Vern?"

He explained again.

The back door closed with a heavy clank. The Counselor was coming, although they couldn't hear his catlike footsteps. Aunt Rinks quickly spun around to get a half dozen selfies with the colorful sky behind her. She tucked the phone away.

"You are witnessing the Northern Lights," the Counselor said. "It is a real-time projection of the North Pole. I thought it would capture the Christmas spirit. I hope you find it inspiring."

"It's beautiful," Marie said. Fritz nodded. If she would have walked into this room alone, she would've thought the back door was a portal.

"When you are ready, there is a staircase on both sides of the balcony. Herr Drosselmeier is waiting for us."

They were mesmerized by the small auditorium, hypnotized by the flowing nightscape, tendrils of color rising into the heavens. Without a word, Uncle Vernon followed the arching banister to the right and rushed down the steps. Aunt Rinks was close behind him.

The staircase sloped along the curving wall. A fir tree was tucked into the corner, its tip nearly reaching the ceiling. The evergreen branches were weighted with gold and silver apples. Almonds and lemon drops and brightly colored candies sprinkled like buds. Tiny lights sparkled like a galaxy bursting out of the trunk. The closer they got to the bottom step, the more it smelled like a forest. Aunt Rinks squatted next to the tree, examining three gift-wrapped presents beneath it, whispering to Uncle Vernon.

"This way," the Counselor said.

Couches and chairs were arranged around a low-lying table. A model spanned the width and length of the table. The details were extraordinary. Stone walls enclosed a courtyard where tiny plastic flowers were planted, and figurines of men and women stood at carts of fresh fruit and vegetables and livestock. There were feathers in hats, long cloaks that reached the ground, and flowery dresses.

Fritz plopped on a couch. His eyes were wide and unblinking.

In the middle of the courtyard was a castle. Turrets of glittering gold branched from the steep walls. It soared above the figurines, a monolith of magnificence, whose scale suggested a hundred flights of stairs climbed to the window at the very top.

"Did you make this?" Marie asked.

"I did not," the Counselor said. "Herr Drosselmeier has been working on this for quite some time. He is a clockmaker."

"Huh," Vern grunted. "I don't get the connection."

"Look closely."

The Counselor gestured with a sweep of his arm. Fritz stood up (the castle was a few inches taller than him). When he leaned closer, the figurines began to move! It was hardly mechanical. They sauntered like living people, stopping to examine an apple or peer through a window. Children in white shirts and green jackets danced to music coming from an open doorway. A man in a green overcoat put his head out the window. He nodded at the children and disappeared.

"Oh... my... word," Aunt Rinks gasped. "That is bananas."

"How are they doing that?" Marie asked. "They look so real."

"Reality is perception," the Counselor said. "Perception is reality."

Aunt Rinks snorted and shook her head at the nonsense. Fritz kept his fingers intertwined to keep himself from reaching in to pluck one of the villagers from their daily duties. Aunt Rinks had no such control. When her hand passed over the wall, everything stopped.

"What happened?" she said.

"The perception was an illusion," the Counselor said.

"Are you *tryin'* to sound smart?"

"The model is one of great craftsmanship. It is also quite educational."

Uncle Vernon paced around the table, scratching the stubble on his chin. This was a challenge. How did Godfather make this thing work? But Marie saw something else. The Counselor was trying to tell them something.

And it was important.

"Ah," the Counselor said. "Herr Drosselmeier is here."

❄

BENEATH THE BALCONY was a white room without corners. The walls were curved where they met each other as well as the ceiling and the floor. It had the illusion of infinity. As they approached the seating area, color bled into the spotless space beneath the balcony. Moments later, it was a cluttered library.

Candlelight flickered on the spines of books filling the outer walls. A man, who hadn't been there seconds earlier, was fiddling at a bank of computer monitors on a sprawling desk littered with random items: gift wrapping, boxes, and trinkets. A white feather leaned in a well of ink. A cane was stored in a tall metal container.

"Herr Drosselmeier," the Counselor said, "your company is present."

He turned with a start. The Christmas music he was nodding along to (and humming merrily, as well) turned down. A smile grew somewhere in a thick beard and shot sparkles into his eyes. "Merry, merry!" his voice boomed. "Welcome. Come in, come in."

He wore an ill-fitting tuxedo that was as disheveled as his long hair. The collar open, bowtie missing. He shuffled over to a comfortable-looking chair positioned just below the edge of the balcony. It was more of a cushy throne than a recliner. With a heavy mug in one hand, he watched them gaze at his surroundings like tourists.

"Let me get a good look at the lot of you."

He had a voice that needed no amplification. It had the richness of a foghorn and carried a smile in its sail. He urged them closer. They meandered around the model with the castle and tiny people and sat on the edges of their seats. Fritz sat next to Marie in a wide recliner.

"Counselor, would you be so kind as to put another log on the fire? Thank you. Did you all get enough to eat? The Counselor worked diligently on dinner. I was the recipient of many test dishes."

He chuckled and thumped his generous belly. He sat on his throne, propped his black boots on a short footstool, and dropped the mug on the armrest. Surveying their expressions—which were somewhere between amazement and shock—he nodded.

"Vernon, my good man, how long has it been?"

"Twenty years, sir. I think."

Godfather shook a finger. "Twenty-two years. It is good to see you. You look fair." Uncle Vernon took this honest assessment of his bad posture and ashy complexion as a compliment. "You are doing quite well with insurance analysis, I hear. I'm proud of you."

Uncle Vernon beamed like a child, told him about an award he'd won, a recent bonus he'd received, and the system he'd rebuilt to assess profit-loss. Godfather listened intently.

"Wonderful!" He slapped his knee. "And Rinks, it is a pleasure to finally meet you. I've heard many a good thing about you. You are quite a photographer, I hear."

The sour expression marring her face transformed under the warmth of Godfather's attention. He was like a sunbeam that unfolded flowers. She gave him the rundown of her social media and all the embellishments that came with it. He looked impressed.

Whether he understood or not. Marie had the feeling he didn't believe the parts she made up. Which was most of it.

"Marie." He turned the sunbeam on her. "You are becoming a lovely young woman, just like your mother. You are excelling in your studies like both your parents, I hear. The apple doesn't fall far. How are you doing, young lady?"

He asked, not like a throwaway conversation starter. It sounded like he really wanted to know, like *how are you doing since your life turned upside down?* She shuddered a little and offered a fragile smile.

"I am honored you are here," he replied, as if knowing she couldn't answer that honestly without popping the lid on a box packed with emotions. "As I am to see this young man. Fritz, the brave soldier. Are you taking care of your sister?"

Fritz looked down at the nutcracker in his lap.

"And what have you there?" Godfather asked. "May I see him?"

Fritz scooted off the recliner. Godfather dropped his boots on the floor and leaned his elbows onto his knees. Fritz held the nutcracker out for him to see. When Fritz attempted to hand it to him, a blaze of light wrapped around it. Godfather's image blurred.

He's an illusion.

It was a projection, just like the library around him. She'd forgotten what Uncle Vernon had said when they'd arrived at the cabin, that he was *never really there.*

"Did the Counselor tell his story of the nutcracker?" Godfather asked. "That is a loyal soldier you have there. He's a protector." He winked. "You must be very special."

Fritz laughed silently and blushed. He hopped back on the recliner with Marie.

"Please excuse my absence," Godfather said. "I would cherish the opportunity to be with you in person, but this time of year is very busy. I hope you understand. It has been a very long time, and I wanted to welcome you to your new home."

The Counselor brought a tray filled with merry mugs. He gave one to each of them. Fritz had hot chocolate. Marie, hot cider.

"Please accept my condolences for your loss," Godfather said. "Your parents were very special to me."

Marie cradled the warm mug in her lap. "How did you know them?"

"Ah, that is a story." He sat back in his throne and propped up his boots. "Your uncle Vernon introduced us. Didn't you, Vernon?"

"I did, yes. I knew your dad in college."

"You never told me that," Aunt Rinks said.

"We were roommates."

"No, that you got him a job."

"Well, I didn't exactly get him—"

"Vernon is very talented," Godfather said. "How long did you work at Avocado?"

"Six years."

"That's right. A trusted employee, you were." Vernon looked at his lap, hiding whatever feelings he carried for being *let go* from his job. "When we had an opening at the company, Vernon recommended your father. There were quite a few candidates, too. Your father came to us with humble confidence, a rare combination. He was skinny with a jaw like a soldier. Quickly became a rising star at the company. He solved a programming conflict that had plagued us for years."

"The Braxton-Milton co-efficient," Uncle Vernon said.

"That's right. He led a team of new and veteran scientists. *Scienceers,* he called them. What they were doing was beyond science and bordered on magic. He was ridiculed by his peers for using that word. Your father was not easily affected when he believed in something."

Godfather heaved himself out of the throne and went to the desk on the other side of the room. He sifted through the clutter (*so he's in that room wherever he is*) and brought back a framed photo. It was a group of young colleagues. They were all in white lab coats. Godfather was in the middle. He looked pretty much the same as he did now: the beard, the belly. He was holding a big pair of scissors over a wide yellow ribbon for the opening of a new research wing. Judging by how Marie's father looked, it must have been thirty years ago.

In the photo, Godfather was next to her father, the bright scienceer, the youngest of the team. His hairline crisply outlined a handsome face. His hair was short. Godfather was beaming in that photo. Marie wanted to think it had something to do with her father, of all the things he accomplished.

And all the things he never had a chance to.

"He met your mother a year later. She was already working at Avocado in the Storyline Division and was transferred to your father's team. He spilled coffee on her the very first day." Godfather's laughter trailed off while he studied the photo. "They were two wires in a single circuit, those two."

He put the photo on his lap.

"They introduced you two, remember that? Your mother brought Rinks to the Christmas party that year. Vernon was standing in the corner, and she introduced her sister. Next thing you know, here you are."

"My sister didn't introduce us," Rinks said under her breath.

"They asked me to be your godfather. Of course, I said yes. I'm sorry we couldn't spend more time getting to know each other. It's been a pleasure watching you grow up."

Counselor sat on the sofa nearest Fritz.

Marie didn't say anything. If she did, it would open the box of emotions she didn't want to let out. So they sat in the silence, listening to the fire pop in the fireplace and the music play from the castle. She was thinking of her parents and wondered if they had told Godfather all about them.

He watched us grow up.

❄

"How are you settling into the toy store?" Godfather asked.

"Just great," Aunt Rinks said. Then she didn't miss a beat. No heat. No hot water. Dirty windows, drafty, dusty, overgrown, rusty pipes, moldy mattress, cracked ceilings. The place was great, she said. Just great.

"Have you been there?" Marie asked.

"Been there?" Godfather's belly jiggled when he laughed. "Your great-aunt was one of my favorite people. The stories she told, oh! She was the heart of this town, Marie. She was the true essence of Christmas, personally responsible for seeding generations with imagination."

He unbuttoned his collar and sagged in the oversized chair.

"One Christmas, I was fortunate to hear her tell a story. The line was quite long, as I'm sure you've been told. I slipped in without much notice. *Corker's Candyland*, they called it. Big sign over the door." He swept a banner with his porky hand. "Very few sweets to eat, though. Children of all ages were there, clinging to a parent's leg or running down the aisles. Teenagers, too. Adults returned to relive a childhood experience. The place had a particular smell. It drew me in like it did all others."

He closed his eyes and inhaled.

"Like pages in old books." He looked around and laughed, suddenly aware of the many books surrounding him. "The toys on the shelves were simple and old-fashioned, teddy bears and wooden soldiers and plastic dolls. They meant nothing to the older children, I'm afraid. They had everything they needed in their pocket."

He pulled a phone from a pocket inside his jacket and tossed it on a small table.

"I stood by and watched children funnel through the front door, guided to a place on the little stage by workers dressed like silly elves." He took a moment to sip from his mug, chuckled at the thought of elves dressed in curly-toed shoes and bells on their collars. "One mother was pulling her little one down the aisle, between other kids who were sitting on the floor and playing. Her daughter was shy. I envied her, the young one. She was about to experience a ride she would never forget. No one forgets their first story.

"A man greeted her. He knew the mother by name, of course. His voice was warm and deep. The mother pried her daughter from her leg. The little girl put her hands over her face, but was peeking through her fingers. He was tall, very tall; stilts for legs. Angular face.

Your great-uncle looked like a butler, the way he stood. His back so rigid you could run a flag up it.

"The little one managed to get behind her mother's legs again and wished he would go away. And then his voice was right next to her. He knelt and said, 'And who is this?' He was as warm as a fire on a winter night and bright as sunlight in the morning. His smile as big as his eyes.

"Of course, the mother introduced her little girl—Hallie, she said —because Hallie wasn't going to say a word. 'Can I tell you a secret?' he said. 'You've come to a magical place. Can you feel it?' Hallie thought magic must feel like clenching fear, because that was what she was feeling. Then he unfurled long, skinny fingers. There, in the palm of his hand, was a piece of hard candy. 'Merry, merry,' he said."

Godfather looked at the ceiling, as if memories were floating above their heads.

"Hallie wouldn't be able to find the words to explain what that felt like, not at that age. It was like a flower blooming for the first time, its petals opening in spring. She followed her mother through the store, sucking on the candy, to a crowded stage in the corner. Mrs. Corker was sitting in her chair, wrapped in her purple blanket. The wire-rimmed glasses on her nose. Her hair white as snow.

"The mother was not shy, stepping between people until they squeezed into an open spot. Hallie sat on her lap, her mother's arms around her. There was an elf behind Mrs. Corker, a tall one. Hallie looked at the elf suspiciously, thinking this wasn't a real elf. She was right, of course. Even at that age, she knew someone was playing dress-up. But it didn't spoil what she was feeling. When bells began chiming, the entire store fell quiet. No one said a word. Not a cough or a sniffle. Not even a mouse."

He winked at Marie.

"Mrs. Corker closed her eyes, gently rocking. That's when she went there, to that storyland in her head. She looked like she'd fallen asleep, but she was smiling. Then she opened her eyes and said, 'Once upon a time...' and took them to a world of toys. Where snowmen lived and reindeer flew. Where Christmas spirit could be tasted in the air. They were spellbound, as was I. Children didn't blink; tears rolled down their cheeks. She took them there, and they felt it. The snow and the cold, the excitement of possibilities.

"To this day, I believe she stoked the imaginations of many who came. Those children were keenly aware, from that moment forward, that the physical world would always have limitations. Even at that age, they knew they might never breathe underwater or sprout wings. But imagination… well, anything is possible.

"The air in the store changed. The toys looked different when it was over, like they would talk to them when they walked down the aisle. Mr. Corker greeted them at the door. He knelt as Hallie and her mother approached. Hallie held her hand, no longer hiding. He whispered to her, 'Do you feel the magic?'"

Chills stormed Marie's arms. *She* could feel it. Just from the way he told it. Fritz had gotten up while he was telling the tale and now stood a foot away from him, holding his nutcracker with both hands. He could feel it, too.

"The toy store wasn't frivolous fun. No, no." Godfather dismissed the notion with a wave of his hand. "They gave the children what they needed, not what they wanted. That is the true spirit of Christmas."

"What was that?" Aunt Rinks said.

He laughed a big belly laugh. It went on so long Aunt Rinks began to frown. The answer was obvious.

"What I meant to say," Aunt Rinks said, crossing her arms, "was why were you there? If it was for children and all. A grown man standin' around is a little strange, doncha think? Right, Vern?"

Uncle Vernon shook his head. He wasn't getting dragged into it. Godfather wiped a happy tear from his eye, laughter trailing off. He paused for a moment, thoughtfully. Then looked at Marie when he answered.

"I was there to deliver a gift."

❄

The Counselor refilled their cups. It wasn't much since no one had really drank what he gave them in the first place. Godfather went to a pitcher on the desk behind him, poured something chocolatey into his mug. He took a sip, wiped his mustache with the back of his hand.

Delivering a gift? Marie felt stunned, for some reason. The way he looked at her when he said it.

"Will you be opening the toy store, then?" Godfather asked.

"Why does everyone keep askin' that?" Aunt Rinks said.

He collapsed in the big chair. "What does your heart tell you?"

"You don't want to know what's in my heart," she muttered.

"Do *you* want to know?" he said, more seriously than he'd spoken all night.

Aunt Rinks looked away, arms still locked across her chest. Still sore from when he laughed at her dumb question. Marie knew what was in her aunt's heart: a dark, self-centered lump of coal. Godfather knew. You only needed to be in the room with Aunt Rinks for two minutes to know how shallow her pool was. Didn't take an X-ray.

"We're workin' on some ideas for the place," Uncle Vernon said. "It's all very new, you know. Just settlin' in. Rinks got some good ideas, though. She's good with people."

"Of course, of course." Godfather took a sip. "I understand."

"Maybe *you* should open the toy store," Aunt Rinks said. "Seein' how you loved it so much. You could make it new, I bet. Just like before."

Aunt Rinks might not have been bright, but she was clever. Here was a man who had enough money to fill a volcano, and he'd just confessed to the importance of the toy store. *The true spirit of Christmas.* His words, not hers.

He didn't take the bait.

"It's your building," he said. "And I have too much to do already."

"What do you do?"

"That is a very good question." He appeared to give serious thought before answering, "I serve."

"Serve?" Now it was Aunt Rinks's turn to laugh hysterically. "Like food?"

"Hope, my dear."

"And who gets your hope?"

"Everyone." He winked. Then he slapped his thigh. "Enough about me. Tell me about yourselves. Better yet, tell me a story."

"A story?" Aunt Rinks howled. That was a sharp turn she didn't see coming. "What kind of story you want?"

"First thing that comes to your mind. It can be anything. Don't overthink it." He got comfortable and looked around, raised his mug of coffee or hot cocoa. "Just go."

Fritz jumped on the couch. Marie shrank into the cushions next to him. The Counselor put his arm around Fritz like story time was about to begin. After a few minutes of nervous chatter, Aunt Rinks and Uncle Vernon started talking. It was more like a report of how they drove all the way here in a beat-up car with bald tires and a broken windshield wiper. Uncle Vernon hardly finished a sentence without Aunt Rinks interrupting about the stupid GPS lady giving bad directions or dumb drivers in the left lane. It devolved into bankruptcy and backstabbing friends. And they never planned to have kids. But you know how that turned out. She nodded her head at Marie and Fritz.

Godfather listened, really listened. Letting them sing their country song of missed opportunities and bad luck.

"And what about you, Marie?" he said abruptly. "You and Fritz."

Marie thought she would dodge the question by hiding in the corner of the couch. Godfather sat forward, leaned a listening ear, waiting to hear her speak her words like they were rare diamonds.

"I... I don't know what to say. You already know about us."

"Then tell me a story."

Marie looked at her brother. He was waiting to hear what she had to say, too. They were all looking at her. The room was as hot as the engine of a long-haul truck. She folded her arms just like Aunt Rinks did, trying to hide behind them. Her thoughts swirled like a winter storm through a broken window.

"I don't have one," she said.

He nodded. "Try this. Think of a story someone told you. Anyone."

"What about?"

"It can be anything. Shoveling snow, digging a hole. Doesn't matter. Close your eyes, tell us a story about the first thing that comes to mind."

She wasn't getting off the hook. Aunt Rinks had a grin the length of a jump rope. Someone else was the dummy in the circle. Fritz put his head on her shoulder. The Counselor squeezed her arm. She closed her eyes, mostly so she wouldn't see everyone looking at her. The silence stretched as tight as a wire on a guitar.

Her father had told her the secret about stressful situations. *Just breathe.* A long inhale through the nose, an exhale even slower. And then it came to her like a fish pulling the line.

"A man went to a conference." Eyes still closed, she swallowed. "He, uh, he didn't like doing stuff like that, getting dressed up and shaking hands. *Droll stuff,*" she said in a deep voice.

She heard Godfather chuckle.

"He met this woman. Her name was... Drea Martenkrugel..." she mused. "He said her name made him hungry. She was a few inches taller than he was, had strong arms that could crush a jug full of milk. And a gruff voice, the kind that could heel sailors on a long voyage."

That was how he had described her. She'd never forgotten that.

"Her eyes were different colors. Brown and blue. Never married. Not that she was after him or anything. Least that's what he told his wife. She was an optics specialist. With eyes like that, it made sense. They spoke about hobbies, like she was into astronomy and ocean life. He was all about the future of human evolution. They even talked about sports, of which he knew almost nothing. And then, out of the blue, she leaned closer. Her perfume was spicy, like she'd rolled in a field of cloves. But underneath it was a hint of straw."

She thought a second, eyes still closed.

"No, like a farm. He was intrigued. *Who smells like that?* And then she whispered, although it wasn't really a whisper—she seemed incapable of whispering—and said, 'I want to show you something.' He couldn't say no. Perhaps to someone else, but not a woman who smelled of cloves and animals. He followed her through the lobby and into the parking lot. There was quite a bit of snow up there. Piles of it between cars. They weren't dressed for it, but off she went across the asphalt, passing under streetlights and not looking back to see if he was following.

"There was a moment it seemed like an awful idea. When they got to the middle of the parking tundra, he called her name. He was concerned for her being out there alone, although he was quite sure she could protect herself better than he could. He followed her to the far corner where a cargo van was parked.

"She was standing by the back doors. He was quite winded at this point and starting to shiver. The wind was raking the lot. Even the streetlights were shivering. He started to say this can wait till morning, but no sooner did he get the words out than she threw open the doors. She reached in and pulled out a chicken."

"A chicken?" Aunt Rinks said.

"The feathers were black, almost iridescent. She held it in the crook of her arm, the bird's neck rocking back and forth the way birds' do. Its beady eyes fixed on him. She told him the bird's name; he didn't remember what she said; he couldn't feel his lips at this point. And then she kissed it on the beak.

"The bird, apparently, didn't like being kissed. It flapped its wings, smacking her in the face, and landed on the ground. Before he knew it, she was in a dash after the mad thing. Feathers flying, Drea calling out the name, calling, 'Blitzen! Blitzen, come back here now!' Blitzen had not been trained to come back.

"He couldn't leave the poor woman. Of course, the chicken wasn't any more keen on him than it was her. He attempted to corner it at a snowbank. Drea had given up at this point, going back to the van. He thought perhaps she was going to drive after it. Instead, she opened the sliding door to retrieve something from inside the van. She put it to her lips and blew.

"Blitzen froze. She blew it again, and the chicken turned its head.

The third time, Blitzen marched straight to her, crawled into her arms, and she hugged it like a child. He said to her, 'Why didn't you blow that cursed thing in the first place?' She put the rooster away and didn't say a word. They walked back to the event."

Marie's eyes were still closed. It was a true story. Mostly. She could see it all happening. Exactly like she did the first time she'd heard that story.

"That's it?" Aunt Rinks said. "That's the ending?"

That was it. It didn't matter whether it had an ending or not. *There are no endings,* her father used to say. *One story leads to another.*

"What did she blow?" Uncle Vernon asked.

Marie opened her eyes, looked around at the expectant faces, and said: "A trumpet."

Uncle Vernon looked confused. Aunt Rinks sort of angry. Fritz's shoulders shook against her. Godfather leaned his head back and let out the loudest, deepest laughter she'd ever heard. His mouth wide open, he cradled his belly and laughed until tears streamed. Marie could feel his laughter in her stomach and started laughing, too. Even Uncle Vernon started giggling. It went on for minutes. Godfather wiped his eyes and leaned forward, eyes wet and twinkling.

"Now *that's* a story."

❄

"Counselor!" Godfather said. "I think it's time."

The gray skinwrapped android moved off the couch as smooth as a figure skater gliding across the ice. He went to the Christmas tree in the corner and returned with the gifts that were under it.

"I have something for each of you," Godfather said. "It's not Christmas, but I won't tell anyone if you open them now. Go on."

The Counselor put a box wrapped in gold paper between Aunt Rinks and Uncle Vernon. Her eyes inflated. It was the biggest present of the three, by far. And every child knows bigger presents are always the best. She clapped her hands and didn't wait for Godfather to say another word, or for Uncle Vernon, for that matter. She shredded the paper like a mouse making a nest. The gift was exposed in two seconds flat.

Her jubilance shrank like a rotting apple core. The thing in front of her had wide wings and big eyes. Aunt Rinks looked up.

"What is it?" she said.

"It's a clock," Godfather said. "I'm a bit of a watchmaker. More of a hobby, I guess."

She turned it around, then upside down, hoping, maybe, there was an envelope taped to the bottom of it filled with cash. "We already have one in the kids' room. It's on the shelf. Right, Marie?"

Marie nodded enthusiastically. It was exactly like that: a clock in the belly and watchful eyes. Aunt Rinks's disappointment was invaluable.

"Of course. I gave one to the Corkers, once upon a time." He chuckled. "This one is for you."

"But I already get the time on my phone." Aunt Rinks lifted her phone, like he might reconsider a better gift.

"What do owls eat?" he said.

"People?" Aunt Rinks said.

"Not this one."

"Mice," Uncle Vernon said.

"I was kiddin'." Aunt Rinks elbowed him. She wasn't. "Mice."

There were no mouse turds in Marie and Fritz's room, now that Marie thought about it. Not that Aunt Rinks would notice. Maybe he was telling the truth. The clock scared them away. Aunt Rinks looked nervous already, turned the clock so the big eyes were looking away from her. She slumped in her chair. Uncle Vernon turned the handle on the back of it. The second hand started ticking. He nodded his approval and said, with mild excitement, "Thank you." As mild as one could get.

Marie wondered if the owl clock was the gift he'd delivered to the Corkers. It was not. And she would soon find out the gift he'd delivered that day was much different than a clock. Not even close.

"Marie." He gestured to the gift in front of her.

She knew what it was before she opened it. It was a thick

rectangle, weighty and dense. She pulled off the tape and unwrapped a leather-bound journal. The surface was worn but smooth against her palm. The pages inside were thick and blank. A white feather was tucked into the pages, a quill to dip in a bottle of ink. It was beautiful. Smelled like old leather and freshly milled paper.

"A journal, dear," he said. "To write your own story. A story no one else can discover but you. And don't forget... look through the pages."

She flipped through them and found, tucked between the last pages, a long white ribbon.

"A bookmark," he said. "Or whatever else you might find it handy for."

"Thank you," she said.

It was a striking gift. The ribbon was nice, but the book was so special she didn't know if she would ever mar the pages with a spot of ink. If the pages stayed blank, that meant anything was possible. When they were blank, they were safe. Unstained.

Aunt Rinks looked a bit cheerier. The owl clock was better than a book. Any book, really. Especially a book with blank pages, the more she thought about it. Besides, a custom-made clock would sell easier. *A clock that keeps away mice.*

"Master Fritz." Godfather swatted his thighs like paddles on a glassy pond. "I haven't forgotten about you, my boy. It's your turn."

The Counselor offered Fritz the smallest gift of the bunch. It was the size of a ring box, tightly wrapped with sharp corners. Fritz put the nutcracker between his legs and turned it over like a puzzle to be solved. He tore one corner, then another. The nutcracker watched with an open mouth. So did Aunt Rinks, stepping closer to see what was in it. A ring, perhaps? Jewelry for a boy who wore a dirty old hat?

Fritz pried open the top of the box and poured out the contents. He cupped it in his hand.

"What is it?" Aunt Rinks said.

He raised and lowered his hand as if weighing its worth. Then held it up between his finger and thumb like a jeweler.

"A marble?" Aunt Rinks said and laughed. "He got a marble, Vern."

"It's a nice marble," Uncle Vernon said.

It wasn't a marble. It was round like one, but not a marble. It was the size of a golf ball with textured stripes. Sort of rough but polished so their distorted reflections looked back. Looked sort of like a walnut. Marie whispered in her brother's ear: "It's lovely, Fritz."

"Come closer, Fritz," Godfather said.

Fritz scooted off the couch. With the nutcracker in one hand, the ball in the other, he went right to the edge of Godfather's projection. Godfather beckoned him closer. Fritz stepped into it. The light streamed around him. Godfather's image was broken from the interference, but he whispered something to Fritz. Appeared to pat him on the shoulder, nodded and winked.

Fritz ran back to the couch with something much rarer than a custom owl clock and an antique journal. Fritz had a smile on his face. A genuine smile. He clenched the ball until his knuckles were white.

That night, the true value of that gift would reveal itself. It was the greatest gift of the night, by a billion miles.

"We didn't get you anythin'," Aunt Rinks said. "We didn't know we were doing gifts."

"I have everything I need," Godfather said. "What everyone needs isn't a place or a thing. It's a journey."

Aunt Rinks snorted. "We ain't on a journey."

"My dear, we're all on a journey." He raised his mug. He looked at Marie. "You just need to find it."

7

The stove burner coil was orange. Rinks spread her hands over it. Her knuckles flexed like hard plastic. She could barely scroll her phone.

She huddled in a blanket like one of those little hotdog treats Vern liked so much. *Pigs in a blanket,* she thought. *Dip me in ketchup.* She chuckled to herself. Despite her steamy breath and terrible night at the full-of-himself rich fat man's cabin in the woods, she was feeling a touch merry.

Likes are up.

Her recent posts were doing better than expected. She subtracted the ones she'd bought—the fake ones—which meant the rest of them were organic. People were catching on. They liked her. They really liked her. She went down thirty-two comments before she got to a negative one (*Your makeup belongs in a circus*) and that didn't even bother her. Most of the comments were about her scarves. She was going to sell them. They were going to buy them.

"Wait till they see this," she muttered.

She searched her photos from that night. Once her followers saw the crazy robot and that whole downstairs setup at the cabin, they'd start spreading the word. Rinks knew important people. She was buds with Avocado, the greatest tech company in the world.

I'm goin' viral, she thought.

She scrolled up and down her photo library. Her face scrunched each time she went through the collection, growing more like a dried apricot each time she did it. She couldn't believe what she was seeing. Her phone never lost its charge (she carried reserve battery chargers in her bag just in case).

This made no sense.

She flipped off the stove, threw the blanket over her shoulder, and started for the bedroom. The kids were still awake. A light showed from below the door. She stopped to listen, pushed her ear against the door. Marie was doing all the talking, like always. Fritz was probably lying there listening to her, ogling that stupid ball he got. (She felt a tad sorry for him. A ball wasn't much better than coal.)

There was a turn of a page. Laughter. Marie was telling a story from the blank book. That irritated her worse than the clock.

Godfather wanted *her* to be the storyteller; that was obvious. Did he know Marie stole that story about the chicken from her dad? Rinks did. She'd heard it three times on one visit to see her sister.

Rinks didn't know they could tell other people's stories. Comedians called that stealing. Rinks could think of a hundred stories better than the one Marie had told, and tell them ten times better. But it wouldn't have mattered. Godfather liked her better. Rinks didn't stand a chance. Never did.

Vern was on their lumpy bed with the laptop on his belly. His face washed in blue-white light. He wore a hoodie with the hood pulled up and a stocking cap on his head.

Rinks aimed her phone at him. "They stole my pics."

"What?"

"My pictures, the ones I took inside the cabin and the basement, they're gone. Like, not even on my phone."

"You weren't supposed to take pics, Rinks."

"Yeah, and it's against the law to hack my phone. I could report them."

He frowned. Who would she report them to? "They probably had somethin' that kept your camera from workin'. You saw the place. Wouldn't be too hard to do."

"I wasn't doing anythin' wrong."

"Except takin' pictures."

"Takin' pics ain't against the law. And I think the world oughta know what they're doin', that's all. I mean, they got all that stuff. That fair? Don't you think people would want to see that robot? I would. That's all I'm sayin'."

He went back to pecking the keyboard, his eyes sinking into the fog of computer life.

"All that garbage about Christmas," she continued. *"It ain't what you want, it's what you need.* You know what we need? Heat. We need heat. We need this place fixed up. He coulda done *that* for us instead of presents. That's what we *need*. Not a clock."

"He ain't Santa Claus, Rinks."

"He's rich!" She threw her hands over her head. "He's got enough money to build a bridge around the world with one-dollar bills. What would it cost to fix up this building? That would be loose change to him." Her knee sank into the pile of blankets covering the dust-mite-infested mattress. "He thinks he's better than us, Vern. You worked for him five years. He should have treated you better than an owl clock."

She scoffed. This usually worked on Vern, getting his blood pressure running in the red. Sometimes she got him madder than she was. She liked that. Like having a pet bull in the house.

"Well." He tapped a key. "At least we didn't get a striped ball. What's Fritz supposed to do with a ball that doesn't even bounce?"

Rinks crawled across the bed. "What do you think he whispered to him there at the end? I don't like secrets, Vern. I'll bet he knew that, did it on purpose just to irritate me."

Rinks had tried to get Fritz to tell them what he said on the way home. The boy had just shrugged. When he finally wrote something on his phone, it wasn't the truth. *The ball is special.* That sure wasn't the truth. If it was, why didn't Godfather just say that? No reason to whisper it. Unless he just wanted to make Rinks quiver with curiosity.

Mission accomplished.

"He was probably just encouragin' the boy." Vern went back to typing. "That's all, Rinks."

He wasn't taking the bait. Rinks bounced on the bed. The laptop shook on his belly. He asked her to stop, and he asked nicely. He was far from upset. Looked bored, in fact. She jumped off the bed and walked around the room. Piles of dirt balls were swept into the corners. The room smelled like wet plaster.

"This clock ain't goin' to keep mice away. You know that, don't you?" She poked the owl face in the eye. It was hard wood. She hated the way it made her feel. Like it was going to swoop down on her in the middle of the night. Vern had put it on a shelf facing the bed. "Like a mouse is goin' to be scared of that. Seriously, you know that, right?"

"I know."

"What's this?" There was a fork on the shelf. She held it like a magic wand. That got his attention.

"I accidentally took it from dinner."

"*Accidentally?*"

"Yeah." He wasn't making eye contact. "You know how I put my fork and spoon in my pocket at supper? It's just habit."

"Oh, yeah. How you just put a fork made of silver in your pocket after supper, sure." She aimed it at him. "You *stole* this."

He shook his head. No more typing. "I'll give it back."

"No, you won't. You're goin' to sell it is what you're goin' to do. Melt it down so they don't know you stole it. You're goin' to sell it and that owl clock. A handmade original clock made by Herr Drosselmeier that's guaranteed to keep mice away."

"No."

"No? Why not?"

"I'm not goin' to sell the clock or the fork, Rinks. He'd find out."

"We need the money, boy scout. Can't feed those kids a clock."

"We don't need money, Rinks. What we need to do is decide if we're stayin' here." He sat up. That was what was on his mind. "Do you really want to live in this building?"

"We own this building, Vern. It's free."

"Well, then we need to start buyin' stuff. Startin' with a new bed. Then a refrigerator and furniture that ain't filled with microscopic bugs. We're goin' to need air-conditioning, too. Summer's goin' to be hot. Kids need their own beds, too."

"Oh, please. The kids got a mattress, probably better than ours. You know, there're kids in the world sleepin' on dirt, you know that? They oughta count their blessings."

"You know someone sleepin' on dirt?"

"Just watch TV, Vern. You'll see. This place ain't bad compared to that. It's basically campin', only better."

"Barely." He closed the laptop and spoke slowly. She hated Serious Vern. "Look, Rinks. This mattress smells. I can feel things in it, and it ain't my imagination. This was a vermin hotel before we got here. Just look in the corners of the room. This ain't a house. We could make it one, sure. We get it cleaned up and all that, but then what?"

He leaned forward with that Serious Vern look: stiff lips and squinty eyes.

"A toy store ain't a bad idea," he said.

Rinks nodded. Not because she liked the idea. She just wanted him to shut up about that. She'd heard the pitch twenty times that day. Good idea or not, it was starting to annoy her.

"Marie stole that story she told, you know that, right?" she said.

"Mmm," went Vern. Which meant he didn't care.

"Just like her mother." Rinks shook her head. A worm of guilt or shame turned in her stomach, knowing where she was going with this. "She just wants all the attention, just like my sister. Marie can't help herself. That's how she grew up, so she's goin' to do that."

She caressed the raised scar on her cheek, suddenly swept back to a memory that still played now and then. When her sister's name came up, that scar would itch. Like it remembered, too.

"You can tell the stories, Rinks. This is your store; you can be the storyteller. Just get a storybook about snowmen and elves and reindeer and stuff. No one cares where they came from. It's not stealing."

He put the laptop on the bed next to him and hooked his arms around his upraised knees. Serious Vern leveled up to Very Serious Vern. "We'll name the store after you." He swept his hand across a marquee. *"Rinks and Toys and Stuff."*

"That's horrible."

"Whatever. You get to design all the toys, too. We'll work up a business plan, have people make them for you. They can be originals; you design the clothes they wear. We'll sell them online, make up stories for them." He stuck out his chin with an alligator smile. "I'll bet Godfather would invest in that."

"He won't. You saw the way he looked at us. He'll want Marie to do it. That's why he gave her that book."

The girl was already telling stories to her little brother in the next room.

"Then we act like Marie is the storyteller. We get him on board. Then after a while, when the ball gets rolling, you take over." He snapped his fingers and drew the marquee again. *"Rinky Toystories."*

Even worse. It wasn't a bad idea, though. And she hadn't seen him this excited in a while, not since the kids moved in with them. It would be her own line of toys. *Original Rinks.* Now, that wasn't bad at all. They would wear her scarves, too. Then she'd sell them to the parents by the busload. She'd go to conferences, be the keynote speaker. Sign scarves and toys. *Playing cards!* There would be photos of her surrounded by adoring faces, kids sitting cross-legged on the floor, listening to her tell stories.

Then, one day, Godfather would come to hear her. He'd sneak through the crowd like he did when the Corkers owned the place, and listen to her from the corner. Afterwards, he would bring a reward for all her hard work. A special gift.

"What gift will he bring?" she said.

"What?"

She lay on the bed next to him, rolled onto her side facing him. "He delivered a gift, remember? Said it was special and then, like, said somethin' about a journey. You know?" She looked around the room.

The walls were yellowed and cracked. "You think it's still here, like he wants us to find it?"

"Is *what* still here?"

"Are you listenin'?" She smacked his arm. "The gift. Maybe he left it here for us to find."

"Rinks, there's nothin' here but mouse poop."

"That ain't mouse poop," she said. "And that nutcracker toy was here."

"Maybe that's what he was talkin' about."

He yawned, opened up the computer to start the pecking again. Rinks rolled onto her back, stared at the water-stained ceiling tiles. Her nose was stuffy. They were going to clean this place up, for real. Get a new bed, new furniture. This was going to be their home. They were going to be famous. *She* was going to be famous. They wouldn't wait for Godfather to mysteriously come by; that would take too long. They'd invite him. He could bring the robot.

"Better not sell that clock," she said.

"What?"

She rolled away from him, dreaming of the taste of fame and hidden treasures. The attention the robot would bring. Maybe Godfather would want to introduce him to the world at *Rinks Toystories'* grand opening. He could tell that weird story about the nutcracker, maybe come up with an ending this time.

"Hey." She looked over her shoulder. "You think I was the queen in that story?"

Vern had no idea what she was talking about. She was too tired to explain. But she was certain the robot's story was about her being the mean little Mousequeen who put a spell on the princess.

That meant Vern had seven heads.

❄

Someone was talking. It was the middle of the night.

Rinks elbowed Vern to turn off the computer. He groaned and scooted away from her. The laptop was closed. There was no movie that he sometimes watched when he couldn't sleep. His dry mouth hung open, heaving waves of morning breath in her direction.

She sat up.

Ghosts. That was her first thought. The place was haunted, and that was why the Corkers left this place. Or maybe *the Corkers* were haunting it. They'd heard them talking about renaming the toy store and weren't happy about it. They came back to stop them.

She shook Vern. His gummy lips clung together as he smacked them and rolled over to the very edge of the mattress. She was about to give him an elbow when she recognized one of the voices. It was Marie. There was another voice, though.

Fritz?

Rinks always suspected the boy was faking it. He was talking when she wasn't around. Who stops talking just because their parents die? She sat real still and tuned her ear. It didn't sound like him, though. Was Marie practicing characters for storytelling? *The backstabber.* Rinks fed her and clothed her, and now she was planning to tell the stories? Not on Rinks's watch.

This had to stop.

It was far too late, and Vern had to work in the morning, and if anyone was going to tell a story, it was going to be the queen of this castle. Those brats were not going to fart around in the middle of the night. Rinks slid into her slippers and wrapped a blanket around her. She snuck out of the room and was going to scare them witless. Maybe make some ghost noises at the door.

The light didn't shine at the bottom of their door.

She stood still and listened. The voices came again. A chilly sensation coiled around her backbone. She almost went back for Vern. Someone was in the storefront. She held very still, thinking what to do. She was almost certain it was Marie's voice. She cracked their bedroom door.

The air mattress was empty.

The owl clock was on the shelf. Below it, standing on the bench, back against a checkered wall, the nutcracker stood at attention. Guarding nothing but squares of wood. She snuck through the kitchen. With her ear to the door, she listened to a conversation coming from the storefront. Something was scratching the floor. Surely, they weren't doing chores. It sounded like they were sanding the floor.

She threw the door open, hoping they might wet their pants a little. A lesson like that went a long ways. It had when Rinks was little. There was a quick flash of light. Rinks put her hand up. Car lights turned the corner, the headlights passing through the windows.

Marie and Fritz were in an empty aisle.

"What do you think you're doin'?" Rinks said. "It's the middle of the night."

"Um, Fritz was sleepwalking again."

"Again?"

"He does it sometimes."

She was lying. It was the look on her face, the way she stuttered. Rinks was a grade A lie detector. Her father was one, too. Passed that skill down to her. It was the little things that gave someone away. These two were guilty.

"Who were you talkin' to?"

Marie shrugged. "I was waking him up so he would come back to bed."

"Uh-huh. That's what all the gigglin' was about?"

"It's just... he made a funny face."

This girl's pants were about to catch fire. Why would they be in the storefront? So Rinks wouldn't hear them in their bedroom, that was why. Fritz had the striped ball Godfather had given him in his hand. For some reason, that felt suspicious. Call it a hunch.

A grade A, lie-detecting hunch.

"Did you find somethin' out here?" Rinks said.

They shook their heads. A bit of confusion on their brows. That looked more like the truth. She still didn't believe them. The first mistake in discovering a secret was trust. She didn't believe or trust them.

"Off to bed. And don't get back up. Your uncle's got to work in the morning. And we got some serious cleanin' on tap. Get your beauty rest."

Rinks remained in the store several minutes after they'd left. She looked around, studied their footsteps in the dust. Just bare footprints. Nothing had been sanded. She was sure she'd heard something gritty on the floorboards. And something else she'd heard. Marie had been talking.

Someone had been answering her.

8

For Marie, life was like a dream. A mostly bad one.
Every day she waited to wake up and everything would go back to the way it was. Every day she woke up, it was more of the same. It still felt like a dream, though.

That night, she had to pinch herself to believe it.

After visiting Godfather, she felt different. It didn't feel real (going to an underground lair with a robot felt far from it), but not in a bad way. For the first time since her life had turned upside down, she was filled with hope and something else. Something uplifting, bubbly. She smiled for no reason because of him.

Because of Godfather.

He believed in her. For no reason, he believed in her. That was why she went to bed smiling.

She sank into the air mattress, her bottom touching the floor, and thumbed through the pages of the book he gave her. They were thick and stiff, rough to the touch. She turned them one at a time, telling a story to Fritz. She was making it up, like she did when she was little and would sit on her mom's lap and pretend to read.

Fritz was half-listening, if he was listening at all. He was more interested in that ball, turning it with his fingertips, staring at his warped reflection. It looked like a big, round walnut made of metal.

It didn't matter if he was listening or not, she enjoyed weaving the story about a boy and a girl who escape into another world with friends and family, where they would spend Christmas and sing songs and do all the Christmassy stuff that was definitely not going to happen this year. They would have a Christmas tree.

"The biggest Christmas tree in the world," she said.

He wouldn't let her hold the ball. Wouldn't even let her touch it. He didn't say why she couldn't touch it or why he was so obsessed with it. It looked heavy and odd. Didn't make any noises when he shook it. Didn't flash any lights or sing a song. He was not at all disappointed Godfather had given it to him. He wouldn't tell her what Godfather had whispered to him, either.

She was about to find out.

He fell asleep with the ball clasped in a fist. Nussknacker was in the other hand. She was sure the soldier would poke her in the back, but wasn't about to take it away from her brother. She put the book on the bench. Out of the goodness of her heart, she thanked the owl clock for keeping the mice out of the room. Whether it worked or not, she was grateful no furry, gray animals scampered around at night.

She put the white feathered quill between the pages of the book and pulled the white ribbon out. With that, she tied her hair back. That was a perfect use for it.

For once, she fell asleep with her hair out of her eyes.

❄

Marie tossed and turned.

Her dreams were filled with scratching sounds. Someone was working an industrial sander. It was occasionally interrupted by gravel turning in a concrete mixer.

She sat up in a pitch-black room. Her bottom was on the hard floor beneath the air mattress. She reached over to find Fritz's side of the bed empty. His phone was on his pillow. She turned on her phone and looked around. The book was still on the bench, but it had been moved.

Nussknacker was standing against the checkered wall.

Fritz must have gone to the bathroom. She turned off the phone. Five minutes later, she turned it back on and got out of bed. The noises were back. *Scritch, scritch, scritch.* Like twisting a bowl on a countertop covered in sand. It was followed by a gritty drag and then *scritch, scritch, scritch.*

A mouse.

She held very still and held her breath, trying to hear where it was coming from. It wasn't in the ceiling. It sounded too far away to be in the wall. She opened the door and listened. When she went to the kitchen, it wasn't coming from there, either.

A voice.

Her heart did a lap around her lungs, then a belly flop into her stomach. Light-headed from a lack of oxygen, she tiptoed quietly to the door that led to the storefront. It sounded like a movie was playing. Fritz couldn't sleep, so he'd gone to the storefront so he wouldn't wake her up.

"You don't need to charge it." The voice had that gravel sound she'd dreamed. Like stones in a glass tumbler. "It'll last, like, ten years. I can give you the exact amount of time, if that's what you want, but just trust me on this, all right?"

There was a pause. Then the voice continued, "The specs? I mean, sure, I can give them, but *you're* not going to understand them. You didn't ask the Counselor for *his* specs, did you?"

Counselor?

At that moment, Marie realized Fritz couldn't be watching a movie. His phone was on the bed. Someone was out there, and it wasn't Uncle Vernon. She eased the door open. The hinges gave her away. A light went out.

"Fritz?"

He was standing in the dark, his messy hair silhouetted by a backlight of streetlights coming through the windows. He wasn't moving in a very scary-movie sort of way. A fist at his side. His eyes were in the dark. She pointed her phone at him. He wasn't blinking.

"What's going on?" she said.

He didn't move. Not a shrug. Not a head shake.

"Were you... were you talking?"

It wasn't him unless his voice changed. Her little brother's voice was trapped somewhere inside him. He'd closed that door when Mr. Trauma introduced itself one afternoon and locked Fritz's voice up in a cell. (Fritz worked with a therapist named Mr. Sean. Unlike Marie's therapist, Teri, Mr. Sean said Fritz's voice was locked in a prison cell instead of a box.) Marie had tried to help Fritz find his voice. She hadn't given up, but she was running out of ideas. Hugs weren't doing it.

"Come on." She held out her arm. "Let's go to bed. It's cold out here."

He didn't move, in true horror-movie fashion. Creepy vibes scampered up her arms like bugs. She didn't know what to do, so she turned for the door and hoped he would follow. If he wasn't back in the bedroom in ten minutes, she'd try again.

And then she heard it.

Her back to him, she was at the door leading to the kitchen when a dusky light turned on behind her.

"He was talking to me."

Marie dropped her phone. It bounced on the floor and scattered light around the room. She turned around. Her heart boarded a rocket ship on a course for the top of her head.

Something was standing next to her brother.

❅

A SANDMAN.

There was no other way to describe it. Think snowman—three balls, the bottom one the biggest and the other two successively smaller. Made of sand. The same height as Fritz. Tree branches for arms. And two sand dollars for eyes.

"Fritz." The word hissed through her teeth. "What is—"

"Surprise!" it said and threw its branches out. Marie jumped and squeaked. "Haha. I told you she'd be *aaahhh*. Hahaha. What'd I say? Oh man, I should've bet you. Easy money."

"Shhhhh." Marie found her voice and rushed at them. The sandman cringed. "Fritz," she whispered forcefully, "what is-is-is... what is *that*?"

"I'm right here," it said. "I can hear you."

Fritz's shoulders were bouncing. *Is he laughing?*

"Listen," it said, "you want the long or short version of this little—what're the kids calling it—this little *getup*."

"Fritz, what's happening?"

"All right, *cool girl*." It made air quotes with the twiggy ends of its arms. "Long or short, you choose."

"What are you?"

"I like that. You're a Zen-present-moment kind of person, I can tell. The imperfection is perfection, right?" It coughed into a fist of curled sticks. A gritty cloud puffed through them. "Sorry. Went over your heads. Short version. *I*... am the sandman. Questions?"

It bowed deeply.

Marie waited. The sandman blinked the big round sand dollars. A smile creased the wet sand just below them.

"I'm going to get Aunt Rinks."

"No! No, no, no, no." It slid towards her like a bag of rocks dragged across the floor. "This is his fault. Fritz, I mean. He did this." It jabbed a stick in Fritz's direction. "I'm not telling on him, it's just the facts. He set me up. I mean, not like a sting. Preferences, is what I'm saying. He made me this."

He presented himself like a runway model.

"A sandy snowman with charm and humor and razor wit. And he took the sarcasm *waaaay* up. Like an eleven. You remember that, kid?" he said to Fritz, poking an elbow at him. "I was like *you sure about this?* He was like *for sure*. And I was like *this handsome and funny?* He was like *why not?* I was like *I can live with that.* You know what I mean? So, his fault."

Marie closed her eyes. When she opened them, it was still there. She wasn't dreaming. Or maybe she was. Maybe this proved the last two years was a dream, and it was finally reaching an absurd end. She was going to wake up any second now in the house she grew up in. There'd be a Christmas tree downstairs and breakfast on the table. Eggs with homemade hashbrowns and a glass of orange juice. She started to leave.

"I'm his voice."

She made it to the kitchen this time. "What?" she said.

"That little thing right there. The one Godfather gave to F-bomb." It pointed a twig. Fritz held out his hand. "That's me."

Marie walked up to her brother, stared at the ball in his palm. The one he'd been staring at all night.

"Neurolink projection," it said. "It took eight hours to link up with his nervous system and access brain waves. We meshed forty-five minutes ago. We're basically best friends." Fritz nodded. "I'm his thoughts, Mar Mar. In the real."

Slowly, she reached for the ball. He let her take it. It shimmered with internal heat, like an engine about to smoke the tires. Pinpricks nibbled at her fingertips. It was heavy, like she thought it would be. She dropped it back in his hand.

"Is this what Godfather whispered to you?" she said.

Fritz nodded.

She swung from confused annoyance to the brink of tears. *He's got a voice. It came in a weird package, but he has a voice.*

"That's coming from the little striped ball thing?" she asked.

"I'm not a *that*. But I'll give you that one," the sandman said. "It's not a striped ball thing. It's a self-powered, neuro-interfacing thought-projector. Courtesy of Avocado, Inc., and not for public use. It's made just for the F-bomb."

"What's the F-bomb?"

"It's him. He's F-bomb."

"Don't call him that."

"Why not?"

"It's a bad word."

"F-bomb? It's the letter *F* followed by *bomb*."

She looked at him. "You know exactly what it means."

A smile dug into the wet sandy cheeks. "Whatever, Mar Mar."

"How does it work? I mean, how am I hearing and seeing your sandman?"

"First of all, I have a name."

"Okay. What is it?"

"I've got many names."

"Sandy?"

"How'd you guess?" The sand dollars opened in exaggerated surprise. "She's smarter than she looks."

"You're kind of mean, you know that?"

"No. I'm not."

"A little bit."

"Not even a little, but I respect your opinion. If you don't like it, talk to him." He leaned toward her and pretended to whisper a secret. "It's his fault."

The elation of her talking to her brother through a projection was nosediving back into a pool of annoyance. She'd do anything to talk to her brother without typing everything on a phone. She sighed, looked at the floor and back up at the sandman. And waited.

"You want to know how it works?" he said. "Simple question, complex answer. I've known you for fifteen minutes, and I can already tell you won't understand." He waved his branches like a breeze blew them about. "No offense. Fritz doesn't understand, either. He also don't care."

"He *don't* care?"

"He turned my grammar setting down. I don't know why."

Marie turned her attention to Fritz, who seemed to be a spectator. "Is this really you talking?"

"It's him," Sandy said.

"Why can't I hear his voice?"

"It don't work like that."

She grimaced. This could just be a goof. Neurolinking thoughts?

Maybe Sandy was no different than the Counselor, just a really cool party trick that had nothing to do with Fritz.

"So he's linked to you?" she asked. Fritz nodded. "He knows your thoughts, says what you want him to say?" She turned to Sandy and asked: "What were Mom's favorite Christmas cookies?"

Sandy's sand dollars disappeared in a long blink. His midsection swelled, and for a moment, her hopes were dashed. *This is just a party trick. And I fell for it.* Her annoyance transmuted into fury that set her cheeks on fire. She was about to grab the ball from Fritz, curse him for goofing on her like that.

"Peanut-butter cookies with a chocolate drop in the center. Right out of the oven when the chocolate's soft and warm. And then a sprinkle of red sugar," Sandy said softly. "She called it Christmas dust."

Marie covered her mouth. Fingers trembling. She could see the cookies. Could smell them. She should've asked a different question, like where did Fritz lose his shoes on vacation or what was his favorite song. The cookies yanked a memory from the box. She slammed the lid tight to keep any emotions from following it out.

He knew. Fritz knew exactly what her favorite cookies were. He didn't forget, either.

She hugged her brother. More like trapped him in an embrace, swung him side to side, and he let her do it. He didn't fight the wetness of her cheek against his, either.

"You really like cookies," Sandy muttered.

"Can you please turn the sarcasm down?" she asked her brother. "It's super annoying."

"I think you mean super funny," Sandy said.

❄

So the striped ball wasn't a bouncy ball. It was an Avocado, Inc., invention. A self-powered supercomputer with neuronetworking that interfaced with the nervous system of its owner. Once it scanned the owner's thought patterns, it would read brain waves and translate them to a projected image. It could be anything. A proper butler or a cuddly grandmother, a stern taskmaster or a suave model. Fritz had picked a sandman. And named him Sandy.

"Couldn't have said it better," Sandy said. Then winked one sand dollar at Fritz, whispered: "Actually, I could've."

"This is incredible, Fritz. I mean, you have a voice. Godfather gave you your voice for Christmas." He nodded with a smile. He hadn't stopped smiling. It spread to Marie. "You don't have to type anymore."

"Please," Sandy said, "you'll make me blush."

"Can you talk with Fritz's voice? Like, let him talk. Not you."

"What's wrong with me?"

"It's a question. Can you?"

"This is his voice."

"It doesn't sound like Fritz."

"Because it's me."

"You're interpreting what he says and turning it into sarcasm."

Sandy pecked at his chin; sand appeared to dribble to the floor. Then pointed. "Sarcasm is a lot harder than you think."

"No. It's not."

Marie had been pacing back and forth. It still felt like a dream, but barely. Godfather had the technology to do something like this, and she couldn't imagine a better use for it. Judging by her brother's expression, neither could he. She could talk to him. Even if it was through an absurd projection, she could talk to him.

"We can't tell Aunt Rinks," she said.

"Oh, no. No, no, noooo. My main man here can't use me in public, either. I'm calibrated like that—just your eyes and his." He twisted his bottom half, grinding it against the floor without leaving a mark. Then said: "And other stuff."

"What other stuff?"

His head rotated toward Fritz. A silent conversation was happening right in front of her. *It's not a conversation,* she thought. *Sandy's just a projection.* It didn't feel like it. They could tell secrets without her hearing a word.

"What is it?" she said. "What other stuff?"

"Well, it's this other thing. We're not sure you're ready for it."

"Ready for what?"

Another long silence. Sandy chuckled. "I know. Right?" he said to Fritz.

"You're talking about me?"

"Uh, no."

"Fritz, tell me. What's he talking about?"

Fritz folded his arms and nodded. His sandman let out a long, slightly annoyed sigh. "Godfather sent me to be Fritz's voice. And also to go on the journey."

"Okay." She looked back and forth between the two of them. "I have no idea what that means."

"Yeah, we know."

When he didn't elaborate, Marie sighed with complete annoyance. "Look, Fritz, it's the middle of the night. I'm going to bed. So are you."

"We're not tired."

"Doesn't matter. Aunt Rinks will have chores for us. We can talk about this when we're scrubbing the ceilings."

"We can't do the journey without you."

She didn't like the sound of this. A journey sounded like running away. If this thing wanted them to pack their bags, she was telling Aunt Rinks first thing in the morning, and Godfather would have to explain giving her brother rogue artificial intelligence.

"You'd better not mean running away, Fritz." She turned to her brother. Because that was who was talking, not a snowman on the beach.

"Running away, what?" Sandy said. "No. It's the opposite of running away."

She pinched the ridge between her eyes. Her brain was swelling. This felt like a night court comedy. She started laughing. *Wouldn't it be great if this entire thing was a dream that ended with a ghostly sandman?* Her laughter didn't stop.

"I think we broke your sister," Sandy said. And this brought another wave of laughter. She covered her mouth, waved her hand.

"I'm going now," she said. "For real this time. You two don't stay up too late."

"Wait! Don't you want to know what Nussknacker said about the journ—"

Sandy vanished when the door leading to the kitchen opened on its own. Aunt Rinks barged through it, dunking Marie in cold panic. Her aunt asked some weird questions. Nothing compared to what Marie had just experienced. She pulled it together and volleyed Aunt Rinks's suspicion with some choice-cut lies.

Her aunt had no idea what had happened.

❄

Fritz rolled onto the air mattress.

The nutcracker was still at his post on the workbench. That was what it looked like, standing guard beneath the owl clock. Mouth half open. Emerald eyes unblinking. Marie thought about the Counselor's story, how the young man stumbled over the Mousequeen on his last step.

She turned off her phone, climbed onto the mattress. With her shoulder blades on the floor, she stared into the dark and listened to Aunt Rinks shuffle around the storefront. Marie kept thinking of the last thing Sandy said, right before her aunt kicked the door open. A field of goosebumps spread across her arms.

Nussknacker said about the journey.

9

There was a path in the jungle. That was what Aunt Rinks called the backyard—the jungle. A tapestry of vines as thick as nautical rope weaved through volunteer trees and shrubs badly in need of a haircut.

Marie was sent to tame it with a cheap pair of pruners and a rake with broken tines. She had started on the patio Aunt Rinks had partially cleared. The chairs were beyond repair, and the pavers were hidden beneath a carpet of matted roots. She was only there a few minutes before she found the gravel path.

It was narrow and winding. She crawled under a tangle of thorns and found a small pond filled with rotted leaves. A tower of flagstones that might have been a waterfall. Goldfish maybe, once upon a time. A little farther and she found herself surrounded by trees and the blue sky above. The sound of traffic was distant.

A bench was opposite the mucky pond. The slats were a patchwork of blue-green lichen; the legs had sunk into the ground. She cut through the underbrush with her hand pruners. Something was on the bench. She swept a mat of soggy leaves away, found a lump of wet fur. It was a teddy bear and a green dragon. There was also an octopus with a pale-yellow body that might have been orange long ago. Their eyes, once glassy, were foggy and blind.

Marie squeezed the teddy bear, and dirty water dripped out of it. She closed her eyes and imagined what it was like to be her great-aunt Corker, to escape into a world she imagined. A world that was kind and pleasant.

A place where the air tasted different.

❄

MARIE LURKED INSIDE the jungle with a view of the truck that stopped at the curb. A heavy door rolled open. The old gate dragged open. Two men were lugging something down the crooked sidewalk toward the back door. They wore blue jeans and matching ball caps. One of them had a red beard flecked with white whiskers.

"This is the place I was telling you about," he said to the guy at the other end of a mattress wrapped in plastic. "Put it down a sec."

They dropped it on the ground. Red Beard took off his cap, wiped his forehead with his sleeve.

"Place is a dump," said the younger guy.

"Last I was here was before you were born. Back then, the place was…" Red Beard shrugged. If he had memories of coming there to hear a story and buy a toy, those days were long gone.

"Habitable?" the younger guy said.

"Something like that."

The gate cranked open again. Uncle Vernon turned sideways to squeeze between the mattress and bushes. The plastic bag he was carrying snagged on a branch and was ripped from his hand. The younger guy helped him put the contents inside the bag from a store called *Larry's Electronics*.

"Thanks. This way." Uncle Vernon held the back door open.

The moving guys hoisted the plastic-wrapped mattress up the steps and squeezed it through the crooked door frame. Marie ducked down when the younger guy looked back. The door slammed shut. A minute later Aunt Rinks was there.

"Murry!"

Marie refused to answer to that name. She was as still as a rock. Aunt Rinks kept calling. Not until she cried out *Marie* did she start crawling out, holding the sodden teddy bear she'd found on the bench. She hid it behind a rotten stump before climbing through the branches. Aunt Rinks pulled her T-shirt over her belly. *Superstar* was written on the front.

"You supposed to clean this." She pretended to wax the patio.

"What are those guys doing?"

"Come on. Inside."

The moving guys were in one of the back rooms. It wasn't where Marie and Fritz were sleeping. The kitchen table had been moved aside to make room for the new cargo. Aunt Rinks's scarves were laid out. They were all silk and hand dyed. Mostly tie-dyed. Marie had showed her how to do tie-dye a year ago. Aunt Rinks thought it was original. Marie had learned it in the third grade.

"Vern," Aunt Rinks hissed. With big eyes, she said: "Somewhere else."

He filled the plastic bag from *Larry's Electronics* with little boxes and bundles of wires and took it to the storefront. Aunt Rinks put on a big fake smile. The one that made animals cringe.

"So, we're gettin' new furniture and a fridge today. A guy's comin' to fix the heat. Gonna make this place a real home. We can't be sleepin' in a warehouse, you know."

"Is that our bed?"

"Oh, no. Your stuff will come later. Couldn't afford it all at once. But it'll come." Fake smile. "I got an errand for you. Fizzy!"

Marie's brother came from the storefront with a bucket of water.

"You and your sister need to leave while we redecorate, okay?" She readjusted Fritz's rosy, worn-out ball cap. "You can finish up later. Go down to the coffee shop and get yourself somethin' to eat. Here." She dropped a wad of money on the table. "Stay down there at least a couple of hours. Don't want you in the way. We got measurements to do and decisions to make. Can't have a couple of monkeys standin' round."

She snorted. None of that made sense. It sounded like a lot of work, and she wanted them to leave?

"I need to clean up," Marie said.

"You look fine. Go on, 'fore I change my mind. Don't put the bucket there, Fizzy. Take it out back on the way. All right, bye-bye."

The movers slid the old mattress that Aunt Rinks and Uncle Vernon had been sleeping on out of the back bedroom. It had stains the color of weak tea. Marie took the bucket from her brother. It sloshed with dirty water.

"You all right?" she asked. He nodded. "You got your thing?"

"What thing?" Aunt Rinks whirled around.

"The nutcracker."

"Oh, that. Leave it. It's in your bedroom, safe and sound." She crossed her heart. "I won't touch your precious toy, stick a needle and all that." She stepped back to make room for the movers and said to them: "You're takin' that with you."

"Yes, ma'am." Red Beard took his hat off. "Is the stage still up front? You mind if I see it."

"You mind if I wander around your house when I'm workin'?"

Red Beard didn't expect that response. It clashed with his memories of the toy store that were bright and shiny and warm. Now a cloudy day moved into the building. He asked Aunt Rinks a few more questions, like what the place looked like, if there were any toys around. Marie elbowed her brother and jutted her chin.

"Where you goin'?" Aunt Rinks said.

"Bathroom," Marie said.

Red beard kept on with the questions. Fritz came back with a bulge under his shirt that Aunt Rinks didn't see. He and Marie were out the door before the movers pulled the spoiled mattress behind them.

"Don't come back for a couple hours," Aunt Rinks called.

❄

AUNT RINKS WAS up to something.

It didn't matter to Fritz. He had a spring in his step, holding the nutcracker in one hand and looking around, feeding the sights and smells to the striped ball in his pocket. Marie wondered if those two talked inside his head. Fritz would sometimes laugh for no reason at all.

Is that good? she wondered.

The streets were crowded. The sidewalks were full; people came and went from the local stores, a different flavor of Christmas music escaping each time a door opened—modern, pop, traditional, bluesy. It didn't feel like Christmas with so many short-sleeved shirts and flip-flops; the blue skies and palm trees were going to take some getting used to.

They passed the game store. The boys were inside. Two of the younger ones watched the older brother play a racing game at a wraparound monitor display. He was wearing the same clothes, this time without a belt. A Band-Aid on his finger.

Fritz held out his phone. There was nothing written on it. Marie took it and said, "Hello?"

"Stop staring at them."

"Sandy?"

"Nussknacker might not protect you this time," he said gruffly.

Marie didn't know what that meant, but moved on before anyone inside the store noticed her. "You're not supposed to be out here," she whispered.

"You see me?"

She didn't. He was on the phone. Then she noticed the Bluetooth speaker in Fritz's ear. So maybe Sandy's voice wasn't in his head.

"There's a park over there," she said, noticing a fountain with benches near a giant Christmas tree. No one was at the picnic tables. "We can talk there."

"You know, people talk on the phone all the time. It's not weird. F-dog is hungry. Go to that coffee shop and spend all that money your aunt gave you."

He wasn't wrong. It was just a phone call. No one would know she was talking to a ball in her brother's pocket. They continued up the sidewalk, past the coffee shop's front window. It was crowded inside.

"Whoa," Sandy said. "Those are some creepy elves."

The mechanical elves were slowly swinging their tools. Marie didn't want to explain that Mr. Corker—her great-aunt's husband (*our great-uncle*)—made them. But, also, didn't disagree. They were creepy. She handed the phone back to her brother.

It was noisy inside. Conversation echoed around the walls and hard floor. Most of the tables were occupied. A small crowd was at the counter. Ms. Trutchen was merrily serving a long line. Ms. Clara, dressed in a frilly apron and a red dress, was sitting at a table with older men and women, telling a story. When she saw them enter, she excused herself.

"Children!" She put her arms around them. She was soft and warm. Smelled like sugar cookies. "Come, come. I have table in corner for you."

She guided them to the back of the store where a beat-up hightop was wedged against a leaning bookshelf. Fritz climbed onto one of the stools. Ms. Clara wiped the table with the rag always over her shoulder.

"Have seat." She pulled a stool out for Marie. "What can I bring you?"

"Thank you. I have money." Marie showed her the wad of green paper. "I want to spend it."

"Ah, very good. What do you want?"

"I'll go look."

Marie excused herself. Ms. Clara leaned on the table. It made Marie a little nervous, but what was there to be nervous about? Fritz was smiling as she told him a story. Marie waited in line, eyeing the glass display. The smells woke her appetite. By the time she reached the counter, her stomach was growling.

"Marie!" Ms. Trutchen threw out her arms. "Merry, merry. What can I offer?"

Marie couldn't help but smile. Ms. Trutchen's joy was a bubbling fountain that spilled on everyone who approached. Her laughter infectious. Marie gave her order, counting up the cost. What was left over she put in the jar. A little stick doll was leaning against it, the branches wrapped in twine.

Ms. Trutchen winked. "Merry, merry."

Marie took the tray of drinks and pastries back to the table. Ms. Clara was wiping a tear from her eye and laughing. Fritz's phone was in front of her. A blanket of anxiety snuffed out Marie's joy.

"You are too funny," Ms. Clara said with a sigh. Then to Marie, "Sit, child. Bring your friend next time. He is good company."

Marie couldn't find words to answer. The phone was on speaker, and Sandy said something in Ms. Clara's native language.

"Oh!" Ms. Clara leaned over the phone. "You from my country?"

"Definitely not," Marie said.

She squeezed Marie's shoulders with both hands, tapped the bill of Fritz's ball cap, and went to greet more people, whom she knew by name.

Marie took the phone off speaker. "What are you doing?"

"I'm charming," Sandy said. "What are you doing?"

Marie looked around and whispered: "You know her language?"

"I know all the languages, kid. Like, all of them. Relax. It's a phone call. No one cares."

Fritz had half a danish in his chipmunk cheeks. Jelly smeared on his chin. Marie sipped her tea and tried to act like she wasn't on the phone with a robot. That was what he was, a little round robot that fit in her brother's pocket. She handed the phone to Fritz.

"Wait!" he said. "We need to talk."

"Who's we?"

"What do you mean *who's we*? You and F-bro and me. Who else is on this call?"

She shook her head. If he didn't speak for her brother, she would've put the phone in her pocket. "What do you want?"

There was a pause. "I missed you. Fritz and I were up all night after Aunt Rinky-Dink ruined the party. You snore, by the way."

"No, I don't."

A recording of snoring played on the phone.

But he was right, no one was paying attention to them or would hear them if they tried. And they couldn't talk at home, not like this. She tore a bite off her banana bread.

"Fritz." He looked up to meet her eyes. "I miss talking to you. It's been so long, and I understand. I just want to know, like... how are you doing?"

"What do you want to know?" Sandy said.

"Like, with everything that's happened. I just want to know you're all right."

He chewed slower and looked down at the table. She knew there wasn't a good answer. It was just something she wanted to say. She did miss hearing him. Sandy's voice was better than nothing, even if it sounded like a monster truck.

"He doesn't like it," Sandy said. "But you already know that. He's glad you're here, though."

"I'm not going anywhere."

"Well, not now."

"I'm not ever leaving you."

"You're seventeen, Mar Mar. You going to live with Aunt Off-Her-Rocker till you're thirty?"

She shook her head. "No, but I'll take you with me when I move out."

That was never anything she ever thought about. She'd be eighteen in a few weeks, the day after Christmas. What money her parents left in a trust would be hers. She wouldn't be rich, but she could get a car and afford an apartment for a while.

And raise my little brother with no job and no degree?

"We can change things," Sandy said.

"Change what?"

"You. Him. Your loony guardians." When Marie shook her head, he whispered, "The journey."

Now it was her turn to look at her food. Her brother was seven years old. He didn't want to talk about Mom and Dad and all this. His silence protected him. He didn't talk to Mr. Sean, his therapist. He just drew pictures. He was doing the best he could, Mr. Sean told her. Just be there for him, he said. When he's ready, he'll let you know.

She pressed the phone to her ear and looked at Fritz when she said, "What's the journey?"

"We have to save the princess," Sandy said.

"Save the..." She had to think. "Princess Pirlipat?"

"Ding-ding."

She dipped her head to catch Fritz's eye under the bill of his ball cap. "Is this a game? Like, did Godfather put this in the ball for us to play?"

"Un, no," Sandy said. "*I'm* the ball."

"Where is she, then, the princess?"

"In Candyland."

"Candyland."

Sandy was just a voice on the phone, not a three-dimensional being scratching the floor. And the journey, which had sounded like running away at first, sounded more like a video game. Maybe one they could find in the game store. A game might be exactly what Fritz needed. She could play the game. Do whatever he needed.

"Where is it?" she said.

"We don't know."

"Is it at the game store? We could—"

"It's not that kind of thing."

"Okay." She sipped her tea. Fritz was making eye contact with her now. "What kind of thing is it?"

"Nussknacker knows where it is. He's going to tell us."

"The nutcracker?"

"Yeah, the nutcracker. He has a name, you know. You're not *the human*."

She looked away from her brother. How did the Counselor know the nutcracker's name? Marie had assumed, after Sandy had appeared, the Counselor had made some mental connection with Fritz. *No*, she thought. *Fritz is just expressing himself through the nutcracker. Nussknacker can't talk.*

"Nussknacker is going to *tell* us? Did he say anything else?"

"Look," Sandy said, "you can just stop with the tone. You think Nussknacker is a toy, fine. Who do you think saved you from that boy, huh? You think, when he was holding Nussknacker over his head, he just dropped him, and his belt *accidentally* broke? That soldier is here to protect Fritz on the *journey*. He's going to take us there."

She put the phone facedown on the table. "Fritz, is Nussknacker talking to you?"

He nodded without hesitation. A quiver shot through her like a bolt of cold lightning. *He's hearing voices.* And this was before Godfather had gifted him with Sandy. She took a long, slow breath and made a mental note. They'd have to address this when the time came to talk to a therapist. For now, *meet him where he's at.*

"Nussknacker told you about the journey?" When he didn't answer, she picked up the phone.

"That's right," Sandy said.

"Okay. Good." She tried to sound authentic and did a pretty good job. "How does he know where Candyland is?"

"Because that's where he's from."

"Right."

"It's not an accident. He found Fritz, not the other way around. He's been waiting for you a long time. He'll take us there. He knows where it's at."

"And then what, everything will be fixed?" She pressed the phone against her ear till it hurt. The look on Fritz's face, the way his shoulders slumped, made her immediately regret saying it. It just slipped out of her. Some people just didn't get it. Some things don't get better. Ever.

"Some things can't be fixed," Sandy said. "But they can heal."

She almost dropped the phone. That was exactly what she needed to hear. Whether it was Sandy who said it or something Godfather had programmed him to say, a warm flood of hope flowed through her like a summer tide.

"If Nussknacker says we have to hop a train, we're not doing that," she said.

"It's not like that."

"Where's Candyland, then?"

"It's at home. You just need to find it."

Home? He was talking about a building. A building where movers were moving new furniture. A building with dirt balls and cold showers. It wasn't home. It used to be a toy store.

"Corker's Candyland," she muttered.

Fritz drained the rest of his drink. With a hot chocolate mustache, he looked across the table. His eyes blinked heavily under the dirty bill of his ball cap.

"Do you believe us?" Sandy asked.

"When I see it, I'll believe it."

"Just like Santa, huh?"

"Santa isn't real."

Sandy laughed so hard she had to pull the phone away from her ear. A smile spread on Fritz's face, and he snorted laughter through his nose. Marie wasn't sure what was so funny.

"Oh. You're serious," Sandy said. "I get it, you're older now. You know everything. That's fine. You don't believe in Santa Claus or that Nussknacker saved you."

"He didn't save me."

"So the boy just dropped him. You're going with that?"

"Fritz, I'll go on the journey, okay? We'll save the princess." She grabbed his arm and squeezed his hand, looked at him with every ounce of sincerity she could muster. It wasn't hard to do because she believed it, with every cell in her body, when she said: "I'm going with you."

He squeezed back. Then he broke off half of the banana bread she hadn't eaten and finished it. She hung up the phone and watched him eat. They stayed at the coffee shop until their time was up. Ms. Clara sat with them for a while and told stories of Christmas when she was a little girl.

Marie listened politely but was distracted by her thoughts. How far would she take this imaginary journey and pretend the nutcracker was real? There was no one who could answer that, no therapists to help her. The answer, she decided, was simple. She would go as far as he wanted.

All they had was each other.

❄

THE ROLLING DOOR slammed on the back of the truck. Red Beard fixed a padlock on it. The younger guy was telling a story, waving his hands. When he hit the punchline, Red Beard bent over laughing and came up wheezing, cheeks as red as a sunburn.

They straightened up when Marie and Fritz came down the sidewalk. She knew who they were talking about and what was so funny. The younger guy—the tag stitched to his gray shirt said Phillip—bunched his leather gloves into a ball and shoved them into his back pocket.

Bernard, written on Red Beard's shirt, wiped his eye, and said to Marie, with a mild aftershock of laughter, "You live here?"

Marie nodded.

"I was telling Phillip here about the place. Your mom wouldn't say whether you were going to open a toy store or not."

"She's not my mom."

"Oh." He looked at Phillip, who shrugged. "She your sister?"

"Aunt."

"Well, your aunt tried to sell us a scarf for a hundred bucks."

"Did you buy it?"

Phillip laughed behind his hand. "I don't need no scarf," Bernard said. "I used to come here when I was your age. Shame it closed. It meant a lot to people. You don't know the half of it." He described the long lines, the stories, the magic air inside the store. Phillip looked bored. "Lot of people would like to see it again, but…" With half a grimace, he said in a gruff whisper, "I don't know about your aunt."

"You all done moving?" Marie said.

"For today." He turned his back and waved before climbing into the truck. "More tomorrow."

The tailpipe coughed and rattled under the bumper. Marie and

Fritz watched them pull away from the curb. She could hear them laughing again.

There was a new couch inside. Beige with extra pillows. A television leaned against the wall, waiting to be mounted. Uncle Vernon was in the corner, sitting uncomfortably on one of the wooden chairs from the kitchen table, hunched over a small table with his laptop. That was his new office.

Aunt Rinks was on the couch, her leg thrown over the back of it, holding her cell phone up. Marie went to the kitchen, where a stainless-steel refrigerator hummed quietly. She opened it to find bright, white light and empty glass shelves.

Protein bar wrappers were next to the sink.

"Where've you been?" Aunt Rinks called.

"The coffee shop."

"I said for a couple of hours. Not all day." It had been almost exactly two hours. Aunt Rinks pulled herself upright. "Like the couch? Got that special coating that don't stain on it. And the TV's goin' to get all the channels once your uncle gets it fixed up."

"Did we get a bed?"

"You got a bed, young lady."

"It leaks."

"Well, we slept on that nasty one. Would much rather have that clean air bed of yours." She stood up and pulled the bottom of her shirt down. "Don't worry that pretty white ribbon of yours. You'll get a bed."

Marie tugged on the ribbon Godfather had given her. It did a good job keeping her hair out of her eyes. Aunt Rinks sounded a little jealous. How many times did she try to get Marie to wear one of her headscarves?

"Me and Vern are goin' to run some errands and get some food. Be gone a few hours. You and your brother stay here and don't leave. Do whatever you want to do. It's free time. We'll bring you supper. You won't see us for a few hours."

A few hours. Got it. "Okay."

"Vern!" He jumped when she shouted. "The kids are home. We're leavin'.'" When he got up to look for his shoes, she added slowly, "Don't forget the computer."

He nodded and muttered something, snapping the laptop closed and tucking it under his arm. She waited for him at the door. With a big fake smile, she said before closing it, "We'll be gone a couple hours."

And then they were arguing on their way down the buckled sidewalk. The back gate clattered shut. Marie and Fritz were confused. The couch, TV and refrigerator looked out of place, like someone moving into a haunted house. And their aunt and uncle had fled like they'd seen a ghost.

A couple of hours.

Something coarse began grinding the floorboards. "That was weird," Sandy said.

10

Rinks loved the smell of fast food. It reminded her of the county fair, where everything was fried. Candy bars, licorice, cake. Her favorite was fried dough. She'd eat those things till her stomach split, then go on rides and throw up afterwards. Barfing made room for chocolate-dipped graham crackers with sprinkles.

She opened the white paper bag to get a huff. A car honked, and she almost dropped it and wet her pants at the same time. She made a rude gesture, even though *Rinks* had walked in front of *their* car coming out of the drive-through. People were lazy. They'd do anything to not walk inside, where there were free refills. Rinks had filled up twice before leaving, and the drive-through had barely moved. *Lazy and dumb.*

Their car was parked next to the dumpster. Vern was in the driver's seat, his face bluish from the glow on the laptop. An employee was hiding behind the dumpster, staring at his phone. That was the other thing. People couldn't look away from their phones when they should be working. Phone addiction was real. That was why he was working at the Burger Hut. She felt sad for him. Going nowhere in life like that.

Rinks squeezed into the passenger seat and handed the cold waxy cup, sweating with condensation, to Vern.

"Where's my drink?" he said.

"We're sharin'. You only drink half anyway."

He smelled the straw poking out of the plastic lid. "Is this diet?"

"No."

"This is diet, Rinks. You know I don't like diet."

"It ain't diet, Vern."

It was totally diet. But she wasn't going to buy him his own drink just to watch him waste half of it. She dumped all the fries and fried fish into the bag. Licked the grease off her fingers. She'd snagged almost thirty packets of ketchup, but a few of them were vinegar. She rolled down the window and threw them in the direction of the dumpster. The employee on break looked up, then went back to his phone addiction.

"Extra crispy, like you like it." She put the bag between them. "You get it workin'?"

He chewed the food, his lips and chin glistening, and turned the computer toward her. "It's a little jumpy, reception not great."

Rinks shoveled a bundle of fries into her mouth. The image on the computer was grainy, but it was good enough. The air mattress was in the corner of the room, all messy and unmade. The leather journal with blank pages was on the workbench. Above that, the owl clock was staring at the camera like it knew.

Vern had drilled a neat little hole into the wall.

The camera was no bigger than a pencil eraser. Looked like a nail when he shoved it in. Didn't need wires or anything. Not the highest quality camera, but their mission didn't need to read words or anything. Just needed to see what those kids were up to.

Rinks had left the drawer on the workbench half open where she'd found the protein bar wrappers. She knew she hadn't lost count the other day. It took every bit of muscle for her to smile when they got home. Like no one robbed her.

"They need to make their bed," she said. "Where are they?"

He reached into the bag. "This ain't live. I started it from the beginning."

"They in there now?"

"I don't know. Figured they might've done somethin' when we left."

"Click over to one of the other rooms."

"We only got this camera."

She smacked his hand. "What'd you mean?"

"I told you, there wasn't time for the others."

She snatched the bag away from him and tucked it between her hip and the door. Gave him a long, hateful eye. He dug food out of his cheek with his finger and licked it, put his hand out like he expected her to give him more after he only put one camera up.

"Vern," she said, sickly sweet, "is half your brain on strike?"

"What?"

"They were *in the storefront last night!* I told you they were doin' somethin'. We got to see everywhere, you melon head. I swear, if you had any more holes in your head, your brains would leak out."

He wiped his hands on his thighs, leaving oily streaks in the denim. He stared out the windshield, running his tongue over his salty lips. Then he said, with all the seriousness of a funeral director, "Apologize."

"I'm sorry, what?"

"You apologize to me, Rinks. I been workin' hard to get that buildin' fixed, bought all that furniture, put that camera in their room —and I didn't want to, I said so, not in their bedroom, but I did it anyway. And then you give me this." He rattled the ice in the cup.

"It ain't diet."

"It is so. I know when you're lyin'."

Rinks lied all the time, and he didn't know the half of it. Little lies that didn't even matter. Like giving Vern diet soda and telling him it wasn't. The worst part: she was going to die on that hill before telling the truth. And she didn't know why.

"I apologize," she said. She didn't say what for. Vern didn't ask.

They shared the bag of fries and stared at an empty room on the laptop. The car had a hot, steamy smell to it. Her cheeks felt oily from it.

"Can you speed it up or somethin'?" She doodled her finger at the screen.

Vern wiped his hands before sliding one finger across the touchpad. Nothing changed except the time stamp. Detective work was dull. It took all her willpower not to look at her phone.

"There!" She wagged her finger. French fries and bits of fish spilled onto the floor. "Go back, go back."

Vern reversed the recording and hit play. Marie walked into the shot. She slowed down and stood in the middle of the room. Rinks leaned over Vern's lap. He pushed her head down so he could see it. Marie suspected something, the way she stood there. The drawer was half open. The book had been moved. She turned around, lips moving.

"Sound. Where's the sound?" Rinks said. "It's not working."

Vern tried some settings, but they couldn't hear nothing. Rinks closed her eyes. He'd messed the sound up, but she wasn't going to say that. Ten seconds later, she started pushing keys on the off chance she might get it to work. The video disappeared.

"Where'd it go?"

He brought the video back and asked her, very politely, not to randomly stab the keyboard. Random was all she knew. He got it back to where Marie turned around. Even though they couldn't hear her, she was talking to someone. And then she stopped talking for a few seconds before speaking again.

"She's talkin' to someone, Vern. Someone's there."

"Maybe."

"Maybe? Look at her... *there!* She's listenin' to someone. Oooooo." She covered her mouth. "It's Fizzy. That little fart smeller can talk, I knew it!"

"Fritz doesn't talk."

She didn't know what made her more mad: how calmly Vern said that or the confidence he said it with. "Then who? Who would she be talkin' to? Unless..." She covered her mouth again. "That girl invited friends over. I told her not to, and she did."

"Stop. Let's just... can we watch this a second?"

She couldn't take the suspense. If there were sound, she wouldn't be on the verge of heart failure. Marie left the bedroom. They were back to staring at the owl clock staring back. He scrolled ahead until it said *LIVE* in the upper right corner. Nothing had changed.

"Great. Just great." She folded her arms. "Let's just go back. I need to know who's there lookin' through my stuff. They could be sittin' on our brand-new bed, Vern."

"Give it a little longer."

His patience was the only thing keeping Rinks in the parking lot. The kids were probably in the storefront doing whatever they had been doing the night before. What Rinks and Vern needed to do was abort mission and get back there. Tomorrow, send them back to the coffee shop so Vern could get the rest of the cameras up. Rinks would go with them. She could get them to relax, ask some questions. Interrogate them until they slipped up.

Detective work was nothing like TV.

She grabbed her phone. Vern kept watching the laptop while chewing through French fries like popcorn. He'd snip one in half with his front teeth and chew it like a piece of meat. Rinks distracted herself from the sound he was making with videos of car accidents and animal tricks. Finally, she held the phone up and shot a selfie with Vern and the laptop behind her.

"What're you doin'?" he said.

"Detective work," she said while typing.

"You're not goin' to post that."

"The kids don't follow me." That sort of irked her. If they followed her, they'd know she was staking them out. That was their fault. They lose. Vern got on his phone.

"What are you doin'?" she said.

"I'm textin' them we're gettin' food, and we'll be home in an hour. And I gave them our location."

"Why would you do that?" She smacked his leg. "Now they know where we are."

"Exactly. It'll put them at ease to do whatever it is you think they're doin'."

"I don't like your tone. *What I think.* They're doin' somethin', Vern; I told you. I got instincts. I know things right here." She tapped her chest. "Sometimes you don't need brains to know things. People think with their hearts way better than their heads. Trust me."

Rinks was a feeler. A deep feeler. And those emotions were pushed way down in the dark, but she knew they were there. Sometimes, when she was up for it, she'd take a peek, and they'd tell her what to do. And right now, those kids were up to something.

She was right.

Marie returned to the bedroom. She put the nutcracker on the bench, facing the checkered wall below the owl clock. Rinks crunched up the bag so Vern would stop eating, so she could concentrate. His breath was in her ear. It was hot and humid. Smelled like a fish tank.

Marie bent over, studying the back of the nutcracker. Did she not know how the thing worked? Pull the lever and the mouth closed.

"What's she doin'?" Rinks said. "Did the camera freeze? She's not movin'."

A few seconds later, she turned her head and called out to whoever was back there. Fritz came in wearing that dirty baseball cap of his dad's. Now the two of them were standing there. All Rinks could see was their backs. The camera angle was too low to see the nutcracker on the bench.

Rinks put two fingers on the screen.

"What're you doing?" Vern said.

"I can't stand that owl."

When she moved her hand, the owl was looking through a smudge left behind from her fingers. She had no idea what the kids were doing, and the owl kept up the accusing look.

"Let's go," she said. "Turn off your location. We'll take off our shoes and sneak in through the back door, catch them in the act."

"I can't turn it off now. They'll know."

"Get out. Get out of the car. You stay here with your dumb phone, and I'll drive back." That was the best plan yet. Why hadn't she thought of that? She opened her door. "I'll come back for you when—"

"What is *that*?" Vern said.

The tone sent a steel rod up Rinks's spine. She'd never heard shock in his voice. Except for the one time her friend Kate Belzinger had caught her hair on fire when she bent over a candle at a candle party Rinks was throwing (and then no one bought candles). This sounded worse.

Rinks leaned over and wasn't sure what she was seeing. At first, she thought the oil she'd smudged on the screen had done something to the video. It looked like someone was with the kids, as tall as Fritz and twice as fat. Three globs of wet sand stacked on top of one another. Bare branches were stuck in the middle ball. It looked like a special effects from one of her social media apps, like the ones that make kitty faces or giant eyes.

Marie turned her head. *She's talking to it.*

"Is that a..." She couldn't bring herself to say it.

"It's not a ghost," Vern said. "It's the ball."

She looked at him. A wide, greasy smile covered his face. The setting sun twinkled in his eyes like little fires. He looked like he was about to cry.

"What are you talkin' 'bout?"

"The ball Godfather gave Fritz for Christmas." He pointed. "It's a projector, Rinks. It's a self-contained character. I seen 'em before, somethin' that neurolinks with the holder. Don't you get it?"

"No, Vern! I don't get it. I have no idea what you're talkin' about."

He grabbed her shoulders. "*It's his voice.*"

It took a few seconds. Several, actually. Then she figured it out all by herself. This thing—this *ghost*—was coming from the striped ball. And it was connected to Fritz, somehow. If that silver butler at the cabin could walk and talk and cook supper, then a dumb walnut ball could make a snowman.

"They didn't tell us," she muttered bitterly. "They're keepin' it a secret."

Vern threw his head back and laughed. The car shook. The employee wasn't slacking at the dumpster to hear it. Vern held up his hand for a high five. Rinks slapped it. It worked. He was right. They caught them. It was time to celebrate.

The kids were working on something Rinks couldn't see. The sandy snowman was pointing his branches, moving them around, giving instructions.

"Let's go," she said.

"We got to bring them food."

"No, we don't. That's their lesson for not tellin' us about that. They can lick wrappers for supper."

"We're gettin' them somethin' to eat."

She leaned back, frowning. Serious Vern was back. Those hard unyielding eyes. He wanted to be the good parent? Fine.

"Go on and get it, then," she said.

He did. He went inside. Rinks watched the video, the kids obsessed with whatever they were working on. They couldn't possibly be trying to work the nutcracker, could they? Vern came out ten minutes later with a bag full of food and four drinks. He handed one to her. It was diet. She didn't say thank you, but she held his hand.

He closed the laptop and drove out of the parking lot. If they would have watched the video just one more minute, they would have seen something even more shocking.

It started with a very bright light.

11

Something wasn't right.

Marie stood beneath the fluorescent light in their bedroom, her shadow sharply cast on a bit of sawdust in the corner. Not much, but enough for her to wonder what that was.

Her journal had been moved. She'd put it on the workbench, right where the nutcracker always stood in front of the wall checkered with squares of wood. Now it was on the corner of the workbench. The hairs on her arms bristled. She felt something was in the room with her. Maybe it was her imagination after hearing all the stories about the nutcracker talking to her brother.

"Fritz!" she shouted. "Did you move my journal?"

"What?" Sandy answered.

"The journal I got from Godfather. Did you move it before we went to the café?"

There was a pause. "I don't know. Maybe."

The hairs on her arms rose again. It was the way Sandy answered the question. He sounded like Fritz.

"Did you come in here when I was in the bathroom?" she asked.

"Nooo."

She shuddered. Fritz was plying butter to a slice of white bread by the sink. He sprinkled it with sugar and folded it over, ate half of it with one bite. Sandy watched with a smile denting his face.

"Was that you talking?" she said to Sandy.

"Uh, yeah. Who else?"

The biting sarcasm was back. "You sounded like Fritz. Just like him."

"I completed calibration twenty minutes ago." He made a twiggy fist in front of his face. Cleared his throat. A perfect imitation of her brother said, "Hey, sis."

"Don't do that." She stepped back.

"Why? I'm his voice."

"You're his voice; you're not him. Don't do that."

She wanted to hear her brother. Not an imitation. Sandy shrugged the pointed corners of his branches. Fritz dug another piece of bread out of the plastic bag. He scooped a dollop of butter from the tub and slathered it like stucco on a wall. The protein bar wrappers were on the counter. Dried flakes of chocolate were stuck to the insides.

"Did you eat these?" she asked.

Fritz shook his head. Marie walked back to the bedroom. The drawer in the workbench was slightly ajar. She didn't need to look inside it to know the wrappers she'd hidden inside there—the protein bars Fritz had taken from Aunt Rinks—were gone.

"She was in our room."

"Who?" Sandy said.

"Aunt Rinks. She found these." She held up the wrappers.

It didn't faze Fritz or Sandy. Marie looked out the window. No one was in the backyard. Aunt Rinks had been acting strange. The fake smile. *We'll be gone for hours.* Marie and Fritz would have had to explain why they were hiding wrappers in their room on any other day. That meant only one thing.

"She knows about Sandy," she said.

"What? No, she doesn't. I was totally gone when she caught us last night."

"She knows we're hiding something. That's why she went through our room. Don't you think she'd yell at us for this?" She put the wrappers in the trash and, unfortunately, didn't notice the empty boxes that came from Larry's Electronics. "When's the last time they left us alone in the house? She knows, Fritz. Turn Sandy off."

The sandman disappeared.

"Go up front, look out the windows. See if you see them anywhere."

Fritz took his white-bread sandwich to the front of the building. Marie went out back. The car was gone. The gate was closed. She would have heard it open if they came back. They could have climbed over it, but Aunt Rinks wasn't much of a climber. More of a walker and a sitter. She scanned through the trees, looked down the narrow path she'd found earlier that morning.

Marie walked around the building. Just in case.

Fritz was in the kitchen, making a third sandwich. "Anything?" she asked.

"Nope."

Sandy pretended to hide behind her brother. So what if Aunt Rinks knew about Sandy. Was it a big deal? *Because Aunt Rinks can't keep a secret. Eventually, she'd post a picture on her social. Then Godfather would send the Counselor to come for the ball. Or it would just stop working.*

So yeah, a big deal.

※

UNCLE VERNON TEXTED they would be home in an hour. He even turned on his location so she could see where they were. It was down the road at a fast-food place. They were going to bring home supper. She felt some relief. Maybe they were telling the truth. Although, it was possible he had dropped Aunt Rinks off to sneak around the back.

The nutcracker was on the table, rigid as always.

"Did Nussknacker tell you where Candyland is?" she asked.

"Not yet," Sandy answered.

"Why not?"

Sandy and Fritz shrugged in unison.

Marie picked up the nutcracker. He didn't squirm in her hand or mechanically kick out a stiff leg. The things Sandy had said about him (or maybe it was Fritz who told him to say it) cutting that boy's belt was ludicrous. She studied the back of the red jacket. She looked closer. Something tiny was written. She'd missed it before, it was so tiny. Like the font on tags found on clothing. Small numbers in a random pattern around an X.

"What's this?"

Fritz turned around. Sandy answered: "The map to Candyland."

"Why didn't you tell me that earlier?"

"You didn't ask." Sandy shuffled over. "X marks the spot."

The projection of his twiggy finger passed through the X etched onto the nutcracker's jacket. "What do the numbers mean?" she asked. "Are those steps? Miles?"

"Ask Nussknacker."

"I am." She addressed the question to the soldier, then looked at Fritz. "What did he say?"

"Nothing."

Fritz searched the empty refrigerator. Apparently, the journey to Candyland could wait until his stomach was full. She should have just let it go. There was still a chance this was all a game he and Sandy were playing. The numbers meant something. She had a feeling.

She took Nussknacker to the bedroom. Every morning, she found him standing in the cubbyhole beneath the owl clock. That was where she put him now, only this time she turned him around so he was facing the checkered wall.

X marks the spot.

Fritz came inside the room and stood next to her. There was a glob of peanut butter on his finger. He had found the jar hidden under the sink.

"Why do you always put Nussknacker here?" she asked.

"We don't put him there." Sandy appeared next to Fritz. "That's where he goes."

"But why?"

Sandy and Fritz shrugged. "He climbs up there at night to stand guard."

"Okay." She decided not to argue that imaginative plot. "You see that?"

She pointed at the square on the wall in the lower right corner. There were thin, whitish scars, the natural sort, that crisscrossed over the circular growth rings from corner to corner. They were hardly noticeable.

"What's that look like?" she asked.

"Do I really have to answer that?"

A twinge of excitement flickered in her belly. It was an X. A coincidence, of course, and not the location of an imaginary land of candy a toy soldier told her brother about. She dug her fingernail into the edge of the wooden tile. It wasn't glued to the wall, but it wasn't coming free easily. She used both hands and, little by little, worked it loose. It fell on the table. Fritz stood on his toes. Sandy leaned through the workbench for a better look.

The wall behind it was painted pink.

"Punch a hole through it," Sandy said.

"I'm not punching a hole in the wall."

"Maybe Candyland's on the other side."

"There's a street on the other side."

"How do you know?"

An argument like this was infinite. Before she grabbed the wooden tile to push it back into place, she looked at the nutcracker. There wasn't just an X on his jacket. There were numbers, too. They were sequential like hopscotch. On a whim, she pressed on the tile to the left of the empty space on the wall, where number 1 would be on the map next to the X. It slid into the empty space where the X tile had been.

What was strange, she noticed, was that the edges of the tile were tongue and groove so that it didn't pop out like the X tile did (which didn't have a tongue or a groove).

"That was something," Sandy said.

She slid the tile to the left of the newly vacated space. It was a game. That tiny spark of excitement fanned into a flame. She didn't expect to find Candyland. But something was here.

She checked her phone. Uncle Vernon was still at the fast-food joint.

She followed the pattern on the back of Nussknacker's jacket. Three more tiles, each revealing a pink cotton-candy painted wall, and then hit a dead end. Nothing would move. "You skipped one." Sandy pointed to the numbers. "Go back one."

He was right. She went back to number two. This time she slid the tile above it down. After that, a couple of the tiles were difficult to move. With a little effort, they came loose and fell into place. Fritz held the nutcracker, and Sandy relayed what move to make next. They got to the last one.

"Dead end," Marie said.

"Try harder," Sandy said.

"I might break it. You sure we did it right?"

"Yeah, 100."

She rolled her eyes when Fritz and Sandy weren't looking at her. The nutcracker wasn't helping them solve the puzzle. If he was talking to Fritz, he could have just told them what to do. Then again, the map *was* on his back.

She tried using both thumbs to slide it up to the empty slot. It gave a little, just enough, to break a vacuum that was drawing it tight against the wall. It popped up and out of the way. The wall behind it wasn't pink.

There was a hole.

Marie took half a step back. She bristled with anxiety and anticipation. Her skin was electrified. They stared at the opening. It looked like a square black hole in the wall.

"Found it," Sandy said.

It was a tiny hole, big enough for a plump mouse to enter. Marie tipped her head to look inside. There was something in there. No whiskers or twitching pink nose. Frigid air leaked out like a refrigerator was open. Fritz reached for it, and Marie grabbed his arm.

"Let me do it."

Marie didn't know how refrigerators worked, but she was certain there was a broken line blowing winter air into the wall. It was colder than inside or outside the building and stung the skin on the back of her hand when she reached in. She was almost elbow deep (wondering if her arm was wagging over the sidewalk outside) when her fingertips touched something. It was a small cube. Her fingers wrapped around the sides of it but not across the back. There was something attached to the top of it.

She expected to pull out a block of solid steel. Instead, it was a red box with a green bow on top of it. *It's the gift,* she thought. *The one Godfather gave to the Corkers.*

"Candyland?" she said.

"That's it. Look."

There was a tag attached to the lid. In small print, a single word was written. *Candyland.*

She felt a bit of relief. All this time it had sounded like they were going to journey somewhere. It was just a present. At the same time, she felt a dark cloud of disappointment. *It's just a present.*

The lid was attached to the box by delicate hinges. She pried it open. Nothing jumped out to bite her hand; poison gas didn't escape. The lid flipped the rest of the way open on its own. They leaned over to look inside.

"Well, lookie there," Sandy said. "Handsome little fella."

It was an orb, sort of like the ball that projected Sandy, only this one was smooth, a little smaller, and not as shiny. Distorted images swirled on the surface like a fortune teller's gazing ball.

It looked like it was floating inside the box.

"Some sort of magnet," Sandy said. "Turn it on."

That seemed like the obvious question. If the ball in Fritz's pocket projected Sandy, then maybe this one would project Candyland. Whatever that was. Right now, though, it was a dull marble with gray images floating on the surface. When she looked closer, there were things inside it that looked like distant forests and rolling hills. If she leaned in one direction, the images changed. There were other things in there, too.

"What are you waiting for?" Sandy said. "Go in."

"Go in what?"

"Candyland. Go in Candyland." He looked at Fritz. "What's the holdup?"

She shook her head. As exhilarating as this little game had been, they weren't going to fit into a box that fit inside the palm of her hand. She turned it around, looked for a button. A humming vibration went up her arm. And the thing was so cold.

She checked her phone. They still hadn't left. "What do you mean, go in?"

"Nussknacker said it."

"Nussknacker said that?"

"Yeah. Who else would say it?"

"Oh, I don't know. You?"

"I don't know any more about this than you do. I'm just telling you what the little soldier is telling Fritzy. He said you found it. He said go in it. He said what's the holdup."

Fritz pointed at the swirling ball floating inside the box. He held the nutcracker in one hand, stuck his finger inside it with the other hand.

"Ask him yourself," Sandy said. "Oh, wait. He doesn't talk to you. You know why? Because you don't believe in—"

Bright light.

A million flash bulbs all at once.

❄

A HIGH-PITCHED WHINE faded when her eyes adjusted. The gift box was on the table. The lid wide open.

Fritz was gone. So was Sandy.

How long had she been standing there? Where did the light come from? She shouted his name. When he didn't answer, she ran into the other room. A jar of peanut butter was on the counter; the lid was off. He wasn't in the storefront or the bathroom or the other bedroom with the brand-new mattress still wrapped in plastic. She went outside and called his name.

Where did he go?

A thousand thoughts squeezed through the bottleneck of her brain. *Call Godfather.* She didn't have his phone number. *Tell Aunt Rinks.* Bad idea. *Call the police.* And tell them what, a mysterious present hidden in the wall vaporized her brother?

She was seized by a panic she hadn't felt since Aunt Rinks had come to pick up her and Fritz on that one day at school, when she'd taken them home to come live with her. An emptiness opened inside her. She couldn't lose her brother. She just couldn't.

The emotional black box inside was rattling.

❄

SHE RETRACED her steps to the bedroom. There were no marks on the floor. No strange smells in the room. Maybe *she* had had an episode, like a brain malfunction from all the stress, and Fritz had gone for help. That was possible. But it wasn't true.

She fell on the floor in the storefront. Her legs crossed beneath her; she didn't have the strength to stand anymore. Not without Fritz. *I can't do this.*

That's a thought, her dad would've said about that. *Can't is a thought. Nothing more.*

She took a long slow breath through the nostrils, like he'd taught her to do when anxiety shook her like willow limbs in a thunderstorm. Long exhale through pursed lips. Again.

Having a thought I can't, she thought. *Having a thought I can't.*

Long in. Long out. Innnnnnn. Outttttttt.

The door at the back of the building banged open. "Murry!"

Marie opened her eyes. She stood up and, calmly, went to the kitchen.

❄

A WHITE SACK was on the kitchen table. The bottom of it stained with oil. It smelled like battered sardines fried in fish oil. Uncle Vernon was unloading groceries in the kitchen, filling the refrigerator with bottles of soda, ice cream, and lunchmeat (the thin round kind that tasted like rubber meat).

"Where's your brother?" Aunt Rinks said. She was tearing open a package of brand-new Bluetooth earbuds.

"I don't know," Marie said.

"Well, go find him. I need to talk with you both."

Marie didn't move. She'd already looked everywhere. She wasn't going to tell her that. She needed to tell someone, though. Aunt Rinks was more interested in syncing her earbuds to her phone than noticing the tremble of Marie's chin. Uncle Vernon was digging into a noisy bag of cheesy puffs, leaving orange fingerprints on the white bag of grease and the cabinets and the drawers.

She thought about running away. Right that second, just bolting out the door and running all the way to the cabin in the woods where the Counselor was planting a garden. Or knocking on Ms. Clara's apartment door above the coffee shop. Anyplace where she felt welcome. Where she was wanted. A place that felt like home. Because this wasn't home.

This was just a building.

"What's with the look?" Aunt Rinks leaned on the kitchen table, a blue light blinking in her ear. "Can you and me just be honest with each other? This is where we live now. It's the middle of December, and we ain't freezin' our toes off. That ain't so bad, is it? Vern, you like it here?"

He grunted while unloading the last bag of groceries. His whiskers were dusty orange.

"Vern likes it here, and so do I. And you will, too. I know it's hard for you, dear. It was hard for all of us when we were your age. You'll get through it, I promise."

Her tone was soft but had that imitative quality. Like someone who's saying the right things because someone told them they were the right things to say. Marie looked at her shoes. She was going to throw up on them.

"We got to trust each other. Right? We got to share each other's success. We're in this together. You, me, Vern. Fizzy. What's ours is yours and yours is mine. You understand what I'm sayin'?"

Marie looked her in her darkly lined eyes, the eyelids thick with sparkly blue eyeshadow. The bag of cheesy puffs crinkled in Uncle Vernon's hand.

"No," Marie said. "I don't."

"You don't understand." Her tone went as flat as a punctured kickball. It was more of a statement than question. "Well, how about when I found you in the middle of the night tellin' secrets with your brother. Let's start there. You found somethin', didn't you?" When Marie didn't answer, she tried the soft voice coated in sugar. "You can tell me, dear. It's all right. We're family. We can tell each other—"

"Rinks, what do you want me to do with these?" Uncle Vernon held up a box of protein bars.

"Stick 'em on the roof, Vern, I don't care. I'm havin' a conversation with my niece." She turned back to Marie. "Where's your brother? What's he doing? He better not be in the shower all this time. Fizzy!"

Aunt Rinks marched toward their bedroom. She was going to see the gift sitting on the workbench. Marie wasn't going to tell her how they'd found it or that her brother had disappeared in a flash of light. At that moment, she was very seriously considering walking out the back door.

"You hear me callin' your name, son?" Aunt Rinks bellowed. She stopped in the doorway to Marie's bedroom, put her hands on the frame, and said: "Where'd you get those?"

Marie hesitated. Aunt Rinks was standing at her bedroom with the door open. Red light was blinking from inside it. Her aunt sounded more upset than startled.

"Vern! Get over here and look at this."

With a bag of snacks in one hand, he trundled across the room, jamming his finger into his mouth, where cheesy puffs had packed into the divots of his back teeth like mortar. He stopped next to her and looked inside Marie's bedroom.

"Well, ain't that nice," he said.

"Nice?" Aunt Rinks said. "How about where'd they come from?"

Marie started toward them. It felt like she was floating on someone else's legs. She braced herself on the couch, then stumbled past the new television leaning on the wall. When she could see between her aunt and uncle, she froze.

Aunt Rinks turned around. "You wanna explain where these came from?"

Marie nodded absently. Walked toward them without taking her eyes off her brother. He stood still, hands in his pockets. Hat pulled down. A smile beamed below the tattered bill of it. Marie squeezed between her aunt and uncle and frowned. Strands of Christmas lights were strung on the walls; tiny bulbs flashed red.

"You lose your voice, too?" Aunt Rinks said.

"Fritz..." Marie cleared her throat. "He found them."

"Found them where?"

"They were, um, they were in an alley."

Aunt Rinks looked at Uncle Vern. Her lips flattened into a straight line that wrinkled her doughy chin. "Right. And you just hung them up before we got home."

Marie nodded. Her aunt was as confused as she was. Never mind where they came from. Maybe they had been in one of the drawers. Even if Fritz found them, how could he hang them up that fast? Her aunt seemed to be asking the same question.

"What else were you doin' in here while we were gone? Did you find anythin'? Huh? Anythin' you want to tell us about—"

"Rinks." Uncle Vernon stopped her before she said more. Aunt

Rinks seemed to understand what he meant. She crossed her arms like a five-year-old throwing a tantrum.

"I found wrappers in that drawer," Aunt Rinks said.

"You were in our room?" Marie said.

"You stole them from me, didn't you? I think that's the point. You ate them when you weren't supposed to. That ain't nice, and that ain't right. I ain't livin' with a bunch of middle school thieves who keep things from me." She stared lasers at Marie, searching for the secrets she desperately wanted to know. "What else you hidin'?"

She didn't ask about the gift because it wasn't on the bench.

"We were hungry. Is that food on the table for us?"

"It is," Uncle Vernon said. He put an arm around his wife. "Let's all cool down and get somethin' to eat. Come on, Rinks."

She didn't budge at first, scanning the room for something out of place besides a mess of mysterious red lights blinking on their faces. Uncle Vernon squeezed her shoulder. She relaxed a little.

"You really don't have anythin' to tell me?"

Fritz pulled something out of his pocket. For a second, Marie was afraid he would show her what the striped ball was for. Instead, he typed on his phone and handed it to his aunt. Marie saw what it said. *I took the protein bars, not Marie. I'm sorry.*

Aunt Rinks sort of laughed, showed it to Uncle Vernon. Then walked out and said: "Clean up after yourselves."

Marie waited a beat before walking over to her brother. She put her arms around him and squeezed too hard and too long. He let her do it as long as she needed to.

Aunt Rinks watched from the kitchen.

12

Christmas shoppers were in full gear. They were coming in and out of stores, peeking through windows, holding colorful bags heavy with loot. Cars circled the area in search of parking.

There was a time when she knew how many days, hours, minutes till Christmas. She and Fritz would turn over days on an advent calendar, then count their presents under the tree, stacking them to see how high they went. Now she had no idea what day it was. Saturday, maybe.

She and Fritz waited to cross the street. He had a Ziploc in his pocket full of orange puffs. His fingers were dusty and wet from licking them. Uncle Vernon had given him two baggies, told him not to tell their aunt. Marie gave her baggie to Fritz.

He had slept like bedrock that night, curled up with his nutcracker in his arms. Marie had stared at the Christmas lights till the early morning hours. When she woke up, he was already out of bed. Nussknacker was at his post, standing guard where the gift had been hidden. Aunt Rinks had sent them out of the toy store without having to do chores, with no money this time. And two secret bags of cheesy puffs.

"You want to tell me what happened?" she asked.

He licked his fingers, one at a time, and reached into his back pocket. He gave her a Bluetooth earbud and held up his phone. Before she could insert it, he jogged across the street when a truck had stopped for them.

"Where'd you get this?" she said.

He didn't answer. It wasn't the new Bluetooth earbud Aunt Rinks had opened the night before. Fritz had dug her old one out of the trash. They stopped in front of a bakery. The smell of frosted cakes wafted through the window. She fitted the earbud into her ear.

"Howdy doody, Murry Poppins," Sandy said. "You like that name? I got more. A whole list."

"Fritz." Her brother had his hand on the bakery window. Generous dollops of red jelly sat on glazed donuts. "You need to tell me what happened yesterday. Where'd you go?"

He turned. He looked at her. Sandy said, "Candyland, m'lady. We went to Candyland."

She didn't like talking about this with people walking behind them. Even if Sandy's voice was only in her ear. She tugged Fritz's green hoodie. They kept walking.

"What do you mean?" she said.

"It means we were there. And it was, like, *amazing*. We could describe it, but you had to be there. You know when you have a dream and—"

"Just tell me."

"I *was* going to paint a picture, but okay. Let's rush it. There were trees and grass and hills, and there was this sky that looked like... you know what? Scratch that. I got one word that sums it up. Delicious. The whole thing was *delicious*. That's what it was."

"Delicious." They waited for an older couple exiting a bookstore. He held the door for his wife, wished Marie and Fritz a merry Christmas. When they were past them, Marie said, "That's your description? Delicious?"

"You had to be there."

"You're saying you *were* there?"

"Yup. One second, bedroom. Fritz touched that little ball inside the gift. Then bright light." If Sandy were there, he would've done jazz hands. "Next stop, Candyland."

Fritz was distracted by an art gallery, stuffing orange curls in his mouth and looking at a wire sculpture of Santa Claus. She remembered the bright light when he had reached inside the gift. It had felt like a train horn that knocked her back. Then the confusion. The panic. She touched his shoulder, just to remind herself he was there. He looked at her with a question in his eyes.

"I thought you were gone," she said. "I thought it did something to you."

"Sorry," Sandy's voice said in her ear. "He said he's sorry."

He hugged her. In front of everyone. That dissolved the tension that had been coiled around her stomach since yesterday. Even with the orange smudge he left on her shirt, it was worth it.

They continued down the sidewalk beneath awnings shading the storefronts. She had no doubt he hadn't been in the bedroom after the bright light, but did she look everywhere? Did she look in the bathroom? She couldn't remember. Maybe he'd fallen into the bed when it happened and got wrapped up in the blankets, and she hadn't noticed.

He dreamed *of Candyland.*

"You can go, too," Sandy said. "It's pretty easy."

Fritz had his hands in the front pocket of his green hoodie. He pulled out a red and white striped box that fit in the palm of his hand. Marie took it from him and put it back in his hoodie while trying not to look guilty.

"Why'd you bring that?" she whispered.

"So you can go to Candyland," Sandy said. "It's in there. In that little box. The floating ball is the way in."

They walked in silence, navigating around a family clogging the sidewalk with little kids and a dog on a leash who stopped to relieve himself on a parking meter. The family took the dog inside a clothing store. Marie looked behind them, then at Fritz.

"You want me to do it now?" She didn't believe what they were saying (quite frankly, it was impossible), but her brother was missing a big step in his trip to Candyland. *He was gone.*

"Not here, kid. You'll disappear, and that'll freak all these lovely people out. Besides, Fritz is hungry."

"Eat the rest of those cheese doodles," she said.

"He's a growing boy. And space travel is exhausting."

"We don't have money, so you'll have to live off fake orange food for a while."

They passed the game store. It was crowded with middle school kids. As far as Marie could see, the boys weren't at the driving game. They approached the three mechanical elves in the coffee shop window, slowly swinging their tools in a bed of cotton made to look like snow. A little girl with a snotty upper lip was knocking on the glass. Her mother gathered her up.

"The old lady will give you something to eat," Sandy said. "If you smile."

He was talking about Ms. Clara. And she probably would. But Marie didn't want to keep asking for handouts. She'd been so nice already. Besides, the tables were full; people were standing in line.

"Not today," she said. "Let's go somewhere else."

"You don't believe us. We get it," Sandy said. "Touching a weird little ball and going to another world, that's nutty boo-boo. If you told us that, we wouldn't believe it, either."

Fritz was looking at her while Sandy continued, "Why do you think F-train brought the gift? So you don't have to believe us. *You see it for yourself.*"

"Uh-huh. And where do I do that?"

"They got a bathroom in there, right? Take it with you." Fritz held out the gift. Marie snatched it before anyone saw them.

If it were Sandy she was talking to, just Sandy and not her brother, she would've laughed. Not the friendly kind of laugh. Like if someone said *No, seriously, you can fly. Just step off this roof and believe.* That kind of laugh. But her brother, the way he looked—the big eyes, the hope swimming in them, the smile that said *c'mon, sis*—kept her lips locked. She would do anything to bottle that feeling he was feeling and keep it on the shelf for rainy days.

"And then what?" she said.

"You'll see," Sandy said. "We did."

She sighed. The elves swung their hammers. "Okay."

"Yesssss!" If Sandy were standing in front of them, he would've high-fived Fritz. "You should take a pic of her right now, F-dog. So exciting!"

Fritz did take a photo of Marie. He held up his hand. She slapped it without enthusiasm.

"All right. Stay out here," she said. He hadn't brought Nussknacker, so no worries about bullies taking him from him. And there were too many people for that to happen again, anyway. But it would be better if he weren't around all those people. That was how she really felt. If someone tried to talk to him and he just looked back without saying anything... she didn't want that to happen. "I'll be right back."

Fritz laughed through his nose. It sounded like a sneeze.

"Oh." She held the door. "How do I get out? Once I'm in the, uh... the place?" She couldn't bring herself to say Candyland.

"Just look up. Aim for the door and jump."

"Right."

She had no idea what that meant. She was just going with it. She touched the Bluetooth to turn it off. Sandy didn't need to be in her ear for this part.

❄

THE BATHROOM SMELLED like cleaning supplies and air freshener.

It was clean. Like eat-off-the-floor clean. There were paintings on the wall and cute sayings. *If you toot-toot, make sure you poof-poof* was next to a can of air refreshener. *Wash your hands whether you work here or not* was above the sink.

She looked in the mirror. Adjusted the white ribbon Godfather had given her to pull back her hair. She looked older than a seventeen-year-old. At least she thought so. Why people pined for being a kid again never made sense to her. Did they just forget how powerless you are at this age? Memories were all sweet smelling from a distance, when all was right with the world, but when things went wrong, you looked like her: five years older than you were.

She looked at the gift. Pried the lid open.

It was more of an orb than a ball. Although, she supposed, those were basically the same thing. Orb sounded more mysterious. A ball would sit at the bottom of the container. An orb hovered. Some sort of magnetic design made it hover. Or gyroscopes (although she didn't really know what gyroscopes did). It was cool, no argument. But the orb had a dullness to it. Like a burned-out light bulb.

She sighed.

Whatever it was, it brought more joy to her brother's face than she'd seen since maybe ever. Before that, the best present he'd ever gotten was a Honer Virtual GameFace. He didn't look like he did now.

She put the gift on the floor.

All she had to do was touch it. If it worked, there would be a bright light. She sat cross-legged in front of it. If there was a flash of light, like what had happened in the bedroom, she didn't want to fall over and wake up on Ms. Clara's hard, clean floor missing her front teeth. She stared at the orb.

She reached for it.

❄

FRITZ HELD HIS HANDS APART, ready to clap when he saw her.

Marie held the café door open for a young couple to enter. Fritz's lips were moving. For a second, she thought he was about to talk. She waited to hear words. Then he pointed at his ear. Marie touched the Bluetooth earbud.

"Well?" Sandy said. "Did you see the chocolate river? Tell me you dipped your finger in it. There's no way you didn't do that."

Marie looked around. Ms. Clara delivered an order to a table just inside the window near the elves. She saw them standing outside and waved. Marie waved back. She leaned close to her brother.

"Let's go to the park."

Fritz skipped next to her, and Sandy was singing a nonsense song in her ear, making up words like random thoughts floating from her brother's head. *Joy, joy, joy and snow to the world and peace and love and dogs and cats forever. I'm warm and sweet and home...*

Marie tried to take his hand, but he didn't want to hold his sister's hand on a crowded sidewalk. Marie turned off the earbud and walked faster. They went to the corner, crossed the street to a big fountain where the water crashed down on a concrete pineapple. There were benches around it and a park beyond it. Playgrounds and tennis courts, baseball fields and people with dogs.

A trailer had been set up not too far from the fountain. A thirty-foot Christmas tree was in front of it, loaded with ornaments and lights that would glow at night. Letters were attached to the trailer, big ones cut from plywood and painted green or red, that read *SANTA'S VILLAGE*. There were plastic reindeer lined up in different poses around a small stage with an empty chair on top. It looked like a throne. Not too different from the one Godfather sat in. People were standing around it.

They were in shorts and T-shirts, throwing Frisbees instead of snowballs. Rolling in the grass collecting bug bites instead of making snow angels. Marie sat on one of the concrete benches next to the fountain. It was warmed by the sun. Mist from the fountain felt cool and refreshing. It didn't feel like Christmas. Nothing about this did.

Fritz sat next to her. Pointed at his ear.

"What's wrong?" Sandy said when she turned the earbud on. "You look mad. Are you mad? You have resting mad face."

She held the gift, no longer feeling the need to protect it. She put it on the bench between them and hung her head. She couldn't look at her brother. Didn't want to see the light dim in his eyes.

"You didn't go," Sandy said. "Was the bathroom gross?"

She sighed, shook her head. She couldn't hide it. Her plan had been to lie when she came out, tell him how wonderful Candyland was. Jump up and down and clap and sing nonsense songs. But when she opened the door to the coffee shop, she just couldn't.

She didn't go. She didn't even try.

It was ridiculous, the whole thing. Touching a magnet wouldn't transport her to another world. It wasn't magic. She'd seen a light when Fritz disappeared, but there was an explanation for that. He hallucinated, fell unconscious. Dreamed of a world made of candy. Of course he did! What seven-year-old wouldn't? And his wingman, Sandy, didn't know the difference. She didn't want to pretend. But that wasn't why she didn't touch the orb. There was a simple reason why she didn't.

She wanted to believe it was true. She wanted that look on her brother's face to stay there as long as possible. And if she touched the orb and nothing happened, she'd know for sure it was just his imagination. This way she could still pretend it was true.

Because she *wanted* to believe.

"I believe you, Fritz. I really do."

"But you have to go," Sandy said. She didn't mind it was more in Fritz's voice this time. "Nussknacker said so. It's your journey, too."

A dad walked by with a little girl on his shoulders. She was eating an ice-cream cone that was melting over her little fingers and dripping in her dad's hair. He didn't seem to mind. Marie slumped on the bench.

"Tell me about it again," she said. "I want to hear every detail of your trip."

"I already told you," Sandy said.

Fritz searched her face for an explanation of why she didn't just go. She took her brother's hand. He let her hold it against the rough concrete bench.

"Please," she said. "I want to hear it."

So he told her. Sandy spoke in her ear about how soft the grass was (like thick fur) and the tree trunks with candy-cane stripes. The air smelled like peppermint, and the sky was the color of pink cotton candy (pink like the wall behind the wood squares). There was a stream of milk chocolate that he dipped his finger in and tasted. It made his toes tingle and head float.

Fritz looked at her the entire time. The more Sandy told her, the more color returned to his cheeks. There were lights in his eyes when she heard about something in the distance that was blurry and gray like a rainy day, although it wasn't raining. The rest of Candyland was just past a sign that was posted in the chocolate stream. Beyond it, all color disappeared.

"What did the sign say?" she asked.

"We didn't read it."

"Why not?"

"Because he was worried about you. So he jumped out."

"You don't have to worry about me." She squeezed his hand. "You can always go there without me. I'll take care of myself."

"We don't want to go without you. It's *our* journey."

She liked the sound of that. Maybe she could find a way to go there, too. Once she heard enough about this world, she could add details to the story. Fill the blank pages of that book Godfather gave her. They could do this instead of the memory game. Make a new story.

She laughed. "You got back just in time. Aunt Rinks was dying to know what we were doing. I don't know what I would have done if you didn't come out."

She almost said *if you didn't come out of hiding*. One day, he would tell her where he went. Maybe there was enough room in his hiding place for both of them.

"We never tell her about the gift," she said.

"Never."

Fritz laughed through his nose. She loved the sound of it. Loved the way his nose crinkled between his eyes when he did it. She let go of his hand. Maybe they could go back to the coffee shop and sit around until Ms. Clara saw them. It didn't feel right begging for food, but Marie had a feeling the old woman understood the situation.

"Hey, I never asked," she said. "Where did the Christmas lights in the bedroom come from?"

Before Sandy answered, Fritz's faded hat went flying into the fountain. Someone snatched the gift off the bench between them.

※

Fritz didn't fish his hat out of the fountain. He spun off the bench and charged in the other direction. By the time Marie turned around, a lanky boy with loopy hair was stiff-arming Fritz and laughing. He clutched Fritz's hoodie at the shoulder.

Acne Boy was back.

This time, the gift was his hostage.

Marie roped her brother around the waist and pulled him away kicking and swinging. Bobby stepped back. His chapped lips pulled back a fierce grin that exposed blocky teeth not too unlike Uncle Vernon's pickets. Sean, his little brother, reached for the gift Bobby had taken from the bench. Bobby swatted him back a step.

No one was paying attention to them. They were all waiting for Santa to come out of that trailer. It looked like kids doing what kids do near the fountain, playing a little not-so-friendly game of keep-away.

Don't run, Bobby, Marie thought.

The last thing she wanted him to do was take off with the gift. Then she'd have to chase him down, tackle him, and take it from him. She didn't want a scene and to scare all these little kids waiting for Santa.

Bobby didn't run. He couldn't care less about the present. He wanted one thing. He wanted their fear. And if he couldn't get that, their anger.

Steam escaped the emotional black box inside Marie.

"That's my brother's," Marie said calmly. "It means a lot to him. Please give it back."

He turned it over like an antique dealer considering an offer. "What'll you give me for it?"

"Please. We haven't done anything to you."

"You got that doll?" Sean laughed when his brother said that. It sounded so serious. "I don't want a wood soldier. Oh, hey. Look at that. Fancy lid."

His eyes were as round as the O his flaky lips made. He didn't open it. He tempted his brother with it and pulled it away before Sean grabbed it.

"Let's see what's inside," he said like a first-grade teacher.

Marie tightened her grip on Fritz. His boots slipped on the grass as he tried to find traction.

"What's wrong with him?" Bobby said. "He looks—what's the word... *wild*." The muscles in Marie's jaw flexed. Bobby saw it. "You get him at the shelter? You know what we do to animals off leash here?"

He winked. It looked like he was imitating something his parents did. Or bullies who bullied him. He kept dodging Sean from getting the gift. He was good at this.

"This must be worth a lot." He shook the box. "Is it gold, yeah? Ooo, a diamond ring. You're going to propose to Santa!" He covered his mouth and turned toward the stage. "I think I'm going to cry."

He fanned his face. Sean looked at Marie and Fritz and laughed. Like squirting lighter fluid on a spark.

Bobby straightened up, said flatly: "You know who he is, right? The guy who's going to come out of that trailer there. That's my uncle Dan. He likes to dress up every year because he's got the beard. Rides a bike, though. A big old hog with louders that set off car alarms when he gasses it. I been on that bike with him. He pulled a wheelie going down Main Cross."

He could tell that didn't impress her. *Is that what he's trying to do?* He shook the box again. Pointed at Fritz.

"You know he ain't real, right?" He looked at Marie, back to Fritz and back to Marie. His laughter was staged. "Oh, man. Oh man oh man oh man. Did I just ruin Christmas? I'm sorry 'bout that, little man, but it's all a lie. You were going to find out anyways. Your mom and dad's a liar. Santa's just a bum dressed up in a red coat. Ain't that right, Sean?"

Sean had given up on the gift, but he was grinning. For once, his older brother was giving the business to someone besides him.

"Why are you doing this?" Marie asked.

"Why? Why does a polar bear turn snow yellow? He just has to."

Sean thought it was hilarious. Not the joke. The meanness. Bobby was holding court. This was what he was made to do: take things and make people squirm. This was what he wanted. That didn't stop Marie from trying to reason with him.

"We don't have any money."

"That's too bad."

He would've taken the money. It wouldn't have gotten Marie the gift, but he would've taken it. He was thinking now. Thinking like it hurt. Like pedaling as fast as you can in first gear. There must be a whole cabinet of taunts cataloged inside his brain, handed down by an older brother or Dad or Uncle Dan. He had been taught this was what you do for fun. Whether he was responsible for this or just another victim was beside the point. There was only one thing that mattered right now.

"Swim in the fountain. You and your wild animal. Do a backstroke around it three times, then stand up, hug each other, take a bow, and tell everyone to mind their own business."

He was good at this. Probably graduated top of bully class. The only straight As he ever got. He was good. Very good. Start with an impossible task and work your way down, that was how you got people to cave. Sean clapped his greedy little hands, a mini-Bobby ready for his own victims one day.

"No," Marie said.

"You're right. Too messy. You could catch cold. Tell you what," he said, "you do this, and I swear I'll give this back. Swear on this little ding-dong's life here." He nodded at Sean. "Mine, too. And you ain't got to do anything embarrassing. See those people over there?" He swung his arm at all the little kids and their parents lined up between the yellow tape in front of the stage. "None of them know you. You don't know them. So it's simple. You start on that end, and you tell every one of them three words. That's it. You get the fancy box back. Deal?"

He held the gift out. She didn't try to take it.

"Three words," he said.

She shook her head. She knew what they were. He could see that, too. He grinned like a mouse in a cheese factory and counted the words on his fingers.

"Santa's. Not. Real."

"I'm not doing that."

She remembered what it was like when she was that age. How special it was to sit by the window on Christmas Eve. Seeing the cookies gone in the morning, the carrots they threw on the sidewalk half eaten. The stockings full. She wasn't going to ruin it for them. Life was hard enough. Let them have this moment while it was here. Get a picture with Uncle Dan in a Santa suit.

"You think telling the truth is bad?" Bobby pretended to be offended. "Or do you think a fat man really slides down a chimney? He lives on the North Pole with elves, rides in a sleigh with flying reindeer to give free presents in one night, really? *Really?*" He shook his head, reliving some awful moment when someone told him it was all a lie. "You look smart. You both do, but you more than him. But you're probably one of those people who gets good grades, like straight As, but can't figure out how to turn on a light."

He made a stupid face and cracked up Sean.

"Can you tie your shoes? Can you?" he said to Fritz. "Tell you what, you count to ten, and I'll give it back. That's all the wild animal has to do, count to ten."

"Don't," she said through gritted teeth.

"How about this? You solve a math problem, and we're done here. What's 345 times 284?"

"97,980," Sandy said in her ear.

She didn't give him the answer. It wasn't going to matter. None of this—not swimming in the fountain or ruining a hundred Christmas wishes—was going to end this. She felt helpless. The feeling left her body. Her arms and legs were wooden. Her chest a steel cage. The tendons in her neck were taut.

A big, brass bell began to ring.

Cheers went up. Little kids on their fathers' shoulders waved. The door on the trailer opened, and a bearded man in a red outfit stood on the top step and waved. A couple of teenaged elves stood with him. The line to see him began to tighten.

"Santa!" Bobby screamed through a bullhorn of cupped hands. "Santa, we got you a present!"

He waved the gift over his head. People were looking at him and laughing. The gangly teen with acne sounded sincere, jumping up and down.

"Uncle Dan! Hey, over here!"

Santa glanced over and ignored him. Climbed the steps to sit on the Santa chair. In seconds, the first of a long line of hopeful wishes walked up to sit on his lap.

"Oh, so stupid," Bobby said with a sigh. "Anyway, better see what we're giving him. Don't want to be embarrassed. Is there a tiny toy soldier in here?" He shook the gift. "Better not be a lump of coal. That would be... you can't give Santa coal, you ding-dongs. *Santa* gives the coal."

"I'll buy you a game," Marie said. "Let's go, right now. We'll go to the game store, you pick one out, and I'll buy it. Just give it back to me."

"Thought you didn't have money?" He was interested. Genuinely.

"I'll get some."

"All right." He sucked a breath between his squares of teeth. The mouse wheel was turning. "Beg for it. I'll give it back."

She put her hand out. She wasn't going to beg any more than she already had.

"What's that?" he said.

"Just give it back."

He put his thumb on the edge of the lid. Looked at her when he said: "You're making me do this, you know." He started to push it open. "This is your fault."

Marie's heart heard a starter pistol and was sprinting around the first turn. The lid flipped over the top and snapped open. He peeked inside and looked surprised. *Please don't touch the orb,* Marie thought. *Not in front of Fritz.*

For a second, she considered falling on one knee. If she jumped in the fountain, everyone would look at them. She could tell the adults who came to help her that was their gift he'd taken from them. It wasn't going to work, but she could try. She had to do something before he—

Fritz slipped from her grip. Hat pulled over his eyes, he charged blindly. Bobby was distracted by what was inside the gift, and he didn't see him till it was almost too late. He hit Fritz with a forearm. Fritz twisted off-balance and tried to catch himself. He sprawled across the ground like a runner stealing second base. Grass was in his mouth. Mud on his cheeks.

Pressure shot from the emotional black box. A switch flipped.

Auto-protection engaged.

Marie bolted forward.

She buried her shoulder into Bobby's midsection and grabbed both of his legs. She dropped to one knee, pivoted, and pulled his legs up while surging her weight forward. She placed her foot behind his knee. The air stampeded from his lungs when he hit the ground.

The surprise didn't last long. He twisted onto his hands and knees to get up. Instinctually, Marie knew at that moment he did not know how to wrestle. He'd given up his back, and she took it. She hooked her legs around him, locked her heels inside his calves. His neck was exposed. She slipped her arm under his chin and clamped onto her forearm, throwing her weight back. He toppled on top of her. She arched her back to apply pressure.

Her arm was petrified wood. Muscles braided cords of steel. She was a sprung trap, her jaw clenched, teeth grinding. His breath wheezed through his chapped lips like an old man breathing through a straw.

Her lips pressed to his ear. She whispered: "Don't *ever* touch him."

Footsteps approached in the soft ground. A shadowy ring formed around them. A woman bent down beside them. Marie wasn't letting go. She saw the gift lying in the grass. Sean picked it up. He looked inside the gift.

No.

She held on as Bobby started to go limp, his face turning red, staring at Sean as he reached inside the gift. His fingers curled around the orb, about to pull it out. The worst part of it all happened right in front of her brother.

No bright light.

No vanishing act.

Fritz got off the ground and saw it, too. He snatched the gift from Sean and took off running.

Marie let go of Bobby and collapsed on the ground. She closed her eyes as more adults came to break them up. She sighed as the lid on her emotional black box sealed shut. She lay on the ground, numb from head to toe.

No Candyland.

13

Three protein bars for lunch. That was how many wrappers were on the table. Rinks didn't count how many licorice sticks she'd eaten. However many half a bag was. Her gut told her it was too many. But that never stopped her from eating more.

Licorice gave her a belly ache. The protein bars, that was just scientific nutrition. It said so on the wrapper. They were solid bars of nutrients wrapped in milk chocolate for a person on the go. She ate them like Vern inhaled packaged noodles, and he was healthy as a clam. The licorice was dessert. A little cheat never hurt anyone.

She took a selfie with a floppy black stick of licorice. Made sure the laptop was in the shot, but not what was on the screen. The kids didn't follow her, but just in case they did, she didn't want them seeing the video footage taken in their bedroom. Social influencing was hard work. It took constant posting of interesting stuff. Not as easy as it sounded. Stuck in this crummy building, she was running out of ideas.

That was going to change. Very soon.

She was watching the footage from that morning. Marie was asleep. The mattress looked like a flat tire. How she slept with those red lights blinking was as big a mystery as how the lights got there. They were lying about it. That was what bothered Rinks the most. *The secrets.* She loved a good secret. They were keeping her from what she loved.

Marie had finally woken up. Rinks fast-forwarded to the part where Fritz came back in the room. She assumed he was coming for the nutcracker (*What'd he call that thing? Crackatooth?*). He stood at the bench, and once again, the angle of the camera was all wrong. She couldn't see what he was doing.

"Can you hear me?" Vern's voice was on the laptop.

Rinks switched to the live stream while she chewed on the rubber stick. Her husband's mouth-breathing face filled the screen. The owl clock in the kids' bedroom was just above his head.

"Move the camera," she said.

"What?"

"Move the camera!" she screamed across the room. "It's too low. I can't see what they're doin' on that stupid table."

"One thing at a time. Can you hear me?"

"Ain't it obvious? Now move the—"

"Just a sec."

He ducked out of sight. That was the other thing. There was a blind spot. She wanted to see the *entire* room. What if something was going on in the corner? She'd miss it. Vern came back into view, doing something on his phone. The blinking red lights made him look... *strange.* Every time it turned him red, he looked like someone else. *Not someone else.* Something *else.*

"We're good," he said. "You done with the laptop now? I got work to do."

"I'll be done when you move the camera," she shouted.

"Rinks, I don't have time."

Rinks rushed into the kitchen. The brand-new coffee machine just finished a full pot. She filled a mug (a clean one), added flavored creamer, and grabbed the bag of cheese doodies. It was mostly orange dust, but that was his favorite. He liked to dust his noodles.

She crossed the room. Coffee slopped over the sides and burned her fingers. She didn't slow down.

"What's this?" He scrubbed his whiskers with the palm of his hand. It sounded like a wire brush scraping paint.

"Special delivery."

He took the mug from her, put his nose over it. His eyebrows rose. After a noisy sip, he ran the tip of his tongue through his mustache.

"You like?" Rinks said.

"I like."

"I bought the expensive coffee for you. The most expensive. And that creamer is—"

"French vanilla." He took another loud sip. "I like it ah-lot."

"That makes me happy. Now can you move the camera?"

"No. I just got the sound workin'," he said to avoid a head-on collision with a tantrum. "I don't have enough time to move it. I'll move it tomorrow. You can listen in on them tonight."

"Well... take down the Christmas lights, at least."

"Why? They put them up. It looks good."

"Not on you." He was too in love with the coffee to know what that meant. "You really think they put them up?"

"Who else would put them up, Rinks?"

She dug into the crinkly bag and aimed a cheese doodie at him. He opened his mouth. She popped it in and kissed him on the lips. His coffee breath was staggering, but now was not the time to talk personal hygiene. He shook his head before she asked about moving the camera again. She stomped around the room.

The owl clock stared at her. She wanted to take that down, throw it in the garbage along with the one Godfather gave them. But they hadn't seen a mouse, so why jinx it. Marie's journal was on the bench, the pages still blank (*not much of a storyteller, is she?*) along with Mr. Crackatooth. *What are they doin' over here?* she wondered. It was something. She could feel it. Then she noticed the square blocks of wood on the wall.

"Have you been over here?" she asked.

"I been everywhere," Vern said, pouring cheese doodie dust from the bag directly into his mouth.

She leaned closer. There was something quite suspicious on the wall. If she had another minute to study it, she might have discovered exactly what the kids had been doing. But just then the back door slammed. Rinks jumped and had one thought. *The laptop is open!*

Before she could escape the bedroom, Fritz almost ran into her. He surprised Vern, and coffee went down his mustard-stained sweatshirt.

"Fritz!" Rinks said in a high register. "What are you doin' here?"

He did a strange shuffle, turned on his heel and went straight to the bathroom. The lock bolted in place. Rinks had barricaded the doorway to keep him from coming into the bedroom if he came out. She turned to Vern and whispered: "He caught us in here."

Vern shrugged, wiping dust off his sweatshirt. "We're admirin' the lights."

"What's he doin' home?"

"Looks like he's got business." He gestured to the bathroom.

Rinks ran on her tiptoes to the kitchen table. The laptop was facing the door with a full view of the bedroom on it. All it would take was a glance. *We'll tell him we're installin' a security system, to keep them safe. We started with their room because, you know, they're most important.* Fritz might buy that.

Marie wouldn't.

Rinks went to the bathroom, tapped lightly on the door. "Fizzy, darlin'? Everythin' all right in there? You're home so soon."

"You think he's goin' to answer?" Vern said.

Rinks swatted him. His coffee spilled again. "What are you doin' in there?"

"Whaddya think, Rinks? Let the boy concentrate."

He got away this time without spilling a drop. Rinks followed him into the kitchen. The kid had to go to the bathroom. Nothing wrong with that. Everyone liked to do business on home base. Perfectly normal. And he'd rushed in without seeing a thing. No big deal.

"Done with this?" Vern held up the laptop.

"Take it. Go."

She grabbed a licorice stick and gnawed it to a nub while pacing around the table. Vern went to the little desk in the corner. Before he got to work, all the lights in the room flickered. The time on the stove began flashing.

"What was that?" Rinks said.

"Nothing," Vern said dully. "I'll check the circuit breaker."

❄

"Is someone knocking?"

Rinks looked out from the kids' bedroom. She'd been waiting for Fritz to come out of the bathroom and found herself staring at the checkered wall. The squares of wood were smudged with rust. Not all of them, just some of them. It looked like fingerprints. Someone with rusty fingers.

She watched Vern get up from the little desk in the corner and look out the window. He opened the back door. Someone was talking to him, saying something she couldn't understand. Then he stepped aside.

"Come in."

Marie was the first one to come inside. That was weird, her knocking like that. Rinks noticed the grass stains on her shirt. She was carrying Fritz's grungy hat. Then two boys followed her, one tall with a mess of hair on his head and muddy knees; the other one was Fritz's age. A woman was the last one in.

"I'm Vernon. That's my wife, Rinks." Rinks stared from the bedroom. No one waved. "Can I get you somethin' to drink? Water? Coffee?"

"No, thank you. I'm Nina."

She shook his hand. Jealousy wrung Rinks's stomach like a wet towel. The woman was slender and fit. Toned arms and angular face. Rinks could see her jawbone from across the room. With the little hoop piercing in her nose, she looked like one of those cool professional types. A gym owner. Or something.

"Everythin' all right?" Vern asked.

"Your daughter strangled my son." Nina folded her fine arms. "It was down at the fountain. Everyone saw her attack him. She got him on the ground and put her arms around his throat. His face was turning blue when someone broke it up. It happened in front of Santa Land. All the kids saw it, too. They were traumatized."

"Marie?" Vern looked at the boy and back to Marie, then at Rinks. "Marie strangled *him*?"

"There were dozens of witnesses. Show him, Bobby."

The boy was staring at the floor, paralyzed with embarrassment. Nina lifted his chin to expose his neck. If there were scuff marks, Rinks couldn't see them. Besides the dirty knees, there was no evidence that would hold up in court.

"Why she do that?" Vern asked doubtfully.

"She attacked him, unprovoked."

"*Really?*" Vern said.

Nina elbowed her son to start him up. "We were just talking," he muttered at the floor. "She caught me by surprise." Like that was the only reason a girl beat him. *By surprise.*

"She attacked you for no reason?" Vern said.

"Yes, sir."

"Marie?" Vern asked.

Marie shook her head bitterly, but said nothing. Her face carved from stone. Jaws clenching and unclenching.

"I'm not calling the police," Nina said. "If she would've touched my Sean, it would be a different story. I don't want her coming around my kids again, or I will next time."

Vern looked around again. He was suppressing a grin and doing a good job at it. "You hear that, Marie? Don't beat this boy up again."

Bobby's eyebrows pinched together, but he didn't say anything to that. Nina clenched her own biceps, understanding the jab quite clearly. Marie nodded tightly.

"Shake hands and apologize," Vern said.

Bobby offered a limp hand. Marie shook it firmly and looked him in the eye. His arm waggly like a noodle. "Sorry."

"It won't happen again," Vern said. "Thanks for lettin' us know. Kids get rough, I understand, but that's no excuse. Especially in front of children. Are you all right, partner?" he asked Sean. The younger boy nodded. Vern rustled his hair. "Thanks for bringin' them here, Nina."

"It was the right thing to do." She seemed satisfied with the handshake and apology. Grownup Vern really nailed it. Rinks would have made a mess of it, said something inappropriate. Nina looked around the room, at the new furniture and moldy walls. "Y'all living here?"

"Just moved in a couple of weeks ago. Still a lot of work to do. The building was in the family. We inherited it and decided *why not?*"

"That's good." She nodded with a tinge of judgment wrinkling her chin. She had yet to smile, just a grim line across her mouth, even when she said: "This place used to be awesome. Are you going to open the toy store? Be nice if you did. I used to come when I was little."

"Apparently everyone did."

"You make these?" She pointed at the headscarves on the kitchen table.

"I do." Rinks raised her hand.

Nina didn't say any more about them. But she liked them. Rinks thought she saw her smile just a little. "Y'all have a merry Christmas. Everyone be safe." The boys couldn't get out fast enough. Vern held the door for her. She peeped back for one last comment. No one noticed how odd it was when she said: "Love the Christmas tree. Just like the Corkers used to do."

Vern watched them through the window. They were talking in the backyard. The gate hadn't closed yet. Rinks knew what good parenting looked like. And that was it.

❄

"You know how to fight?" Vern said. "You see the size of that kid, Rinks? Oh my... he was *huge*. And you just—"

"She couldn't hurt a fly." Rinks locked her arms across her chest, tapping her foot. "What was that all about, Marie?"

"Where's Fritz?" Marie said.

"He's hidin' in the bathroom." Rinks met Marie halfway across the room, blocked her from going around the couch. "I know there's more to it. That boy wasn't sayin' somethin'. And why do you have Fizzy's hat? Now, you're goin' to tell me what—"

"He deserved it!" Marie hit her thighs with balled-up hands. "He and his brother were teasing Fritz, calling him an animal. They threw his hat in the fountain, laughed at him, made fun of him. I tried to be nice. I was calm and polite. But he hit Fritz and knocked him down, and I—"

"Took him down," Vern said. "Is it karate or somethin' else?"

"She strangled him, Vern. That ain't karate."

"I choked him," Marie said. "There's a difference."

"That so?" Rinks planted her hands on her hips. "Well, at least somethin' makes sense because none of what I heard a minute ago did. They were just teasin' you for no reason, just out of the blue. You were mindin' your own business, and they decided to throw his hat in the water. Is that it?"

"They were the ones from before, at the coffee shop."

Rinks took a second. She'd forgotten all about that. "What about them?"

"They took the nutcracker from Fritz. Ms. Clara made them leave. They were probably sore about that. No one was around to stop them this time."

"So you took him down," Vern said.

"Vern, would you stop saying that?"

Marie was biting her lip. The girl looked disgusted with herself. She'd lost control, hurt the boy. Maybe that wasn't what was eating her up. Maybe she enjoyed it. She had a bunch of stuff packed down inside her, emotions all bottled up, and that burst of anger had uncorked it like champagne. Now she felt ugly.

Rinks knew the feeling.

"So we got ourselves a fighter," Vern said.

"No, we don't. That little stunt's gonna ruin our reputation. People'll be talkin' about us, not in the good way. They know we live down here. Suppose we open the toy store like everyone wants us to do. Things like this is gonna scare them off. We'll lose followers on social if we go around beatin' up everyone that throws a hat in the fountain."

"He knocked Fritz down," Marie said.

"Let adults take care of it. What you did has consequences. You're lucky she ain't gonna press charges. We're new on the block, girl. They all live here; they all know each other. You got to think of more than just yourself."

Rinks was filled with pride. This was an award-winning speech she was giving. Too bad Vern didn't have the cameras set up in the kitchen to record it. This was high-level parenting, like Nina the gym owner had done. The lesson was sinking into Marie's brain, weighing on her. Wisdom was heavy for kids. Takes them a minute, sometimes years, to make sense out of it. Marie was staring at the floor, grim-faced and tense. She'd get it, though. She'd understand.

"Where you goin'?" Rinks said.

"To see if Fritz is okay."

"He's in the bathroom doin' what one does in the bathroom. Give him some space. He's just shook up watchin' his sister beat the tar out of some—"

"Bully. He was a bully."

"It don't matter."

"So don't stand up for Fritz?" Marie spouted.

"Don't put words in my mouth, young lady. You're not hearin' me. You did that in front of all those people, scarring those little kids. You heard what Ms. Nina said."

"Rinks," Vern said.

"Don't *Rinks* me, Vern. She ain't tellin' us everythin'. She got secrets, don't you, Marie. What'd I say the other night about—"

"Rinks!"

Vern was standing at the door leading into the storefront. He was staring all confused like. It sent a shiver over her skin. She almost didn't want to look at what he was seeing. He pointed through the doorway. For the first time, she thought maybe she didn't want to know the secrets.

"What's that?" he said.

※

IT WAS A TREE.

Eight feet tall, maybe ten. The branches were soft and feathery. The top of it hooked to one side like a cartoon. A star was attached to the tippy-top. It was so bright, it hurt to look at.

It was littered with ornaments. Not the store-bought kind with reflective surfaces or plastic snowflakes. They were made with scissors and glue. Things found in a kitchen junk drawer or third-grade art class. Paper snowflakes sprinkled with glitter, tongue-depressor reindeer, Styrofoam snowmen with googly eyes. Santa faces with cotton-ball beards, pretzel-made sleighs and hand-shaped turkey cutouts painted red, green and yellow. Strings of popcorn and cranberry hung from the branches.

In the corner of the store for the whole world to see.

"I'm goin' to ask one time," Rinks said. "Real simple. Did you put this up?"

"No." Vern was gawking at it. "It's somethin', though."

"How'd it get here, then?"

"When would I put it up? You been with me all day."

"Check the camera."

"We ain't got no camera out here, Rinks. You wanted audio in the…" He looked around, then whispered: "In the kids' room."

Rinks didn't like the way this made her feel. It was fully decorated. Not a branch left unhung. It hadn't been there that morning, and neither one of them had left the building. Not for a second. It was impossible to pull this in without making a sound.

Physically.

IMPOSSIBLE.

"Marie!"

A minute later, Rinks's niece came from the back of the building. She seemed not at all surprised to see an eight-, maybe ten-foot tree in the storefront. She squinted at the star's radiance.

"You know anythin' about this?" Rinks asked.

"It's nice."

"How'd it get here?"

"What'd you mean?" A solid liar, this one. Not even a flinch.

"What I mean is, how... did... it get here? It wasn't here this morning. And now it's here. How?"

She shook her head. She was feeling the same gooseflesh on her arms that Rinks was feeling. The weirdness was like a static charge. A ghost dancing around the room. Then Rinks remembered something Nina had said right before she left. A fresh wave of gooseflesh crashed over her. *Love the Christmas tree. Just like the Corkers used to do.*

"Maybe one of the locals snuck it in," Marie said.

"She's got a point, Rinks. Every one of them keeps bringin' up the toy store."

"You're tellin' me... someone snuck in here... and did this while we were here?"

"I mean, yeah," Vern said. "We don't lock the front—"

"No one snuck a CHRISTMAS TREE IN!"

She was feeling light-headed. Too much oxygen or sugar or Christmas spirit. *Something!* First the lights in the kids' room and now this. It didn't make a lick of sense. She was on the verge of freaking out, and these two idiots acted like someone had left a note on the window.

"Go get your brother."

"He's still in the bathroom."

"Kick it open."

"I'm not kicking open the door," Marie said. "He's been through enough. How else would a tree get in here? Someone is pranking us."

They stared at it for another minute. It didn't disappear. The ornaments didn't look like they'd been pulled out of storage. They were fresh. Newly made by little hands. Like an art station was next door. Rinks took a long deep breath. There was a reason it was here. It wasn't magic. Someone would confess, sooner or later.

But no one would confess.

She would find out where the tree and the lights came from. Sooner than later, she would know all the secrets.

14

It sounded like a landscape company in the next room.

Uncle Vernon snored on the exhale like a stubborn lawn mower that wouldn't start. Aunt Rinks was more like a chainsaw running on bad fuel.

Red light flashed across the ceiling. Marie's back was on the floor, cushioned only by a thin layer of deflated plastic. Fritz was curled up with the nutcracker, his hat, still damp, pulled over his eyes. She didn't want to get up. Her body weight was keeping his side inflated. But she was sore. And anxious.

She rolled off gently, watched Fritz sink as the air mattress recalibrated to her absence. He didn't notice. She pulled the covers up to his chin. Tension jolted through her. Sleep was so far away. Her body didn't care how late it was. Thoughts were working third shift like they were behind on deadlines.

Quietly, she opened the door leading directly from their bedroom, which was the workshop in an earlier day, to the storefront. The hinges didn't squeal anymore. Uncle Vernon had sprayed down all the hinges. Aunt Rinks didn't like the sound they made. The room stilled smelled of oil-sweet lubricant.

The storefront was dark. The star had been unplugged. Aunt

Rinks said it was using too much electricity. Besides, it was drawing too much attention. Everyone could see inside. *And it'll blind someone drivin' by, and then we'd get sued for it,* she had said. Marie liked it dark. It was how she felt on the inside.

She didn't want anyone to see her sit cross-legged on the floor. It wasn't a perfect tree. It was crooked and hooked at the top, like it was falling over in super-slow motion. The branches shot out like a bad haircut. The ornaments, though, were so real. Like the ones she and Fritz had brought home from school. The ones Mom and Dad would say were their favorite, even more favorite than the ones from the year before. Mom had a box of all the ones she'd made when she was little. Every year, she would hand out the ones that made the cut. And she'd tell a story each time.

This one Gramma made when we didn't have much money. It was a yellow foam cat with pipe-cleaner whiskers and missing an ear. *And this was my favorite. I carried it around school all year long.* That was the glass drummer boy.

There were no presents under this tree.

Marie propped her chin in her palms. It was warm next to the tree. Like the last embers of a fire just before they went out. Tears welled up, tracked down her cheeks, and pooled in her hands. The past was still too close. It was a bruise still tender. It was easier not to feel it with Aunt Rinks around. She was an odd blessing in that way. There were no reminders of what Christmas used to be like around her.

Marie didn't want to forget. She just didn't want Christmas to hurt like this.

"Hey, kid," a scratchy voice whispered.

Marie wiped her cheeks. Fritz was coming down one of the aisles. The shelves were still leaning, some broken. Spiderwebs filled in the corners. Most of the mouse turds had been swept away, but the floor was still gritty. He was dragging the blankets through it, holding pillows under one arm, the nutcracker in the other. Sandy was shuffling behind, his colors muted to avoid being seen by a passing car.

Fritz stood next to her, staring at the mystery tree in the corner where the dirty windows met.

"Can't sleep?" Sandy said.

"Just thinking."

"About Mom and Dad?" he said, sounding more like Fritz.

Marie nodded with a shudder. Fritz flopped on the floor next to her. They sat side by side, knees touching, watching the Christmas tree like a movie that was about to start.

"I'm sorry about today," she said to him.

"It wasn't your fault," Sandy said. Marie nodded, but she didn't believe it. The weight she carried wasn't fair, but it didn't go away. "Marie," Sandy said softly, "it's not your fault."

She nodded, feeling the emotional fabric she wore like a motheaten sweater beginning to fray. And the emotional black box quivered. Her voice betrayed her, cracking a little when she said, "I know."

Fritz threw the blanket around them. Gave her a pillow to sit on. He leaned his head on her shoulder. She tried not to shake too much.

❄

"You want to know where the tree came from?" Sandy asked.

Marie didn't want to know. She knew what he was going to say. She stayed silent, knowing Sandy was going to tell her anyway. Fritz put the gift on the floor in front of them. The red and white wrapping was burgundy in the dark. The green bow on top still perfectly looped. Even after it flew from Bobby's hand and rolled in the grass, was scooped up by her brother, who ran home with it, it still looked brand new.

How long can I do this? she thought.

She shook her head, holding her tongue. Fritz was escaping into an imaginary world of candy canes and chocolate streams. How long would that help him? Or was it just going to make the return to reality a crash landing? The past couldn't be changed. They would have to accept what things were, someone had told her. After the grieving was over. Fritz was still wandering through a world of delusion.

That's why he's not talking, Teri, her therapist, had said.

"When we came home, you know, from the battle royale—"

"Sandy." She shook her head.

"Sorry." He started again, without the snark. "When we got home, we went straight to the bathroom. Aunt Rinky Dink and Uncle Vermin were in our bedroom, doing I don't know what. Which was fine, because they didn't bother us in the bathroom. We had to know if it was real. Like you said, maybe we just dreamed it the first time. Then that ding-dong—for the record, that's what Bobby called his brother—touched the orb, and nothing happened. So, you know, we had to try, just to see."

Sandy's bottom twisted and scuffed across the floor until he was between them and the tree. He threw his sticks out to the sides.

"Guess where the tree came from?"

Marie shook her head again. She didn't want to hear it, so she said without much effort, "Candyland."

"That's right. Just like the lights."

"But Sean didn't go there when he touched it, Fritz."

"We can't explain that one. But we have a theory. It's more Fritz's theory than mine; he's pretty smart, you know. He thinks maybe it doesn't work outside the building. Which makes sense, if you think about it."

None of it made sense.

"We proved it, Marie. We went there again. In the bathroom. When you got home, we were there. The Christmas tree was there, too. That one, right there. And now it's here. What else do you want?"

"Sandy." She turned to her brother. "Fritz, I think, maybe... I don't know."

The ever-present hope didn't fade from his eyes. He believed. She wished she had that childlike innocence. She'd grown up. And with that came responsibility. For both of them.

"Try it." Sandy poked at the gift. "Go ahead."

Her heart went into another gear. She just wanted to look at the tree and drift off to sleep. Sooner or later, she was going to have to prove it didn't work. Was Fritz ready for that? *Am I ready to crash-land his dreams?* She was carrying the weight for both of them. The emotional black box was getting heavy. Add the regret of all those kids watching her choke Bobby out. *I can't carry any more.*

Fritz flipped open the lid.

The orb was spinning on an axis like a high-speed planet. A little spot of color zipped around on a globe of grays. It was the size of the lump in her throat.

"Fritz—"

"If it doesn't work, it's all right," Sandy interrupted. "Maybe Nussknacker is wrong, and it's not for you. Because, you know, you don't believe. But you got to try."

Fritz grabbed her hand and squeezed. Just like she did to him when things got heavy. He showed her the nutcracker like a symbol of courage. The solid jaw and square mouth that had bitten Bobby's finger outside the coffee shop. He turned blurry as tears welled in her eyes once again.

She didn't want to hurt him. His hurt would pile on top of hers. And that, she was afraid, might break her. She felt like an assembly of toothpicks poorly glued together. Maybe now was the time to move forward. *Would there ever be a good time?*

She sniffed.

Fritz let go of her hand. She reached for the gift.

❄

IT WAS A MAGNETIC FIELD.

When her fingers drew close, it grabbed her like a high-voltage wire. When she yanked her hand back, a white light filled the room like the eye of a freight train. The dark image of the Christmas tree hovered in her vision.

She couldn't see.

A flashback of when she'd last seen that light haunted her. When she'd searched the building for Fritz. When she'd looked around, blindly, for him. When she'd called his name. She took a deep breath and tasted something.

Peppermint.

It was like drawing a deep breath of winter. Cool, minty air filled her chest. The white ribbon fluttered in her hair. Her eyes stung, like a menthol breeze had blown over her face. She staggered a step, then another (*When did I stand up?*) and caught her heel on uneven ground. She put her hands behind her. Instead of hitting the floor, she thought she landed on the pillow Fritz had brought into the room. But it wasn't soft.

It was spongy.

It felt like a shaggy, foam mattress. Long silky fibers slid between her fingers. The ceiling was pink. *Pink?* The color of candy with fluffy patches of cotton. A black square was cut from the middle of it, like a door to an attic.

Nausea spun her stomach in a blender, sending sticky sweet fumes into her head. Her lips felt puffy, her tongue a balloon. She didn't want to turn her head or blink her eyes. She just wanted to lie there and breathe the cool, minty air. Because she knew the ceiling wasn't pink. There weren't cotton clouds painted on it.

With molasses pumping through her veins, she rolled her head. Grass blades tickled her cheek like fragrant fur. There were no windows or walls around her. But there was a tree. There were lots of trees.

Their trunks were striped like barber shop poles. The limbs heavy with frosting that sparkled with sugar in the diffuse light that floated down on yellow sunbeams. She reached up and touched her rubber face. She couldn't decide if she was dreaming or having a cavity filled in a very strange dentist's office.

A small wooden sign was stuck in the ground. *Christmas Wood,* it read in sloppy red paint.

White light erased the forest of candy-cane, frosted trees. They were back an instant later, like the world's biggest flash bulb had gone off. There was coarse rustling. A shadow passed over her. She looked up. The pink sky was blotted out by a ball of sand and two sand dollars.

"Told you so," Sandy said.

❄

His voice was different. Thicker. Like a radio personality with a slight echo.

Fritz was next to him, looking down with a smile that cut his face in half. He pushed the ball cap back on his head and grabbed her hands. She came up like a bag of sticky rice. Her legs folded into a pretzel. She started to fall back, pulling Fritz with her, when something speared her in the back. Adrenaline surged. She sprang up and spun at the same time, swatting at whatever was poking into her shoulder blades. Her hand connected with something cold and dense and gritty. She had a fistful of wet sand.

A chunk of Sandy's midsection was missing.

"Oh, great. Don't move. Stay right there." He shimmied closer to her, twisting on the emerald green grass like a buffing machine.

The sand was heavy and real. Sandy leaned toward it like she was feeding an animal at the zoo. She panicked, threw it on the ground. He looked different. More colors and shades, the way his body undulated when he moved. The sound it made. He smelled like the ocean.

His head twisted back and forth when she threw the sand on the ground. He moved like a slug, hoovering up the lump of desert like an amoeba merging with another amoeba. And then the divot she'd carved from his midsection was gone.

"What—" She covered her mouth. Her voice had an echoey feel to it. It vibrated like an instrument. "What's happening?"

"Candyland is what." He threw his knobby branches out to the sides. "You believe that?"

She took a slow breath. This wasn't a dream. She didn't know what this was. She could feel it and taste it. Hear the gooey burble of the chocolate stream, the musical creaking of tree branches. Her tongue inched between her lips to lick the sweet air.

"How... how is this..."

"How does a phone work?" Sandy said. "I don't know. You don't, either. Same thing."

"I don't believe this," she whispered, looking at her hands. Her skin was creamy and smooth. The hair on her arms swayed like fine strands of wheat.

"Taste the grass. Seriously, eat it." He fell forward and began grazing on the thick carpet. Fine blades of grass pulled into a hole in his face. "Key lime, I swear."

Fritz was laughing that nasal laugh and holding his stomach. Sandy looked like a lumpy cow that hadn't eaten in weeks. Marie reached down. Her finger sank into Sandy's wet bum. Grains of sand stuck to her finger.

"Hey, hey, hey!" He jumped back.

"You're real."

"Yeah. So are you."

"But... you're not." She looked at Fritz. "He's not real."

"I am. Case you haven't noticed, this ain't like out there." He pointed like something was up there. "This. Is. Candyland."

He raised his stick in the air like a war chant. Fritz slapped it. Flakes of bark fluttered off. They took off across the small clearing, Sandy scootching after Fritz. They were hemmed in on three sides by the candy-cane trees. There was a sign, like a memorial placard, posted where the trees were absent. Beyond it, the colors dissolved into a watery, gray world of blurry shapes and fuzzy lines.

"Marie, get over here," Sandy called. "You got to try this."

Fritz was on his hands and knees where a chocolate stream cut the ground like a wound. Milk chocolate bubbled over large chocolate drops. Little things popped out of it and wiggled before diving back into the stream. Marie knelt next to her brother. When the next wave swam up, he cupped one in his hands.

"Let me see, let me see," Sandy rattled.

Fritz slowly opened his hands. A little goldfish cracker flopped in his palm with a smile etched on its face.

"You can't eat that," Sandy said flatly. "Throw it back."

Marie rubbed her face. The feeling was coming back, but the nausea was still cooking in her stomach. These two acted like this was recess. If this was real (and she had zero evidence to prove it wasn't), then this was their third trip. Despite everything her senses told her, she couldn't get over the hurdle of doubt.

This is Candyland.

"What is this place?" she said.

"Really? You're still stuck on... she's still doing this. Hey, you're awake. You're here. We came into a tiny world locked in a cute little present hidden in the wall that a nutcracker told us about. Does it sound crazy? One hundred percent. But then I don't make the rules, and neither do you. We just live in them and—what is *that*?"

Just on the other side of the chocolate stream, near the edge of the candy-cane forest, clumps of frosted grass shook. A pair of eyes parted the long, skinny blades. Pink light reflected off them like windshields driving into the sun. A pair of round fuzzy ears twitched.

"Fritz," Sandy said, "you shouldn't—okay. All right, we're doing this."

Fritz had leaped over the stream, his bare foot slipping on the edge, toes dipped in muddy, brown chocolate, and raced toward the eyes. Scaring whatever was back there into hiding. Fritz stopped and took a knee. He put out his hand. There was nothing in it, but he held it there. A few seconds later, an animal crawled out to investigate.

It was a bear. A tiny one, as big as a pillow. No teeth or claws. It wobbled on stubby legs. Black nose twitching.

"Is that a—"

"Teddy bear," Sandy finished. "Yeah, I think so."

The teddy bear crawled into Fritz's lap. He hugged it with both arms, swaying back and forth. Marie smiled despite the head-spinning confusion. Thirty seconds later, something else hobbled out of the trees.

"And that's a dragon," Sandy added.

It was a dragon. A purple one with tiny wings and a pot belly. It galloped like a newborn pony, the belly shaking like a bag of beans, stumbling in the grass before leaping into Fritz's arms. He fell on the ground. The dragon licked him with a felt tongue. Fritz laughed like a barking seal. Marie and Sandy watched from a distance. The joy radiated from Fritz like heat waves on a summer beach.

"I guess he doesn't need me anymore." Sandy looked like he was melting.

Fritz heard him (of course he did) and carried the bear and dragon like sacks of grain, one under each arm. He leaped over the stream, clearing it this time, to introduce his new friends. They were toys. Of course they were.

"What else would they be?" Marie mumbled.

"What's that?" Sandy said.

"Nothing."

Sandy warmed up to them in a hurry. He got a hug from the teddy, leaving a coat of sand on the little guy's fur. The dragon high-fived him. Then a gigglefest erupted. Fritz and Sandy rolled on the ground like they were puppies.

"I love you, too," Sandy sang.

※

MARIE FOLLOWED THE CHOCOLATE STREAM.

At the edge of the clearing, where color bleached away, there was a gate. It was more ceremonial than functional. A couple of pretzel sticks and almonds and raisins hung from the arbor arching over them. She pushed open a pretzel curl attached to one of the pretzel sticks. A sign was posted in the middle of the stream. The sign was an oversized graham cracker.

On the other side of the stream, the world was a watery blur where blacks and whites bled into a gray landscape. The pink sky melted into a colorless slate. It was hard to tell what was out there. It was hills, maybe. A mountain in the distance. She tried to step over the stream. When she did, nothing happened. She just appeared to be standing in front of the sign again. She reached her hand over it, tried to touch the other side. *Click.* She was back to standing in front of the sign.

Words were etched into the graham cracker placard. Crumbs were scattered around the freshly chiseled letters. She ran her fingers over them.

O' the Land of Candy,
Where dreams and thoughts do lend,
A world of Christmas spirit,
For your story to begin...

She read it two more times. The third time she read it out loud. It was more than just a limerick. It *did* feel like Christmas spirit here. She was breathing it, tasting it. Feeling it warm her heart like a fire on a cold winter night with family and friends. The kind of feeling that made you smile for no reason.

The gray landscape, though, was lifeless.

She searched the sign for a switch or a button. Crispy flakes fell from the edge into the gooey stream below. *Is that part off-limits?*

"Marie. Marie, watch." Sandy shimmied toward her with the dragon in his branches. A trail of grit glittered behind him. "Ready?"

The dragon's tongue lolled from her mouth like a dog happy to see you. (The dragon felt like a girl; Marie didn't know why.)

"Do it," Sandy said. "Show her."

The dragon squirmed in his arms. Whatever the trick was, she wasn't going to do it. Then her stomach swelled like an inflating balloon. A rainbow of hard little rocks fell from her mouth.

"You see that?" Sandy said. "It's candy. She pukes candy. Fritz, get over here! She did it again."

Sandy tried to rake the candy into a pile, but they were too small for his twiggy fingers. The dragon and teddy imitated him. Fritz picked pieces of candy up and popped them in his mouth. The three-second rule didn't mean anything in Candyland.

"Cherry soda," Sandy said. "The red ones are cherry soda. The green ones—oh, gross. Blech."

Marie looked back at the gray world beyond. As amazing as this was (she still wasn't 100% convinced this was real), she already felt confined. There was something more to this than taste-testing dragon candy. *What's out there?*

"It's a riddle," Sandy said.

"What?"

"The little poem there. It's something that will open the rest of Candyland."

"How do you know that?"

"Nussknacker."

She looked around. "Where is he?"

Sandy shrugged. He told her all the guesses they'd made so far to answer the riddle, which were different versions of *open sesame*.

"Open sesame?" Marie said. "Aren't you a computer? Don't you have algorithms?"

"Technically," he whined. "But you're the one who has to answer it."

"Me? Why me?"

"Because he said so."

"Who? Nussknacker." She answered before he did. It still didn't spare her the condescending sand-dollar look. "Got it."

The nutcracker wasn't here. Fritz had had him when he came out of the bedroom to sit with her in front of the Christmas tree. That got her thinking. She grabbed Sandy's branch before he slid away. It pulled out of his body. He looked offended and embarrassed.

"Sorry." She jammed it into him like an umbrella on the beach. "Hey, how long do we stay here?"

"As long as we want."

"How do we get back?"

"Same way we got in."

He pointed up. The black square was still fixed in the pink sky. She was overwhelmed with vertigo. *Are we really inside the box?*

Sandy slid over to where Fritz was sitting on the ground. The dragon was now spitting candy, one at a time, into the air. Every time Fritz caught one in his mouth, the toys clapped. Sandy cheered like a foghorn. After three successful catches in a row, they jumped up and joined hands and sticks and danced around the pile of candy like it was a bonfire.

The ever-present worry swirling inside Marie mixed with something new. It was as unavoidable as the sweet air she was breathing. It was dancing in a circle. It was a world of Christmas spirit, just like the sign said. Before she asked Sandy just how they were going to get through the square in the sky, she ignored the gnawing in her belly.

For the first time in a very long time, she danced.

15

Rinks woke to the smell of coffee and clean sheets. She lay in the darkness behind her sleep mask, wondering why she didn't wash the sheets more often.

Sunlight greeted her when she peeled off the mask. She blinked and rubbed her eyes. It felt like a spotlight coming through the window. *Is that the sun?* She held up her hand, squinting. She'd been up late, well past midnight, but it felt like an afternoon in August. When her eyes stopped aching, she noticed there wasn't anything unusual about the daylight.

The window was clean.

She crawled out of bed and looked closer, tapped the glass to make sure it was there. *Huh.* It was just like her mother told her to wash them. Leave no streaks or smudges. Make it look like it's not even there.

Cleaning Vern must've got out of bed. He got like that, where he couldn't take the chaos. Not very often, but when he did, he was a one-man cleaning service. The place would look like a hotel. She looked around. He hadn't picked anything up, though. Just did the windows.

She flopped back on the bed, went through her morning routine.

Check social posts, count likes and read comments. The likes were going down. Her last post was coming out of the shower and showed a little shoulder. *Gross*, someone commented. Nothing like a kick in the stomach to start the day. Then she noticed the mildew on the shower behind her. That was what they were talking about. Because the filters made her look smooth and glowing.

The bathroom was locked. A game melody was playing as little blocks slid into place. She knocked on the door. "Hurry up."

Vern grunted.

Rinks listened at the kids' door, could hear someone breathing. She went to the fridge, cracked open a soda and, sipping the carbonated fizz off the top, grabbed the laptop from Vern's corner. She'd been up late watching the kids in their room. Marie had a Bluetooth speaker in her ear. Rinks didn't know she had one, then realized it was her old one, the one she threw away. She was talking to someone on it, really quiet like. Rinks couldn't understand a word, even with the volume turned up. Vern needed to fix that.

It looked like she was talking to Fritz. The air mattress was nearly flat. They needed a real mattress. It was the right thing to do. They could get one for Christmas. What with the things Godfather got them, they didn't need anything else. *Christmas isn't about what you want.*

Rinks unwrapped a protein bar and washed it down with a slug of soda. It stung her throat and watered her eyes. She went through the video history to see if anything had happened after she fell asleep. It didn't take long to hit paydirt. Marie tossed and turned, walked around the red glow of the Christmas lights on the walls.

She's goin' to do it. She's goin' to do whatever they been doin'. Rinks was sure Marie would expose whatever secret they had in the privacy of their own room. The anticipation twisted her stomach between chocolatey bites and swigs of soda, watching the girl pace, stopping on occasion to stare at the blocky wall below the owl clock. There were still smudges on those squares.

Then she walked out. Went through the door leading to the storefront.

She didn't come back. A few minutes later, Fritz rolled out of bed with his dumb little soldier and followed her. Rinks waited and waited. It was killing her. They were doing something out there again, and she couldn't see it. She jumped ahead in the video.

The red lights in their bedroom flickered.

She stopped the video, rewound it. Something else happened. A bright light flashed under the door coming from the storefront. It was too bright for a passing car. It looked more like an explosion. Nothing shook, though. Not even a sound.

Then a second flash.

"It's all yours," Vern announced.

His bare feet sounded like sandpaper blocks on the dirty floor. It needed a good mopping. A good activity for the kids.

"'Bout time."

He tried to kiss her. She pushed him off. His hands were wet. *Gross.* She raced to the bathroom and held her breath. The seat was still warm. When she came out, he was pouring the last bit of coffee. One pot down.

"They're up to somethin' again." She sat at the table, wiped the grit off her feet. "They went out front in the middle of the night and then this."

She showed him the video. He stood behind her, scratching his butt and smacking his lips, nodding with detached amusement. For a genius, he was an idiot. None of this was sinking in—the Christmas tree, the lights. Explosions.

"Nothin'?" she said. "You think that's nothin'?"

"Probably a car."

"Unless a car drove inside the buildin', that ain't a car."

He shrugged. Burped. He was useless. She waved off the fog of coffee breath and a gross smell of hard-boiled feet. He grabbed her before she could get past him, threw his arms around her. His whiskers scrubbed her cheek like a steel brush.

"You stink," she said.

He sniffed his armpit, then gave the other one a whiff. He debated whether it smelled bad, then hauled his coffee mug toward the bedroom. Rinks went to the door leading to the storefront. Yawning, she opened the door and threw her arm up. Daylight streamed into her eyes.

She shuffled in. The floor was smooth and cool. When she took her arm down, squinting into the sunlight, the can of soda slid from her hand and cracked on the floor, spilled suds over her feet.

❄

"This ain't a bad thing," Vern said.

"You're jokin'."

He was wearing the same smelly shirt. He hadn't made it to the bedroom before she started screaming. Cars on the street would've heard her. He slurped his coffee like this was normal. Like it was lucky. He looked around, went up to one of the shelves, ran his finger across it. It wasn't that the shelves weren't dusty or the spiderwebs were gone.

They were fixed. All of them.

Straight lines and clean surfaces. The floor was spotlessly buffed and shined, waxed with something wintergreen. They could see faint outlines of their reflections when they looked down. Not a dirt ball in sight. The room smelled like a forest. And the windows. The windows. Like the bedroom window. Sunlight poured through them. Rinks was still squinting.

"Saved us some time and effort." He held up a dustless finger. "Whoever it was."

"That's all you got to say?"

"What else is there?"

"Oh, I don't know. How about *how is this happening?*"

He looked like that hadn't occurred to him. "Well, I guess maybe—"

"Maybe what? Someone broke in with buffin' machines to scrub the floor? Did you hear buffin' machines last night, Vern? Did a gang of do-gooders sneak in with buckets and squeegees to clean the windows? Did you see the window in our bedroom? *They did that, too!*"

Marie and Fritz entered the room. Their sleepy eyes squeezed down to slits in the stark morning sunlight. Fritz with his dirty hat; Marie with her dumb ribbon in her hair. They looked at each other, looked around. Looked at each other again. *They knew. Oh, they knew.*

"What happened?" Marie answered.

"You tell me." Her foot tapped rapid-fire, waiting for an answer. "You came out here last night, didn't you? Middle of the night. Explain that. Explain the bright lights that went off."

She was thinking of lying. Rinks was sure of it. The gears were clicking in that pretty little head. But that look in ole Aunt Rinks's eyes set those excuses on fire as fast as they churned out. Then Marie said: "How'd you know we came out here?"

Good volley. Rinks didn't see that coming back. How did she know they were out here? "I heard you get up," she answered sharply. Nodded at Vern, but Vern was admiring the new-looking shelves. "You woke me and your uncle up." *Well played, Rinksy. Although that didn't explain the lights.* Marie didn't notice. "What were you doin' out here?"

"I couldn't sleep after what happened yesterday. I came out here to look at the tree. Fritz came out later. We fell asleep on the floor, went back to the room when it got cold." She looked around. "It didn't look like this."

"That's all you did?"

She nodded. The little liar. Something was left out. Maybe they were looking at the tree, but she wasn't giving up the whole story.

"Hey! Look at this." Vern put his coffee on the shelf and shook two things above his head.

"Not now," Rinks said. "What else did you do?"

Marie and Fritz watched Vern approach. He had two stuffed animals. One was a bear, the other a dragon with plastic teeth. Mint condition, the both of them. Clean fur, clear eyes.

"They were on the shelf. Right over there," he said. "How about that?"

"That's what surprises you most?" Rinks said. "Toys? Not someone or somethin' buffin' the floors and wipin' down the windows and fixin' the shelves in the middle of the night without wakin' us? You're okay with that part, but toys? Are you kiddin' me, Vern?"

He held them like puppets. "Why you mad?"

"I'm not mad!" She took a deep breath, stared at her reflection in the floor. Said more calmly: "I'm not mad. I'm just worried. You should be, too. This ain't normal, Vern. None of this—the tree, the lights, all this—it ain't right. Am I the only one who gets it?"

"No, I get it, Rinks. It's weird all right. But it's all fixed; it's all clean. It's better, and it's free. I don't care how, just that it is." He held the toys at his sides. Something bounced around his feet. "Look at that," he said.

Colorful little rocks of candy ricocheted off the floor. They scattered in different directions. He shook the dragon. The belly was full of it. Fritz picked one up.

"Don't eat that," Rinks said. He did anyway. She pointed at Marie. "You did this."

"Me?"

"You had somethin' to do with it, and you ain't tellin'." Rinks was quivering. The anger and frustration were frothing over the dam of self-control. She wanted to go in that bedroom right that second and start tearing things apart.

"Rinks," Vern said, "how in the world would they fix everythin' and clean it up? It'd take all night."

"That's what I'm sayin'! What did you find, huh?" The sound her back teeth made was like a grinding stone wearing down rocks. "Tell me. You're good at keepin' secrets, ain't ya. I know you ain't tellin' us something, Murry."

Just like her mother. Rinks's sister would write all her private thoughts in a journal and hide it. Wouldn't share her stories about boys. Didn't take her to parties. Didn't help her make friends. It was all about her.

Fritz handed his phone to Marie. She read it, showed it to Rinks. Vern read it over her shoulder.

"You think Godfather's doin' it?" Rinks said.

"He said a gift was coming," Marie said.

"That's not what he meant." Rinks crossed her arms. *You have the gift, you little liar.*

"I think she's right." Vern pointed with the teddy bear. "Think about it, Rinks. He's got people all over the world workin' for him. And the technology is beyond what anyone could imagine."

Marie nodded vigorously.

"If anyone could do somethin' like this, it's him," Vern continued. "Puttin' up lights, a tree. Fixin' all this up. Like little elves comin' in the middle of the night, makin' things right."

"Elves?"

"You know what I mean."

"You said elves."

"I mean, he's got all sorts of things that can do anythin'. You saw that butler at the cabin. It was dang human! Nobody ever seen anythin' like that. This right here." He swung his arms. "This ain't nothin' compared to that. None of us knows the half of what he can do. And think about this." He shook the toys. Their heads bobbled. "How many times did he say somethin' about the toy store, huh? He wants it back, Rinks. He's just helpin' out."

"Did we ask for help?"

"So you don't want any of this? You want to do all this ourselves? Clean and fix and spend money." He jutted out his whiskered chin, narrowed his eyes. "'Cause I don't."

The line between Rinks's lips pulled straight and tight. She racked her arms over her chest, squeezed her biceps. They had her stuck. There was no way of getting the truth out of them, not now. But she didn't need them. She could find it on her own.

"Then call him," she said quietly. "Thank him."

"He won't admit to it," Vern said.

"Call. Him."

Vern nodded. He handed the toys to the kids, gave the bear to

Marie, the dragon to Fritz. Then fetched his coffee cup. He was pleased with himself. Nothing made that man happier than free stuff.

"What's that?" Rinks said.

She pointed at Fritz's foot. It was dark and muddy. He tried to hide it behind his other foot. It flaked off in dried chunks. Marie swept them up with her hands.

"He stepped in a puddle yesterday," Marie said. "I thought he washed up."

Rinks's eyebrow arched. "Barefoot?"

"He was looking for something out back."

"Get cleaned up," she said to the kids. "I want you out of the house today. Don't come back till supper. Get some exercise, but stay away from the park. I don't want to hear about another fight today, you hear? Vern, give them some money to eat. Not too much, just enough to keep them from lookin' hungry."

They followed their uncle. Frankly, she didn't care where they went. That was how Rinks grew up. Out of the house in the morning, home by dark. No one asked where she was or why. And she survived.

She was going to close the door on all these lies. Vern was going to set up the rest of the cameras. Rinks was going to dig. She was going to start in the kids' bedroom.

No one could keep a secret from her.

16

"I don't know what to say," Marie said.

Fritz had chocolate frosting smeared on his lips. He shoved another bite of Ms. Trutchen's famous double chocolate fudge brownie in his mouth before swallowing the first bite. And chased that with foamy hot chocolate.

The coffee shop was crowded and loud. The Christmas music was barely audible over conversation. They had a little table in the corner where no one noticed them. Not even Ms. Clara.

"You can start with thank you," Sandy's voice said on the Bluetooth.

"The lights and tree... and then the storefront. I don't understand it. It's like... it felt like a dream. Don't you think?"

Ever since waking up, she couldn't quite wrap her head around what had happened. The memory was warped and strange, like dreams are. She didn't believe it until Aunt Rinks woke them up with screaming. Before they walked out front, she knew. She could feel it in her bones. *It happened. It really happened.*

"Ow!"

Fritz pinched her arm and smiled with chocolate-painted teeth.

"You're not dreaming," Sandy said.

"Yeah, I know. I'm just saying where did the lights and tree come from? How did the storefront get, you know, *fixed*. And the toys!" She lowered her voice and leaned over the table. "The toys that where there. How did they get *here*?"

"No idea."

"That's what I mean. How does it work? It's just a little ball inside the gift."

"I'm just a little ball in Fritz's pocket. How do I work?"

"You're a projection and a voice. I get that. The other thing... *Candyland*," she whispered, "is another world. Big difference."

"Is it?"

"We *went* there."

Fritz looked at the empty chair at their table. For a second, Marie was worried Sandy was going to appear in front of a crowd of caffeinated locals with cameras on their phones. Fritz was nodding, and Marie suspected he might be hearing their grainy snowman *and* seeing him. That wasn't something she wanted to talk about. There were already too many wildfires to deal with.

"Think of it like this," Sandy started. "If you showed a caveman—or cavewoman—a phone, what are they going to think, mmm?" Fritz held up his phone, submitting the evidence.

"I know what a phone looks like," she said.

"Or a plane. Or a computer or a bridge or building or ballpoint pen or—"

"I get it."

"Magic, right? They would throw someone into a volcano to thank the gods. And there's nobody who could convince them otherwise. Do you know how a computer works? You do not. Neither do I. And neither does Fritz. None of us knows how Candyland works. It just does."

"Sandy..." She shook her head, had to remind herself whom she was talking to. "Fritz, you *disappeared*. You touched the orb and *actually went inside*. How is that possible?"

Her brother popped the last bite of double chocolate brownie in his mouth and shrugged. He was right. That was the way to go. It happened. Why did she have to know how it worked? *Because I need to know if this is real.*

"Why are things appearing?" she said. "The tree and lights and... what else? I mean, what's stopping more from happening?"

There was a long pause. Then, "Oh, you're asking. We don't know." Sandy explained how the red lights had been in the Christmas Wood the first time they went inside. The Christmas tree had been next to the sign the second time. And now the toys.

"They're coming out," she muttered.

"Seems that way. Fritz wants to know if you're going to eat that."

He took the chicken salad sandwich off the little plate in front of her. Marie hadn't touched it.

"You're not worried about that?" she said.

"Why? Ms. Clara said her chicken salad is the best—"

"No. Things coming out of the box," she hissed.

Fritz looked up before taking a second bite. He looked slightly confused, then continued eating. "Um, he's seven, Marie. He's not worried about big-picture things."

Sandy was right. Why was she asking her little brother that? These were things *she* had to watch. If they kept going in, would things keep coming out? So far it was just little things. Well, not little. But what if that was the point? Maybe it was things to restore the toy store, like Uncle Vernon said.

"What am I thinking?" she said to herself. "Those things can't be coming *out*."

"You really think Godfather had elves clean the room and deliver a Christmas tree? That was Fritz's idea, by the way. The Godfather alibi. It was a good one. They bought it, too. At least your uncle did. But I think you're missing the obvious part, kid."

"What's that?"

"I was a *reeeeal* boy," Sandy said in a squeaky tone.

"You're not helping."

"Come on. You tore a hole in me, remember? I remember. I could feel Candyland, just like you did. The way it smelled and tasted. It made us happy. You danced! Remember that? And you know why? That's Christmas spirit in there. Am I right?"

She couldn't argue the way it felt. It was like distilled Christmas magic. The hope and excitement and cheer were in the air. *Only we didn't spritz it from a bottle. We went there!*

"You see what's happening, don't you?" Sandy said. "The toy store is coming back. That's what Godfather wants. Fritz made that excuse up, but he wasn't wrong. I mean, elves didn't clean the place up. Or maybe they did."

"I thought you said this was about a journey to save Princess Pearly Pat."

"Nussknacker said it. And don't pretend you don't know her name. Princess Pirlipat."

"Why, though?"

"Why what?"

"What's the journey for?"

"It's a journey. We find out when we get there. What's the problem?"

She pushed away from the table, resisting the urge to get up and walk around. The conflict was winding a spring inside her. Her head was going to pop off if she didn't make some sense out of it.

"What's the problem? We disappear; things coming out of a gift. Those things are *impossible!*"

"I feel like we've covered this. Caveman. Airplane."

"Shrinking and disappearing, that's my problem. It's against physics. If Candyland is real—"

"It is. We did it. Admit it."

"*If* it is real," she repeated, "then it's technology that's light-years ahead of its time."

"Yeah, and cavepeople were around ten thousand years ago. They'd say the same thing about that thing in your ear you're talking to me with. Get it? It's like saying reindeer can't fly and Santa doesn't deliver presents."

She didn't want to answer that last part, not in front of Fritz. A little part of him still believed a fat man visited every house in one night.

"Kid, it wasn't a dream. We were there, all of us. You, Fritz and me. We can't all have the same dream. The question isn't *if* it's happening. The question is *what's next?*"

She couldn't explain how things happened, not the tree or the lights or how things got repaired. But the toys. *I saw those in the backyard. They were dirty. Someone could have cleaned them.* There was an easy way to check that. See if they were still back there. She didn't know how that would make things better.

"What do you mean what's next?" she said.

"Solve the sign. We can't go on the journey till we know what it means."

"That, right. And why would it be a riddle we have to solve? Why can't we just go?"

"You're asking us? Maybe it's important to the journey. I just know we'll be stuck dipping our fingers in the chocolate stream till we do. Princess Pirlipat is out there."

She took long slow breaths. There was no point in figuring out how or why it worked. Sandy was right. It happened. *It's happening.* Just accept it, go downstream with it. If she was honest, things were better than they had been before they found that gift in the wall. At least she knew what to expect from her aunt. But maybe they'd find a bed in Candyland.

"Solve the riddle," she said, nodding. "Okay."

Fritz nibbled the rest of the sandwich, leaving the crusts on the plate. He lifted his hand for a high five. Marie tapped it lightly. If for anything else, she'd do it for him. Because look how happy he was.

❄

"You don't have the gift with you, right?" Marie asked.

"Nope," Sandy said in her ear. "It doesn't work outside the building."

That wasn't a fact, even though it hadn't worked when Sean had grabbed it in the park. "Where is it?" she said.

"Back where we found it."

"In the hiding place?"

"Where else?"

If he put it in a drawer or, worst case, left it on the bench, then things would get more complicated. If that was possible. "Aunt Rinks can't know about this."

"We've been over that."

"I mean it. If she knew what was happening, it'd be all over her social."

"Roger that."

She looked at Fritz. He nodded enthusiastically, added a thumbs-up. Everything Aunt Rinks touched got messy. This would be like giving her the keys to a nuclear power plant. Things wouldn't just go sideways. They'd go in all directions.

"She's watching us." She stacked the empty plates and finished the rest of her tea. "She knew we went to the storefront last night."

"About that. Don't you think that's weird?"

"No. She's a spy."

"Not that," Sandy said. "She saw the lights flash when we went to Candyland."

"Of course she did. The light is blinding. Probably lit up the building and the street." Marie hadn't thought about that. They needed to be careful where they did it.

"But she sleeps with a blindfold."

Marie started to reply and stopped. Something didn't line up. How had she heard them get up? They hadn't been making noise. And if she'd seen the lights, why wouldn't she come out? There was more to this. Her bloodhound thoughts might have sniffed out the answer, but Ms. Clara interrupted her.

"Children! You don't say hi when you come?" Her smile dimpled her rosy cheeks.

"I'm sorry, Ms. Clara. It's so crowded, and you were busy."

"Nonsense. There is always time to say hello and merry, merry."

She grabbed the stack of plates from the table. "You leave crusts, young man. Crusts are best part. Did you get enough to eat, skinny one?"

She squeezed Fritz's shoulder. He shook his head with a chocolate smile.

"We had plenty, Ms. Clara," Marie said. "We were just going to walk around."

"It is beautiful day. Go get vitamin D."

She whispered to Fritz. He would grab a big, salted pretzel on their way out. Ms. Trutchen would hand it to him in a paper bag with a jolly laugh for free.

She hugged them when they stood up. "Come back tomorrow," she said. "We close soon."

"You're closing?" Marie said.

"Christmas very busy for us. We have much travel to do. I want to see your smiles before we go."

Christmas was still a few weeks away. Maybe they had family to visit in another country. They weren't from around there, everybody knew that. But nobody really knew where they were from.

17

The owl clock didn't see Rinks pull the last drawer out of the workbench.

Rinks felt like prey under its big, angry eyes. The wings spread like it was about to take flight and snatch her by the hair like some dirty little rodent. Rinks finally turned the clock so it was staring at the wall.

The drawers were scattered around the room. There were no hidden switches or secret buttons that tripped a trapdoor. No levers that opened a door in the wall. No notes or boxes or treasure maps. She got on one knee. Nothing taped underneath the workbench, either.

The blood rushed to her head. Her blood sugar was low. She'd skipped lunch. Not even a cracker. She checked her phone. The kids just left the café, were heading toward the park. They shouldn't be back for another three hours. *Better not be.* This mess was going to take an hour to put back together.

It had been a week since the windows got clean and the storefront fixed up.

Every night, the video glitched. She'd watch the kids get up. Sometimes that sandman Vern was all excited about would be there.

He'd sworn her not to say anything. It would just make them more secretive. It wasn't in Rinks's nature to be quiet. She put her curiosity in a compartment in the corner of her brain where it pouted. Then she'd watch the video from the night before. A bright light would go off. Then the kids were gone. Something about that light was turning the cameras off. Like the kids knew it. Like they had something to block the cameras.

Vern still hadn't fixed it.

Two nights ago, Fritz had come back to the room muddy. He took a shower in the middle of the night. The bathroom was a mess the next morning. There was chocolate all over the sink. *They're stealin' my protein bars again,* she thought. *And goin' outside.* She spent the rest of that day searching the backyard, looking for buried treasure. None of the protein bars were missing, though.

She leaned on the workbench to catch her breath. The toy soldier was two feet in front of her, eye level. He didn't judge her, not like the owl. His look was all business. The bushy eyebrows and stiff legs. Pinewood breath.

Rinks looked over her shoulder. A tiny lens, no bigger than a pinhead, was embedded in the corner, right where Vern had put it. If it were three feet higher, she would've known exactly what they'd been doing. She bent over, stared the nutcracker in the eyes.

"You standin' guard, mmm? That what you're doin'? What is it they were doin' here, little man? You tell me."

She picked him up. Fritz didn't care if she touched him anymore, not like when he found him that first day.

"He doesn't care about you anymore, you know that? Just leaves you behind like yesterday's Big Wheel. You know what that is, a Big Wheel? Probably not." She pulled the lever on his back, looked around just in case it triggered a surprise. "What's this?"

A pattern of numbers was written on the back of his jacket. Looked like something a gang of nerds protecting the world from prime numbers would do. She pulled the lever. The mouth opened and closed. She put it to her ear, hoping he'd whisper the secret to her. *I'm losing my mind,* she thought. But she kept pulling, felt the square jaw rub against her ear, hoping something would happen. And then it did.

A squeaky voice said: "Your husband's hot."

Embarrassment flushed her cheeks. She shoved her husband against the wall.

"Hey, hey. She's mine, you little splinter." Silly Vern pointed at the soldier. "I'll turn you into kindlin'."

"Shut up," Rinks said.

He thumbed his nose and threw a right hook. His broomstick arms looked like a third-grade shadow boxer. If she had to wager, the soldier would get two to one odds.

"Is the camera fixed?" she said.

"It ain't broke, Rinks."

She shook her head. "They ain't disappearin', Vern."

"I replaced it. And I did this."

He opened the laptop. There were three new video feeds—the front of the building, the kitchen, and their bedroom. Now they had the whole house. Unless the elf army redecorated the bathroom, they were going to solve the mystery.

"All right," she said. "Guess we'll find out now, won't we?"

"We will. Only I was thinkin', what if they don't come back?"

"Who you talkin' 'bout?"

"The ones who brought the... you know." He tilted his head.

The suspicious git didn't want to say it out loud. The Christmas tree and the red lights in the kids' room and the toys. Nothing new had happened in a week. He was still hoping more free stuff was on the way.

"You know who did it."

"It wasn't the kids, Rinks. Whoever's doing it, what if the cameras scare them off? I mean, the walls need paintin', the bathroom needs doin', there's, like, a week's worth of landscapin'. And that." The air mattress was a vinyl pancake. "Kids shouldn't be sleepin' on the floor, Rinks."

"I know."

Despite the obvious betrayal, she hadn't forgotten about the bed the kids were sleeping on. Or lack thereof. It wasn't right. The crazy thing was they didn't complain about it. Not once. She had to respect that.

"You goin' to explain to the kids someone robbed them?" he said.

Empty drawers were stacked against the walls. The blankets were thrown around, the string lights pulled down, the workbench moved, clothes overturned. There was no way she'd get it all put back together.

"They won't be home for three hours," she said.

"Good enough. And what are you lookin' for?"

She looked at him with contempt. "You seriously don't know?"

"I know." He chuckled. "Of course I know."

"Get out."

"Rinks." He grabbed her arm and wouldn't let her go. "Seriously, what are you lookin' for?"

All she could do was shake her head. Did he really not care what was happening? It was eating her up like an infection. She had a stomachache and not from eating boxes of chocolate protein bars. And now she was dizzy. Either he was better at compartmentalizing (something she'd totally lost control of) or was a moronic genius.

She couldn't tell him the real reason. *I'm obsessed with being left out.*

"They stand here, Vern, and do somethin'. Then there's the light, and then there's all the new stuff. And because you ain't moved that camera, I can't see what they're doin'. So I'm tearin' this place apart screw by nail."

"Okay." He nodded along in listening mode. Empathy Vern narrowed his eyes to hear her feelings, really hear them. She felt better until he said: "What did Knackadoodle tell you?"

"Leave."

"Did you ask nice?"

"Out. Go." She shoved him. He tickled her. The wall of bitter rage bent to his cackling. She regrouped and pushed him again. "If you don't leave, I'm shovin' this up your nose. Boots first."

She held the soldier like a weapon. He threw his hands up.

"So you asked him what they were doin'?" he said.

"I did. Nicely."

"What'd he say?"

"That you should brush your teeth more."

He breath-checked in the cup of his hand. "He say that, really?"

"Serious, Vern, if you ain't goin' to help, then move that camera so I can see what they're doin' here."

She put one of the drawers back. It got stuck and didn't slide in till she knocked it with her knee. The wood splintered. *Great.* Her back hurt, her knee hurt, her stomach hurt, and she was no closer to finding anything out. She kicked the flap of vinyl bedding. Last thing she wanted to do was reward them with a new bed.

"He say anythin' about that?" Vern pointed at the square blocks on the wall below the owl clock. "Is that right?" Vern said to the nutcracker. "Cheesy puffs, you say?"

She didn't know how much more of Silly Vern she could take before her hair started falling out.

"Hear that, Rinks? He likes cheesy puffs."

She went to the bathroom. She stayed on the toilet long after she'd done her business, flipping through her accounts, trying to think of something to post. Maybe a photo of the bedroom she'd destroyed. *Kids,* she'd write. *Can't live with them.*

That's not bad.

She tried to think of something wittier. Vern would get bored. Pretty soon, he'd hunker down in the corner with his second wife, Mrs. Laptop, and she could get back to the investigation. Ten minutes later, though, she could still hear him tinkering around in the bedroom. She lost the boredom battle and surrendered to find him hunched over the workbench.

"What're you doin'?" she said.

He was holding the soldier in one hand and mumbling. Only this time, he wasn't poking fun at her. He was talking to it. And during his imaginary conversation, he was pushing at the little blocks of wood on the walls. One of them was lying on the workbench.

"Don't do that," she said. "I already split that drawer and—"

"Shhh."

The blocks were sliding around like checkers. Reminded her of a game on her phone, one where you fit together different shapes and sizes; and when you did, there were fireworks and electronic music and prizes. *Prizes!* That was exactly what she'd win on her phone, shiny presents and fountains of coins.

Only the game Vern was playing was with ugly little pieces of wood that were grooved and had orange smudges. *Cheesy puffs.* She'd seen that last week, when Vern and Fritz had gone through a whole bag of them. *And he brought home a bag yesterday.*

"This goes there." *Snick* went one of the pieces. "That one there—no. Not there." He pushed it up instead of down. "You know why it's hard to be a thief in winter, Rinks?"

"What?"

"A thief. You know, steal." He slid a third block into place, this one to the right. "Petey and I used to dig through garbage cans when we were kids. Just after Christmas was the best time to do it. People'd throw out the old to make room for the new, and we'd be there to take. Their old was our new. Our old man, he was terrible at Christmas. Used to give us used tools and things he didn't want. Petey and I did our own shoppin'."

Snick.

"We'd walk down alleys and dig through trash cans. If we saw somethin' in a backyard, we'd take that, too. Basketballs, pogo sticks, kites, remote control cars. One time an old video game, still worked. We'd fill up a wheelbarrow full of this garbage. But then we started peekin' in garages. One year, we seen these bikes. Christmas bikes. The stickers were still on the handlebars."

He kissed his fingers like a chef.

"The car wasn't in the driveway. The door was locked, but there's this doggy door with a flap. It's for a small dog. Petey can't fit through because he's fat. I'm the runt, you know. The mouse. It don't take three seconds for me to squeeze inside. Next thing you know, Petey and I are peelin' down the alley on new bikes. No one sees us, either.

We ride straight home, throwin' snow off the back tires, pulling wheelies. Best Christmas ever."

He looked up, remembering. Then *snick*.

"We put the bikes in our garage, 'cause the old man ain't goin' to notice. If he does, we'd tell him we bought them with snow-shovelin' money. He wouldn't care anyhow. So now we got new bikes. We're in our bedroom talkin' about where we're goin' to ride the next day when someone comes to the door. It's dark out. The old man is conked on the recliner, but he wakes up before we get downstairs."

His story stalled. He hit a dead end on the wall, backtracked a few moves before working it out. Rinks didn't know which was a bigger waste of time: the wall or the story.

"So it's cops. They're with a dad we've never seen. Said they're lookin' for bikes. Petey and I play dumb, but that don't hold up because the cop takes the old man out back. They go straight to the garage and find the bikes shoved behind a sheet of plywood. No one saw us take them. Know how they caught us?"

He thumbed another block smudged with orange fingerprints. The last block slid up. This one was different. There wasn't a pink wall behind it.

"If you follow the tracks, you find the mouse."

❄

SHE KISSED him on the mouth. Not a bird peck, either. It was long and wet. Her fingers in his hair, his whiskers scratching her chin.

"You did it," she said, breathy. "You found it."

"I did."

She bent over to look inside the square hole in the wall. There was something in there. It wasn't moving, but she couldn't be sure it wasn't alive.

"What is it?" she said.

"I don't know."

"Reach in there."

He used the nutcracker like a stick, poking it into the hole boots first.

"What're you doin'?" she said.

"Checkin' for traps."

"There ain't no traps. Just reach your hand in there."

"Someone went to all this trouble to hide whatever's in there. You don't think there might be somethin' else?"

She crossed her arms, watched him poke the hole like it was a fire that had just about gone out. Next, he leaned in and blew into the hole (like that was going to do something). Rinks didn't say anything. He could sing a song into that opening, just as long as he reached inside it before the kids got home.

A minute later, he did exactly that. His hairy knuckles clenched around something square. He slid it onto the bench. They stepped back. Rinks clenched her hands beneath her chin.

"This is it," she whispered. "What they were hidin'."

It was a present. A little red and white gift with a green bow. Expertly wrapped without a cobweb on it. Rinks remembered what Godfather had said about finding the present. She thought it was hogwash, but there it was. It was beautiful and came with a side dish of redemption that tasted delicious. *You can't hide it from me no more.*

She reached for it without thinking of booby traps. Only visions of jewelry or diamonds inside it. The lid lifted on hinges. Shoulder to shoulder, they leaned over it and peered inside.

"What is that?" she said.

It was ugly, whatever it was. It looked like something that would fall out of a car wreck. This had to be a joke. *The kids! They put that in there 'cause they knew I'd find it!* The elated feeling she'd felt a minute ago hardened into a lump of coal. She had the urge to find a hammer and start knocking holes in the wall.

"Oh my." Vern's hands fluttered in front of his mouth like he was looking at a winning lottery ticket. His eyes weren't blinking, shifting from her to the box to her. His lips moved, but only weird squeaks came out. It sounded like he was choking.

"What?" she said. He pointed at the dumb thing. "What?" she repeated.

He scrambled toward the door, turned around, held up his hands. "Don't touch it! And don't take a picture!"

"What are you—"

He ran back and scooped it off the table. "How much time before the kids get back?"

Hours, she said. Which was true. He took it to the kitchen, came back for his laptop, and giggled. Rinks followed him. It wasn't a diamond in that box.

Vern said it was better than that.

❄

HE SAID ALMOST NOTHING. Just typing and sweating. Occasionally, laughing like a middle schooler watching cartoons.

"I can't believe this," he would sometimes say. Rinks would say, "What?" And he would keep going. And this went on for an hour. She'd eaten three protein bars and drank two sodas. The thrill was almost gone. She went back to the bedroom. Her husband, the idiot genius, had followed the cheesy puff tracks Fritz had left behind on the blocks of wood. It had taken nine moves to find the hole. *How did they find it?* she wondered. *Someone must have told them.*

The nutcracker lay on the bench, staring at the ceiling. She narrowed her eyes, thinking of how Fritz was always holding that thing.

"Rinks!"

Vern was at the kitchen table. The gift was next to the laptop, lid still open. Round magnet still floating. He scooted back his chair and pointed at it, making those weird sounds again.

"Just talk, Vern."

"This is it."

"It's what?"

He turned the laptop. She couldn't make sense of it. It looked like a chat board. She gave up reading in five seconds.

"Can you just settle down and tell me what's got your shorts in a bunch?"

He did. She understood next to nothing, but she let him go. It was like letting off pressure for him, spouting all these smart words that made her feel dumb. Density and electromagnetic fields and compressed data and symmetrical circuitry. He'd heard whispers of the thing back when he worked at Avocado, Inc. It was a black-box project, whatever that meant. No one was supposed to know what it was, but there were rumors.

He finished blowing off steam, slumping in the chair and huffing like he'd completed a marathon. A stupid smile leaked on his face.

"So what is it?" Rinks said for the thousandth time.

"A story orb."

"A story orb?"

"A self-contained, virtual-reality story orb."

She nodded and hummed. Then said: "I don't know what any of that means."

"When do the kids get back?"

She checked her phone. They were on Main Cross, walking in the opposite direction. They weren't due back for a little longer. She told him so.

Vern grabbed her hand. His palm was slick. He told her to sit down.

"You ready?" he said.

"You're scarin' me, Vern."

He nodded and smiled that dopey smile. A bag of worms began to dance in her stomach when he grabbed her wrist. She saw him stick his finger into the box.

Then tasted peppermint.

18

The sun had dropped behind the downtown buildings, bruising the sky in colorful streaks.
    Marie dragged down the sidewalk, feeling the dregs of a late afternoon nap on a concrete bench at the park. The late nights were catching up to her. She hadn't planned to fall asleep this afternoon, just wanted to do some cloud gazing. Then Fritz was shaking her awake. For the past week, she and Fritz spent the day at the coffee spot or wandering around. At night, they locked the door and opened Candyland. Thankfully, nothing followed them back. Aunt Rinks had even stopped asking questions. Just told them to make themselves scarce in the morning.

Fine with Marie.

She hugged herself against the approaching evening air, thinking of crawling under the blankets when she got back to the building. Not even bothering to blow up the mattress. Fritz was half a block ahead of her, standing in front of the toy store. The Christmas tree was glowing from inside the window. Marie lumbered by him. When he didn't follow, she went back.

He wasn't looking at the tree. There was something in the back corner of the storefront. The aisle shelves were blocking their view, but lights had been added. Uncle Vernon was standing on a ladder. It looked like there were new shelves on the wall. *Did they paint the store?*

Marie and Fritz rounded the corner and went through the rusty gate. Two plates were on the kitchen table. Fritz began spooning the heap of noodles drowning in orange tomato sauce into his mouth, hardly chewing before throwing in the next scoop.

Something was creaking. Like old wood bending in a storm.

Marie crept into the storefront. She didn't know why she was sneaking. Maybe she wanted to change her mind before she saw something she didn't want to see.

"A little to the left," Aunt Rinks said. *Creak.* "Right there."

They were on the little stage in the corner, on the step-up platform. The wood planks, once littered with mouse turds and dust bunnies, were now lacquered to a shine that reflected dozens of string lights hanging from the ceiling. It looked like little stars. Aunt Rinks sat in an antique rocker with a purple blanket on her lap. Uncle Vernon was on a stepladder. He was dusting the clock embedded in the owl's belly.

"What's going on?" Marie said.

"Oh!" Aunt Rinks clutched her chest.

Uncle Vernon teetered on the ladder and jumped off before he went down on his head. They began laughing at their fright. Uncle Vernon took a knee, grabbing his stomach. He laughed so hard his nose was dripping.

"Oh, oh." Aunt Rinks turned the rocking chair to face Marie. "You scared us half to death, young lady. We need to put a bell round your neck."

"Where did all this come from?"

"Surprise!" She threw her arms up. The purple blanket fell at her feet. "You like it?"

It wasn't their style. A mural of reindeer and clouds was on the wall. Santa in a sleigh with a village below with steepled roofs and puffing chimneys and blankets of snow. The shelves were loaded with trinkets and figurines. Snow globes swirling with white bits.

Snowmen and snowwomen and snowkids made with foam. Reindeer in different poses, some sleepy, some frolicking. One big and angry.

And there was more. Lots more. Way more than would fit in a storage trunk or closet.

"We made it just like it was before," Aunt Rinks said. "*Storyteller Corner.*"

Uncle Vernon gestured to the letters painted above the shelves, a stylish script.

"You did this?" Marie said.

"Yep. We did. We got the *Christmas spirit* today." She looked at Uncle Vernon and chuckled. "I don't think she believes us, Verny baby."

"It's just... it's a lot to take in," Marie said.

"Oh, it wasn't hard," she sang. "We made a few calls, had some help. Everyone wants a toy store."

"I thought you *didn't* want a toy store."

"We're warmin' to the idea, sugar."

She winked at Uncle Vernon. A wink and a smile. Marie didn't like that. It felt like someone sticking out their tongue. Marie stepped onto the stage to look around at the garland and paper snowflakes. It looked like a hundred feet of string lights hanging from little hooks in the ceiling.

Aunt Rinks took a mug from a small wooden table painted red as a rose. She slurped whatever it was (probably soda) and smacked her lips. A long curly whisker was growing from her chin. Aunt Rinks had been too distracted by her scar to see it.

There was a vase of candy canes on the little table. And an old book. The leather cover was scuffed and worn. The corners bent. She saw the title on the spine. A shiver trickled down her back.

"Where'd you get that?"

"This old thing?" Aunt Rinks opened it on her lap. The binding crackled. "Someone gave it to us. It looks like the real thing, don't it. I looked for Aunt Corker's name and didn't find it. But we can pretend it's hers."

She turned a few pages.

"Want to hear a story?" Aunt Rinks put on a pair of tiny, wire glasses, then looked over them. "*Once upon a time...* there were two children, a boy and a girl, who were on the naughty list—"

"There's food in the kitchen," Uncle Vernon interrupted. He was scratching a rash on his neck. "We already ate, so you go ahead. It should still be warm."

"Yes, where *are* my manners? Go on, hon. Get somethin' to eat. Me and Vern got a few things left to do out here."

"I think I'm going to bed."

"Bed? It's barely suppertime."

"I'm really tired."

"Why you so tired, darlin'?"

Marie didn't answer that. It didn't sound like a question. She turned to leave.

"We straightened up your room for you," Aunt Rinks called. "Made it all good again."

Marie stopped like she'd hit a wall. Something cold and heavy thudded in her stomach and recoiled into her throat. "You cleaned our room?"

"Like I said, we got the *Christmas spirit* today."

Then she laughed again. It was more of a cackle. Uncle Vernon was scratching his neck with both hands.

※

THE BED WAS full of air. The nylon membrane stretched like a balloon with a few new patches on it. Their clothes, once piled in the corner, were folded on the workbench. The nutcracker was at his post. Marie's book was next to him. It was open. The pages still blank.

She stood as still as a deer listening for a twig to snap. Nothing moved. Nothing out of place.

Her aunt and uncle were talking loudly. Their voices coming through the door. Fritz had wandered out to the storefront to see the new decorations. They regaled him with excessive laughter and broad smiles that split their faces.

Marie looked at the owl clock. It was facing the wall. She turned it around. They must have taken the one from their room to put on the shelf. The checkered wall below the owl clock was still in place. She moved the nutcracker to examine it. The block with the X—the first one they took out to move the pieces—was right where it should be. She put her thumb on it. It snapped into place.

We probably did that, she thought. *Didn't put it all the way back.*

She wanted to believe that. What other choice was there? Aunt Rinks wasn't smart enough to figure it out. Uncle Vernon, though.

Aunt Rinks began reading to Fritz the fake story about a boy and girl on the naughty list. "Once upon a time..."

The name of the book Marie had seen, the one Aunt Rinks had on her lap, was embossed on the spine in shiny letters. *Tales from Candyland.*

Marie moved quickly, turning the nutcracker around to follow the sequence. The orange smudges had been scrubbed off the blocks. If they hadn't been, she would've been more than suspicious. By the time she opened the mouse hole, Aunt Rinks was still telling her fake story, and Marie reached into the dark. Her heart dropped like she'd missed the last step on a staircase. Then her hand grasped the gift.

She didn't find it.

That brought some relief. She crawled onto the air mattress with it cradled to her chest.

❄

Someone shook her awake.

Sand dollars as big as moons were in her face. She rolled away from them and groaned. Sleep pulled her eyelids down like shutters.

"It's gone," Sandy said. "Hey, wake up. The present's gone."

Marie sat up, shedding the final grains of sleep from her eyes. It took a few moments for her head to stop swimming. "What time is it?"

"Time? You're worried about the time?" Sandy said. "The gift is gone!"

"Shhh."

Marie held up a finger. She was suddenly one-cup-of-coffee alert. She turned her head, listening. Fritz and Sandy looked at each other, waiting. When she heard a duet of snoring from the other room, she reached under the corner of the mattress and pulled out the bright, red and white gift.

Sandy's celebration sounded like a bag of rice being tossed around. He turned in a circle and shook his round bottom.

"Wait," Sandy said. "Why was it there?"

Marie shook her head. It took several moments for her thoughts to warm up. "They were acting weird," she whispered. "I just had this feeling they might have found it."

"You think they solved the puzzle?" He aimed a stick at the wall. "No offense, they're not that smart."

"We need to be careful, that's all. Maybe put it in a different hiding place."

"Great. Let's go."

Marie pulled the gift away before Fritz snatched it. She looked a little desperate. "Now?"

"Yeah, now, while the lumber yard is sawing. When else we going?"

He looked at Marie like she was the dumb one in the room. How he made those sand dollars roll was remarkable.

"We've been there every night. I'm tired."

The truth was, she wasn't any closer to solving the riddle. The thrill had worn off, hard as that was to believe. They were visiting another world—going there—and Marie would rather sleep.

"The journey doesn't care if you're tired. It's the journey. Sometimes it's hard. Now grow up and pop the top. We're going in." Sandy swelled like the chin of a bleating frog. "Nothing cures a blue day like some *Christmas spirit*."

Another dose of willies laid claim to Marie's backside. *That's what Aunt Rinks said.*

Fritz and Sandy were going with or without her (she realized she thought of them as two people now). And she wasn't going to get any sleep until then. Marie locked the bedroom door. There was no point in hiding the gift. If Aunt Rinks kicked the door in, they weren't going to be there.

❄

Fritz and Sandy were off to Christmas Wood again. The dragon and teddy weren't there. *They're in the storefront.* The lights, the Christmas tree, and the toys. Nothing had happened in the last week, though. But now Storyteller Corner appeared. *Where did that come from?*

They leaped over the burbling stream of chocolate like school was out.

Marie went to the sign. The pretzel post was plunked in the middle of the chocolate stream, the thick, milky current cutting around it. Beyond, the world was pale and murky. A coloring book yearning for color, wanting to be discovered. Her head was clear and shivering. The sharpness of each breath sent tingles through her body. She longed for what was out there. She didn't know why. At the same time, she was terrified of it. That made no sense.

O' the Land of Candy,
Where dreams and thoughts do lend,
A world of Christmas spirit,
For your story to begin...

She was never any good at riddles. Never in her life had she ever solved one, always turned to the answer page no matter how long she thought about it. And then, as always, the answer seemed obvious, like it was never hiding in the first place.

What has four wheels and flies? A garbage truck.

Despite the joy all around her, despair rolled through her like the cool front of a thunderstorm. It was a familiar feeling. Like driving a car into a snowy ditch. She was stuck with no way to go back, no way forward. If she didn't move, she was going to be sandwiched by the past and future. Wind up an oil stain in the present. At least, that was what Teri, her therapist, said.

"Look!" Sandy and Fritz pranced toward her. Gummy worms

squirmed in Fritz's hands and between Sandy's sticks. "There's, like, a whole family living in a stump."

Fritz had a chocolate mask drying on his face. After he'd fallen in the stream the last time, she made him take a shower in the middle of the night. Uncle Vernon and Aunt Rinks didn't wake up. Although Aunt Rinks looked a bit suspicious the next day. Marie thought it would be smart to clean up beforehand. She wiped his face and hands while Sandy was telling her the name of each of the gummy worms. They came in different stripes of yellow, green, red and orange and giggled each time he held one up. Sandy said they weren't for eating.

"Hey, hey. Easy on the clean-up," Sandy said. "You act like this is a crime scene."

"You can't leave like this, Fritz. You want to take another shower?"

He resisted her attention. She had to scrub to get it off his cheeks. Forget getting it out of his fingernails; she could explain that.

"You all right, Mar Mar?" Sandy said. "You want to eat some grass? It might take the edge off."

"That. Out there." She punched at the lifeless landscape beyond the stream. "Remember the journey? That's why we're here in the middle of the night. This isn't recess, you two."

Sandy looked like he'd put his sticks in an electrical outlet. Fritz went limp. His face sagged, and his eyes shot up in surprise and hurt. Something hard had sprung out of her. That something she tried to keep a lid on. *Where'd that come from?*

She knew where. The emotional black box was bulging.

"I'm sorry." She stopped fussing over the smudges on his chin. She sighed, hands on hips, looking at the breezy grass. "Look, I get it. This is cool and amazing and mind-blowing. I'll come here any time you want as long as Aunt Rinks doesn't know about it. But right now, middle of the night, is not why we're here. Nothing's changed, and I'm tired. If we don't figure out that riddle, there's just this... this chocolate stream and grazing grass and-and-and—" She waved at the gummy worms. "And I'd rather be sleeping."

A long moment of silence. The gummy worms meeped like chicks. Sandy held one up to the side of his head and nodded.

"Hey, Marie. You know why the chicken crossed the road?"

"What?"

"Just answer the question. Why did the chicken cross the road?"

She sighed. "To get to the other side."

"There you go. You solved a riddle. Now let's take this one line at a time. Come on, we can do this. *O' the Land of Candy*. That's easy. Candyland. Fritz, you take the next one."

The two of them took turns reading the sign and making obvious observations. Half the conversation—when Fritz answered Sandy through their mind-meld or whatever they did—Marie didn't hear. It devolved into telling unrelated riddles. *Which fish costs the most? A goldfish.*

Marie fell on the ground and crossed her legs. She plucked blades of grass and minced them between her teeth. They tasted like sugared mint leaves. She'd give it five minutes; then she was leaping out. She'd given up searching her phone. The internet didn't have an answer to the riddle. It was hopeless. And hopelessness was an iron jacket.

"What has a neck and no head?" Sandy asked. "A bottle. Get it? Hey, kid, don't give up. What's the hurry, anyway? We'll get there when we get there. Fritz agrees, don't you? So does Ernie." He dangled a rainbow-striped worm in front of her. "This place isn't so bad. We make new friends every time. It feels better than it smells. And it smells awesome. It's wonderful being *here*."

"What's the hurry? I think Aunt Rinks knows about it. If she doesn't, she will. And then what? I'll tell you. Forget about the journey. She'll turn this place into an amusement park."

That felt worse than being stuck. Marie didn't know what Candyland was or how it worked, but it wasn't meant to be a theme park.

"She doesn't know about it," Sandy said. "The gift was still in the wall. You think she'd put it back if she found it?"

"You believe they did Storyteller Corner? The chair and the way they were smiling. Did you see the book? It was called *Tales from Candyland*."

"No, it wasn't."

"Yeah, it was. You think that's a coincidence?"

"All right, I'll give you that. Weirder than their weird smiles." He chiseled his chin with a knobby stem. "It could still be a coincidence."

"Really?" She threw her head back, stared at the exit floating in the pink sky. "I'll bet that book came from here! Just like the lights and the toys and the Christmas tree!"

Her voice echoed in Christmas Wood. Sandy and Fritz stepped back. The gummy worms squealed. Paranoid rage simmered inside her like a pressure cooker with a leaky seal. She was tired and hungry and irritable. Anger came out in bursts. Guilt came along for the ride when it did.

"Did she read you a story?" Sandy said. "She's not a storyteller, you don't have to worry about that. Trust me. No emotion. And kind of mean. Two children on the naughty list? Horrible."

He babbled on like the chocolate brook, casting doubt on Aunt Rinks's storytelling skills. Like that was what was bothering Marie. That book was old. It was authentic. That was what bothered her the most. That book wasn't a coincidence. If Godfather had anything to do with this journey, why didn't he just give Marie the answer? Or was it her great-uncle Corker who did this? He was a game maker, Ms. Clara had said. *Maybe that's all this is. A game. A game of wonder pretending to be a meaningful journey.*

"She kept telling the same story over and over and..." Sandy said. "*Once upon a time, there was a boy and a girl...* Terrible."

Marie turned her head. An idea struck her like an aluminum bat. She stood up. Sandy was talking to the gummy worms now. Fritz held them in both hands so they could listen. Marie opened the Almond and Raisin Gate to look at the sign.

O' the Land of Candy,
Where dreams and thoughts do lend,
A world of Christmas spirit,
For your story to begin...

Aunt Rinks kept telling the same story. Every story began the same. All stories did. They started with one line. Marie whispered, "Once upon a time..."

In the distance, a bell chimed.

❄

Pink bled into the grayscape like watercolor on a linen sky. Grassy carpet rolled down a slope where a deep crevasse carved the landscape. Trees popped out of the spongy soil, branches unfurling puffy seeds that floated on a peppermint breeze. It unfolded like dominoes to the horizon: glassy cliffs spilled frothy waterfalls, distant mountains slathered in rich icing and topped with sprinkles. And in the center of the valley, a dark brown monument reached for cotton-candy clouds. Spires forked from the sides.

A chocolate castle rose in a distant village.

"You did it." Marie felt dry twigs on her arm. "You did it!"

Fritz and Sandy hugged. The gummy worms danced on their shoulders. The peppermint breeze blew up from the valley and stung their eyes. The chocolate stream began to overflow its banks. The signpost crumbled in the current. The graham cracker slate with the riddle carved into its surface floated like a runaway raft.

Branches out, Sandy's midsection expanded. "Let the journey begin!"

Marie hadn't moved. She was rooted into the ground, breathless in the face of the world expanding before them. It was like standing on the edge of a cliff. Her legs quivered. A hesitant fragility quaked up her thighs and rattled her stomach and froze her chest.

"Stop!" she shouted.

Fritz had one foot on a chocolate drop. The stream was gushing around it. The grassy banks were falling into the current.

"We need to hurry," Sandy said. "In case you hadn't noticed, this chocolate fountain sprang a leak."

Fritz grabbed Sandy's stick when the chocolate drop he was standing on melted around his foot. Marie pulled her little brother back to shore before he was swallowed up. Sandy's arm came with him. The current was growing stronger and thicker, belching fudgy bubbles.

"You're right. Okay, little help." Sandy swung his remaining branch as he began sliding into the stream. His bottom started to melt. "I don't want death by chocolate!"

"Jump!" Marie shouted.

He gave it his all, and it wasn't much. It was enough to hit the shoreline. Marie and Fritz did their best to pull him out. They came away with clumps of wet sand, but he managed to claw his way out, rolling in the grass with two panicked sand dollars staring at the pink sky. Fritz stabbed the stick into his side.

"Thanks, kid."

He pushed himself up and surveyed the damage. He was a foot shorter. "Hey, where's my... oh no. This is permanent. Here, give me that."

They slapped the wet sand they'd pulled off him when trying to get him out. It filled a few holes, but he didn't grow an inch. He moaned and shivered. The gummy worms hopped on the ground. They were cheering.

"You do?" he said. "I'll be right back."

He slid away with the bright, rubbery worms in the lead, leaving a dark, brown trail behind him.

Marie and Fritz stepped back. The chocolate stream had become a river growing wider by the minute. The Almond and Raisin Gate was swept away in broken pieces. The post that held up the sign was gone. Maybe her answer had triggered a self-destruct landslide. She looked up at the square in the sky. It wasn't too late to get out.

Candyland begged them to stay.

❄

"CHECK IT OUT." Sandy was back to his normal height. His bottom half was speckled with bits of colored grains. It looked like a dance floor. "Too loud? I don't care, I like it. The gummies said it was castings. I don't know what that is, but I like it."

Castings was worm poop. Marie didn't tell him that.

He turned in a circle and made more of a slithery sound than a gritty one. The gummy worms cheered him on. He shook his bottom. Marie guided Fritz and the dancing sandman away from the encroaching flood.

"So what now?" Sandy had to shout over the gurgling current. "It looks a little strong."

"It's a warning," Marie said.

"Yeah. Wait, what?"

"Not to go on. It's pretty obvious. I think we need to get out before it gets worse." The ground was spongier than before. It bounced like a bladder of lava. "Sorry, Fritz."

Her brother shook his head. She kept him from going any closer to the river. The whites of his eyes were billboards.

"Can I ask a question?" Sandy said. "Do you even *want* to go on the journey?"

Marie swallowed the hard stone in her throat. She couldn't answer. Her emotions and thoughts swirled in a blizzard. She didn't know what she felt beneath the crushing anxiety. Not since she put a lock on the emotional black box. Dry twigs curled around her fingers. She was trembling.

"We *have* to go, kid."

"Why do we have to go?" she muttered.

"Because we can't go forward," he said, "if we don't look back."

She expected a different answer. Like Nussknacker said so. What Sandy said, for some reason, terrified her. She didn't know why. Across the meadow, the valley was so beautiful. She did want to go. *What's stopping me?*

"You know how to get across," Sandy said. "You solved the riddle. You can do it."

Her lips were dry. The minty air hot in her chest. She wanted to go back to the flat mattress and life in the toy store, even though she hated it. She wanted her brother to be safe. He didn't want to go back. He was looking at her, waiting for her to take him across.

Above the noisy river, bells were ringing in the distant castle. It was Christmas music.

This is a story. That's how I solved the riddle. And every story starts with a blank page. You write the story, Godfather said.

She took her brother's warm hand. Sandy's grip tightened around her other hand. She stood tall. They weren't going back. And things couldn't stay the same. They were going to write their story.

"Once upon a time," she called, "there was a bridge."

❄

Pretzel posts erupted from the ground on both sides of the river.

They were solid and stout and coated in salt, two on each side. More of them heaved from the soil, these longer, skinnier and twice as long. They pushed out of the ground and fell over the dark, brown river. Black licorice whips (the kind Aunt Rinks snacked on) snaked out from the ground and whipped and snapped and lashed the pretzels together. Next came the pretzel logs, rolling across the supports. They thudded against each other like bowling balls on a return chute. Black licorice slithered and cinched them tight.

Marie looked at her brother, then at Sandy. They returned the look. The river began to recede. There was new grass on the other side. The air coming across was stronger and sweeter, like vaporized breath mints that stung their nostrils. Marie wiped a tear from her eye. The scent was strong, but it was more than that. Music called from far away. She could feel it in her chest.

The castle was calling.

The trees began to tremble on the other side of the stream (it was more like a creek again). The branches shuddered on both sides of the open field. The forest looked alive, like it was an organism waking from a long sleep. Leaves fluttered to the ground. On the right, between two stout tree trunks, a bunny hopped out. Its plastic nose twitched; glass eyes blinked. It was joined by a floppy-eared dog with a long velvet tongue. Then a wooden puppet and a bouncy ball. An orange octopus. They came in all sizes and colors. A herd of toys bounced and hopped and danced into the field, filling it from tree line to tree line. Staring at them from across the bridge.

"I'll be honest," Sandy said, "I didn't see that coming."

"I think they're waiting for us," Marie said.

"They're definitely waiting for us."

But Marie felt their goodness. She could taste it in the air. They were happy to see them. All her fears, all her anxiety, had vanished.

"Where's Nussknacker?" she said.

"He's here," Sandy said. "You'll see."

She didn't know what that meant. The journey would soon reveal that mystery.

19

They wore jogging shorts and running shoes. Some of them had holsters for water bottles, patches to measure their glucose, arm pockets for their phones. Then there were the bikers with tighty-tights and clappy shoes, numbers on their shirts to remind everyone they didn't ride on skinny wheels just for fun. They were in it to win it. There were normal people at the coffee place, too. The ones in sweatpants and T-shirts, the blue-jeans mom with flip-flops and the cargo-pants dad with work boots. They were happy. Super happy. Their caffeinated eyes jittered out of their heads.

It made Rinks sick.

They were faking it. She could tell. A bunch of road rats on the treadmill, running as fast as they could to get absolutely nowhere. That was why she never left the house; she couldn't stand the fakeness of their laughs, their smiles, their caramel crunch Frappuccinos. They had no idea what true joy felt like. Rinks did.

It was in a tidy little gift box hidden in a mouse hole.

She was going to send the kids out that morning, tell them to come back for supper like she'd done that entire week. The plan was to dive back into that lovely land of sweets. But then she'd reviewed the video from the night before, when she and Vern had been sleeping. The kids had gotten up in the middle of the night.

That was what had changed her plan.

Vern carried eight small plates. Three on each forearm and one on each hand. He weaved through the crowd like a street performer. He nearly collided with a skinny runner who used to be fat (extra skin hung on his arms like a trophy; he wore a tank top to show it off) and made it to the corner without losing a crumb.

"It all looked so good." He filled the round table with cupcakes and muffins and macaroons and fudge. "There's not much left up there. They almost sold out."

"You ask them to turn the music down?" Rinks said.

"Um, no. I can barely hear it."

Neither could Rinks. But if they turned it down, maybe all these posers wouldn't talk like caffeine addicts on a long-distance call.

"They're practically givin' the food away." He shoved a pastry in his mouth. "Nice people," he muffled. "Feel like I met them before."

It was embarrassing the way he ate. Like a squirrel in a nut factory. She threw a napkin at him. He wiped his fingers.

"Kids still asleep?" He pointed at the laptop resting on her thighs.

"Shh."

She could barely hear him. But someone just might, like the lady at the next table. She could be pretending to read that boring book. Rinks turned the laptop toward the wall. Vern craned his neck to see.

"So what is it?" she said.

The time stamp was 12:45 a.m. Marie was in the still-inflated bed that Vern had patched (*you're welcome*). Fritz got up with the nutcracker tucked under his arm. And the metal ball Godfather gave him in one hand. He nudged his sister. When she didn't wake up, the sandman came out.

"Right on time," Vern said. A soft morsel fired from between his teeth and stuck to the monitor. He wiped it off with his finger. Thank God, he didn't eat it. "He's a projection. Like an avatar, you know."

"That ain't an avatar. It's a... a sandman."

Three balls of dirty sand, sticks for arms and seashells for eyes.

Standing right in the middle of the kids' bedroom. A week had gone by, and they never sang a peep about it. Rinks had even asked what that dumb little ball from Godfather was for. Nothing. Just keeping their secrets to themselves. Rinks had to bite her lips and sew them shut.

That's who she's been talkin' to all this time. The little liars.

"Godfather had somethin' like that when I was there. They must've gotten it down to a personalized pocket pod. I imagine they'll go public with it in a few years. Probably a prototype Fritz has." Through a fresh load of donut jelly, he said, "He gave Fritz a voice."

"Don't get all goody-goody for the boy. He's keepin' a secret. And don't act like you know what it is."

"It ain't a ghost, Rinks. I know that."

"Then how's it projectin' from his pocket?"

He shrugged. "I didn't work on it. But that's what it is. Probably neural circuiting tech. They got that for exoskeletal assist for people who can't walk. It's probably not much different than Candyland."

"Shhhh."

She was tired of his fancy talk.

He leaned in and whispered and not without sarcasm. "*Candyland,*" he whispered. "It was amazing. You felt it, right?"

She didn't know why she was cranky. Most people would say that was her default mode. Candyland, one would think, would've cured that. It felt like home. Maybe that was why she wanted to scream. To break things. *I want to go back!*

"Here. Eat this." He offered a cannolo. "It's good for you."

She refused. Two bites was all it took him to finish it, wiping cream off his lips and sucking all his fingers. A bear claw was next. The stuff went right through him, never stuck to his hips or butt. It was so easy to hate him.

"What about the sign?" she said.

"What about it?"

"*O' the Land of Candy...* it sounds like a clue."

"It's not a clue, Rinks. It's a poem."

"All right. What about the rest of it. The... you know—" she waved her hands "—the blurry part. There's somethin' out there."

"It's not done. You know, like, not programmed. There's that little candy field and the chocolate river and that's it. What else you want?"

"She talked about the journey." Rinks turned the laptop toward him but not too much. He hadn't studied the recordings like it was a final exam. "How can you stuff your face like that? I know you're Mr. Computer Man, and all this ain't that special, but there's more goin' on here, you ding-dong. They're goin' on a *journey*. And they're plannin' on leavin' us. They're gonna hide the gift so we can't find it, and then what?"

Vern sounded like a dog licking a bowl.

"Stop for a second, all right? Listen to me," Rinks said. Vern dropped a jelly donut, leaned over the table to hear her whisper. "Marie's suspicious," Rinks said. "She didn't believe we did Storyteller Corner."

"You think?"

"What's that supposed to mean?"

"It means there's *no way* we did all that. Then you told that dumb story about naughty kids, just rubbin' their noses in it."

She cringed. What that sandman thing had said about her not being a storyteller and clearly not smart was a kick to the shin. She didn't need Honest Vern piling on. Rinks wasn't a fan of the truth. She liked to lock it up, compartmentalized deep inside her where the light never shined. She liked to see the world the way she wanted to see it. It was so much nicer that way.

"Why we here, Rinks? If you ain't goin' to eat anythin', why didn't we just stay home and send the kids out?"

"Because I want them to go in."

"Well, you're goin' to have to explain that one to me."

She broke a corner off the brownie. "We're goin' to follow them."

"Brilliant."

The sarcasm was thick and pasty. It kicked her right in the bruised feelings. Tears threatened to rise to her eyes; she swallowed them down with a bitter bite of fury. Having a dirty snowman call her stupid was one thing (the thing wasn't real), but that look on her husband's face had a sharp edge.

"Listen to me." Her lips tightened and started to crack. "You're goin' to stop being an idiot and listen. I want to know what the journey is. Maybe there's gold at the end or lottery tickets or nothin' but a pretty picture. I don't care. Those two little weasels have been goin' in there for a week or maybe longer. They're after somethin'. I want it. You hear? Now there's only one way I'm gettin' it. We're goin' to sit here and watch. When they disappear, we go straight home and follow them inside."

"Disappear?"

"Disappear, Vern. Watch the video, you ignorant toad."

"Rinks, no one disappears. It's virtual reality. All senses captured. It's impossible to *go in there*." He gave a snort and started feasting on banana bread. If the place weren't crowded, she would've smacked it out of his mouth.

He hadn't watched the video of when they were at the kitchen table and he grabbed her hand. There was a flash, and they were gone. It wasn't a glitch, which was what he'd say if he did see it. That was exactly what he'd say. But it had happened. And he was going to get on his knees when she proved him wrong. And it was going to feel so, so good.

❇

"Merry Christmas!"

Rinks slammed the laptop shut. A doughy, old woman came at them. She looked like a sack of potatoes with an apple face wearing glasses. Wiping her hands on a damp dishrag with a smile on her wrinkled mug, she said, "You are Rinks and Vernon."

Rinks looked at Vern. "How's she know us?"

"Your niece and nephew talk so much about you. I'm very glad you come here. It is pleasure to meet you."

"What'd they say about us?"

"Well, they say many nice things." There was a lie in there. "They say you move down street in old toy store. Very exciting. You found home, I think. You have been searching awhile."

"They said that?" Rinks said. "All that?"

"Yes, of course. They are lovely children. A shame about your sister. It breaks my heart. My sympathy to you. I do hope the children find their way."

The old lady looked back and forth between Rinks and Vern, wiping her hands like they were permanently stained. Rinks didn't like the way she was looking at her. It felt like an X-ray machine. Reminded her of Mother, the way she sniffed out a lie just by looking.

"You ain't livin' with them," Rinks said, "so they ain't peaches and cream."

The old woman's cheeks turned pinker when she laughed. "Family, yes. It has challenges."

"You can say that. The lies, the secrets." Vern shook his head at her, but she kept going. "Those two can be bad. Very naughty."

"Oh, not to worry. They are not on naughty list." She patted Rinks on the shoulder. She smelled like cinnamon. "How was the food? Good, yes?"

Vern polished off the last bite and gave her a thumbs-up. When he tried to speak, crumbs flew from his lips.

"He liked it," Rinks said.

"What about you?"

"I got too much on my mind. Christmas ain't for everyone."

"I'm sorry to hear that. We have tea for upset stomach. I'll be back."

She scuttled toward the counter before they could stop her. She was stopped twice on her way—once by a sweaty lady in yoga pants, then again by a little girl holding a cup with both hands. She took a knee to talk with the little one, rather effortlessly got up. Maybe not as old as she looked. When she made it to the counter, where another old lady served drinks, Rinks turned to Vern.

"How'd she know us?"

"Seems like she knows everyone."

"We never *met* her, Vern." A bad feeling rumbled through her. "She's spyin' on us."

"Or," he said, licking his finger to pick up crumbs, "she's friendly."

She was already coming back. No interference this time. "Tea for your tummy. And this for children." She put a lumpy paper bag on table. "Banana in there, also. Good for digestion."

"Thanks," Rinks said. "I don't think we brought enough money to—"

"No charge."

"Excellent!" Vern said.

"Today last day we open," she said. "You enjoy."

"We will," he said. Whatever was in there wasn't going to make it to the kids.

"Merry, merry," she said. "Best of luck on your searching."

Rinks smelled the tea. It was peppermint. Smelled just like Candyland. But she hated tea. When the old lady looked back, Rinks pretended to drink it. Vern was looking in the sack. The idiot didn't even hear what the old lady said.

"We're leavin'," she said.

"Why?" He cracked the laptop open. "Kids are still sleepin'."

"You heard her. Best of luck on your *searchin'*." She looked for eavesdroppers, then for hidden cameras and microphones. She hissed: "She knows, you ape."

"Rinks, you're just bein—"

"You hush that fat mouth. I don't like this place anyhow. Bunch of phonies suckin' up to those two... two Santa Claus wannabe old ladies."

He sighed. "Whatever. I need to talk to a man about a reindeer." He pushed away from the table. "If you know what I mean."

"You're disgustin'."

"Might be a minute."

She didn't want to sit there another second. But what her gross husband was about to do to the bathroom brought a micro-smile to her face. When he came out of the bathroom, she was tempted to make him sit down at the table so she could see who would follow his diseased colon. She was really hoping it was Mr. Bike Pants.

She carried the laptop, tea and sack out to the sidewalk. The little bell rang above the door. Someone shouted merry, merry as she left. Rinks raised the cup of tea without looking back.

The sidewalk was warm. Sweat pricked her scalp beneath the headscarf as she scrolled through her social. She hadn't posted yet that day. Her account was beginning to cool. She held up the phone for a selfie. The mechanical elves were behind her. Creepy little things looked like an advert for a horror movie. She deleted it.

Vern came out sucking his coffee-stained teeth and adjusting his belt. He looked in the window. "Those look old as dirt."

Everyone in the café was staring at them. She threw the tea in the garbage.

❄

RINKS WAS ALONE in the car. The meter was expired.

Vern was inside the store. The banner on the window read *40% OFF!* That was a rip. They jack up the price 50%, then call it a discount? Vern climbed onto another mattress, hiked up his feet and laced his hands behind his head. The lady helping him stared at the big toe sticking through his sock. Poor woman. Those feet smelled like recycled trash bags. And he'd been on every bed in the place.

Fritz was awake.

Rinks looked in the rearview mirror. Several sprigs of gray hair were springing out from above her ear. That was new. Her mother hadn't had a gray hair until she was in her seventies. Her father had had jet-black hair past that. Even worse, she saw what was on her chin. She plucked it off, a slick of tears rising in her eyes when she did, and held it in front of her. It was a whisker as thick as a toothbrush bristle. And there were two more. She attacked them like roaches in a cupboard, tossing them out the window and cursing. She searched her ears and her upper lip for more, then checked her social to make sure none of those were in her last post. She imagined the comments.

Shave much?

There were no comments like that. Actually, nothing but good things to read. She felt better and clicked over to the kitchen camera. Fritz went through all the cabinets, peeked in the refrigerator. When he popped his head back out, there was a protein bar in his mouth. The little scamp found her hiding spot. Rinks's skin began to peel.

Naughty list. That old lady had no idea what she was talkin' about. Rinks had an idea to drive back to the coffee place and show her what awful children looked like. *Naughty list kids.*

He ate a bowl of cereal with his face inches from his phone, slopping milk all over the note Rinks had left that morning. He had three bowls. Fortunately, he didn't steal another protein bar. Her head would've exploded. He rinsed the bowl and put it in the dishwasher. It was going to take more than that to get him off the naughty list.

He stared at his phone another five minutes. Then he started for the storefront. Rinks sat up in the passenger seat of the car, leaned closer to the laptop. Eyes wide and watery. She hadn't blinked since he woke up. A tear streamed down her face as he put his hand on the door. He stopped with it open. Rinks didn't click over to the storefront camera. She knew what was out there.

Fritz was on his way back to the bedroom.

Marie got out of bed. The sandman thing was out again, sending strange vibes up Rinks's neck. A sci-fi movie was playing in her house, and she was watching it on the laptop. Marie followed Fritz to the storefront. They came back to the kitchen in a hurry. Marie read the note. Then checked the location app on her phone.

And we're very far away.

Rinks honked the horn. Her eyes were burning. She rubbed them with the heels of her hands and honked some more. The lady inside the store was looking at her. Rinks rolled down the window and pointed. The lady shook Vern's leg.

Rinks went back to the laptop while her husband put his shoes back on. The kids were already in the bedroom. A minute later, they were sliding the blocks on the wall.

"Go on, little chickens," Rinks said. "Lead the way."

❄

They parked a block away in a boot store parking lot.

The back gate began to squeal. Rinks grabbed it before it announced their arrival. Slowly, she pushed it open. Sweat dampened the back of her shirt. She pulled off her shoes and pointed at Vern to take his off. Tiptoeing down the crooked path, they snuck up the steps and stopped at the door. Rinks checked the laptop, clicked through all the cameras inside the building. The rooms were empty. Unless they were both in the bathroom, she knew exactly where they were.

She opened the door even slower than they did the gate. It felt like minutes before they were inside. The note was on the table. Sliding their feet across the living room to keep the wood floor from creaking, they stopped at the kids' bedroom. Not a sound. A slow turn on the doorknob. The door caught on the hook set in an eyebolt.

Rinks almost put her fist through it.

Vern dug through his wallet. He poked a credit card between the door and the doorjamb, sliding it up and lifting the lock out of the eyebolt. It clattered against the door frame.

Rinks's pulse shifted into passing gear.

They opened it just as slowly as they did the back door. The bed was empty. The sheets a mess. The owl clock watched them peek into the room. The nutcracker at his post. Next to him, the lid flipped open, was the bright and shiny present.

"They're gone," she whispered.

Vern shook his head. Thankfully, he didn't argue the impossibility of physically travelling inside a box the size of a cupcake. "They musta left."

Rinks checked her phone. She showed him what she saw. The kids were in the building. Their phones weren't anywhere in sight.

"If they're not in there," she whispered, "how'd their door get locked?"

He opened his mouth. It hung that way with no stupid words coming out. She was right. They couldn't lock the door if they left.

"Okay," he mumbled. "I can't explain it, but they ain't in there, Rinks."

"I'll go first."

His whiskers sounded like bristles in the palm of his hand. "This a good idea?"

"We're surprisin' them, Vern. We'll know what they're up to as soon as we do."

He sighed, shaking his head. Rinks didn't get what his hesitation was all about. He peered into the open gift. Then pointed. "Look at that."

The floating orb wasn't gray anymore. It was full color. Like a model planet hovering between the four walls. *They up to somethin' now.*

Rinks jammed her finger at the orb like it was a button on a vault of gold coins. There was white light. The falling sensation. The smell of peppermint and silky grass on her feet. A few seconds later, Vern was next to her. His complexion was a bedsheet.

"You disappeared."

She lapped up the sweet taste of victory and looked around. Things had changed.

Candyland wasn't so little anymore.

20

"You got to see this!" Sandy said.

"Everything all right?" Marie said before she was fully awake. She jolted off the bed, looked around. "Where's Aunt Rinks?"

"Never mind her; come on."

Fritz had a smudge of chocolate on his face from the night before. Sandy followed him into the kitchen. The lower half of his bottom was a speckled patchwork of funky gummy castings. Marie rolled off the mattress (still half-filled with air) and went to the bathroom. When she came out, the door to the storefront was open. Fritz and his sidekick were waiting.

"They followed us." Sandy's sand dollars looked like Frisbees.

Dust particles floated through beams of late morning sunlight. The shelves looked cluttered. She stepped across the spotless floor, shading her eyes from the bright light. When she lowered her arm, she saw what was on the shelves.

Toys.

They were piled and stacked from the bottom shelf to the top. Bunnies, octopuses, dragons and bears. Robots with TV heads and stretchy muscle men in tight shorts. Baby dolls and purple monkeys, rainbow birds with leather wings, little white puppies with velvety tongues, lanky puppets made of wood with hinged jaws. It was them, the toys that greeted them after they crossed the bridge. They came from the trees and flew down from the sky, took their hands and climbed on their shoulders. Dancing and trotting and twirling as they went with contagious laughter.

Marie, Fritz and Sandy had walked all the way to the valley and stopped at a cliff. Below, a stream trickled over brittle slabs of glassy candy. The scent wafting up was perfumed. *That's the Orange Brook!* Sandy had said. (It was much later when Marie would remember how he knew its name.) They had walked for hours. The castle didn't look any closer. Marie barely remembered coming back out to fall in bed.

Marie checked her phone. Aunt Rinks and Uncle Vernon were across town. *A furniture store?*

"There's more."

Sandy tried to grab her hand. His stick passed through it. She followed him into the kitchen. There was a bowl of bright-colored gummy worms on the table with a note next to it. The ink was leaching in soggy milk stains. She read it to herself. Sandy told her to read it out loud.

"Morning, sleepyheads. Looks like Godfather's elves paid another visit. Haha. :) Me and your uncle went shopping. No guesses and no peeking where we at. No chores today because it's Christmas time. We'll be back at supper. Have fun and do whatever you want!"

"Did she put a smiley face at the end?" Sandy asked.

She checked her phone again. They were twenty minutes away. *Did someone kidnap Aunt Rinks? The note sounds nothing like her. The only time she uses smiley faces is on social media.*

"We're going in," Sandy said. "It'll take all day to get to the castle."

It would take more than that. A week, maybe. If the trail was easy. "Wait."

"Wait, what? No. They're not coming home till tonight. You see where they're at."

"She had to see the toys." She shook the note. "She doesn't even sound surprised."

"And that's... *bad*?"

It was suspicious. Marie looked around. It felt like someone was watching them. *Did they put their phones at a furniture store and sneak back?*

Fritz was dancing in place like he needed the bathroom. He nodded at Sandy. "We're going," Sandy said.

"Wait, wait. I just... I need to get something to eat."

She was still waking up, and these two wanted to go. Candyland wasn't imaginary. It ached in her bones. Her feet were sore from a two-hour hike. And they wanted to get to the castle today? On top of that, she hadn't eaten in twenty-four hours. Hadn't showered in two days. And her thoughts tossed about like sheaves of paper in a winter storm. Still, she wanted to go, too. The journey was just beginning.

"Don't eat the worms," Sandy said.

❄

"Well, this is a bummer," Sandy groaned.

They were at the Almond and Raisin Gate, staring across the valley. The sign with the clue was gone. The bridge was still there. It felt more like a video game: respawning at the beginning. There was no way they would make it over the vast stretch of land in a few hours. Even if they rode horses (there were none to ride, toy horses or otherwise), it would take all day.

"You know, we could do a sleepover at the cabin with the Counselor. Take the gift. He'd probably go with us," Sandy said. "I'm just spitballing."

That was never going to happen. Even if Aunt Rinks let them go, the gift wasn't going to work outside the toy store (that was a working theory). It was a dumb idea. Their spirits sank like an iron sled on the Arctic Ocean. Fritz didn't even dip his toes in the chocolate stream (which had receded to its meager current) or search the Christmas Wood for new friends. Sandy slumped like a snowman in August.

"Journeys are supposed to be fun," Sandy said. He sounded like a machine losing power. "This isn't fun. Or funny."

Journeys aren't always easy, Marie thought.

She sighed. The other two sighed. The riddle wasn't easy, but she thought that was just a test. Travelling that distance was impossible. Unless they stayed in Candyland a week. That would mean telling Aunt Rinks, which would create a bigger problem.

It feels like a video game. Marie had played video games with her friends. The kind of games where one level had to be solved to get to the next. There was usually something that linked them together, though. A common thread. A weapon or charm that allowed them to pass to the next level. *What have we done so far? We solved the riddle.*

The riddle gave them the bridge.

"Come on."

They searched the Almond and Raisin Gate for buttons or levers or secret compartments. It was a pointless gate that didn't keep anything in or out. Maybe it would transform into a monster truck or a flying carpet. A sled that slid down sugar-coated fields of grass. Fritz poked at the gummy raisins stuck to the posts while Marie twisted the almonds. Sandy hopped across the bridge and back.

"What are we looking for again?" he said.

"I don't know. Just... just look."

It was officially hopeless when Fritz began licking the peanut-sized grains of salt off the pretzel posts. Sandy helped him break off a chunk to dip in the stream. They'd given up and decided to eat.

Marie crossed the bridge, sat cross-legged in the field (*Candy Meadow* was written on a little sign posted on the other side of the bridge), picking sweet blades of grass and mincing them between her teeth. *What's the link?* Most riddles—good riddles—were misdirection. The answer was obvious, just not where you would expect it even when looking right at it. What had they solved so far?

For your story to begin...

The journey had started when she solved the riddle. Perhaps it was more than just a riddle. The answer was more than an answer. This was a story. And a story started with blank pages, just like the one Godfather had given her. And in a story, anything was possible. She stood up, looked at the pink sky.

"Once upon a time... we were at the castle."

Her words were strong and deep. They bounced off the trees. A tremor sent ripples through the stream. Fritz looked up with chocolate-smeared lips. They felt it, too. But nothing happened. They was still in Candy Meadow.

"Present tense," Sandy said. "We *are* at the castle."

She tried that. It didn't work.

Sandy snapped his fingers like breaking twigs. "Helicopter. Do a helicopter."

"Once upon a time, a helicopter was in Candy Meadow."

Another tremor, this one knocked caramel-dipped fruit off the candy-cane trees. They gathered sticks and leaves as they rolled across the ground. Nothing, however, dropped from the sky or erupted from the ground. Marie thought a helicopter wouldn't do them any good. *We don't know how to fly a helicopter.*

Sandy spouted nonstop ideas that included four-wheelers, motorcycles and jetpacks. Airplanes, parachutes, dragons, dinosaurs, pogo sticks, and hot-air balloons. Marie didn't bother. She was onto something, though.

Candyland heard me.

It just couldn't comply. She looked at the candy-cane trees and cotton-candy clouds. The Christmas music that played from the muddy castle a hundred miles away. This place had a theme. A story had to be congruent. A historical romance didn't have laser guns. Some did, but that didn't work here.

What's the theme?

It was toys. It was music. It was the feel of winter and essence of joy. It was happiness and wonder. Outside, through that square in the sky, it was that time of year. *Christmas spirit.*

"Once upon a time," she said, "there was a sleigh with flying reindeer."

The ground shook this time. Tree trunks swayed, and candied fruit bombed the sparkling ground. The pretzel bridge crackled and leaned. Fritz and Sandy hurried over it. The earthquake rumbled into the distance. The Christmas music stretched out on long notes, then resumed its cheery refrain. A peppermint breeze blew a lock of hair that had escaped Marie's ribbon.

She heard bells.

Tiny bells chimed everywhere at once. It was like a cricket that couldn't be located. It came from the trees. She expected to hear a hoof scratch the turf, or see a snout poke out from the shadows. The bells grew louder. They were coming from the right. She took a step in that direction when *whuuump!* A shadow passed over them.

It was cool and large, like a cloud flying over the sun.

They looked up in unison. Four cloven hooves pedaled the air. The antlers looked like tree branches. Behind it, sagging from thick straps, was a red sleigh with golden rails. It sparkled in the sunlight. Each stride the reindeer took cut the air like giant limbs swinging through the air. *Whump. Whump. Whump.*

It circled Candy Meadow twice, then came straight for them. Marie, Fritz and Sandy ran to the left. Spongy dirt and soft sprigs of turf shot up as the hooves bit into the ground. The sleigh bounced on one rail, then the other. It skidded behind the reindeer. A musky smell mixed with the peppermint breeze. The reindeer came to a stop. He shook his head, bells ringing on the harness over his shoulders, and turned a black eye toward them. A frightening snort rattled his nostrils. Wet steam shot out.

"It's a reindeer," Marie whispered.

She wasn't sure. It was more like a mutated bull. The antlers were as wide as a truck. And the look in his eye could melt ice. He dug a trench in the dirt with his front leg as easily as a backhoe ate the earth. He dropped his head to graze, looked back at them with tufts of grass disappearing between black lips.

Marie, Fritz and Sandy weren't moving. It was like a bear had wandered into the meadow to eat berries off a tree, and they were afraid to move. So struck by the reindeer's size and intent, they hadn't even looked at the sleigh.

And when they heard a voice, they jumped a foot off the ground.

"Merry, merry!" An elf leaped from the bench inside the sleigh. He was as round as a beach ball with a tumbleweed beard that was braided in two strands. "Ronin Express, at your service. I am Garl. Short for Garland, if you're wondering. Named after me grandpap. That there is Ronin."

Garl executed a very short bow. His hand barely reached the middle of a generous belly—a belly so big it was doubtful he could see his feet. Even feet as large as his. They were size 30s (if there is such a thing), and bare. Tufts of fire red hair on the knuckles of his toes.

"Ronin is the ninth reindeer in Santa's crew. You've never heard of him. No one has. Also, I'm obligated to inform you not to touch him."

"Why?" Sandy asked.

"Look at him." Two streams of steam shot from the reindeer's nostrils. A big, black eye turned on them again. "Would you like to hear his story?"

"We're in a bit of a hurry," Marie said.

"You know what they say about hurries," Garl said. "Hurries make blurries."

A smile turned his cheeks as red as the hair on his toes. Sandy said, "That doesn't make sense."

"We're looking for Princess Pirlipat," Marie said.

"Fine choice. Fine choice, indeed." He snapped his fingers, but no sound was made. "The king and queen's daughter, yes. Poor girl. You've heard the rumors. I'm not one to gossip, but her face..." He wiggled his hand in front of his nose. "And her head..." He extended his hands. Then more upbeat, he said, "So, you want to go to the castle?"

"Castle, yes."

"We can't take you to the castle."

"Why not?"

"Road's too narrow. You see that." He pointed at Ronin's antlers. They fanned the air when he turned his head. "Can't fit. Road's too sticky. Not good for sleighs. It's always crowded and—hey, no touching!"

The tip of Sandy's stick was reaching for Ronin's hindquarters.

"He'll swat you like a bug. Grind your bones into dust." Garl shook his tiny fists. "He'll stomp you so deep into the ground you'll need an elevator to climb out."

Ronin lifted his head and loosed a howl that shook the trees. It vibrated in Marie's chest. It was raw power. A layer of sand trickled off Sandy. Ronin swung his head around and fixed a baseball-sized eye on Garl.

"Eh-hem." Garl nodded. "Very well. It seems he likes you."

"I knew it," Sandy said. "So I can touch?"

"Go on. Be quick."

Sandy poked Ronin in the leg. Fritz reached up to stroke his fur. Muscles rippled beneath the dense hide. His tail swished about and knocked Sandy's arm off. Garl snickered. He began to lecture them about what he said. As impressive as this reindeer was—somewhere between the size of a rhino and an elephant—Marie wanted to get to the castle before Aunt Rinks came home. Garl was sweet, in an odd way, but just as distracted as her brother and his sandman were. Why did they need someone to take them where they wanted to go? *This is a story. We can start anywhere.*

"Once upon a time," she started, "we were at the castle."

They looked at her. She thought about clicking her heels.

"Your journey starts in Candy Meadow," Garl said. "Besides, you asked that already."

"Then where can you take us?"

"Now that is a fine question." He raised a finger and began.

They could go to Orange Brook, which he said was fine this time of year, but a little sweet for his taste. Lemonade River, which was a bit sour right now. Molasses River came highly recommended. It was deep and rich; the salted nippers were spawning. Gingerbreadville was a tourist destination. Far too crowded at any time of year, as far as he was concerned. Bonbon Town was for locals. A nice art scene, if they were into that (he wasn't). Paper Land was industrial. All anyone wanted to do there was work for King Chocolate.

"And Confectionville. The hub of this great valley that surrounds Marchpane Castle."

"That castle?" Marie pointed at the mud castle.

"That one. It was much finer at one time. You should have seen it. The walls gleamed, and the spires soared. A beacon of hope, a symbol of home. Now, it's, uh… it's that."

"What happened?" Sandy asked.

"Things change." He cleared his throat.

"Is Confectionville the closest we can get?" Marie said.

"It is," he said. And they'd best be going before the Yellow Throated Sour Picklers began to swarm. Whether that was bad or not didn't matter. Marie was ready to go. They climbed onto the bench behind Garl that was cushioned and warm. Sandy bounced around and settled in. Garl seemed a little annoyed at the mess he was making—sand all over the floor—but didn't say anything.

"Hands and feet inside the sleigh at all times. This sleigh does not move until seat belts are fastened. We aim to amuse and serve here at Ronin Express. Above all else, we do it safely."

He snapped a long belt around his waist. Marie and Fritz did the same. Sandy did, too; although it didn't seem like that would help him should something happen. He would just crumble.

Ronin snorted. Garl asked if they were ready.

Marie was so caught up in the moment, she forgot to check her phone. If she did, she would've seen her aunt and uncle driving toward them.

❋

THEY HAD BOARDED A ROCKET.

Heads thrown back, the sleigh jiggled. The ground below them walloped with hooves as heavy as falling trees. Bits of dirt and debris showered down on them. The wind drew tears from their eyes and howled in their ears, shearing whatever Garl said into distant nonsense.

Marie grabbed Fritz. Fritz grabbed Sandy.

They knocked into each other, tossed back and forth as the sleigh wobbled. It teetered on one rail, then the other, shooshed through the grass. Then suddenly... their stomachs dropped into their socks and pinned them to the back of their seat. The sleigh dipped below Ronin's churning legs. He pedaled like he was scaling a mountain. Up, up, up they drove toward the pink sky. The black square hovered above them like a four-cornered moon.

Marie caught tiny gulps of air. Fritz ducked his head, holding his hat to keep it from flying off. It was like being strapped to an airplane wing. She was about to duck behind Garl's seat when the wind began to die down. In seconds, it was silent. She wiped her face. They were peacefully sailing high above the valley.

"That's better," Garl said. "I thought you would want to experience the raw takeoff."

Fritz was gasping. Sandy was a narrower version of himself. A layer of sand had been sheared away. A strange bubble wrapped around the sleigh. Like looking through water.

"It warps the view," Garl said, "but at least we can breathe. Anyway, everyone still buckled? Good. We're going to be turning in a minute—"

The turn came sooner than that. Ronin leaned sharply to the left. The sleigh swung like a water tube behind a speedboat. Marie smashed into Fritz and Sandy like a collapsing accordion. Garl, meanwhile, pointed out the sights as the sleigh turned on its side. The muscles on Ronin's back rolled like waves.

"Orange Brook," Garl shouted. "The perfume is quite a treat, a bouquet of vanilla pudding and cherry raisins."

That smell was lost in the musky scent of Ronin's efforts. A turn in the other direction sent Sandy and Fritz crashing into her. (She didn't understand what all the turning was about.) They soared over Lemonade River; its sunshine water rippled in sugary waves. Up ahead was Molasses River, a richly dense body of water that cut into the valley like a vein of silk.

"Funny story, the Molasses River. It was discovered at the Gumdrop Mine by accident. They thought they'd hit a vein of taffy when the first drops of molasses oozed out. Before long, it was flowing—hang on, quick drop."

Ronin plummeted so quickly he disappeared. The screams Marie had bottled up were drowned out by the terrorized shrieks coming from Sandy. He clawed at Fritz like a cat going over a waterfall. The sleigh was going down. Ronin extended his legs and glided like a flying squirrel. Garl continued the story about the Molasses River that no one heard.

Ronin arched his back. Slowly, the skydive arced into a gradual descent.

"Approaching Icing Road," Garl announced. "All passengers return their seats to an upright position. We thank you for flying Ronin Express and hope you fly again soon."

They drifted toward what looked like a white frosted lane. Toasted houses zoomed past on both sides. A moment of silence was abruptly broken by thumping hooves. The sleigh bounced three times before it began skidding on the rails. Ronin was in full stride. The end of the road sped toward them.

Ronin locked all four legs in front of him. The sleigh bumped into his rear. Ice shavings flew from the deep tracks carved beneath his hooves. The shavings were sweet and tangy as they melted on Marie's face.

"Oh no," Garl said. "Brace!"

Marie didn't like that sound. She knew what he meant by the narrow road. Where Icing Road ended, a one-lane road paved with spongy gumdrops continued between two-story gingerbread structures. Ronin's antlers would destroy them like a plow through snowdrifts. His hooves dug deeper. The sleigh began tipping forward. The seatbelts kept them from tumbling onto Ronin's backside. The grinding hooves cut deeper.

Boom!

The sleigh dropped on the ground. Marie collapsed into her brother. Sandy looked like a slushy poured into the seat. A few seconds later, Gurl popped up from the front.

"Perfect landing!"

※

Gumdrop Alley, Garl called it.

A skinny road paved with lumpy treats that would knock your teeth out if you drove too fast. The gutters along the curbs were slick tracks of shiny fruit tape. Gumdrop Alley was lined with two-story gingerbread buildings. The seams were spackled with white icing, the walls (toasted to perfection) decorated with candy beads and breath mints, marshmallows, and raisins. Flower boxes spilled bundles of candy corn beneath awnings propped on cinnamon sticks.

The jellybean sidewalks were mostly empty. Those who were walking on it had stopped to watch Ronin stick a landing that was inches away from tearing down a wall or two. Marie expected them to be afraid. Relieved, maybe. They started wandering toward the sleigh, a motley bunch of rag dolls and plastic dancers, superheroes and smiling goblins. There were also gingerbread people and mini-elves with giant feet, gremlins with pointed ears.

Doors began opening. Heads poked out. They started toward the sleigh. Walking, at first. Then hopping. Then sprinting. Marie grabbed her brother. She was wrong. They weren't afraid or relieved. *They're angry.*

The mob was coming for them. Garl jumped out of the sleigh and waddled to the front. He slung a sack over his shoulder. Ronin lowered his head and snorted. *What's in Garl's bag?* Marie thought. She wondered if they leaped out of Candyland now, would this stop before someone got hurt?

"All right, all right!" Garl shouted. "Everyone, please. Get in a line."

Their pilot dropped the sack on Gumdrop Alley. The mob jockeyed for position, coming together in a single file down the middle of the multicolored road. It formed ten feet from Ronin's snout, which snuffled at Garl's sack. Garl tugged the twine that tied it shut.

"Mary Popkins, you're first."

The shaggy doggy with a pink bow between her ears trotted closer. Garl reached into the sack and pulled a grassy cube out. He gave it to Mary Popkins. The toy doggy balanced the treat on her pink bow. Ronin gave it a sniff, then pulled it between his rubbery lips. Mary Popkins hopped with joy.

"What's happening?" Sandy said.

Marie was caught up in the spectacle and, for a second, forgot where they were and why. Her heart was still recovering from the death ride through the sky. That wasn't what she had in mind when she'd wished for a sleigh pulled by a flying reindeer. *What is this place?*

It was a story that had already been written by her great-aunt Corker, she guessed. And Great-Uncle Corker had turned it into a game. Marie looked at the black square in the sky again. *These people don't know they're not real.* They weren't people, but she didn't know what else to call them. A bout of vertigo swirled her head like a bowl of noodles. *Is this real?*

The longer they were in Candyland, the easier it was to forget. This world smelled like sweets, felt like a song. *It's inside a ball!* she reminded herself. *This isn't any more real than a video game.*

The castle loomed in the distance. It was difficult to judge how far away it was. It was a mountain of fudge that pierced the hovering clouds of cotton candy. The details were smudgy and faint. The day was bright and pink, but she felt like they were standing in the castle's shadow. A hard, cold breeze wafted from the castle like it was a block of ice.

Fritz and Sandy leaped out of the sleigh. Garl let them cut in line, put blocks of grassy food in Fritz's hands for Ronin to grind between his teeth. Marie leaned over as Garl called up the next in line, a blocky robot with light bulb eyes.

"Garl," she said, "how much farther?"

Garl rose a foot taller when he stood on the toes of his giant feet. "The line, it goes back a block, methinks."

"Not the line. To the castle."

"Oh, that. You can walk there in a day."

"A day?" Ronin nudged her before she fell into him. "It'll take us a day to walk there?"

"Me, a day. I've got these." He wiggled his blocky toes. "You, half a day. But what's your hurry?"

"We're on a journey."

"Well, then, good news. You're already here."

A small family of trolls with fiery hair approached. They vibrated as they walked. Fritz helped pass out the reindeer treats. When he stroked the trolls' hair, they squeaked. What would happen if Marie wasn't there to remind him where they were? Would he forget what that black square in the sky was? This was a journey, not a destination. They belonged out there. Did anyone understand that?

"Garl, do you know where you are?" she asked.

He turned his head on blunt shoulders. Then he lifted one hand and saluted her. Said, "Do you?"

That struck her as odd. Did he know where he was, that this wasn't real, or did he give her another riddle? She seemed to think it was neither. His answer meant something else, and she didn't know what. *He knows why I'm here better than I do.*

"You know, I hear cookie cutters go quite fast if you take them down the gutter. Too bad there isn't a store." He handed her a treat.

"Not that I know of."

Ronin raised his head, careful not to bash anyone with the bony trees growing out of the sides of his head. His nostrils flared, blowing hot air into her face. Her reflection looked back from his black eyes, which blinked slowly. She held out the treat. He took it with guttural appreciation. This was the journey. What was her hurry?

The longer the journey took, the more nothing would change. That was the secret hope she clung to, the reason she believed Fritz and Sandy when they told her a little toy soldier had told them they had to go on the journey.

Journeys lead to change.

Gumdrop Alley was nothing but edible rowhouses. No one was selling cookie cutters (whatever that was). Not a single storefront in sight.

"Once upon a time..."

※

TWO LOLLIPOPS WERE under a red awning. They were side by side, spinning like pinwheels, the colors bleeding in a dizzy vortex. The window behind them, broad and foggy, had words painted on it as thick as cake icing. *Hussar Peregrinations,* it read.

Something went wrong, was Marie's first thought. She'd wished for a cookie cutter store. She'd also wished for a monster truck and got the Ronin Express instead. Written in small print, stenciled in red goo from a piping bag, was a line just below the storefront name. *Licensed Cookie Cutter Specialist.*

There were hazy objects on the other side of the window. She cupped her hands against it.

"Party's back there, kid." Sandy and Fritz reluctantly walked up. The crowd around Ronin had grown larger and stranger.

"That's not why we're here."

"Hussar Peregrinations," Sandy read. "This is what you wished for?"

The doorknob was a jawbreaker the size of a cue ball on a slab of hard candy. She opened the door and ducked under the low frame. There was no bell to greet them. Only the smell of burnt maple syrup and peanut butter. There were stacks of cookies as big as trash lids, pretzel logs against the wall, apple crates filled with button pops, buckets of pixie sticks. A narrow alley wound between the clutter to a countertop dusted with flour and doughy stars that hadn't been baked. Behind it looked like a short-order kitchen with tickets on a wheel. It smelled like an apple pie had just come out of the oven.

"Push." The tip of Sandy's stick clicked on a puffy button below a handwritten sign that read exactly that. Marie wasn't in time to stop him.

It set off a chain reaction of mouse traps and dominoes, a clawing crane, a fan blowing a Ping-Pong ball. A baseball fell into a catcher's mitt and rolled behind the cook's window. It fell into a metal bowl. A few seconds later, a bell went off.

Something shuffled. Toothpicks snapped. There was a drilling sound, then hammering. A small door opened below the cook's window. A plank stuck out like the tongue on a cuckoo clock. A soldier stood on it. Big hat, square jaw, bushy eyebrows. A scabbard on the belt. Not Nussknacker, the tuft of white hair on the chin was different, and the jacket was green. But a nutcracker, all right.

He took one stiff-legged step onto the dusty counter. His head turned mechanically, first toward Fritz, then Sandy. When he saw Marie, his jaw snapped closed. He gave a crisp salute in her direction.

"Welcome to Hussar Peregrinations," he barked. His wooden jaw clapped up and down when he spoke. "How may I serve?"

"Do you have cookie cutters?" she asked.

"This is a bike store."

"Looks more like a *parts* store," Sandy said.

Marie poked him. Sand trickled onto the floor. "Are you Hussar?" she asked.

"No. I *am* a hussar."

"Right. What's that?"

His eyebrows pinched together. "A soldier, of course. Peregrination is my assignment."

"That's it." Sandy tapped the counter. "Wandering journey. That's what it means. Clever. We're in the right place, Mar Mar."

"I believe you are. Pate is my name. What kind of bike interests you?"

"A fast one," Marie said.

"How fast?"

"The fastest."

"I see. And where will you go?"

"To the castle." When the eyebrows pinched together again, she added, "Marchpane Castle. We're looking for Princess Pirlipat."

"Ah, yes. Poor girl," he said and shook his head. "I have many options to offer, then. There is a dough beater that will get you there in two hours. It's reliable, very comfortable. The Slim Jim slider will take an hour. It's stylish. Very popular with the muppets. We also have—"

"How about the cookie cutter?"

His jaw hung open for a long moment. Then he said, almost reluctantly, "Two minutes."

"We'll take it."

"I don't think so."

"What? Why not?"

"Have you ridden a bike before?" he asked.

"Since we were five years old," Marie said.

"I mean truly ridden a bike. Become one with it?"

"We know how to ride a bike," Sandy said. "We want the cookie cutter."

Pate marched back and forth on the counter, his head twisting in their direction each time he turned. He stroked the tufted beard with his left hand. His right arm dangled loosely at his side. It wobbled in the socket with each step.

"I only have one," he said.

"One?" Marie considered wishing for another, but she had a feeling that wasn't going to happen.

"I'm very slow these days. You can't just slap a cookie cutter together with jam and peanut butter."

"I hope not," Sandy said.

"It takes time and precision to make what you're asking for. One wrong turn and you'll be a pat of butter on the pavement. I am a licensed cookie cutter specialist. Only the best and nothing less."

He was stern and verbose. His voice projected in military rhythm that could make them do what he wanted. He was also wasting time. She was about to just ask for the Slim Jim slider when Sandy spoke.

"It's the arm, isn't it?"

Pate's head swiveled like a turret. His eyes narrowed to slits. Air hissed between rows of wooden teeth. Then he said: "They were hiding in the abandoned Gum Drop Mine. No one had thought to find them there, but we'd received word they were. They were multiplying deep underground. The tunnels go everywhere throughout the land, under the rivers and lakes, beneath the roads. It's dangerous belowground. Easy to get lost. But not for them."

"Who are *they*?" Sandy asked.

"Mice." Pate hissed the word. "No one believed they'd returned, but the rumors are true. We had them cornered in the Cinnamon Swirl corridor. Desperate and hungry, they mounted a counterattack." He lifted his good hand to his eyes, shook his head. "I lost a good many hussars that day. I was lucky to survive, sent here with this."

His right arm swung like a string.

"But now we know they are coming. The return of their leaders is imminent, I'm afraid. Now I make bikes."

"And we'll take one," Marie said. "Can we just—"

"Who are the leaders?" Sandy said.

Pate dropped to his knees. They hit the counter like wooden knobs. He fell to one hand, his left hand. Sandy and Fritz leaned in. Marie did, too.

"The Mouseking," he whispered. "And Mouse—" He snapped his jaw shut, shook his head.

"What were you going to say?" Sandy said.

"It's bad luck to utter her name."

"It's okay. We won't tell."

This time he added, "The Mouse *Queen*."

"Queen?" Sandy repeated. "You couldn't say the word *queen*?"

"When they return," Pate continued, "the mice will rise up. They will nibble at the foundation of Marchpane Castle, eat all of the king's lard and sausage, and continue to curse Princess Pirlipat (poor girl). Darkness will fill the skies for the rest of time. The battle will be lost if not for the return of the lost hussar."

"Who's that?" Sandy said.

"No one knows." He stood up, saluted. "Not even the lost hussar."

❆

MARIE LOST TRACK OF TIME. The sense of urgency disappeared in the hussar's story. She was missing something in what Pate was saying. This was part of the story, somehow. She repeated over and over in her head what he'd said but couldn't find the answer. She felt a sharp twinge in her side.

"Marie." Sandy poked her again. "Yes or no?"

"What?"

Pate waited for an answer to a question she didn't hear. "One cookie cutter?" he repeated.

"Yes. Yes, we'll take it."

"Great. And what will you give for it?"

"Pardon?"

"It's not free. I have bills to pay like every citizen in the Alley."

Marie dug into her pockets. She dumped a crinkled wad of one-dollar bills on the counter. Fritz threw two quarters, a dime and three pennies next to it. Pate stared at the money. Just under four dollars wasn't enough. Marie checked her back pockets.

"What's that?" Pate said.

"It's three dollars and sixty-three cents."

The eyebrows pinched. He kicked the bills and poked at a quarter with the toe of his boot.

"I think he means *what's money?*" Sandy said.

It was just paper and round wheels of metal. It meant nothing here. He booted the bills onto the floor. "Come back when you have something I can use."

"No, wait," Marie said. "Peregrination. We're on a peregrination."

"Aren't we all." He saluted with his good arm. "Best of luck. And clean up the sand on your way out."

He did a crisp one-eighty and marched toward the cuckoo-clock plank to return to the back room. The broken arm swung wide when he turned. It rattled and flopped against his stomach and around to his back before slapping his stomach again.

"Wait!"

Marie pulled the ribbon off her head—the silky white ribbon Godfather had given her—and tied it into a loop. Her hair fell into her eyes as she motioned for Pate to step closer. She took his right arm gently.

"Does that hurt?"

He shook his head. She went about fashioning a sling that held snug against the front of his brass-button jacket. When she was done, he bent at the hip. The arm did not flop forward. He twisted back and forth, bending his knees. It held firm. Finally, he brandished the sword in his free hand. It slinked from the scabbard, its silver edge glinting. They watched him slice the air, pivot and parry, spin and leap, sticking the toothpick-length blade into the countertop. He stood as stiff as a flagpole and, once again, saluted Marie.

She saluted back. It seemed the thing to do.

He stepped back onto the cuckoo-clock plank, leaving his sword behind, and returned to the back room. Marie held her breath, wondering if she'd done something wrong. Somewhere in the back, a gear turned, and a latch clicked. The start of another mouse trap had begun, only this time it did not end with a doorbell.

Pate returned to the counter. He plucked the sword from the counter.

"I am indebted for your gift. I will return to the battle, to fight for our land. To honor our king and queen."

A door opened next to the counter.

"May the Christmas spirit guide you."

❄

Now she knew why it was called a cookie cutter. It wasn't what she expected. No steel wheels or sharp edges. Two giant cookies were attached to a frame of toffee sticks. The seat was long and curved and yellow. It was a banana.

It did not exude speed. In fact, there were no pedals or chain (or licorice whip) to drive the back cookie wheel. Just crude handlebars and a set of foot pegs. She wheeled it across the bumpy road.

"This is the fastest bike?" Sandy said, hopping across Gumdrop Alley. "It's definitely dangerous, but fast?"

Crumbs fell from the wheels, leaving a trail from the store. Pate had already turned a sign in the window that read CLOSED. Marie went to the slick gutter between the road and gingerbread buildings. An egg-shaped toy was on the sidewalk, licking a lollipop. A plastic tongue darted from its mouth, watching them center the cookies on the gutter.

Marie checked the time on her phone. They had an hour before Aunt Rinks came home. Maybe two. There was no way they would reach the castle on this. Halfway, maybe. There was also the issue of Sandy. There was enough room on the banana for her and Fritz. Sandy would crumble if they put him on it. She considered leaving him behind, but she needed him. So did Fritz.

The building behind the lollipop-licking egg was under construction (new walls had been pasted together). A pile of gingerbread crumbs and icing were on the sidewalk. She found a long strand of red licorice in it. She lassoed it through the frame and tied loops at the other end.

"What's that for?" Sandy said. She harnessed the licorice around his midsection and lower half. "You're kidding," he said.

"Either this or meet us there."

"Seriously? I can walk faster than that cookie machine. You don't even know how it works. It doesn't have pedals!"

That much was true.

Fritz climbed onto the front of the banana. Marie was behind him. They grabbed the hard-baked handlebars. The seat was mushy and formed to their behinds. The banana skin didn't split. So far, so good.

"Give us a push," Marie said.

"You want me to push us all the way to the castle?"

"Just get us started."

Sandy's sticks jabbed into her back. He just poked at first, barely trying. "We could've walked there by now," he whined. "You got robbed, you know. The ribbon is worth way more than this."

The little egg blinked its painted eyes, pointed the lollipop at the bottom of the bike. She put her foot on one of the pegs. It vibrated on the sole of her foot, sending waves through her leg. It tingled up her spine. She gripped the handlebars tighter.

"It's not a total loss," Sandy continued. "You hungry, Fritz? I am. Maybe just a nibble off the back wheel."

"A little faster," Marie said.

"Sure, make the sandman do all the work." The sticks dug deeper into her back. "Why don't I just carry you?"

The momentum picked up. Marie put both feet on the pegs. Fruity fumes wafted from beneath her. The cookie cutter stopped wobbling. It had locked into the gutter. It paused like a slingshot pulling back.

"Hold on," she whispered into Fritz's ear.

Sandy said, "Are you even helping? I'm about to sprain a—"

WWWWHHHHHHEEEEEEE!

The cookie wheels were brown blurs. Two disks that didn't even appear to turn. The only sounds were the howling wind and Sandy's screams. Marie's hair whipped across her eyes. Tiny specks spit from the front wheel and stung her cheeks. She didn't dare let go of the handlebars or look behind her. The cookie cutter, somehow, remained steady in the center of the gutter. The buildings on both sides of the road became one long beige smudge.

The castle grew like a stain spreading into the sky.

A red hue began to color the surroundings. It looked like the sun was setting at the end of the road. Marie hunkered against Fritz, peering over his shoulder. Tears streamed from the corners of her eyes. The glow was getting brighter. It was coming from a red puddle up ahead. As they sped closer, it turned into the sun-bleached color of Fritz's worn-out hat.

Where the road ended at Rose Lake.

❄

Marie took one foot off the peg. The high-pitched vibrations that had numbed her legs dropped a pitch. The spray of cookie crumbs felt less like a sand blaster on their cheeks. She dropped her other foot. The lake was still approaching at full speed. In a matter of seconds, the cookie cutter slowed as if it had hit a puddle of slag. Their hands—aching from the grip—hung on tight enough to keep them from flipping over the handlebars.

They came to a full stop before driving into the deep end of the rose-colored water. Ears ringing. Eyes itching and faces chafing. They looked around, panting. The road continued to their left and right. It was crowded and diverse. The sidewalks filled with tents and tables of goods—trinkets and food and such. A market that seemed oddly familiar.

Marie's attention was drawn to Marchpane Castle.

It blotted out much of the pink sky. And they still weren't next to it. Rose Lake went around it. The castle was a deep bruise on an island. Even the lake's rosy hue didn't affect the dark monolith. Scaffolding was anchored into the walls; a multitude of spires forked upwards and pierced the delicate sky. It was mean and gorgeous at the same time. Immoveable and fragile. A mesmerizing essence that was hard to look away from. It emanated a breath of its own, a coldness that carried over the rosy water like the promise of a storm. It filled her head; sank its teeth into her bones.

Something about it didn't feel right. It pretended to be beautiful while hiding a secret.

"You cold?" Sandy was shockingly slender. He'd lost half his body on the ride there. His voice had gone up an octave. "You look cold."

She was shivering and couldn't stop. The castle beckoned her to come closer and begged her to stay away. It was a terrible contradiction. An itch that hurt to scratch.

"Once upon a time..." she started, but couldn't finish. The words lodged in her throat. She swallowed hard and tried again.

Fritz took her arm. It startled her. She jerked away, said she was sorry. He shook his head. Sandy said in her brother's voice, "What's wrong?"

"I... I don't know."

The journey—this peregrination—had become a dizzying drop into conflicting emotions and confusion. A destiny she couldn't avoid.

"Hey there. Pardon me." Sandy slid into the road. "How do we get over there?"

He'd stopped a line of dwarves. Seven of them. Each wearing frumpy clothes of vivid colors. Thick white beards and thicker eyebrows. Hair grew from their ears. The lead dwarf stopped, and the others bumped into each other in succession. Each dwarf looked at the dwarf behind like falling dominos. The last one in line looked at the busy market.

"Marchpane Castle?" the lead dwarf asked. "No visitors allowed."

"Why not?"

"To protect the princess," the second in line said. Then all of them said, "Poor girl."

A barge was in the rosy water. It would take a good walk to get to it. Marie wasn't going to take the cookie cutter through such a crowded market. The barge was being loaded with crates.

"What if we found a boat?" Sandy said. "Would someone stop us?"

They shook their heads. "Boats sink," the third dwarf said. "It's the water."

That didn't make sense. The barge wasn't sinking. "What about that?" Sandy pointed at the barge.

"Shipment from King Chocolate in Paper Land," the fourth dwarf said.

"To make the castle bigger," the fifth one said.

"Thicker," said the sixth one.

"One day," the last one squeaked, "it'll swallow Rose Lake."

As if that was all the words they had, they began their march with bulky sacks thrown over their shoulders. Humming as they bounced on their heels. Sandy followed them with more questions.

Marie watched the barge get heavier. *To make the castle bigger.*

There were street performers wandering in the crowd. Skinny jugglers with elastic arms. Dancers spinning like tops. Twirlers threw themselves above the crowd as Christmas music echoed across the water. Dwarves and elves, toys and animals, and things she couldn't explain walked or rolled or sprang or hopped. They entertained and argued, laughed and danced. A thriving collection of this world's inhabitants. *One day the castle will swallow Rose Lake.*

Why is it getting bigger and thicker? Is that the journey, to stop the castle from growing?

Her thoughts spread out and followed all the possibilities. She thought of how they could get across the water when she realized she was looking at a tall couple in the crowd. They were wearing cloaks with the hoods drawn over their heads. It wasn't their size or dark clothing that struck her as odd. Her heart ached to stop them.

They're human!

"Hey!"

She waved her arms and ran towards them. They couldn't hear her shouting over the crowd and music. She was slowed by dancers and jugglers and a wobbly cart rolling on rotting apple cores. The cloaked couple walked in the direction of the barge.

"Stop!"

She jumped onto the sidewalk and ran around tents. Sandy was calling her name, but she couldn't stop. She had to get to the couple. She could feel it like the castle calling her and pushing her away. She tripped over a skateboard rolling on its own (was it alive?) and stumbled into a cart. It tipped over. A thousand nuts spilled into the road, bouncing between legs and wheels. The hussars minding the cart (*Support the Troops* was written on the side) gaped at the nuts rolling away, their square jaws dropping open.

They helped her up. "I'm so sorry," she said. "Who is that?"

She pointed at the cloaked couple, who were even farther away now. They had reached the barge and were conversing with the crew loading boxes from King Chocolate in Paper Land.

"The king and queen," one of the hussars said.

Marie's hands involuntarily balled into frightened fists. Her jaw clenched and unclenched. A fresh wave of cold anxiety passed over her. Gooseflesh rose on her arms. She'd lost all will to run.

"Marie." Sandy looked around at the mess. The hussars were already cleaning up. "Look, look."

Fritz handed her his phone. At first, she didn't know what she was looking at. Her vision was blurred, her attention distracted. It was his location app.

"We have to go back," Sandy said. "Now."

❄

THE AIR WAS UNPLEASANT. It was thick and oppressive. Had the stink of rotting wood and clothes that needed washing. The colors were bland, even the red lights on the wall.

Marie's knuckles ached. She unclenched her hands. White crescents dug into her palms. Her cheeks raw. She felt as fragile as a dry cookie.

Fritz quickly snapped the gift closed and put it in the wall, sliding the blocks into place. Sandy was gone. They stood still, listening for movement outside their bedroom. She wiped the cookie cutter crumbs off her clothes. Fritz did the same. They checked their phones again. Aunt Rinks's and Uncle Vernon's locations still weren't showing up. It was an hour till supper. Marie opened the door to the storefront. Nothing had changed. Nothing from the market had followed them back.

They circled around to the kitchen. No dwarves with lumpy sacks were at the table. No aunt or uncle, either. She peeked out the window, told Fritz to see if the car was parked out front. She opened the door to their bedroom. Her journal was on the workbench, the pages still empty. Nussknacker stood guard. He felt different somehow. More intimate. Like she could feel the stiffness of his body.

Will we have to start over? she wondered. She would go back to Candyland that night. If they appeared in Candy Meadow, she could make better time getting to Confectionville and the market. *All the way to the barge.*

This wasn't a game. This was a journey she had to finish.

"Marie." Sandy slid into the bedroom with Fritz. "There's no car. You have to see this, though."

They went out the kitchen door. Something had come back with them. The backyard jungle was gone. Lights were strung through the tree canopies. The paths were cleared and the patio clean. New chairs faced a warm fire in the firepit. Off to the side, a fountain was bubbling in a koi pond of rosy water. A hint of peppermint was in the air.

How were they going to explain this? Godfather's elves had come during the middle of the day and no one saw them? And what if someone had been driving by when it happened?

They would never have to explain that, though. No one saw it. And Aunt Rinks and Uncle Vernon wouldn't come home that night.

Marie and Fritz waited by the fire until it was dark. The moon was out. The lights in the trees looked like stars. Every time she checked her phone, nothing appeared. Neither of them had an appetite. Marie read the note Aunt Rinks had left that morning. Then she remembered something. A small clue that told her exactly where her aunt and uncle were.

She got up. She went to their bedroom and stood at the door. When Marie and Fritz had gone to Candyland that morning, she had locked the door. When they returned, the latch was undone. There was only one way that could have happened.

"Nussknacker knows where they are," Sandy said.

21

It smelled different. Like a wet dog in a peppermint bath that still smelled like a dog.

The amazement Rinks had felt the first time she'd dropped into Candyland had dulled to a passing head turn. This was just a next-generation video game as far as she was concerned. Cool, at first. At the end of the day, just another video game.

Candy Meadow was empty. The chocolate stream and the dumb, useless gate was all there was. And the rickety bridge. Something rustled in the candy-cane woods. Twigs snapped from the right.

"Go look," Rinks said.

Vern hopped over the chocolate stream, not before dipping his finger in it for a taste, and stepped between the red and white striped trunks. If the kids were in there, he wouldn't find them. He couldn't find the car if he was sitting in it. Rinks knew where the brats went. They were on the other side of the valley. Toward that brown stain on the horizon.

Turd Mountain.

It was probably an amazing castle up close, chocolatey walls carved with smiling gargoyles wearing elf hats and throwing presents every time the bell rang. From this distance, it looked like an accident. She didn't want to walk that far. Not now, not ever. There were other ways to catch her traitorous niece and nephew.

The bridge was a little wobbly. The pretzel posts were leaning. She climbed over it instead of wading through the stream. The grass on the other side shimmered with a coat of sugar water. Something had dug a long patch of divots. The grass had been turned over and pawed at.

"Vern!"

He came trotting along the stream, chewing on a branch like jerky. She didn't ask why he was eating a tree. Only pointed at the ground. He grunted, nodding like he did when something puzzling came up. She waited for him to say it, counting down in her head, and then right on time he said it.

"Interestin'."

He got on one knee, brushed his fingers in the dirt. Smelled them. Ate a clump of it like it was cake. He looked back over the bridge, over the trees beyond. He raised his hands like he was framing a picture. Rinks rolled her eyes.

"Somethin' landed," he said. "Then took off again."

She didn't see how he got to that. Then he pointed to the long dents in the ground. There were two of them that trailed through the divots. They went about thirty yards and stopped.

"Look at the size of that," he said. "Look."

He held his hands a foot apart like he was showing her what he caught with a fishing pole. She took a closer look, noticed the cloven print about the size of a frying pan.

"What is it?" she said.

He palmed the stubble on his chin. "Well, that's a moose print, for sure. Or the world's biggest caribou."

"You know animal prints now?"

"No. But those lines right there look like rails. Like it was pullin' somethin'."

He looked at her, waiting for her to put it together. She didn't know exactly what a caribou was—like a big deer or elk—but she knew where he was going with it. Something made those tracks, and an animal was pulling it.

"What're you sayin'?" she said.

"I'm sayin' a reindeer picked the kids up."

"You said caribou."

"Reindeer. Caribou. Same thing."

"It ain't the same thing."

"Whatever, Rinks. It's a flyin' one. And it was pullin' a sleigh."

She started laughing. The kind of cruel laughter a school-ground bully would do before making fun of an idiot.

"Look around, Rinks. This place is Christmas. Rules don't apply here like they do up there." He pointed at the box in the sky. "You hear the music out there. You don't think Santa's reindeer are grazin' round here? Anythin's possible!"

She couldn't argue that point. Those were caribou or reindeer prints. Those were sled tracks. *And anythin' is possible.* If the kids got a ride, they were probably already at the castle by now. Vern stuck his fingers in his mouth and ripped a high-pitched whistle. Then called out Santa's reindeer names. He got as far as Vixen before having to sing the song to remember the other ones.

Nothing dropped out of the sky for them.

"Let's go back." She sighed. "We can wait for them to come out, surprise them in their room."

"Why?"

"Because that big pile of mud is, like, five hundred miles away. We ain't walkin' to it."

"It ain't that far."

"And we don't even know that's where they went. What, we're goin' to just walk around and hope we find them pettin' a reindeer that stopped to take a leak?"

He thumbed his phone. This was ridiculous. If they'd come home earlier, they could've caught them before they left. Now they could be anywhere.

"They're at the castle," he said.

"You don't know that."

He showed her his phone. An icon with Marie's face was far away from them and in the direction of the castle. That meant the location was working (which seemed odd, but what else was new?).

He powered off his phone. "Turn your phone off."

"So what if they know we're here."

"We want to catch them by surprise, don't we? Let's just walk a little ways down there. Maybe one of those reindeer is grazin'. We can catch a ride. It can't hurt, Rinks. We're already here."

He took off with a bounce in his step. Rinks looked up at the box in the sky before following him. It was the last time she would see it for quite some time.

※

That rustling they'd heard in Christmas Wood was following them. The sugar grass had become a narrow strip hemmed in by the trees. It sounded like little things scratching around in fallen leaves. She didn't like it.

And she was starving. Her last meal had been breakfast, and that had been a protein bar. Vern was munching on a handful of grass, the frosted blades sticking out between his lips like a cow. He stopped suddenly, put his hand out.

"Smell that?" He took several whiffs. "I think there's a stream right down the way. I'll bet it ain't water, either. Like lemonade or sports drink or something." He snapped his fingers. "Soda stream!"

The trees were near them on the left and right when she could hear water, too. Vern broke off a branch and handed it to her, told her to try it. He gnawed on it first. She gave it a nibble. It tasted like cinnamon toast. The buttery kind her mother used to make. She ate the whole thing. Vern kept on walking. Rinks went deeper into the trees to find a different branch. This one smelled like maple syrup on French toast with whipped cream. She took two bites. When she looked down, something was between her feet, holding up a twig for her to grab.

"Aaah!"

Rinks ran back to the field. The rustling grew louder. It was all around her now. Shadows were moving everywhere.

"Vern, come on. Let's go."

She was frozen in place. Something scurried out of the trees. A mouse stood on its hind legs, sniffing the air. It wore what looked like a tiny helmet. And it was holding a stick in its pink hand. A stick with a shiny tip.

"Don't move," Vern said.

Another mouse joined the first one. Then a third. After that, they came out in lines. Helmets and spears and swords and daggers. Standing up to sniff at them. Beady black eyes looking. There were hundreds of them. Maybe a million. They came from both sides, circling around them and lining up in formation. Many were injured. Blocks of rodent militia standing at the ready. Weapons at their sides.

"What are they doin'?" Rinks said.

Not a mouse was stirring or whisker did twitch. Eyes unblinking. Then the formation parted in the middle. An aisle opened between them. The last of the rodent army emerged from the trees. This one twice as big with a tail three times as long. The rat's fur was gray and coarse. He limped on his back feet, using a spear as a cane. He stopped five feet from Rinks, tested the air with his pink nose. He put a front paw on the shiny plate that covered his chest.

He bowed. They all bowed.

"What's happenin'?" Rinks said.

"They're bowin'."

"I see that. Why are they bowin'?"

Vern looked at her. "They bowin' to you."

That was how it looked. Why they were doing it couldn't be answered. The rat raised the spear and squeaked. Vern bent over to listen. The rat gestured with both hands, pointing toward the castle, pointing at Rinks.

"He wants to show us somethin'," Vern said.

"You speak rat now?"

"I don't need to speak it. Look at him."

"Ask him if it's the kids he wants to show us."

With that, the rat leaped and pointed. Hopping up and down like a subway rat that found a pizza box, he waved at Rinks and Vern. Clearly, he wanted to show them something.

"It's obvious, ain't it?" Vern said. "The way they're all lookin' at us. *At you,* Rinks. They don't want to hurt us."

"They got weapons, Vern."

"If they wanted to hurt us, they would've already."

Vern scratched his neck. The rash was bright red. Bumps were growing on the skin, but he didn't seem bothered. He wanted to follow them. What harm could it do just to look? Besides, if things got hairy, they could just leap out.

They didn't bother checking to see if the box was still in the sky before following the army into the trees.

❄

THE CANDY-CANE TREES were replaced by bramble. Tangles of salted pasta wrapped around their feet and arms, stung their eyes when it caught in their hair. Twice Rinks almost turned around. The food forest cleared into glazed slabs of granite that stuck to the soles of their shoes and palms of their hands. The edges were brittle and sharp. At the bottom of a descending climb, they stepped in pasty mud that smelled like gooey peanut butter.

A narrow path led to a hole in the side of the hill. The mouse army lined up on both sides of the trail. They raised their weapons as Rinks and Vern approached. The rat captain or general or whatever he was—the important vermin—waited at the entrance. He raked a matchstick on the ground. A flame broke out. Sulfur wafted up. He hopped into the dark tunnel. Rinks and Vern peeked inside. Little spots of flickering light went way back.

The cave smelled like rock candy. The colorful rocks she used to eat when she was little.

"Seriously?" Rinks said.

"We come all this way." Vern shrugged. "Should at least look."

Rinks didn't follow her husband at first. She gave a hard think about turning back. She looked up, but the trees were overhead. She'd have to climb back to the clearing to see the box in the sky. She never thought it might not be there.

Sweet dust filled the cave. Rinks pulled her shirt over her mouth. Vern was a shadow ahead of her, coming into focus when he passed a matchstick stuck in the wall. The ground became thick and muddy, made sucking sounds with each step. It oozed over her shoes and soaked through her socks, cold and sticky. It smelled like fudge.

"I don't like this!" Her voice echoed the length of the cave.

Vern didn't answer or hesitate. He trucked ahead. A few steps later, Rinks felt a warm breath on her face that smelled like everything else. Yummy. The sound of the ocean slowly began to rise. A beige halo was at the top of a gentle slope. Vern stood at an opening with his hands braced against the walls. Several mice were at his sides with flaring matchsticks. General Rat held a tiny torch in each hand, watching Rinks slip on the floor.

She grabbed the back of Vern's shirt, wiping her hands on it before pulling herself next to him. There was a giant bowl in front of him. There was a handle on it. *It's a teacup.*

"It's beautiful," he muttered. "Look at it, Rinks."

It was a cavern, like the ones you paid money to go see. Instead of cheesy lights and clear streams, this one dripped from sugar-cone stalactites. A milk chocolate waterfall crashed on chocolate boulders. A river ran through a ledge that circled the cavern.

The rat general tapped the giant teacup with his matchstick. The flame sparked. It reminded her of one of those rides at the carnival, the one with spinning teacups that made you puke up an elephant ear.

"What's he doin'?" Rinks said.

"I think he wants us to get in."

"I don't think so."

"That's what it's for." Vern pointed down the slope that entered the cavern. "It's a ride."

"Are you outta your mind? I'm not gettin' in that thing, and neither are you."

The rat general tapped it again. It rang like a china plate.

"This ain't real, Rinks. It's just pretend. How can we *not* go on this ride?"

She stared at the stupidity dripping from his face. "How? How? We don't know where it goes."

"They do. That's why they brought us in here. Look at them." The mice waited patiently as their matchsticks burned close to their little pink fingers. "Besides, it's not like we're stuck here. If somethin' goes wrong, we just get out."

Vern wasn't thinking straight. First, he didn't understand that getting out required jumping at the door in the sky. They couldn't see the sky, for one. There was another problem they weren't aware of just yet.

"See? Look," he said.

The mice were jumping in actual teacups, the kind you drink from, and shoving down the slope. When they hit the stream, they floomed into the current, twisting and turning along the curved outer wall, circling down into the chocolate toilet bowl.

"It's just a ride." Vern threw one sloppy leg into the teacup. "Maybe we'll see the kids."

That was the one thing keeping Rinks from running out of the cave. It didn't hurt that the mice kept bowing to her. She didn't hate that.

"If we die," she said, "I'm gonna kill you."

Vern scratched his neck. "No one ever died on a chocolate slide before, Rinks."

He helped her into the teacup. There were benches inside it. And seatbelts. *Great.* The rat general and his minions gathered behind them and started to push. The mice chittered with excitement.

"Take us to the kids," Rinks said.

❄

There had been a log flume at the amusement park when Rinks was little. This was worse.

It started slowly enough. The cup circled as it dipped into the flow. Around the perimeter it began. Rock candy imbedded in the walls like unmined jewels. Farther down were jagged chunks of chocolate bars.

They picked up speed through the foam pit. The taste of coffee and cream on their lips. Bubbles in their hair. "I don't like this!" Rinks shouted.

Vern didn't hear her over the gurgle of a caramel geyser. The syrupy explosions splattered on racks of toffee. The teacup dropped down between spongy layers of cheesecake. Crumbly crust sprinkled over them. Rinks grabbed Vern's arm. She bent forward, kept her head down. She smelled cinnamon dust. Bright sprinkles rained into the teacup. A blob of ice cream melted down the back of her shirt.

"Vern! I want to go—"

She didn't see the last descent. They corkscrewed deeper into the hidden folds of the chasm. The slushing stream had become a gushing roar. The teacup shot up a steep incline. For a moment, it slowed. It was long enough for her to peek through sticky fingers. They were approaching the final drop.

Her screams were gobbled up in the rushing wind. She scratched at Vern. They held each other as close as the seatbelts would let them. Rinks in terror. Vern smiling through laughing shrieks. Above was a blurred excavation of desserts.

Then it was black.

They shot into a tunnel as dark as outer space. The roar had become a locomotive hurtling through their ears. Mushy specks stung their cheeks. Unexpected turns threw them one way, then the other. It was an endless waterslide through sticky nothingness.

Rinks babbled. Even she couldn't hear what came out of her mouth. It soothed her to rock back and forth, holding her stomach down to keep it from springing into her throat. It went on and on and on. It grew colder. She couldn't tell what direction they were sliding. Up or down or sideways. She just wanted it to end. When it did, she would make Vern pay.

At some point, they were going upward. Definitely upward. It warmed as they began to slow. The teacup wasn't spinning. She could hear herself panting. Her hair, matted and tangled, draped down her neck instead of flying behind her. They tipped one last time.

The teacup docked to a standstill.

Vern's face looked like an abstract painting. She was too weak to smack the goofy grin off it. Rinks wiped the mess out of her eyes. She'd passed through a confectionary birth canal and wanted to cry. Her clothes were ruined. Her scarf had flown off her head somewhere in the birth canal. Even worse. Her phone was soaked in a puddle of syrup. Everything was ruined. This whole thing was a bad, bad, bad idea.

Someone would pay for this. Not just Vern. The kids would pay dearly. This was a trap. And her idiot husband fell for it.

❆

VERN CLIMBED OUT. Something was dripping. It sounded like a room, where they were. A humid, dank room. Her nose was clogged with vanilla ice cream and caramel and whatever else had flown in her face, but she could smell new things around her. Vinegar and vegetables. Fruit, too. Large things hung around them like bodies.

Vern was smelling them. Turning them around, fingers running up the sides of salted slabs of meat. He had his nose right up against it.

"All that," she croaked, "for a cellar? A cellar, Vern? We're in a cellar!"

He scurried to a wall and shelves filled with jars of pickled roots and preserved peaches. He sniffed his way to the far side of the room. Rinks struggled to get unstrapped. The buckle was slimed and slippery. By the time it clicked, a beam of light fell from the ceiling. Rinks threw her arm up to shield her eyes. A ladder unfolded. Vern climbed up on all fours.

"Vern? Vern, wait. Don't—"

She flopped out of the teacup. The dirt floor wasn't a sponge cake, and for some reason, Rinks was relieved. She wanted to breathe regular air and drink water. Above her, where the stairs led to a rectangle of warm light, came the clanging sounds of pots and pans.

❄

It was a kitchen as long and wide as any house she'd ever lived in. Big, black wood stoves, copper pots and pans, rows and rows of butcher knives and big spoons and silver bowls. A fireplace blazed in an old stone hearth.

Vern had lost his shoes. Barefoot, he hunched over a huge table. With a grease-glistened mustache, he held up a half-eaten sausage. Lines of meaty links circled around tubs of lard and bowls of potatoes, onions, and beets. Juicy sounds of chewing were interrupted only by his moaning. The last thing she wanted to do was eat. The first thing was to hit something.

Rinks took her shoes off. The floor was warm and uneven. She threw her shoes across the room. They almost bowled over a regiment of mice standing at attention beneath a washtub of dishes. The mice were all around with their little weapons and helmets and breastplates. She wanted to grab one and shake it, find the stupid General Rat and tell him to take her back. *I want out of here!*

General Rat stood on a table in the corner. It was dull silver, dented and grooved from a lifetime of chopping things. It didn't hold any food, though. There were no meaty links or bowls of lard. There were shiny things. Her feet slapped the stones. The closer she got, the slower she stalked toward it. Her pulse picked up (as if that were even possible).

Scarves. Beautiful headscarves, just like the ones she made. They were folded neatly in lines and in all patterns and colors. Jewels, too —brooches and rings and diamonds and such. Shirts and skirts and designer shoes she couldn't afford. And protein bars! Black sticks of licorice! And there, on a pedestal, sitting on a stand all shiny and new, was the thing that gave her life meaning.

A brand-new phone.

The screen lit up. Her apps were on it, too. Her photos.

In the middle of this treasure were eight crowns. Seven were gold bands with boring details etched around them. The sort of design a kid might wear on his birthday at a pizza party. The last one, though, was delicate yet sturdy and encrusted with diamonds and pearls and rubies and sapphires. A gaudy thing that would make a woman feel truly special.

General Rat picked up this crown of ultimate value. He walked it toward her, lifted it with a bow of his head. She reached for it, but he pulled it back. Waved for her to come closer. She got on her knees. Eye level with the furry general, he placed it on her head. She tingled with entitlement.

"Where are we?" she said.

Vern didn't hear her. He was scooping lard out by the handful. But she wasn't asking him. Wasn't asking the big rat still prostrating himself toward her. She could feel the thick walls around her, the heavy ceiling above. The weight of the building vibrated in her bones. In that moment, all the anxiety fell away like old skin.

She smacked Vern on the back of the head. The rash on his neck was angry red bumps that shined like boils. Three on one side of his neck, three on the other. "Don't eat that," she said. "You're breakin' out."

He scampered off.

Rinks broke open a protein bar. It tasted better than ever. She sighed, let it melt in her mouth. When she was finished, she dropped the wrapper. A mouse dragged it away. She slapped her hands together, no longer thinking of the sky or the way out. She was thinking something entirely different.

"Take me to the top of this turd."

22

The gift sat on the kitchen table. The lid open. Marie had closed it for a while. Now they stared into it, waiting for their aunt and uncle to come springing out like an unshaven Jack-in-the-box wearing a headscarf and clothes too tight. The room was dark. The clock on the stove cast green light.

Fritz put his head down.

Elbows on the table, Marie looked into the box, watched the hovering ball slowly turn. The colors swirling and changing. Her eyelids grew heavy. When soft snores came from across the table, she stood up. Fritz didn't wake up when she shook him. She picked him up, cradled him like a child, and carried him to their room. She stared at the mattress. The patch had given up half the air. She went to their aunt and uncle's room.

She tucked him into bed. He would sleep on a real mattress tonight.

She returned to the kitchen table.

❄

A BOTTLE WOKE HER UP.

It danced on the floor. Marie sat up on the couch, blinking at the early morning light. Fritz was in the kitchen, holding the refrigerator open. Bottles and cups and jars were all around the table. She'd put them there before lying down, a makeshift alarm system should her aunt and uncle pop out of the gift in the middle of the night.

She rubbed her eyes. Something fell on the floor. The nutcracker had somehow ended up on the couch with her. She didn't ask Fritz if he'd put him there to keep her company.

"Well?" Sandy slid toward her. He was half the size, a mini version of what he had been before they went to Candyland. He'd lost so much of himself on the bike ride. Why wasn't he back to normal? *Because it's real,* she thought. *Candyland is real.*

She shook her head. It might be why Sandy was skinny, but Candyland wasn't real. She couldn't think that. If she did, they'd never go back.

The gift was still open. The orb still turning. The colors, however, were muted and muddy. Something had changed. Did something happen to them? Did they not know how to jump out?

Maybe that's the journey. The gift was for them. Aunt Rinks and Uncle Vernon won't come back. That, she thought grimly, *is a true gift.*

Fritz sat at the table with buttered cinnamon toast. "What now?" Sandy said.

"I need to shower."

She climbed off the couch. Stretched the ache in her neck. The weight in her head was heavy. How did this get so complicated? The answer seemed clear enough: go back in, find them, help them return. That would be the right thing to do. Explain where they'd found the gift, what they'd been doing, and why they hadn't told them. *It would all be a mess after that.*

Her decision got even heavier when she looked across the room. In the corner, on Uncle Vernon's desk, the laptop was closed. Marie stopped and went toward it.

❄

Marie didn't know what she was looking for on the laptop. It wasn't what she found.

At first, she was confused by what she was seeing. It was security footage. It took a moment to recognize the room she was seeing. There were blankets on the floor and an old workbench on the wall. It felt like she'd missed the last step on a long staircase. Her stomach surged with panic. She grabbed the desk.

"Go to the bedroom!" she said. "Our bedroom, go there now."

Fritz looked up from his second piece of toast. "We didn't do anything," Sandy pleaded. There was a hurt look in Fritz's eyes.

"You're not in trouble. Just... I need to see something. Go in there, stand there for a few seconds, and come back."

Fritz did exactly that. Marie held her hair back. Her brother came on the screen. He looked around. Sandy was next to him, shrugging. Marie ran to the bedroom with the laptop open. She looked in the corners, at the ceiling, tracking the view on the screen, turning in the direction it was watching her. *There.*

A hole had been drilled into the corner, no wider than a straw. A beady, black dot had been inserted into it.

"What?" Sandy said.

She dropped the laptop on the bench that was suddenly hot. The screen jittered and returned to normal. Marie paced with her hands on her hips, struggling to breathe. *Slowly,* she reminded herself. *Breathe slowly.*

"Hey, look. We're on TV." Sandy waved.

They've known all along! They've been spying on us this entire time!

Of course they knew. That was how Storyteller Corner had appeared. They'd been in there already. They'd pretended to leave yesterday, to follow us in. And then what were they going to do? Her worry for them soured.

She went to the kitchen. The gift was open on the table. She looked through scowling slits at the hovering orb. Reaching behind the box, she pried the lid loose. It snapped closed.

"What are you doing?" Sandy said.

"I've got to think a minute."

"What if they're in there?"

"They are in there!"

Her arms stiffened; fingers clinched. Jaw clenching and unclenching. Fritz recoiled, at first, like she was transforming under a full moon. She closed her eyes, whispered an apology to him through wooden lips. Disgust coated her throat.

"I really need a shower."

※

SHE SHOWERED. She ate breakfast.

She found the cameras in the other rooms. Learned how to scrub back the footage and watched Aunt Rinks and Uncle Vernon come into their room. First, Aunt Rinks reached into the gift. Then Uncle Vernon.

Marie ate lunch.

She spent the afternoon in the backyard, listening to the pond trickle. The teddy and dragon she'd found on the bench that had been covered in weeds now sat in a chair next to her. She closed her eyes and counted her breaths, emptying her mind of prickly thoughts. Angry, redemptive thoughts that didn't go away.

※

"WHAT'S THE PLAN?"

Sandy woke her from a nap. The sun was already heading toward the horizon. Fritz was stacking wood in the firepit, tucking kindling in between logs he'd found by the building. He had a feeling she wasn't in a hurry. She stood up to stretch. Her legs stiff and cold.

"I'm going for a walk," she said.

"Where you going?"

"I don't know. Stay here. I'll be back."

She went on a long walk, past the coffee shop (it was dark inside; the elves were gone from the window) and through the park. She sat near the giant Christmas tree and listened to Christmas music. For a moment, all the thoughts and worries disappeared. Like bubbles in the fountain, that blissful moment would eventually pop. For now, she waded in the tranquility. If not for her brother, she could keep walking and never come back. Get a job, start a new life. Become someone else.

Abandon the journey.

It was dark when she got back. A fire was burning in the ring of stones in the backyard. The little lights blinked in the canopies. A warm glow flickered on Fritz as he played a game on his phone. The nutcracker on his lap.

Sandy didn't say anything when Marie sat next to them. She watched her brother smile. Sandy looked over his shoulder, pointing at the phone, telling him what to do. Making fart sounds. Fritz coughed up a laughing fit.

She could stay here like this. Put the gift in the wall and go on living. They'd be happier. Definitely happier. This was her family, right here. Her brother and an oddball sandman. No one would ask about Aunt Rinks and Uncle Vernon. Maybe they were happy in Candyland. Maybe they belonged there.

The town square clock rang in the distance. A Christmas song played. It was Christmas Eve tomorrow.

Marie wanted Christmas to just be this moment right there at the fire. One thing bothered her, and it wasn't her aunt and uncle. It nagged like a sliver under the skin. She could go back to Candyland sometime later, could finish the journey when she was older. If she hadn't seen the king and queen at the market, she might have done just that.

When the flames died to an orange glow, she turned to her brother and said, "Hey. We need to crash. Got a long day tomorrow."

They slept in the big bed.

❄

In the morning, their backpack was loaded. Marie packed anything of value: Uncle Vernon's watch, Aunt Rinks's headscarves, knives and forks, T-shirts, a screwdriver, a hammer, and a bottle of orange soda.

There was just enough room for the owl clock.

They each took a shower, put on clean clothes, and ate breakfast. The town clock rang at the top of the hour. It played a different tune this day. This day was special. It was Christmas Eve. Fritz was in the kitchen. A glass of milk on the counter along with two unwrapped protein bars on a plate. He was slicing a carrot into orange discs.

"You can't take those with us," Marie said.

She didn't know why he couldn't. He took the milk, protein bars and carrots out the back door. Marie watched through the window; he put the milk and plate on the armrest of one of the chairs, then scattered the carrots on the ground. Sweet boy was leaving them out for Santa. And carrots for his reindeer.

They went to their bedroom, put the gift on the workbench. The orb inside was still muddy and blurred. With Sandy's striped ball in his pocket, Fritz reached into the gift.

Flash.

Marie felt a blow of loneliness inside her. Her brother there one second, gone the next. The walls around her felt cold and bare. She picked up the nutcracker. The red jacket and gold buttons, the sword in his belt. His mouth fell open.

"You're coming this time."

She checked her phone one last time. Aunt Rinks's and Uncle Vernon's locations were still dark. If she would have checked her aunt's social media, things might have gone differently.

But she didn't.

23

Rinks loved it on top. The very tippy top. She always wondered what the view would be like looking down on poor folk. She knew what it felt like looking up. Wishing. Wondering what it was like at the top.

It's pretty great.

The air was sweeter. Like sticky buns in the airport, the tempting smell following wherever you went. When the breeze eased through the window, it felt like a lover blowing in her ear. A high school crush who finally smiled at you. She smiled back. A smile so big the cucumber slices almost slid from her eyes.

She was melting in a full recliner. The rhythmic scritching she heard would sometimes lull her into tiny naps. *Mouse naps,* she thought. And smiled again. Little hands kneaded her arms and legs, her shoulders and feet. Massaged almond oil into her cheeks until they were delicious. Her pores opened, and the sweet sticky bun air seeped inside her. She was full. So full.

Pretty, pretty great.

She was drifting into another mouse nap (*scritch, scritch, scritch*) when a pile of something brassy crashed in the next room. One cucumber slice fell off her face. The other slid down her cheek. She stared at the glittery ceiling. It had been muddy chocolate when she arrived. *Enough with the chocolate!* she had ordered. It was smothered in diamonds an hour later.

"Vern!" she shouted.

He muttered. He was always muttering now. Nonstop nonsense. Having conversations when she wasn't in the room. He hadn't slept since the teacup ride.

Rinks pulled the cucumber off her face, dabbed it in a bowl of powdered sugar and took a bite. The Jojos continued rubbing and kneading her with little pink feet. They would massage until she told them to stop. They were like Vern: never tired. They wore little headscarves (she designed them). Tiny jars of oil dangled from belts that crisscrossed their backs. Lemon oil, coconut oil, almond oil. Vanilla. Whatever she was in the mood for.

She studied her nails. They'd been filed to points, painted red and white and coated and buffed. "Very nice, Jojo." She blew on them like a fancy lady would. "I like the feel."

She called all the mice Jojo. She tried to name them, but there were too many of them. The first one she named Jojo. That was as far as she got. It was better than *mouse*. More personal. The Jojo who had done the nails on that hand bowed. His emery board took the place of his weapon. She stuck out her pinky.

"I'm feeling a hangnail."

He went to work. *Scritch, scritch, scritch.*

The foot squad had done an impressive job on her toenails. They shined like the hood of a sports car. They were sanding the calluses on the sides of her big toes. A pile of dead skin fell like parmesan cheese.

Two new cucumber slices were hauled up to her eyes. She ate them instead, bathing in the shiny room, surrounded by everything she ever wanted. Figurines and dolls and metal cars and expensive paintings. Wigs, sweaters, eye shadow, hats. Three shelves of flip-flops. If she thought of something, she said it out loud. It appeared. There was even a shelf of trophies with her name on them. First place for tennis. Winner of bowling. World champion sprinter. Billiards, wrestling, and archery. Cheerleading was the biggest of them all. The gold figure on top with spiky pom-poms.

She scrolled through her phone. Her last three posts since she got to the top were killing it. More likes than ever. And she hadn't paid for a single one. She'd suggested to a Jojo it would be nice if there were more likes. Maybe he had something to do with it. The last post —her lying in a pile of gold coins—was trending. *I just want to be me,* she had written.

She sighed. *Pretty, pretty great.*

A cottony cloud eased past the open window. If it came closer, she would reach out and tear off a bite. It would melt in her mouth. She'd done it twice already. The pink sky was flawless. As the cotton-candy cloud moved closer, she sat up. She frowned. Someone had cut a hole in the pinkness.

A black square hung like an odd-shaped moon.

She flung the cucumbers against the wall. The Jojos scattered. The bowl hit the floor. She slipped off the recliner, her feet soft and oily, and almost rolled herself in the powdered sugar. She leaned out the window.

"Vern!"

She could feel them now. They were out there. Smelled the little goodie-goodies coming to do goodie-goodie. A sick feeling coated her throat. Her lips contorted. Her face wrestled over a frown and a smile.

"Couldn't stay away, could you?" she muttered. "Come on, you little brats. See what mama built."

The exit in the sky was open for a while. And then it was gone. *They closed it! They didn't even come looking for us!* By the second night, Rinks didn't want to leave. She only wished the little turd brains would come back. She wanted them to see what mama had done to the place. This lump of chocolate had become something worthy. Ask any Jojo. It was a silly castle with a silly princess locked inside (they hadn't found a princess anywhere, but that was the rumor). Rinks made it sturdy. She made it thick and hard and unyielding.

She made it a big deal.

She turned her back and lifted her phone. The angle was right.

She could get a selfie with Rose Lake below her. Confectionville beyond. A post like that would blow her followers' minds. They'd swear it was fake. In just two days, her face had narrowed. Her cheeks had hollowed, and her nose glowed a pretty pink. The crown, though —oh, that crown. A million-dollar crown for a million-dollar lady.

"Lady Rinks."

She was too distracted by the bling to notice the white hair on her nose. She had had several plucked from her chin that morning (hurt worse than a waxing). There were three times as many now. Thick and pokey.

Vern crashed into the room. All the things he was carrying went to the floor. Vases and coins, polished rocks and knives and forks. He searched every floor, every room (they were endless), stuffing what he found in pockets and pouches. When they filled up, he stuck them in corners. He was bent over from hauling this stuff around. A hump had formed on his back. He must have just raided a wardrobe because no less than twenty silk scarves were wrapped around his neck.

"What?" he said, gathering his loot.

"Forget it." His whiskers were stiff and white and an inch long on his upper lip. She thought of doing a selfie with him, but gross. "The kids are comin'."

"They can't have any."

He twitched like a broken toy. Eyes big in their sockets. He looked sick. That rash on his neck might be infected. She was glad the scarves covered it up. There was probably a doctor down there somewhere. Probably not one for humans. He would be all right. He seemed happy.

"Go," she said.

He scurried off. His conversation faded down the hall. At least he had himself to talk to. Rinks snapped a selfie. *Love yourself,* she wrote. Then looked out the window.

"Come to mama, little chickens."

24

"So good to be back," Sandy exclaimed. He drew a deep breath (as if he really breathed). *Are we really breathing?*

Marie grimaced. Sandy didn't notice the air smelled different. Something foul was beneath the cool draft of peppermint. She marched through the Almond and Raisin Gate and over the bridge, unaware Nussknacker—whom she had been holding tightly when she entered—was no longer in her hand.

"Once upon a time…"

She waited on the other side of the bridge. The bells rang, and the shadow circled like a dense cloud. Ronin hit the ground like an armored truck. The earth shuddered. The sleigh slid to a stop.

Garl leaped up and said, "Merry, merry! Ronin Express at your—"

"Take us to Confectionville." Marie climbed onto the back seat. "Straight away. No tours or stories. Put the shield up, or whatever it is, to keep the wind off us."

Ronin looked back. Black eyes twinkling, he pawed a rut in the turf.

Fritz and Sandy sat next to her. Garl stroked the braids in his beard. With a nod, he said, "Right."

In moments, they were in the air. The wind did not erode Sandy.

They rode without talking, clenching the seat as they sped straight for Gumdrop Alley. When they landed, Marie was stepping out before the sleigh came to a stop. She ran her hand along Ronin's flank and ducked under his swaying antlers.

"Thank you, Ronin." She continued walking. "Once upon a time…"

❄

A SPACE between the gingerbread rowhouses opened, and Hussar Peregrinations grew out of it. Marie went inside and pushed the button. While the dominos and springs worked their way to the back room, she unzipped the backpack. When Pate came out on his cuckoo-clock tongue depressor, the owl clock was waiting for him on the counter.

"I need a cookie cutter. This is payment."

Pate's eyebrows rose. While his eyes didn't show it, amazement beamed off him. His wounded arm dangled at his side (she wondered where her ribbon had gone). The bell over the door rang as Fritz and Sandy entered. Pate paid them no attention. He stroked the owl wings with his good arm.

"Give this to the hussars at the market." He raised his arm when she dug in the backpack for something else. He went to the back room. A moment later, the cookie cutter came out.

"I need something else," she said. "A shield or something to keep the wind off my friend."

She pointed at Sandy, who was half the size he had been the last time they were in the store. Pate returned to the counter with what looked like a fruit cake. Jelly beads imbedded in the dense loaf. He told her what to do with it. She offered what was in the backpack. He wouldn't take it.

At the gutter, she stuck the fruitcake on the handlebars. With Sandy prepared to waterski on the back of the cookie cutter, she put her feet on the pegs. They blazed past the gingerbread buildings without the wind in their ears or grit on their faces.

The castle approached.

※

IT WAS TALLER THAN BEFORE. The sides of it were thick and lumpy. It glittered with cheap jewels. It was fat with excess. The hard shell of a prison littered with scaffolding. The center spire speared the puffy clouds in the pink sky.

It was gross.

The bell tolled somewhere on the castle. The tinted water of Rose Lake rippled. All around them, the inhabitants of the market leaped and cheered. They threw arms and limbs around each other and began to sing.

It's Christmas Eve, it's Christmas Eve. Time to smile and not to grieve.

"Stay here." She climbed off the cookie cutter. "I'll be right back."

She worked her way through the celebration, bumping into the line of dwarves they had seen before (now with their arms around each other, singing with big grins) and through a formation of twirling ballerinas.

Family and fun and all loved ones will be with us together.

The hussars were marching around their cart of nuts, below the banner that read *Support the Troops*. Their jaws snapped open and closed as they sang. Marie placed the owl clock in front of them.

"From Pate," she shouted. "For the troops."

They halted as Pate had done. Their finely pressed uniforms creased as they raised their arms to salute her. Then they ogled the owl clock like fine art. She turned to leave, but they stopped her. One of them dug through a pile of walnuts and pecans and Brazil nuts. He came up with a hard-shelled nut with black and white striped grooves. It looked just like the ball Godfather had given Fritz. And just as heavy.

"What's this?" she said.

"It is yours."

She ran her thumb in the grooves. It was as solid as granite and heavy as iron. It was then she realized the nutcracker she'd picked up in the bedroom was no longer with her. It was like he disappeared. *Why didn't I notice?*

She put the heavy nut in her pocket.

The chime of the last bell faded. The marketgoers gave one final huzzah, hugged whoever was next to them, and went about their business as Christmas music played. Two figures in hooded cloaks walked among them. Marie didn't hesitate.

She gave impolite chase toward the only humans she'd ever seen in Candyland. *Aunt Rinks?* she wondered. *Have they been here long enough to hide from us?* Marie apologized as she knocked things over and scattered produce from baskets, but she didn't slow down. No matter how fast she ran, she didn't gain ground. The distance between her and the hooded royal couple remained the same. She pushed harder, ignored the irritated pleas of those she offended.

The barge was up ahead. Square-headed workers were untying the mooring rope. A bassoon horn blared from the crates stacked three high on its deck. *King Chocolate* was written on the sides of the crates. The couple, arm in arm, boarded the ramp leading up to it.

"Wait!" Marie shouted. "Wait for me!"

The ramp was pulled on board. The barge drifted away from the port. Just as she approached the widening gap in full sprint, she leaned back and skidded to the edge. The couple was somewhere in the stacks. She looked down into the raspberry water. The waves rebounded off the port. There was something odd about it.

She didn't see herself in the water. No clouds above or shadows below. Just a pure body of water of nothingness.

❅

"We have to cross on our own," she said.

Fritz nodded. He knew the journey ended in the castle. That was where Princess Pirlipat was. Where the cloaked couple was leading them. Marie knew, somehow, no matter how many times she returned, she would never get to the market in time to catch the barge.

"Once upon a time, there was a boat."

A storybook rowboat appeared on the shore. There were two bench seats and two oars. Painted across the flatback stern was one word. *Nussknacker.*

"Whoa, whoa," Sandy said. "Remember what the dwarves said about boats."

"We don't have a choice. It's too far to swim."

"When it sinks, what do you think we'll be doing."

"It's not going to sink."

There wasn't a cloud in the sky. Not even a breeze. The water was as smooth as a window. They were going to paddle across it because that was the story she was telling.

No one at the market was alarmed that a rowboat appeared. They didn't stop Marie and Fritz from climbing onto it. Sandy worked his way onto the back bench next to Fritz. The bow of the boat rose out of the water even with Marie in the front. She shoved off with an oar and leaned back to counterbalance their weight.

She pulled long, easy strokes. The rosy water hardly rippled around the paddles. They dipped beneath the surface and found purchase when she pulled. The shore receded. They cut effortlessly toward the hulking shadow. Each stroke raised gooseflesh on the back of her neck, cool and damp.

They were a third of the way across when her arms started to burn. The boat, for some reason, had leveled out. They were no longer heavy on the stern. In fact, the bow was starting to surge down with each stroke. Marie leaned forward a bit. She pushed the oars out of the water for a rest.

The market was starting to stir.

It was as if they had just noticed a boat was on Rose Lake. The good-natured laughter and cheer sounded a bit strange. They were agitated, jumping around and running to the sidewalk. Marie put her hand above her eyes and squinted. The hussars had abandoned their cart. They pulled their weapons and shouted orders. The public got out of their way. The clang of metal sounded like tiny pins dropping on an aluminum sheet.

"Look!" Sandy pointed at the shore.

Something small had leaped into the water. Something followed it. Then a horde of little things followed. The surface of the lake shimmered. Torpedoes were coming.

"Go!" Sandy shouted.

Marie dug until her shoulders were on fire. Each pull was harder than the one before it. The rowboat slugged forward only when the oars moved. The water hadn't changed, but it felt like rowing through molasses. Sweat gathered on her brow, streaked down her back. Fritz came up to help her. Water splashed over the bow.

"No. No, go back."

They were heavy up front. The weight had shifted, like something was pushing them back. Water lapped against the bow. It sprayed on her back each time she leaned into a stroke. Puddles formed in the bottom of the boat. Fritz began scooping it out with his hands. Marie dared a look behind her. They were past the halfway point. Maybe three-quarters.

"Oh, gross." Sandy's skinny head spun around. The sand dollars were full circles. "Mice."

Marie could see them now. The little torpedoes were gaining on them. The pink noses above the water; tails whipping behind them. Tiny legs paddling below in a migrating V formation.

Marie closed her eyes. And pulled.

Breathing hot exhaust, the perfumed air roasted her lungs. She could feel the castle like a magnet pushing against them. Her skin hummed and itched. Her back was soaked. Her bottom slid on the wet bench. The splashing against the bow grew louder. Each stroke pulled a wave into the boat. Fritz used his hat to bail the deepening pool.

"They're going back!" Sandy shouted.

Marie eased her next stroke. The rowboat stopped. The torpedoes shattered into chaos. The mice struggled to stay above water, turning around and swimming back to the shore. It looked like a nest of giant water bugs climbing over each other.

The bow bobbed inches above the water. The stern hovered off the surface. "Go to the back, the very back," she told Fritz. "Hold the boat down."

They did what she said. It helped a little. Water sloshed around her ankles. The bow barely moved. She pulled the oars again. *One more,* she chanted. *One more.*

The rowboat wobbled side to side. Water surged from front to back with each stroke, and they were hardly moving. She dug deep into her arms to find another pull, propped her feet on the bench behind her and leaned. *One more. One—*

The tip of the boat went under. It didn't come up.

Crimson water poured in. The back of the boat rose off the lake. Fritz grabbed Sandy. Sandy's branches wrapped around him. Marie scrambled over the benches for her brother. The oars plunked into the lake behind her.

"Grab your sister, kid." Sandy shoved Fritz at her. "Hang onto her!"

Fritz landed in Marie's lap. He was holding one of Sandy's branches. The boat heaved to one side. Marie put her arm around Fritz's chest. The water was frigid and heavy. She paddled at it with one arm.

"It'll be all right." Sandy was perched on the corner of the boat. "You're going to make it."

The world turned rosy red.

25

Rinks had camped at the window for hours, elbows on the ledge, eye to a telescope. Canvasing up and down Gumdrop Alley and along the market. A Jojo on each shoulder, working out the kinks in her shoulder blades. One on her back. A Jojo on each foot.

If you've never had a Jojo scalp massage, she thought, *you've never had a massage.* The tiny feet. They get right in there. They found exactly what she needed. Like they read her mind. A little to the left...

Perfect.

The market was slammed with weird things. Creatures, she called them. *What else do you call them?* They were toys and cookies and dwarves that made no sense. They were flat and small and boxy and twisted. Ugly, most of them. And they didn't even know it. Weirdos.

The bells went off at the top of the hour. The countdown to Christmas followed. The castle walls vibrated with each gong. The freakos at the market did what they did when they heard it. They danced with no rhythm, twirled and jumped and scooted and marched. From this far up, she couldn't hear them sing. Thank God.

"Look at them," she muttered. "A bunch of stupid muppets."

She had watched enough to know it never changed. They went about the day like the world's kookiest musical.

"Tell me somethin'," she said, "do they even exist if we're not here?"

The Jojo on her head squeaked an answer. It sounded neutral. She didn't speak Jojo. It was a good question, though. She felt smart for thinking it. Like that one about the tree falling in the woods.

"A little to the right."

The Jojo found the spot. She closed her eyes and melted.

"What about you?" She looked at General Rat. "What were you doin' before we got here?"

Squeak.

"Here's another question. Why do you fight the soldiers? They look down on you, is that it? Think you're less than them?" She went back to the telescope. "Well, look who's lookin' down now. Am I right?"

Up and down Gumdrop Alley, no sign of Miss Pretty-Pretty. Maybe they were waiting for Rinks and Vern to come out. They could wait all day and night. They weren't coming out any time soon. Far as she was concerned, they could lock that gift up and throw away the key. Rinks was fine and dandy where she was. Vern, too. If the kids did come inside the castle, they were just going to make trouble. Them and those soldiers. She just knew it. So she kept watching.

"Somethin' to eat," she called. *Squeak-squeak.* "Surprise me."

The pitter-patter of feet went down the hallway. She liked that. The obedience. It was pure. Maybe she was getting the hang of speaking Jojo. The subtleties of the squeak. Vern had picked up on it right away. In some ways, he was smart. Dumb as a chocolate drop in others.

The fools were still dancing the day away in the market. She panned all the way to the end. The boxy robots were still loading the barge with crates. Special deliveries from King Chocolate. Pure cacao to make the castle bigger and better and thicker. A rock of tastiness. She'd never met King Chocolate, of course. He was an ally, for some reason. Why, she didn't know. The crates came like clockwork. Once she sorted out her niece and nephew, she'd tour the land, meet this ally of hers. She wondered what he looked like. Tall and skinny? Probably fat. And weird.

Maybe it's better not to meet him.

Two Jojos arrived with a coconut bowl filled with strawberry milk (the instant kind like she had when she was little) and a hollow Twizzler. She gave it a stir and sucked it through the Twizzler.

"Mmm." She nodded her approval. Pointed at her shoulders. The Jojos went back to work.

She slurped while she watched. You'd think a freak show like that would never get boring. They were done dancing and singing, back to milling around selling nuts and springs and googly eyes for sock puppets.

Something was different. In the middle of the squatty and skinny and twisted were two tall figures who wore hooded cloaks. They didn't seem in a hurry. Rinks focused the telescope. It was hard to tell, but she thought they were holding hands.

"Who's that?"

The squeaking did her no good. It wasn't Marie and Fritz. They were too tall, for one. They held hands like a couple, also. She couldn't see their faces, hidden deep in the cowls, but she'd bet a bowl of strawberry milk they were people.

They stopped at the barge.

"Hey! Hey, hey, hey. What are they doin'? I didn't say they could come here." She turned to General Rat. "Tell them to get off."

The big-bellied rat saluted. Then gabbed a bunch of squeaky nonsense.

"Vern!"

Back to the telescope. The loading robots ignored them. The idiots were supposed to bring crates only. Not people! This was not cool. Something had to be done. Rules. *Laws!*

"Look, I can't understand you," she shouted at General Rat. "Learn English, you furry squid. Use your hand to write it down. What are they doin' on my barge? Vern!"

Chains rattled. A box closed. Her husband was dragging something in the hallway just outside the room. A rank smell of body odor ruined the vibe. Rinks told a Jojo to light a candle.

"It's the king and queen," he said from the hallway.

"Who?" Rinks said.

"The people down there, on the barge. He said it's the king and queen."

"What king and queen? We're the king and queen." She looked at General Rat and declared, "We're king and queen!"

"He says the king is mad at us."

"For what?"

"For eating the lard."

"Lard... what in the... what does that even mean?"

There were voices in the hallway. A brief conversation. Laughter.

"Who's out there with you?" Rinks said. "Vern?"

"It's me!"

She jumped. His reply was tempered and sharp. More things rattled and thumped. He was sorting through the things he'd found. It was nonstop, the way he stuffed his pockets. "Stop hoarding! We live here, Vern. This is *our* stuff now. *We* are the king and queen. These are *our* soldiers." The Jojos saluted. *Our soldiers.* "Listen, all of you. Go down there. When the barge docks, tell those two they don't live here anymore. Candyland is under new management. There's plenty of places for them to live, not here. No vacancy, get it? Hotel full. Tell them to beat it. If they don't, run them down. Got it?"

They saluted. Then they were off, scrambling through their mice holes and down however many flights it would take to get to the first floor. *A hundred?*

"And someone make me another coconut bowl!"

Back at the telescope, the barge had shoved off. It was a slow-moving thing, but not slow enough. She didn't need royalty wandering the halls and screwing up this sweet gig. If it was war they wanted, Rinks had a bazillion Jojos to throw at them. What were their wooden soldiers going to do, crack walnuts at them? Jojos had needle teeth and soft, little hands.

The soldiers in the market didn't even seem to recognize the king and queen. If they were royalty, why didn't they have a guard? Rinks focused on a display of nuts. There was something on the cart she recognized. It looked just like—

"What's the owl clock doin' here?"

A second later, she caught sight of someone running through the market.

❄

"THE KIDS ARE HERE!"

Marie had been talking to Fritz. That sandman was there (and fit right in with the weirdos). He'd lost some weight. A whole bunch of it. Looked like he'd stared into a fan too long. They were on the shore, looking at the castle. Rinks wasn't ready for them. She just wanted them to go away now that she had the king and queen to deal with. There wasn't a bridge to cross, and they'd missed the barge.

"Wait. Is that a..."

She refocused. Maybe she'd missed it before. She could've sworn there was nothing on the shore.

"They can't cross," Vern said.

"Well, they got a boat, Vern."

"The general said it won't work."

"Do you know how boats work?" she shouted. "They're gettin' into the boat. And now... yep. They're rowin' it, Vern. They're rowin' the boat and *crossin' the lake!*"

General Rat squeaked orders to the remaining Jojos in the room. Just in case he didn't understand what was going on, Rinks made it crystal.

"Stop them! I don't want them over here, you understand me? Do something!"

"General says they have to go around. Get them from the market side."

"I don't care if you shoot them from a cannon. Stop. THEM!"

Not a single Jojo was left in the room after that. Even the general scrammed. Vern was muttering to himself in the hallway, dragging chains and stuff. Rinks switched between the barge and rowboat. Her pulse quickened. She was going to puke a fountain of strawberry milk if something didn't happen and soon. This was Marie's fault. She made her sick. She had a way of making Rinks feel small. Useless. Even after all Rinks did for her.

"Just go away."

The market was in chaos. Rinks thought, for just a second, they were cheering on the rowboat. The weirdo traitors. The red water began to ripple. It looked like an arrow pushing off the shore, aimed for the little boat.

"Oh." Rinks fanned the sweat on her cheeks. "My little Jojos, go. Go with your little feet. Stop those wicked little ones."

Finally, someone was on her side. *Someone's fightin' for me.*

The wave closed in on the rowboat. Marie was getting tired. The weak girl couldn't even row across a pond.

"Surround them. Push them back, my little darlin's. Send them home and tell them never come back. Make them—what are you doin'? No. No, no, no... *go back!*"

The Jojos, for no reason at all, turned around. They were heading back to the market. Did they not get the memo? This wasn't an exercise. This was a mission.

"You're goin' the wrong way!" She waved her arms. No one was in the room to help her. "Go back! Go—"

The boat, however, was stuck. It heaved forward. The back end rose out of the water. And then, just like that, it was gone.

"Huh." Rinks scanned the lake. It was as smooth as polished marble. "You were right," she said to no one. "Yay, Rose Lake."

Did they drown? She never thought to ask.

❄

A SHOWER of relief washed away the nausea. She was in the mood for a nosh. Maybe a plate of string cheese with some fruit roll-ups. There were no Jojos to get it for her, though. General Rat trotted into the room. He hopped on her leg, climbed up her arm.

"One problem solved," she said. "You, my furry general, are in line for a medal. I need you to find our royal guests and send them packin'. Maybe send them for a swim with my niece and nephew. Can you do that? Good." She kissed the general's pink nose. "Off you go, stinker."

Say what you will about rats, that general is a loyal soldier. She had no doubt he would see to the king and queen. If that was what they were. Could be bums, for all she knew.

Rinks was alone with her telescope and Vern's racket. Worse than the banging and clanging and scraping and hoarding was his constant chatter. He was like a room full of people with a room full of opinions.

"Vern, can you cut it for a second? I'm gettin' a migraine listenin' to you. Shut up!" There was silence, then whispers. "I've been thinkin', it's time to make us official king and queen of this dingbat land. There needs to be a ceremony. Somethin' to introduce us to the people… or whatever they are."

The whispering grew louder. This had to end. She put up with his snoring at night. She wasn't going to listen to this all day.

"Did you hear what I said?"

She shoved out of the recliner. Pinpricks tingled on her soles. Her feet had fallen asleep. She bit her lip as the feeling slowly came back, wobbling across the room. Vern wasn't in the hallway. It wasn't hard to find him. All she had to do was follow the scarves. She'd lost count of how many he'd been wearing around his neck. He wasn't muttering anymore. The idiot probably overheated and passed out.

"Vern?"

The trail of scarves, some tattered and chewed, led her to an arching doorway. The idiot was eating perfectly good scarves! The room inside was spacious. A mountain of stuff was piled in the corner —blankets and chairs and hats, framed paintings and footstools and boxes. A giant glass display case was against the wall, and deep gouges were in the floor where he'd dragged it across the room. The shelves inside the display were full of shiny things. Vern was on top of the pile, digging like a squirrel hiding a nut. He was gabbing to himself.

Rinks stopped to listen. There was something odd about the voices, something she hadn't put her finger on until now. They all sounded like him. But they were talking at the same time.

"Vern?"

He jerked around with a snort and a squeak. "What?" he said. And said it seven times.

Rinks threw her arm up and looked away. She closed her eyes. Maybe she didn't see that right. The light was an odd color, and she was a bit stressed. Slowly, she looked between her fingers.

No. She saw it right.

It was worse than a car accident. She lifted her phone to snap a photo. No one was going to believe this.

26

Marie woke on a soft shore. Water lapped her waist. Hair soaked.

A dark monstrosity was behind her, soaring up and disappearing into a delicious pink sky. Little things crawled along scaffolding like insects, packing globs of chocolate onto the walls. The spires like drip castles made of sand.

She rolled onto her side, wiping her face. Rose Lake tasted like a honeyed tonic of flowers. Mud squeezed between her fingers like soupy cookie dough. She coughed and sputtered, blowing strings of snot from her nose. Colorful beads dotted her hands.

"Fritz."

She climbed through the slop, clawing at soft, chocolatey boulders wedged against Marchpane Castle. Her brother was curled between sloping wall flares, shivering and weeping. His hands clutched to his chest. She pulled him close and wrapped her arms around him. The lake was pristine: not a wave, not a ripple. Across the way, the market was back to normal.

"Hey, hey." The bill of his cap dripped sweet-smelling water. "We made it. We're all right."

He was inconsolable. Something lay near their feet. She reached into the water. Marie looked around. She held him tighter, rocked him back and forth. His cheek, pressed against her chest, convulsed. The black square stared down from the sky. *This wasn't supposed to be like this.*

The journey sounded fun. Exciting. Discovery and adventure. Now they were marooned at the foot of a monstrous lump of castle. Marie holding a tree branch.

"He's all right." She squeezed her brother. "He'll be back, I promise."

The barge was docking at the castle. The gate lowered on massive chains; colorful links looked like loops of cereal. Boxy robots waited to unload the cargo. Two hooded figures slipped between the crates and entered the castle.

"We have to go." She picked him up. "We'll never finish the journey if we stop now."

His legs buckled like loose hinges. They made it three steps before he collapsed. A sand dollar fell from his hands. There was nothing more she could say. *He'll be back,* she told herself. *He has to come back.*

She hoisted her brother onto her back. His arms hung like wet socks over her shoulders. She trudged along the castle wall, footsteps sinking into the mud. Her legs like boneless putty. Arms weak from rowing.

"We can do this," she told him. And told herself, "We have to."

Why? Why do we have to do this? Because the journey wasn't optional anymore. *We'll have to do it at some point.*

❋

THE LOADERS on the barge didn't stop them from climbing to the gate. They waited for them to pass before rolling a crate through the bay door. Crates were parked along an endless hallway. Some of the tops had been broken up. *Paperland* was written on the sides.

Candles flickered on candy dishes mounted on the walls. Drippings of chocolate puddled under them. The air was dense and sickly sweet. The sound of distant Christmas music from outside quickly muffled away. Even the loaders barely made noise when they dropped a crate.

Fritz walked alongside her now. Dark smudges colored his cheeks where he wiped his face. He sniffed every now and then. Their footsteps were dull thuds on the firm floor. The doors along the hall were locked when they tried to open them. Farther down the hallway, pictures appeared in ornate frames. Each one posted above a candle. The dim candlelight made it hard to see them. One looked like a beach. Another of a ski slope. A decorated Christmas tree.

They were familiar.

She tried several doors, all of them locked. *How many more doors are there...?* The end of the hallway still wasn't in sight. She whispered at her brother lagging far behind. Her voice died in the thick air. He was looking at a photo. She went back to get him. Stopped when she saw what he saw. It was a picture of a house.

What's that doing here?

It was white with green shutters, the kind of shutters that were decorative and not functional. Wooden steps led to the front porch, where a swing was chained to the ceiling. A swing where you could idle on a summer day and drink soda and tell stories. She knew the handrail leading up to the porch was rotting, something that was always meant to be fixed but never was. She didn't have to see the railing to know it hadn't been fixed.

It was the house they grew up in.

They put their arms around each other. His longing was a cold wind that echoed inside an empty canyon. It was in her, too. She tried not to feel it, to stuff it back in the emotional black box. She couldn't look inside it. If she did, she wouldn't be able to hold her brother up.

Doubt took hold of her. It turned her back toward the open door, where the barge was pulling away from the castle. She thought about taking her brother outside to look up at the sky and leap through the exit. They could go back; they could close the gift forever and never look back.

Then the hooded figures exited a room.

"Hey! Stop!" Marie shouted. "Help us!"

They didn't stop, walking calmly away. The candles snuffed out as the figures passed them. Darkness fell around them. Marie held onto her brother. She dragged her hand along the soft wall, leaving tracks in it, feeling it curl under her fingernails. Slowing as it grew darker. Something was ahead of them. A large structure anchored in the middle of the corridor. Carefully, they approached, reaching their hands out to avoid running into the unexpected.

It was a staircase.

The hall met with another hall that went perpendicular in both directions. This was the center of the castle. They stood in the intersection and looked up. A vertical tunnel bored straight up a silo. A railing and steps spiraled around the perimeter, an infinite corkscrew that would reach the sky. Somewhere up there, footsteps were climbing.

I can't do that, was her first thought. *I can't climb that far.*

She didn't have the strength, even if she wasn't carrying her brother. It was too much. "Wait!" she called. "Please."

The mysterious couple didn't come for them. Their ascent faded with each passing minute. Fritz put his hand in hers. They stood there, looking up, when they heard more footsteps coming from behind. Maybe the cloaked couple hadn't gone up the steps after all. Relief filled her with a temporary surge of strength. She couldn't see anyone coming, though. And the footsteps were different.

There were a lot of them.

The pitter-patter was joined by tiny metal clangs. Nothing, however, was there. Then she noticed, more like felt, the floor moving. It looked like a wave coming down the corridor. As it passed through a candlelit section, just before vanishing in the dark, she saw it.

She threw her brother behind her. Marie felt her legs stiffen and arms harden. Her jaw swelled and jutted out. She felt heavy, unyielding. In the dark, something about her was changing. When an idea occurred to her, she softened, felt more like herself when she said: "Hang onto me."

Fritz threw his arms over her shoulders. She locked his hands together, told him to close his eyes and not let go. There was no going back. The journey had only one direction now.

"Once upon a time..."

※

A STRAP DROPPED down from above.

She wrapped it around her hands several times, yanked on it to make sure it was secure. She raised her arms. Her heels lifted off the floor. Then her toes. She began floating. A bright red balloon bobbed over their heads.

A mouse leaped and caught her shoestring. A little metal breastplate banged against the sole of her shoe. She kicked it off. The mouse fell with it, his helmet rolling across the floor like a die. The vermin army jumped up and down like popcorn on a hot skillet. Throwing toothpick spears that clattered back to the ground. Many of them flooded toward the stairs.

Soon, she couldn't see or hear them.

Up. Up. Up.

The air grew colder. They floated in silence. Only the sound of Fritz's chattering teeth in her ear. They were going all the way to the top. This was where the journey was taking them. Deep down, Marie knew she'd been avoiding this trip. The emotional black box began to quake inside her.

"It's going to be all right," she whispered to Fritz. Then to herself.

27

"What happened to you?" Rinks said.

A garble of overlapping voices replied. Seven of them, to be exact. Because there were seven heads. Seven mousy heads crammed onto her husband's shoulders. Each wearing a crown. One head was bigger than the rest. That was Vern. The rest had sprouted from those boils on his neck, all jammed together and yammering at Rinks.

"Shut up!" she said. "I'm talkin' to Vern."

"I am Vern," they said.

She had to look away. All his personalities were on display, busting out so their voice could be heard. Sad Vern. Happy Vern. Angry Vern. Sweet Vern. Serious Vern. Fun Vern. It was all very disturbing, the way they were crammed together and twisting about. Made her stomach curdle.

"Are you okay?" she said softly. "Does it hurt?"

"Hurt?" they said. "I'm just lookin' for my…"

They all said something different. *Snack, belt, button, cup, key, ring, hat.* He dug like a squirrel looking for acorns. Things flew between his legs: pots, pens, feathers, flowers, pillows, shirts. The heads argued where to look and what to grab. Like seven captains steering a boat.

"Vern!" When she had the attention of all seven, she said, "It's goin' to be all right. This is all make-believe, like you said. When we go back, you'll just be, you know... *normal*."

They twisted and turned to each other, their crowns sliding one way or the other, muttering to each other. Confused. Thing was, Rinks didn't plan on going back. And as long as she was here, this was her husband. She could get used to it. Maybe. But the yammering? *One Vern at a time, please.*

"Right now, we have a problem," she said. "They're comin' up. When they get here, they're goin' to take *aaaaaallll* this stuff away. Unless we stop them."

He gathered an armful of bedsheets. "Who's comin'?"

"Who do you think? The general and the Jojos went to stop them. If they don't, we have to be ready. Are you ready to fight, Vern?"

His hand went to the jeweled hilt of a sword. (*Where did he get a weapon?*) Knuckles big and hairy. *Gag.*

"We're king and queen, Vern. You and me. This is ours now. You understand?"

He sniffed the air, nose twisting. Long whiskers twitching. Rinks shivered and swallowed a knot of disgust.

"Go clean yourself up," she said. "We need to get ready. You smell like a litter box. And here, put this on."

She pulled a coat from the pile. It was long, the material soft and clean. More importantly, it was huge. She held it up. Vern climbed off his treasure, let her drape it over his shoulders. She pulled it up and over the heads and tucked it down in there.

"Ack!"

"I can't breathe!"

Vern threw it off. The six heads she'd tried to hide huffed like she'd tried to suffocate them. She hadn't thought of that. Maybe they could be twisted off like warts.

"What are you tryin' to do?" they said.

"That's not goin' to do, Vern. That look." She painted him with a gesture. "You're hideous."

"Me? Look at you."

"What about me?" She fixed her crown.

He scrambled up the pile. Things cascaded down and clanged and rolled. He came back with a copper frying pan. Held it up. Her bronzy reflection was soft and distorted. Her hair was a nest of gray sprigs. And her eyes were shiny black balls bulging from their sockets.

She touched her face, felt the pointy end of her nose, the bristled poke of whiskers around the scar on her cheek. She threw the pan across the room.

"Lies!"

Vern chased after it. He bumped into the glass display. It teetered off balance but stayed upright. He buried the pan under a loosely rolled rug. Sat on it like a goose on a golden egg.

"Is that all you care about, this stuff? Do you even care about me?"

There was a brief discussion. Then they all said: "Yes." Then they said, "This, too. I like you and this."

She straightened her collar and smoothed the kinky hair on her head. "I will make you noodles, Vern." *Well, the Jojos will.* "Noodles and cheese. You like cheese?"

Their tongues licked wet, black lips.

"We can have whatever we want, Vern. But we need to protect each other. We need to protect this castle so we never get hurt again. Ever. No one can touch us in here. You understand?"

The sharp blade slinked from the scabbard on his hip. The tip gleamed as he leveled it at her. She fell back a step. Maybe they changed their minds about what was important. If they turned him against her, she was truly alone. They squirmed like a litter of freakish puppies, trying to look behind her. She turned around.

A hooded figure stood in the doorway.

It stood still, watching. Wispy clouds steamed from the blackness inside the cowl. Rinks recoiled from a sudden wave of pain and discomfort.

"Get it!" She pointed. "Get it, Vern!"

The threat startled the mystery person, who Rinks assumed was the exiled queen coming to take everything from them. Rinks jumped into the hall, watched her go. The cloak brushed the floor behind her.

"Vern, we have to—"

The door slammed shut. The sound of trinkets being buried came from inside the room. Pretty clear what was more important. Rinks ran in the opposite direction of the queen. She turned left at the first hallway. This way wasn't familiar. She turned around and went right instead. The doors all looked the same. There were no windows. The walls muddy brown. *I don't remember the walls curvin'.*

"General!" She was running now. "Where are you?"

Totally lost, peeking around corners to avoid running into the queen, she ran. She just wanted to get back to her room. Finally, at the end of a long corridor, pink light filled an open doorway. She ran to her room and slammed the door. It was chilly inside. Cold sweat ran from beneath the hard band of her crown. The Jojos must have turned on the air conditioning. They knew she was hot. Sweet things.

She put her back to the door. Her chest burned; side stitched. When she opened her eyes, things got worse.

The queen was already in the room.

28

The staircase spiraled down a hundred stories. The mouse army wouldn't reach the top any time soon. Her skin was raw from the bindings she'd wrapped around her wrists when the balloon carried them up. Fritz held her hand tenderly with concern.

"I'm okay," she said. The hallways went in different directions. "Stay close, okay? Don't leave me."

She was fragile and scared. Her bones were cold. She questioned everything now.

"We need to find a window, see the sky. In case we need to leave. Okay?"

He nodded.

They went in one direction, tried some of the doors. They stopped to listen. When they backtracked, the halls were different. Like they had shifted with new openings and more doors. The walls grew thick around her. The weight was stifling. There was a dead end when they turned around. And no windows. She focused on her breath to slow it down before she careened into anxiety.

What if we can't get out?

Fritz picked up a scarf. The edges were frayed. Holes chewed through it. There were more scarves up ahead. Voices grew louder. They stopped outside a door to listen. She put Fritz behind her, kept a hand on him, and opened the door just a little. There was an argument inside the room. Marie stuck her head in.

"No!" they shouted.

Marie closed the door. She resisted the urge to close her eyes. What she saw was... *unthinkable*. This wasn't what she expected. None of this was. She grabbed Fritz by the shoulders.

"Don't look. Close your eyes and stay right behind me."

He nodded. She grabbed his wrist and squeezed a little too hard. The door swung open. The thing she'd seen was on top of a mountain of debris, grubbing things to its chest and stuffing them into bulging pockets.

"Uncle Vernon?"

He was a rat. A giant, human-sized rat wearing a crown. His eyes bulged from the sockets. And there was more of him. Heads, that is. Smaller versions of Uncle Vernon had sprouted from his neck, bunched together and twisting to have a look at her. Each with a different expression. Each with a crown.

"Stay away. I'm warnin' you. You can't have it. None of it."

"Hey, kids," one of the heads said. "It's about time."

"Hungry?" another one said.

"Hey, buddy," another said. And, "Isn't it your bedtime?"

They were all talking at the same time, saying different things in different ways. Marie took a step closer. *Is it really him?*

"Stop where you are!" they all said. "Not one more step. Mine! This is all mine!"

"I don't want anything," she said.

"Well, you can't have it!" Confusion rolled their beady eyes. They looked at each other. "Mine. Mine."

Marie looked around. It looked like a giant nest of shiny objects. A glass case was against a wall, objects shoved onto the shelves. *Where's Aunt Rinks?*

"Go to your room," one of them said. "I don't want to hear another word from you."

Marie's legs stiffened. Her chest tightened into an impenetrable shell. Candyland had turned her uncle into a monster she couldn't have dreamed up. He was hard to look at. Her jaw clenched.

"I don't care about any of that. Where's Aunt Rinks?"

They struggled with conflicting thoughts, snapping at each other with sharp teeth. A consensus was reached. In unison, they bellowed, "Huzzah!" and slid down the pile, plowing through objects with wide feet and sharp nails, and reached for their belt. The sword slid from the sheath. *Ting!*

"Mine!"

Marie went rigid. Her skin tightened and tingled. Muscles turned to fibers tough and flexible like the trunk of a tree, swelling inside her clothing. The sound of her teeth snapped like a trap. She felt something in her hand, hard and cold. She pointed it at the seven-headed Mouseking.

Where did I get a sword?

That thought was distant. Like she was far away from herself, becoming something else. Her sword was curved and silver with the edge of a razor. Her uncle, the Mouseking, stumbled back.

"Not one more step," she said. Her voice as sharp and steady as the blade she held.

The Mouseking babbled and cried, shouted and spit. He threw a box. It splintered on the wall. He threw a pillow that she split in half. Feathers snowed around them. He threw forks and spoons, cups and plates. She dodged them deftly. Her remaining shoe slipped off her foot. She picked it up and threw it at him. He ducked behind the glass display. When he did, the entire thing tipped over. Glass shattered on the floor, sending shards across the room.

Marie felt a sharp pain in her left arm.

The Mouseking crawled back onto his nest of stolen goods, swearing at her, asking if she was hurt, telling her to go away, wondering if she wanted some noodles to eat. This wasn't where Marie needed to be. This wasn't their journey. *This is Uncle Vernon's journey.* She reached behind her, to pull Fritz closer, to shield him from her uncle's obscenity.

"Fritz?"

The doorway was empty. She ran through it, looked down the hall. He was walking away from her, holding the hand of one of the cloaked figures who had boarded the barge.

"Fritz!"

She sank the tip of the sword into the floor and went after them. The Mouseking's cackling faded behind her, then disappeared when he slammed the door.

"Mine!"

29

"How'd you get in here?"

Rinks grabbed the L-shaped doorknob. It rattled up and down. The door shook in the frame but didn't open. She grabbed it with both hands, leaning against the door for leverage. Fingernails, long and curved and sharpened to a point, bit into her palms.

Rinks pinned her back to the door. The queen watched from the other side of the room. Tendrils of condensed breath huffed out of the darkness inside her hood and disappeared on their way up to the ceiling. Rinks grabbed a trophy from the shelf. The cheerleader figurine that looked like her poised on top, with a frozen pom-pom aimed at the queen.

"Stay away. You're not supposed to be here. You left! This is my castle now. I'm the queen!"

She had the absurd urge to whip out her phone and show how many followers she had. How many likes her last post got. People loved her, and she could prove it. The phone slipped from her quivering hand and tumbled to the hem of the queen's cloak.

"Vern!" She slammed the door with open hands until her palms stung. "Help me! Get in here, now!"

She tried opening the door again. *Why is this locked?* She felt movement, spun around with the trophy in front of her.

"Don't move! I'm not afraid to use this." Rinks moved to put the recliner—the one where the Jojos had made her hands and feet pretty—between them. "I swear."

The room was freezing. Rinks could see her own breath now. The blackness inside that hood was crippling. Like some outer space, bottomless hole that ate planets and moons and stars. It was unsettling. Sent a shiver through her belly button. *Did she gargle perfume?* Rinks thought. It smelled pleasant and familiar. Brought a memory of her mom teaching Rinks and her sister how to put on just the right amount. *Spritz a cloud and walk through it, girls.*

The scar on her cheek burned.

"I have an army, you know. A thousand mice. A million. They love me, too. How do you think I got here, huh? They love me! You leave now, and they won't hurt you. I swear. But if you don't…"

The queen was motionless. The robe unmoving. Only perfumed clouds wafting out and evaporating. Slender fingers dangled from the oversized cuffs. Not even twitching.

Rinks relaxed her grip on the trophy. She straightened the crown that was crooked on her head. Made sure the queen knew who wore the crown now. She smoothed her springy hair. The scar felt hot on her cheek. She stood upright, pulled back her shoulders and puffed out her chest. Something royalty would do.

"What do you want?"

She bent over without taking her eyes off the queen, pushing clutter around to find an emery board the Jojos had used to file her nails. She tossed it at the queen. She was aiming for the black hole in the hood. It bounced off her sleeve. The queen didn't flinch.

Maybe she wasn't real. *Does Marie have somethin' to do with this?* She could. That little liar could be trying to scare her.

Rinks moved closer, sliding a footstep at a time. The perfume grew stronger and sweeter. It burned in her eyes. It buzzed under her skin, in her head. The scar began to itch. Rinks covered it with her hand. Stiff whiskers pricked her palm.

"Seriously, what do you want? You just goin' to stand there starin'?"

Nothing.

Rinks went back to the door. With the trophy raised above her head, she brought it down on the L-shaped doorknob. Once, twice. The third time, the cheerleader snapped off and danced across the floor. It jigged under the recliner and came to rest against the queen's cloak.

"Look what you made me do. That was my best trophy. These are all mine. All of this!" She swept her arm at the walls. "But that was my favorite!"

The queen was not moved.

Rinks looked around the room. Everything was gingerbread this or gingerbread that, or bolted to the floor or screwed to the wall. Nothing solid except... she shuffled around the recliner, the jagged end of the trophy aimed at the cloak, till she got to the window. She snatched the telescope. The tripod tipped over. Rinks threw the broken trophy down and took that telescope like a baseball bat to the doorknob.

The lens shattered. The eyepiece snapped.

The L-shaped doorknob broke off. She pulled it out of the door and yanked it open. The hallway was empty. She could hear voices, though. Her husband and all his malignant heads going on about *mine, mine, mine!*

Rinks didn't run. She'd done that already, and look what happened. Whatever this was, she couldn't outrun it. She turned with the bent telescope on her shoulder. "Best you leave before they come for you. They won't be friendly." She aimed the telescope at her. "You ruined my life."

It was an odd thing to say. She didn't know why she said it.

Nonetheless, nothing happened. Rinks could bar this room closed and never come back to it, leave the queen in it forever. But this was her room. These were her trophies.

"You deaf?" Rinks dared a step toward her. "I said you need to get out of my life forever."

One more step, then another. She was breathing slower now. Calmer than ever, she inched her way forward. With one hand on the telescope (if the queen flinched, she'd get the homerun swing), she reached out with the other. Grabbed the coarse sleeve of the cloak.

"Come on."

She tugged. It was like pulling open a freezer where slabs of meat are kept. The tip of her nose went cold and started to drip. The perfumed breath drew water from her eyes. The breathy cloud disappeared. The queen stopped breathing.

"Let's go."

Rinks gave it a yank. It was like pulling the lever on dry ice. The next exhale enveloped Rinks in a cloud that nipped her earlobes and kissed her cheeks. She dropped the telescope, let go of the sleeve. Swung her arms in search of the door. One step, two. Ten steps. She didn't find it. Didn't run into a wall or stub her toe on any clutter. She waved at the smoky air. Her fingertips were numb.

She folded her arms over her chest. She was cold, but that wasn't why she tucked her arms against herself. She just did. The smoke began to swirl. Wind in her ears, she was spinning in a vortex.

Instinctually, she closed her eyes, locked her knees. The balance of gravity settled inside her like a child's top standing still. Metal blades ground in firm footing. Tears streaked across her temples. The gravity bloomed in her stomach, opening like a flower. Joy surged through her veins, filled her body and flooded her head with lightness and smiles.

She knew this feeling.

Lost in the experience, she pushed backward. Pulling one leg up and behind her, dug the other one into the ice. Came out of the spin with a powerful surge, drifted on the edge of a metal blade. With her arms out and winter nibbling her ears, she soared like an angel.

Flying beneath a gray sky.

Alone on a frozen lake. The lake she grew up on, where they swam in the summer. Played hockey in winter, practiced their spins when the boys weren't around. Ankle burning, leg held high, she etched an arching line in the black ice. Curving around her father's ice fishing hut, where he and her uncle would cut a hole and drop their lines.

This feeling she'd forgotten. It was buried under so many scars. Now it was clear and present. It was graceful beauty. Pure instinct.

It was as free as she ever felt.

※

THE SMOKE CLEARED.

Her father's ice hut was gone. The lake and gray sky. That freedom still trickled through her. It turned to ash when she realized she was back. Not in her room high atop the castle.

There were trophies on a shelf. Ribbons, too. The Golden Skate Award (she had forgotten that one). A tennis racket and more trophies. Behind her, the recliner was replaced by a bed with a quilted comforter and a pile of pillows. Posters on the wall. A dresser with Christmas cards, a jewelry box, a jar of pennies that read *Be The Change*. A photo of a boy Rinks had a crush on. A boy who barely knew she existed. Marco only spoke to her if she answered the door.

A tiny blue flame ignited in her belly. A furnace began to warm oils of resentment.

She took a medal from the dresser. A red and white ribbon was strung through a loop attached to it. It was thick and heavy, began to spin as she held it up. She read the person's name engraved on it. *First Place* was etched on the other side.

Her skin began to sizzle.

Car doors slammed shut. Panes of glass were frosted on a rectangular window. Outside, her parents were in the front seats. Her dad backing out of the driveway. In the back seat, her sister was on her phone. Smiling at something she read. A text from Marco.

Rinks stood there long after the car was gone, on its way to a competition. Her sister would bring home another ribbon. She'd throw it on the pile, close her bedroom door, and call Marco. They would talk. He would come over. Rinks would hear them through the wall of her bedroom.

She remembered what she had done that day. Even if she could change it, she wouldn't. She gave in to the bonfire cooking her thoughts into blackened coals. The trophies went on the bed. She didn't place them carefully. They were thrown one by one, chipping and scratching. Plastic figurines snapping. Then the ribbons and medals. The certificates. The Christmas cards, the picture of Marco. It all went onto the bed.

She bundled them in the bedspread.

Rinks was barely aware she wasn't *actually* there. She didn't think about the room in the castle or the hooded queen with the icy breath. She dragged that bedspread by four corners down the steps, through the living room, and out the sliding glass door. In stocking feet, she pulled it through the snow. Onto the frozen lake. Balled-up ice crystals stuck to her socks. She fell three times, spilling the loot, packing it back up, pushing farther out onto the ice.

The hole inside her father's fishing hut had frozen over. A hatchet he kept under a folding chair did the trick. She hacked it to floating pieces. Her face red, eyes swollen. She screamed with each swing, satisfied each time the blade sank into the ice.

Bye-bye, first-place ribbons. *Bloop.* So long, state champion. *Bloop.* See you later, medals and trophies and certificates and pictures. Some bobbed momentarily. Then the icy darkness took them all the way to the bottom of the lake. First in her class, gone. Regional winner, fish bait. Boyfriend, have a drink. She clogged the ice hole with the bedspread. Go away and never come back.

❉

RINKS WOKE TO CRYING.

She couldn't remember falling asleep or even coming to her room. She lifted her head off the pillow and listened to the sweet sounds in the next room. The wailing turned to growling. Then a scream blew frost off the window. There were muffled thuds and loud ones that shook the wall. A picture fell over on Rinks's dresser. She put her hands behind her head and soaked in the misery. It was art, what she did. Award-worthy. *What do they call it? Performance art.*

So caught up in her thoughts of accepting an award for her courageous act, she didn't notice the thuds moving down the hall. Her door slammed against the wall, the knob punching a hole in the drywall (which her dad made *Rinks* fix). Her sister, still wearing her winter coat, leaped across the room. Rinks rolled off her bed, but not before catching a fist to the side of the head. Her ear caught fire, and her head rang a long high-pitched note.

The worst of it was when she hit an open dresser drawer.

Her sister was on top of her, knees pinning her shoulders to the carpet. Rinks covered her face. Warmth flowed from her cheek, which was sticky between her fingers. Her sister's face was flaming. Rage turned the princess into a snarling ogre making garbage-disposal sounds.

Squeak, Rinks heard.

Rinks's mom grabbed her sister, wrapped her arms around her, and dragged her across the room. Legs kicking, body twisting. Her dad came in next, wondering what the fuss was all about. Rinks's sister told them exactly what Rinks had done. They listened in disbelief. Then saw the proof. The looks on their faces stole all the joy from Rinks's work of art.

"Your sister worked so hard," her mom said.

"The efforts she makes," her dad said.

Rinks curled up against the dresser. She wanted to feel sad, to feel regret. But that furnace in her gut only burned on envy, pure, 100% envy that pumped out globs of hate. That look of hurt on her sister's face was the tip of an oil rig tapping a deep deposit under years of pressure.

Squeak.

"Because of you!" Rinks jumped up. "Is it really so hard to figure out? You deserve it!"

The cut from the open drawer—the cut that would become a thin scar to remind everyone of that day—bled along the ridge of her jawbone. The cut her parents didn't ask about till hours later. The ride to the hospital in fuming silence. The lock they put on her sister's door so Rinks could never perform again.

"I was good, too," Rinks said to her sister. That wasn't what she'd said when it actually happened. She hadn't said any of that, really. She had curled up in a ball on the floor until they made her get up. But she said all of that now.

Now she said to her sister: "You never cared about me. Admit it."

Squeak.

There was a rat on the floor. Rinks stepped back in horror. It leaped up and down, shook a tiny spear at her. Rinks looked back. The recliner was empty. The queen was gone. The fake trophies on the shelf. No cloak on the floor, no nippy air in the room.

Rinks with her hand to her cheek.

Squeak.

"Where'd she go? Where's the queen?"

The general tapped his spear three times and began running down the hall. Rinks went after him. She wasn't done with her sister.

The furnace was burning hot now.

30

"Fritz!"

Fritz and the cloaked figure were taking a stroll. They turned right. Marie followed. Each stride thudded in her ears. The walls shook. The air stagnant and humid. When she made the turn, they were farther away.

The corridor was narrow.

Her pumping arms scuffed the walls. She huffed hot air. Sweat streaked her back. She wiped her eyes. They made a left turn. She couldn't gain on them. They were casually walking, looking at each other. *Is Fritz talking to him?*

Two more turns. An ache buried in her side. Her shoulders bounced between the shrinking walls. She pushed through the burn, the pain, the struggle to breathe. Her legs were hollow. She'd lost her way. This had become a maze of turns and tunnels. Finding her way out wouldn't matter.

Not without Fritz.

The chase ended. Fritz stood with the stranger, still hand in hand, at a dead end. The passage was long and narrow. So narrow she had to cock her shoulders to squeeze through it. Fritz and the other stood side by side in front of double doors. The hood of the cloak had been thrown back. It was a man. Marie wiped her eyes with her sleeves. Blood from the cut on her left arm, when the Mouseking's glass case shattered, smeared across her cheek. The coppery taste of iron on her lips.

Through the sweat and thick air, it was hard to tell what the man was wearing on his head. As she drew closer, she realized Fritz wasn't wearing his ball cap. They turned their heads, saw Marie coming for them. They were too far away to see their faces or expressions. But she saw what the man was wearing.

He had Fritz's hat.

They reached for the doors. Marie was closing the distance. When they opened them, bright white light blazed from the next room. It was stunning. Her knees wobbled. She pressed her hands against the walls, their ghostly images imprinted in the whiteout. She ran through blindness, dropping one foot in front of the next. Calling her brother's name.

A gale of frigid wind cooled the slick of perspiration on her face. It soothed her burning eyes and itching throat. Fritz appeared out of the whiteness so suddenly that she almost tackled him. She picked him up and held him tightly, buried her face on his shoulder. Looking around for the man who took him.

"Are you okay? Did he hurt you?" she choked into her brother's ear. "Where's your hat?"

Fritz shook his head. He didn't look at her with fear or sadness. A palpable calmness possessed him. He wasn't winded or afraid. He looked through the doors they had opened. The light had dimmed. What was inside was not what she expected.

We're here, she thought. *We made it.*

❆

IT WAS A CATHEDRAL. The big church kind, but older. The king and queen kind, where subjects and landowners brought offerings. Pillars as big as redwoods. Arching ceilings fifty feet above. Carvings on the walls, wintery scenes with sleds and snowballs, snow angels and snowmen, snowflakes and ornaments and presents and Christmas trees. Plump elves looking down from the ceiling.

Ice. All of it made from ice. Frosted ice and clear ice. Ice with sparkling crystals. Black ice on the floor, buffed and smooth as marble. In its depth, tiny specks glittered like a galaxy of stars.

Marie took it in through squinting eyelids. It seemed far too big to fit at the top of the castle, but she'd stopped rational thinking a while ago. Candyland operated by different laws. This was the end of the journey. The quiver in her stomach told her this was the place.

Her heart wanted to escape its cage.

At the far end, chiseled from the tip of a jagged iceberg, were two empty thrones. They were side by side with wide arms and soaring backs of spearing icicles. The king and queen were missing. But standing in front of the thrones, facing them with her back to Marie and Fritz, stood a girl.

Fritz took a step inside. He tested the black ice, took careful steps. He stopped and held out his hand. Marie was as solid as the pillars holding up the intricate ceiling. This was why they had come. This was the end, and she hesitated. Something about it told her to run and hide. It was dangerous to her, but not to Fritz.

It threatened her, somehow.

He kept going without her. When he went too far, she slid after him. The floor was a flawless mirror. It was like looking into the universe, skating over endless black space. It burned the soles of her bare feet. She'd lost one of her shoes to the mice, the other to the Mouseking. Barely halfway across the cathedral and she could not feel her ankles.

She didn't notice her reflection was missing.

Fritz waited for her to catch up. They joined hands and shuffled toward the empty thrones. The girl did not turn around. She wore a white cloak of fine silk. Red trim along the hem and cuffs. It bunched on the floor around her feet. Her hands hung from the sleeves like shriveled leaves. The hood covering her head was enormous. *She's been cursed.* Marie thought of the nutcracker story the Counselor had told. The Mousequeen had avenged the Mouseking with a curse. *Poor thing.*

Marie squeezed Fritz's hand.

They were ten feet away when Princess Pirlipat turned to face them. Her head was the size of a county fair pumpkin. Misshapen like a potato dug from the dirt. Her nose a twisted root between two dull green eyes. A lipless mouth cut a line from ear to ear.

Marie took a step back, her hand to her mouth. Legs melting hot rubber. Fritz tried to pull away. Marie held onto his hand, determined not to let him go again. Marie couldn't look away. Horrible air was sucked through tiny nostrils with each breath the princess took. She didn't tremble or hide her face. But the pain was there. The pain was in her eyes. She'd been abandoned. Forgotten. Alone in this tower for so long.

Marie could feel the pain. It rang like a wineglass struck with a knife. The vibrations quivered in her stomach, singing its song in her heart. Loosening the lid on the emotional black box.

"What do we do?" Marie said.

The princess's mouth opened like a wound. No words came out. Only the struggle for another breath.

Marie remembered the Counselor's story. She searched her pocket for the nut the hussars at the market had given her. It would lift the curse. Her pockets, however, were empty. It had fallen out at some point during the running and jumping and fighting. It could be anywhere. She had to find it. Had to put an end to the curse.

Fritz put something in Marie's hand, closed her fingers around it, and hid behind her from the sight of the princess. It was hard and heavy, oblong and furrowed. Marie opened her hand. When the princess saw what she was holding, she grunted and snerked a retched breath. Her head shook like it was attached to a spring.

The ball was heavy.

It was the ball Godfather had given him, shaped like an oversized walnut that hummed with warmth. She turned her back to the princess, to face her brother. She didn't understand what he was doing. Sandy had washed up on the shore of Marchpane Castle, but he would come back when they left Candyland. She was sure of it. Besides, this couldn't be it.

"Crackatook," Marie whispered.

He looked up with heavy eyes, put his hand to his mouth like he was biting an apple. This was the nut that would lift the curse. The hardest nut in all the land. The Counselor had told the story. It wasn't just a story, though. He was telling them about this very moment. *Godfather gave us the crackatook.*

"Fritz... this is *Sandy*."

He nodded. It broke her heart (as if there were any pieces left to break) to see him like that. Putting his hand over hers, closing her hand around it. She closed her eyes.

The crackatook must be cracked open in front of the princess.

The kernel handed to her with closed eyes by one who had never shaved or worn boots.

Seven steps backwards without stumbling.

Marie had never shaven. Had never worn boots (that she knew of). How was she going to crack the nut? This was the job for the nutcracker. *Where is he?* He'd never come with them to Candyland. Even though she was holding him when she came in. Even though Sandy insisted he was always there.

"I'm not the one," Marie said.

A part of her wanted to turn and run, look for the door in the sky to leave and never come back. The princess was hideous. *I don't want to be the one.*

But she knew. Deep down, it had to be her.

❈

THE CRACKATOOK WAS like iron between her teeth.

She bit down, tentatively at first. The hard shell didn't give one bit. A little more and her eyes watered. She was about to stop when she felt the first fracture. *Pop!* A bitter taste was on her tongue. Pain spiked in the roots of her teeth, but still she bit harder. The shell fell in two pieces between her lips.

The kernel was golden yellow.

The princess held out her withered hand. The fingers like dry leather. With Fritz behind her, Marie closed her eyes. She reached out and felt the princess's cold, coarse skin brush against her palm. Spidery fingers took the crackatook kernel from it.

Marie stood barefoot, listening to the kernel crumble, crushed between wet gums in a lipless mouth. A warm light began to glow. Marie resisted the temptation to peek, to see the transformation. There was still more to do.

Fritz stepped aside. Marie put her foot back. *One. Two.*

A drip of water fell on her head.

Three. Four.

The sun was in front of her. She clenched her eyes against the brightness. The floor crackled beneath her. Without stumbling, she continued.

Five.

Six.

With confidence and eagerness to see Princess Pirlipat, she took the seventh and final step.

31

The distant sound of tiny feet echoed in the stairwell.

A deep pain dug into Rinks's side. She stopped to put her hands on her knees. The air was dense and hot, like she was huffing it straight from an exhaust pipe. Her teeth, pointed and sharp as needles, pierced her bottom lip. All of that was nothing compared to the hollow pain in her chest, like she'd taken a right hook from a world boxing champion.

The general kept hopping. Rinks raised her hand. Her words puffed out. *Go,* she thought. *I know where she is.*

Her sister had a familial smell. Rinks had grown up with that scent on the bathroom towels and the clothes she borrowed (stole). She raised her chin, nose twitching in the dead air.

I'll find you.

There was no love lost between her and her sister. No love had existed. They were bad roommates. Reluctant classmates. Sibling rivals wasn't it at all. It's not a rivalry if you don't care. Rinks couldn't care less. She'd taught her sister a valuable lesson by throwing out the trophies. Her sister never thanked her for it. None of them did. They didn't understand how attached she was to those things. She was addicted to success. Rinks made her see that.

"You see me now?" she muttered.

The pitter-patter of tiny feet grew louder. Pairs of beady eyes bobbed in the dark. *Squee-squee-squee.*

"Come, chickens. Come to mama."

Rinks staggered a few steps, then caught her stride. The stitch in her side cinched tighter, but she powered through it, fueled by righteousness. Her sister needed to recognize her true self. She needed to admit how she'd treated Rinks. She needed to apologize to Rinks. Right to her face.

"Vern! Get out here." She pounded the door with open palms. "Now!"

The clutter of things fell, an avalanche of things gold and silver. The slap of bare feet. The door opened. Seven heads poked out. Each held a different expression.

"Shut up. All of you. If you want that stuff, then you better follow." She was running again. "I mean it!"

It wasn't clear if Vern would leave his treasure behind, but soon Rinks heard the clunk and clatter of precious loot jangle in pockets and pouches. The rattle of her husband's saber in the metal scabbard. Beyond him was the distant rumble of tiny feet.

Squee-squee-squee.

She followed the scent—left, right, right, left. Stagnant air scratched her lungs like vaporized wool. Her legs grew heavy. She pushed around the final turn, where a white laser blasted her between the eyes. Her head snapped back. She tumbled into her husband's lumpy belly. Seven sets of whiskers tickled her face.

Through fingers that had grown knobby and pale, she squinted into the light. The sun was fifty feet away. It hurt her brain. But she could smell her in there. Her sister and something else. A walnut or pecan. Bitter and spicy.

A horde of Jojos filled the corridor behind them with musky odor. Balls of fur flooded toward them. Swords and spears raised. Rinks elbowed Vern in the doughy midsection. He pulled his saber. Rinks lifted her fist.

"See me now!"

She led the charge into the light, a gasping, haggard queen with a tilted crown on her head. Eyes closed, following the scent of her sister, to confront her for all the wrongs, to make her beg for forgiveness. Apologies Rinks would gobble up like Christmas dinner. She licked her lips. How delicious it would taste, her sister admitting she was wrong after all this time.

Through the doorway.

Into the light.

Suddenly, she was on the frozen lake where she grew up. On one foot, arms waving, sliding and twisting. Peels of ice curling under her toenails. She leaned forward and back, side to side, but without a blade to catch the frozen surface, she couldn't gain her balance. Her feet flew out.

Rinks landed on her back.

An explosion of stars twittered in a dark cloud. Arms and legs spread, she spun like a hockey puck. Arching beams turned overhead; glittering crystals moved across the ceiling. Slowly, she came to a rest. A tender knot swelled on the back of her head. She looked up at the ceiling and thought of church or a citadel or something special. A stupid smile bloomed on her lips.

It withered when a shadow fell over her.

32

Adrenaline raged a steady drum.

Numbers appeared like flashcards as she counted the steps. There was no one to stop her. Only Fritz and the princess. The taste of anticipation on her lips. On the last step, the final step, her heel landed on something soft and gagging.

Marie stumbled. Fell.

Bright light grew painfully brighter. It ran through her arms and legs, rang in her head, hardened her ribs. She lay as still as a felled cypress. Clumsily, Marie climbed to her feet. Legs stiff, joints creaking. Inside her, a little black box fractured. A pilot light of blue flame flickered. Heat coursed through her, lighting emotions leaking from the black box like wildfire through dry pasture.

The empty thrones cracked.

The sound of crackling wood was in her ears. Embers glowed in her heart. Geysers of ignored emotions, packed down in that black box, shattered the brittle shell that contained them. She stepped toward the tilted thrones. Her feet, clad in heavy black boots, splintered the ice. Cracks ran over the floor and up the crystal walls. Spidered the ceiling.

The snap of her teeth echoed like a gunshot.

"Where are they?" she said.

Her voice, dark and brooding, shook the pillars. The princess, gone. Her brother, gone. The thrones empty.

Someone scampered on the floor. A half human, half mouse clawed at the ice. Her crown tangled in a nest of gray. Toenails carving tracks but not finding purchase to stand. Marie snatched her aunt by the tunic. As effortless as lifting a doll from a tea party, she held her at arm's length. A wild animal kicked and spat.

Marie was growing.

Her boots, her starched red jacket, a patch of whiskers on her chin and shaggy eyebrows eluded her. She had no idea what she had become. The burning question consumed her.

"Where are they?"

The power. The rage. It spilled from her in plumes of smoke. A mighty column holding up the ceiling shattered. Frozen boulders punched holes in the floor. Fumes smoldered in the cuffs of her jacket. Pellets of ice rained down and danced. The Mousequeen dangled like a puppet. Her throat was swollen where Marie's seventh step had landed. She tried to speak, turning helplessly on a hook.

"WHERE ARE THEY?"

This wasn't what Marie had wanted for Christmas. This was not what she *needed*. She continued to swell, growing another five feet. Her body sounded like trees bursting in a forest fire. The Mousequeen's clawed feet twittered high above the fractured floor; she sank her needle teeth through Marie's white glove. The tunic slipped through Marie's fingers. The seven-headed Mouseking was there to pull his queen away. Mice formed a circle around them. Clad in breastplates and helmets, they launched metal-tipped spears that bounced off the looming wooden soldier. Marie stomped the floor and sent them tumbling. Some fell through cratered holes.

Marie doubled in size again.

The hat on her head punched through the ceiling. Shards shattered on the floor. A patch of pink sky shone through. A black square nestled between cotton-candy clouds.

The thrones fell in pieces. Columns collided and crashed. Broken lines were all around. She swung tree-trunk arms at the injustice of it all. Unsheathed her sword at the unfairness of a cold, uncaring world. Beneath the merry air of Candyland was a current of ugliness and sorrow that suffocated her.

The chocolate shell that coated the castle fell in slabs, exposing shiny walls beneath it.

Marie swung wrecking balls at the emotions that hurt. She kicked at the feelings of pain. She could not get her hands on the sensations that smothered her. An inferno blazed inside her. Untapped rage ran unchecked.

The army of mice scattered.

The Mousequeen and Mouseking were gone.

Marie swung around, picked up her boots, kicked the debris. She was alone in the wreckage. She had failed the princess. She'd failed her brother. Her parents.

There was no one left to fight.

The walls fell around her. The treasures her uncle had hoarded spilled down into Rose Lake. The chocolate shell fell away, swallowed by the rose-tinted waters without a splash. The castle glittered, once again, in all its glory. The castle she had seen once before, an extraordinary model in the basement of a cabin deep in the woods—but that memory incinerated like tissue paper.

The inhabitants of Candyland, as tiny as mites, marveled from the shoreline.

Snow came in big, beautiful flakes tinted pink. From below, she heard the cheers welcome it. The snow swirled around her, landed delicately on her wooden nose.

Above her, the black square had vanished.

Marie stood atop the tallest spire, completely exposed. Fully vulnerable. This was who she was. This was what she had been hiding. This ugly beast. This vengeful torrent of rage. This was the journey, and the journey betrayed her. Her greatest fear had been realized. They saw her for what she really was. Her all-consuming anger at the world for wrecking her family. Her ugliness was out.

The black box is open.

33

"Where are they?"

Rinks didn't recognize the voice that shook her into consciousness. The ceiling sparkled high above. Fractures swept across the beams holding it up. A pink sky shone through pockets that had opened. At the last second, she rolled away. A jagged chunk of ice shattered next to her. Fragments sprayed her face. She struggled to breathe. Her throat had nearly swollen shut.

She panicked. Scrambling on the slippery floor, she went nowhere. Her royal tunic began choking her. She clawed at her throat, felt her feet rise off the floor. She tottered back and forth. Rinks knew she was becoming a mouse. Her husband, he had seven heads. But what was holding her like an unspun yo-yo shocked her.

It was a nutcracker.

The toy soldier was ten feet tall and growing. The strange thing that sent shivers down her hairy back was it was alive. It was holding her. And to her nose (which had become quite sensitive), it smelled like her sister.

"WHERE ARE THEY?"

Rinks struggled to breathe. She flailed; she scratched. The Jojos were rushing in, standing behind her seven-headed husband like useless bugs. What were they going to do? Seeing as she was dangling from a wooden monster, who was currently destroying the castle, what could they do?

Rinks helped herself.

She managed to pull herself up and plant her teeth into the nutcracker's finger. It was enough to get loose. She landed like a bag of jellybeans. Her Jojos surrounded her, her loyal chickens, and sailed their useless weapons at the swelling titan. It was her husband who pulled her away, dragging her on her backside.

"No," she muttered. "The castle."

The nutcracker would destroy everything. There would be nothing left if they didn't stop her. It wasn't just the walls. Its stupid hat punched holes through the ceiling. Debris fell like bombs. The floor was caving in. And the floors below that. Vern's treasure (however many rooms away that was) was crashing through the devastation.

Vern threw his arms under her. He lifted her head and pointed at the pink sky. Snow was beginning to fall in big, fat flakes. The peaceful kind of snow that dampened the world's troubles. She resisted what he was telling her. But he was right. There was no other option. She whispered to the Jojos, told them to run.

She would be back for them.

❄

WHITE SPECKS SHOT from the open gift like a snow machine.

It swirled around the bedroom. The red string lights rattled on the walls. The air mattress flapped. Loose clothes whirled beneath the workbench. The blank pages in Marie's journal flipped.

Vern slammed the gift shut.

The gift wrapping on the side of the gift tore down the side. The frigid cyclone was over. Rinks sat against the wall, the red lights draped over her head. The scar on her cheek burned. She panted like a dog in summer. A storm still overturned thoughts in her head like loose change. Was any of that real? When her husband turned around, her question was answered.

"You okay?" one head said.

"You hurt?" another said.

"Get up!" said another.

Rinks hid her face. The whiskers on her upper lip poked the palms of her hands. "Ah!" she cried.

"What? What?" Vern said. "Are you okay?"

"Okay?" She jumped to her feet. "Look at us! Oh my god. Ohmygod... *we didn't change!*" She reached for the gift. "We have to go back."

"No! She's destroyin' it, Rinks. She'll take us with it."

"She? Where were you? It was the..." She pointed around the room, looking for that dreaded toy soldier Fritz played with. "The nutcracker lost his mind!"

"Marie!" said one of the neck heads. "The nutcracker is Marie!"

"We saw her change," another head said.

"When she stepped on you," said another.

Rinks shook her head. The brainstorm was still howling. *Marie? She smelled like my sister.* "That's... that's *impossible.*"

"We saw it!" they all said.

Well, Rinks supposed, anything was possible in that box. After all, she was part mouse. "We have to stop her. That's our home in there. And we look like this. We can't be out here like this. We got to stop. We have to—"

"We can't, Rinks. You heard what she said."

Where are they? Rinks had heard it loud and clear. Her ears were still ringing from it. "Fizzy. She was looking for Fizzy." No, wait. *They. She was looking for Fizzy and*—"She's lookin' for *them.*"

"Who?"

"My sister. Her parents. Who else?"

"They ain't here," Vern said. "And they ain't in there."

Yes, they are. "Keep that closed. We got to think. Where's Fizzy?"

"He's in there."

"No, he's not. He was in there with her; then he wasn't. *Think*."

All seven of Vern's heads started whispering to each other. Fritz had been in that ice church when they got there. When the ceiling fell and the door in the sky appeared, he was gone.

"He's out here," Rinks said.

Vern and all his heads nodded.

❄

"Stay away from the windows," Rinks said.

It was coming up on midnight. Most people were at home waiting for Santa to come deliver their Christmas loot. But if a car drove by and saw a seven-headed mouse eating slices of cheese over the kitchen sink, they were going to stop. Worse, they'd take a photo and post it. That was what Rinks would do.

"Look in the bedrooms. Check the bathroom," she said. "He's around here. I can smell him."

Maybe it was his clothes she smelled. Didn't matter. They needed to find him. He was their bargaining chip. They could send a message into Candyland. Make a deal with Marie. Her brother for their castle. Or what was left of it.

Rinks looked out the back door. The yard was brand new and inviting. She didn't dare go outside.

"Fritz!" Rinks called. "Hon, come out. Aunt Rinksy needs a talk, darlin'."

She went to the storefront. The shelves stuffed with toys were, thank God, just regular toys. It was creepy, though, in the dark. The sound of her toenails on the floor made her cringe. She checked the aisles, behind the counter, peeked under the tree.

"He's not here," Vern said, nibbling on a slice of cheese.

"I can see that. Keep lookin'. He's around here somewhere."

"Look where?"

"I don't know, Vern. Under the bed, in the closet. The shower. He's hidin'. Sniff him out!"

The heads snapped at the last bite of cheese like hogs at a trough. "You shoulda been nicer to them, Rinks."

"I am nice!" She threw a stuffed cheetah with purple stripes. "I gave them a home and food and clothes."

She cleared a shelf with a sweeping hand. Her fingers long and knobby and gross. The toys tumbled at her disgusting feet.

"What about me? When do I get what I want? I ain't a mistake. I got nothin' to give, and you want me to be nice? That what Marie wants, she wants me to be nice? Just because she lost her parents? I GOT NOTHING!"

She kicked a baby doll down the aisle.

"My parents were *never* nice. They *never* talked to me. And Marie's special? Why, because she's a kid? She'll learn life ain't fair. There ain't no rule book to all this. Not on Christmas or any other day. It is what it is, and that's what you get. Deal with it. She's throwin' a tantrum, Vern. A spoiled brat makin' a fuss because she don't like what life dealt her. Boo-hoo and cry on your pillow. Get over it."

Rinks grabbed the last bite of cheese from one of Vern's seven mouths, mashed it on the floor. It squeezed between her long toes.

"Now I look like this. You look like that. Is that fair? And she's wreckin' our castle while we're out here. That's ours in there. *Ours.* That ain't fair at all. I don't belong out here lookin' like this. I never belonged out here."

That was the truth of it. She never belonged. She didn't want to be here, either. Marie wasn't going to take that away from her.

"Where you goin'?" Vern said. He grabbed her arm. "We got to stay here, Rinks. Hide out for a bit; let things settle down."

Rinks was shaking.

"We never have to leave the store," he said. "We'll put the boards back up. Order food. Build a nest of our own. It'll work like that, Rinks. And when it's time, we go back. We stay here for now, temporary like. We can have our own children, too. We can do that."

Rinks rubbed her eyes. "We got children, Vern. We left them *in there.*"

The Jojos had been running scared when Rinks and Vern had leaped out. Falling in those craters Marie had been making. Throwing their tiny spears to protect their mama. And she'd left them.

"They're safe." The breath from seven mouths was in her face. "They're in the tunnels. Remember the tunnels? The Jojos will be waitin' for us down there when we go back. They'll be waitin' for their queen."

She waved away the breathy stink, a mix of coffee and cheese, and paced in a circle. He was making sense. They couldn't rush back. Marie the nutcracker was probably the size of a skyscraper by now. She'd snatch them out of the sky if they leaped in now. Let her get tired. Distracted. They could go back then, find her little Jojos underground.

Vern rubbed his greedy hands, licking his lips. All his lips.

They could stay here, make their own nest. Be as normal as two half-mouse people could be. "Okay," she said. "All right."

She picked up a headscarf from the floor. It was paisley with bright colors. She found two more and draped them around Vern's neck. Tied them together.

"It's hard to breathe in here," the neck heads muffled.

"I just want to talk to you, Vern. Not them."

"I am Vern!" they chorused.

Rinks put her hand on his cheek. The whiskers were long and pokey. "You're my Vern."

He leaned into her hand, nose twitching. Smelling her. Black eyes blinking, he took a knee and bowed his head. He spoke—they all spoke—and chills straightened the coarse hairs on her back.

"My queen."

She could get used to this. They could make this their nest. Throw those owl clocks out and have Jojos of their own. And when the time was right, they'd go back to claim their kingdom. Rinks put her hand on the crown on his head. A royal gesture accepting his allegiance. For the first time in her life, she felt special.

Something floated between them. It looked like a fuzzy dust bunny dancing on a draft and landed delicately on the back of her hand. When it began to melt, she realized what it was. She turned around to see more wafting out the open door that led to the children's room, where the gift was.

It was snow. Pink snow.

※

A PEPPERMINT BREEZE carried snow into the storefront.

It gusted in waves, rattling sheets of paper and sending the rocking chair in Storyteller Corner back and forth. The red string lights in the children's room tapped against the wall. Snowflakes melted on the floor.

Rinks and Vern knew what was happening.

They slipped on the floor where the snow had melted in tiny droplets. Three steps closer to the room, they were hit with a gale that blew the crowns off their heads. They chased them down (what is royalty without proof?) and started again. Doors banged off the walls. The toys Rinks had shoved on the floor tumbled like weeds. More tipped off the shelves. The Christmas tree chimed in the corner.

They worked their way close enough to grab the doorframe, holding their crowns on their heads. (Four of Vern's crowns were lost.) Snow streamed from the gift like a confetti gun. The air mattress was thwapping like a loose sail. When the current changed directions, it swept it off the floor and slammed Rinks and Vern square in their pointed noses. They skidded down the aisles, fingernails etching white lines in the floor.

They rolled against the front door. The shelves were cleared. A mountain of toys cushioned their stop. The pink snowstorm howled around the storefront like a horde of ghosts, sweeping anything loose into the corners. Ornaments flew off the Christmas tree and burst like light bulbs.

"We'll go around to the back door!" Vern shouted. He reached up to unlock the front door. "It's the only way—"

"No!" Rinks pulled his arm down. "Are you out of your mind?"

There was nothing that could chase her outside. She didn't care if the town was deserted for a thousand miles.

The children's room was puking pink ice now. It plinked off the metal shelving, bounced across the floor. Pelted Rinks on the face. She used a blue whale as a shield. If that gift was going to freeze them out, no big deal. She grew up in long winters. She could take it.

The first hunk of gray fur flew out like a bouncy ball. It ricocheted off the rocking chair (no longer rocking on its side), caromed off the ceiling, and landed in the Christmas tree (also on its side). The branches pushed apart. A pink nose twitched.

General Rat climbed out. With his helmet on sideways and sword twisting on his belt, he hopped through the toys and leaped into Rinks's open arms. The fuzzy general nuzzled in her embrace. He popped his head up, let out a squeak.

Rinks didn't need Vern to translate. She understood.

❄

ALL THE MICE followed the general. Ten thousand in all. Disheveled, yet dutifully uniformed.

They were tossed out of Candyland like food poisoning. A volcanic eruption of fur and tails bubbled into the storefront, blown to the far side into waiting arms. The swarm of vermin mauled their queen, squirming over her and around her. Only her face could be seen.

She loved it. The warmth. The love.

It lit a fire in her. Should anything dare come out of that room to hurt them, it would deal with her and her seven-headed idiot.

The snow accumulated on the floor and shelves, drifted in the corners and frosted the windows. A foot of the pink stuff piled on the stage of Storyteller Corner. The temperature plunged despite ten thousand mice panting steamy breath swirling in the eddies.

When the last Jojo came bouncing out, the wind died. The storm was over, just like that. Only the ticking of the old building settled around them. Nothing stirred. Not even a mouse. Patterns of crystal lattice crept over the windows. In the tense silence, she appreciated its beauty.

Vern stood up. Mice fell off him like fallen leaves. If he ran for it, he could close the gift and weigh it down with the refrigerator before another pink snowflake popped out. He took one step.

Clop. Clop-clop.

A shadow stretched out of the children's room. On the back of a tiny, plastic steed, a smartly dressed hussar sat. He was no taller than a mouse standing on its hind legs. It was pretty clear one of Rinks's little soldiers could take the hussar in a straight-up one-on-one. The toy horse danced in place, its hooves tapping the floor, as the hussar surveyed the storefront. When his eyes narrowed, he unsheathed his sword. Raised it above his head. Chills ran down Rinks's neck, the kind that said *run now!*

General Rat was unimpressed. He squealed orders.

The mouse army scrambled for position. They fell into ranks, lining up with weapons at their sides. However, they were crammed into the corners and digging through snow, crawling over each other to see the hussar slowly approach. If that wasn't bad enough, the storm opened up again. Hussars poured out the doorway. Some were on horseback. Most tumbled out like the mice had. The wind blew what little order the mice had assembled into a squirming ball of chaos.

Rinks was buried in panic. She clawed her way out, standing up to breathe. The general's orders changed. They were doomed if they stayed where they were.

"No! No, no, no!" Rinks slapped at her Jojos, but they persisted. The general was right. They needed space. They needed room to organize. To defend their queen.

The floodgate flew open.

The mice billowed through the front door. They fled the storefront, where hussars appeared one by one, two by two and more. The soldiers filed into formation and raised their weapons. Above the howling storm, the wind and ice, their little voices cried.

"Hooah! Hooah!"

They marched, line by line. Plowing through the snow, slicing through the ice. Columns of uniformed soldiers filled the aisles. Sleet shot over their heads like artillery. It tinked off the glass, bounced into the street.

Rinks crawled against the window. Vern huddled next to her. He'd given up all hope of running around to the back door. The entire building shuddered. It was going to fall like the castle. Under the general's orders, the mice gathered around their queen and guided her outside.

The building exhaled snow through the front door. It whipped high into the night, swirled over the buildings. The peppermint current glittered like fairy dust. It was thick and dazzling. Plumes of sparkles cartwheeled down the sidewalks and up the sides of the buildings, rustled awnings and rattled locked doors. It raced under parked cars, swirled around the fountain and shook the branches on the great Christmas tree.

The long exhale ended when the final hussar emerged.

There were a thousand of them in all. They marched into the street, locked in step, chanting as they went. "Hooah! Hooah!"

The mouse army crowded the sidewalks on both sides of the street. Their queen and king (but mostly their queen) they guarded in the doorway of Happy's Candy Emporium. The armies eyed each other, waiting for orders. The plastic steeds held steady. Weapons were at the ready. There were no caves to escape to, no streams to cut off a charge. This was it.

The toy store breathed again.

The peppermint air coughed a steady stream of snow and ice. It piled on the curbs and rested on awnings. Coated windshields with frost.

"My crown!" Rinks watched it roll down the street like a loose wagon wheel.

"No!" Vern grabbed her. "Stay here!"

"We can't leave," a head said.

"Don't be an idiot," another head said.

Rinks struggled to escape his iron grip (his hand felt like a trap on her arm). She felt naked. Without her crown, she was just a big ugly mouse. But then from the front door, the first of many came rolling onto the asphalt. It came to rest across the street, popped up, and shook off the snow.

It was a dwarf.

Six more followed. Then came the other weirdos who had crowded the market at Rose Lake. The dancers and robots, the slinky springs and twirly tops. Lollipops and licorice whips, rolly dusters and mini-busters. Gnarly rooters and shooter tooters, pop-its and shove-its, wheelie-makers and frog-stakers, cookie cutters and ditch rutters.

Candyland barreled into the real world.

They ignored the tense standoff, running and dancing, hand in hand and leg in hook. Singing. Laughing. They climbed over parked cars and stared through store windows. The buildings had taken on a sugary glow.

A car stopped at the corner. Its headlights beamed into the chaos. The driver and passenger got out. Snow fell on the hood of the car. Jaws dropping, they reached for their phones. When they found they mysteriously didn't have reception, they tried to take pictures. When that didn't work, they got back in their car. When it didn't start, they honked the horn.

"The toy store is haunted," the driver said. In a sense, he wasn't wrong.

Candyland crept over the town. Bricks turned into gingerbread. Rivets and bolts became chocolate drops. Tires transformed into cookies.

Lights came on in the apartments above the stores. People looked down on the improbable snowfall and the impossible mob. Giant flakes of pink snow drifted down from a starry sky. It muffled sound and condensed breath into fog.

Once again, the wind died.

If a picture were taken at that very moment, it would've been fit for a holiday calendar. A scene imagined by the mind of a twisted artist who stayed up late on too many nights. It was still and magical. For a brief moment, everyone and everything looked up. They felt Christmas nearing. Sugarplums invaded children's dreams. The sound of Santa's sleigh bells. It was peaceful, it was.

The toy store exhaled one final time.

34

Toxic emotions seeping from the pores of her wooden body smelled sulfuric and rancid.

They condensed like storm clouds, filled her lungs. It was a bottomless black box full of roiling pressure that was somehow empty and full at the same time. An all-consuming emptiness pulled on every aching fiber in her body. It highlighted a gaping black box. Nothing could escape its gravity.

The lid on the box was gone. Blown to pieces.

She wanted the box gone. Covered up like a turd in a litter box. To make it go away. Wishing it never existed. But she couldn't look away. It had become her.

I don't want this!

The mighty sword cut the air. It shattered the thrones. The remaining walls crumbled and fell over the edge. She searched the remains for the missing piece in her life, the thing that would make her whole again. There was nothing but smoke and rubble.

"WHERE ARE THEY?"

The words rippled down the castle. Floors shook. The chocolate walls continued to fall, turning end over end on their way to Rose Lake. They dropped into the rose-tinted water with barely a splash.

She kicked the stump of a once-pristine pillar over distant mountains. All the power made the ache worse. Even with the villagers watching from below, the endless stretches of candy-striped forests and chocolate-dipped hills, the caramel waterfalls and faraway kingdoms—she was alone.

"WHERE ARE THEY?"

A dark violet wave bruised the pink sky, rolling through it like an ugly sound wave. A box flickered in its wake. The outline remained long enough for her to see it. The lid to the gift had been closed. Her aunt and uncle had escaped. They'd locked her inside. Her brother was out there. She could feel his absence. Her search, her answer to this dull, unimaginable pain—this idiotic journey—wasn't in Candyland.

It's out there.

She raised the mighty sword. The central ridge along the flat length gleamed. There was no sun in Candyland. No moon or night. Yet the sword flashed its brilliance. *Yes,* it said. *It's out there.* She stood on the toothy ledge of the castle, a peppermint breeze fluttering up the sides to ruffle the tufted beard on her square chin. The tip of the sword slashed through cotton-candy clouds. Onto the toes of her boots, she jabbed deep into the pink sky.

It struck something hard.

She drove the sword higher. The lid was heavy and resistant, but a flash of red light briefly escaped through the opening. The string lights in the bedroom were visible for a moment. She moved closer to the edge, leaning further onto her toes. With all her might, she thrust the sword upward.

Clink.

The red lights. They began turning. Marie let go of the sword.

She was falling.

※

THE HAT FELL AWAY. The sword turned somewhere below her. For a moment, she was weightless. Drifting downward like a boulder breaking from the side of a mountain. There wasn't much impact, not like you would expect. Falling into water from that distance would break anything into little unrecognizable pieces. But this wasn't ordinary water. This was Rose Lake.

Marie sank below the surface as smoothly as dipping her fingers in a bowl of tea.

Rosy light quickly dimmed above her. She paddled her enormous arms and kicked her tree-trunk legs. They swirled in the dark water without purchase. Even wood would not float. A current dragged her down. She expected to find a hard bottom to kick off from and surge upward and outward. To escape her pain.

There was no bottom.

The world became a dark shade of scarlet. It turned to burgundy silt. Coldness sank into her like serpent teeth spreading icy venom. She fought the grip of the current, twisted and turned. Her screams came out in bubbles that were swiftly pulled into a riptide. Even they didn't escape.

Marie sank deeper.

Time had stopped. It was a continuous present moment that did not move. The panic to breathe subsided. She was a wooden soldier. She had no lungs. No stomach or organs. She was not going to die. The harder she fought, the deeper she sank. There was nothing she could do. She had the sense Rose Lake wanted something from her. A key that would allow her to be free.

It wasn't like Rose Lake was talking. There were whispers in the water, but not exactly words in her ear. No rosy mermaids singing to her. She felt it. She felt the wishes as if the water itself was a current of thoughts. It wanted her to give up, to let the current take her where it was going. To be a leaf in the river. A stone in the ocean.

To surrender.

No, she answered.

Felt herself tumble head over boot, not knowing if there was an up or a down. The numbing waters were inside her. She felt their cold hands rush through her and gush into the emotional black box, swirling its contents.

NO!

She snapped her jaw. Shockwaves erupted. The black box slammed shut, seams bulging. She kicked and screamed and swung her arms. She didn't want this. She didn't ask for this. She wanted it to go away, to leave her alone. *To never have happened!*

There would be no surrender. Not today or tomorrow or ever.

She pulled her knees to her chest, locked her arms around her shins. Lacing her fingers together, tucking her head against her knees (the hat had floated away), she folded her body as tight as a clam. As impenetrable as the pearl inside it.

NO! NO!

Her knuckles as white as the gloves that covered them. Arms and legs creaking under the strain. Joints popping. Weightless, she hadn't noticed she was no longer sinking.

Eyes squeezed shut.

Mind blank.

She no longer heard Rose Lake's invitation. Whether it whispered to her or not, she repeated a single word over and over in her mind. Her mantra of resistance that kept her hard and unyielding.

NO! NO! NO!

Her feelings encased in a concrete shell, she hung in the silence, a numb ball of wood. Seeing nothing. Feeling nothing. Becoming nothing. Rose Lake heard her answer.

It answered back.

❄

From deep below, a current rose like a volcanic vent opened up. It swept her upward like the remains of a shipwreck. She was spit out into the frigid air. Marie remained clamped down, spinning over the raspberry-tinted water. Soaring like a cannonball fired from the deck of a warship. Wind whistled past her ears.

She landed in the snowy bank, half buried in the soggy earth. She uncurled on impact. Arms unfolding. Legs springing outward. Her eyes snapped open like shutters. Disoriented, she'd forgotten what she'd become. *What am I?* was her first question. She didn't see that her arms and legs, her chest and back had become wood beneath the red coat and white gloves. Then, looking up at the sky, she thought, *And what is that?*

The world had turned upside down.

Snow was falling in the wrong direction.

Her red jacket with brass buttons was drenched. The white gloves on her hands soaked. Her head rested in the soft embrace of the snowy shore. Hooked candy canes had erupted from the ground like striped streetlights. They sprang up like weeds. Pink snow swirled above her. It wasn't drifting down from the sky—although a thin layer of the pink stuff had accumulated on her square jaw. *It's snowing upward.*

It sounded like a full-throated carnival had begun.

There were shouts of joy. Screams of fun like children coming down a slick waterslide. Hats tumbled upward. A funnel was turning in the sky, sucking snow and carts and toys and dwarves and hussars into its vortex. There were mice and plastic horses, crates of chocolate, dust storms of sugar pulled from rooftops, walls of gingerbread, and gumdrops from Gumdrop Alley.

They were falling into the black square in the pink sky.

Marie sat up. Her gloves sank in the snow. The world wasn't upside down. Candyland wasn't falling down through the black square. *It's being sucked out!* The landscape around her was rising off the ground. She didn't turn around to see what had become of the castle. Even if she had, she wouldn't have appreciated what she would've seen.

A pilot light ignited fumes of anger. It began to warm the deadwood shiver inside her. It incinerated emotions leaking from the box.

Rose Lake erupted again. An enormous burp ejected what belonged to her. It spun like a helicopter blade. *Whoop, whoop, whoop.* And speared the ground next to her. Next came the hat with the looping chain, falling with a sodden *thwap.* She fixed the hat on her head. Grabbed the sword that had been spat out from Rose Lake, and looked up at the black square.

The gift was open.
She'd lost the princess and her brother.
She knew where to find them.

❄

Marie crawled through the front door of the toy store.

She pushed her way through, splintering the frame and cracking the windows. She stood to full height, staring directly at people in their second-story apartments chattering in the winter chill. Looks of shock and amazement.

Her steely gaze took aim at the scene below. It locked onto each thing and every person. The hussars stood before her in formation on the plastic horses. They parted like a curtain and pushed through the snow that threatened to bury them. The horses dug through it. Marie took one step. Her boot hit the pavement.

The buildings shook.

Snow fell from the sky like ash. It clouded the space between the buildings. None of this mattered to her. She was in the real world and made of wood. All of Candyland had escaped with her, and none of that mattered to her.

Mice were clotted at a candy store like a swarm of bees. Buried in the shadows, she saw the twitching noses. The fire crackling in the hearth of her chest smoldered. Puffs of gray smoke leaked from beneath her vest. One earth-shaking step was all it took. The mice scattered.

The Mousequeen and Mouseking ran for it.

The hussars charged. The vermin army turned tail. It was a slow retreat through the piling snow. The hussars barely managed to dig their way out. Marie stepped over them. With each plodding stride, the blizzard grew. The buildings were fading shadows. It felt good to run. She needed to escape the emotions burning her alive.

"WHERE ARE THEY?" she released.

Windows shattered. Alarms went off.

Her wooden legs numb. Her stomach a knotted ball of snakes; her chest a metal cage. Christmas cheer tainted by the foul breath in her mouth. She ran harder. The snow came thicker. A toy here. A car there.

Sirens whined in the distance. A snapshot of spinning red lights.

She outran everything except the snow and the memories glittering on their crystal edges. Her memories poured out of the black box like ghosts. They stuck to the snow, petrified her limbs, saturated her with fear heavy and cold. She ran blindly into the storm.

Running and running and running.

35

This isn't happenin'.

Rinks was a mouse. Her husband had seven heads. The buildings were gingerbread. For some reason, it was a twenty-foot nutcracker that was most unbelievable.

Smoke puffed from its sleeves. Vengeance burned its eyes. Boots that would smash her army like ants on a sidewalk. They were useless to her. Worst of all, the nutcracker reeked of ungratefulness.

The brat.

Marie's eyes scanned the area, looking for Rinks. "Hold still," Rinks said. "Everyone, be still. She won't see us."

They huddled deeper into the doorway beneath an awning sagging under the weight of discolored snow. The mice went limp, their tails lying like cords of rope. The tiny heartbeats pitter-pattered against Rinks. Whiskers tickled her face.

"Vern, shut your stupid heads up."

The bickering didn't stop (they were arguing about the best way to escape), but it dropped to whispers. There was no way Marie would see them. It would look like a discarded rug piled against the door. A rug with tails. If the peppermint wind kept blowing, they would become a snowdrift. She was plenty warm under the tiny bodies. In fact, she was starting to sweat. They were going to make it. When Marie was down the road, they would run in the other direction.

Vern sneezed. The idiot.

Rinks peeked out. There was so much going on already, Marie didn't hear it. But then one of Vern's heads said, "Bless you."

"Gesundheit," another one said.

"Shut up," another said.

"RUN!" said another.

That did it. An avalanche of fur scattered to the sidewalk. They burrowed into the snowbanks and ran along the gutter. Hussars raised their swords. "Hooah!"

"Get back here! I'm your queen! Protect the queen!"

She was alone in the corner, just her and her mutant husband. Vern scrambled onto his stumpy legs and hurried off. Trinkets fell from his pockets as he waddled for safety. Her little chickens were gone. Was it because she had no crown? Did they forget? A second ago, they had been dutifully hiding her. Now she was completely exposed. A giant weirdo on the street.

Steam shot from Marie's nostrils like a mechanical bull seeing a red cape. A steam engine pumped to life somewhere in the enormous wooden head. Then the eyes fell on her like wrecking balls. With one step, a heavy boot cracked the pavement. The awning ripped open and dumped a load of pink snow on Rinks. Not enough to hide her. Too late for that.

The ground thundered. Sent waves of terror to the top of Rinks's head. She bit her lip and tasted blood. It was over. Everything she fought for was going to end any second now. As soon as her selfish niece put that oversized glove around her, that would be it. *Fine*, she thought. *I don't belong here anyway.*

"What are you doin'?" Vern returned. "Come on."

"It's goin' to be all okay," a head said.

"RUN!" said the one.

Vern pulled her off the concrete. The general squealed in her ear. They ran close to the building, where the snow was the shallowest.

The mouse army had abandoned their weapons. The hussars gave chase on their stupid little horses. "Hooah!" Most of the hussars, though, were lining up on both sides of the street. They were clearing a path for the oncoming giant. Like Marie was a one-person parade. They saluted when she neared.

Vern tried to open the door to the video game store. It was locked. The next one was a clothing store that sold candles. Locked. The coffee shop, locked. Marie's footsteps knocked them off-balance each time one of the boots shattered the pavement. Rinks wobbled against the window of the coffee shop. The mechanical elves with their wooden tools were gone.

It was too late to try another door. He fell on the ground with her, wrapped his arms around her neck. The general climbed onto her head. Nearby mice returned to her side and scurried into her lap. The general called for reinforcements, and more mice came from the snowdrifts. The hussars ignored them as they got in line to salute the wooden menace.

Marie smelled like sulfur. Snow melted around her and ran down the gutters. Vern leaned into Rinks. At that moment, she loved the smell of coffee breath. The way his sharp whiskers poked her cheek. Vern put his lips to her ear (it wasn't one of the neck heads; it was her Vern) and whispered, "My queen."

She shivered with delight.

If they survived, she would love him. All of him. Maybe she'd twist a few of the heads off, just the mean ones (definitely the one that said RUN!), but she'd keep the rest. Because she loved him. He got her.

She closed her eyes. *He sees me.*

The footsteps drew near. Rinks and Vern were bouncing off the sidewalk now. A heatwave fell over them like a runaway wagon of burning hay was coming. The snowmelt soaked their clothing. Her bones rattled.

"WHERE ARE THEY?"

Rinks held very still with her only family that loved her. She smiled a fangy smile in her wet clothing. Still a queen.

The next footstep didn't bounce her as high off the concrete. The next one only tickled her bum. She didn't open her eyes, imagining that steam engine of rage leaning over them. Rinks wouldn't give her niece the satisfaction of seeing her quiver.

Squeak.

The general had climbed out of the pile. He leaped on her head and squeaked again. Rinks peeked through one eye. The back of the nutcracker was fading in the pink snowstorm.

"She didn't see us," Rinks said. Marie was blinded by pettiness. Probably saw something shiny and got distracted. "Dumb girl."

The hussars followed the nutcracker into the pink haze. She was just a fuzzy patch of red and then vanished in the storm. The mice were hopping with excitement. The general raised his weapon (the only one not to drop it). Rinks was on her hands and knees, watching to make sure Marie didn't return. She stepped into the street.

We're safe, she thought.

Marie didn't want anything to do with her. She saw Rinks, looked right at her, then walked on her way. That opened all sorts of possibilities. Marie might be marching all the way to the North Pole, for all Rinks knew. And now that the buildings were candy and the weirdos were playing in the street, that meant one thing. Rinks didn't have to go back. Her kingdom had followed her into the real world.

And I'm the queen, she thought proudly. *Get ready, world, for the Mousequeen.*

She wouldn't have to hide her whiskers. She could be exactly who she was. And she was going to show the world. She searched for her phone. What better time to post a selfie than now?

The watermelon snow was starting to accumulate now that Marie wasn't melting it. Only now it was drifting sideways, she noticed. There was no wind, not even a breeze, but the delicate flakes were floating into her face and moving down the street. Before she turned around to see where it was going, she heard Vern.

"My crowns," all seven heads muttered.

Someone had the crowns he had lost. There was also a big one crusted with jewels. Rinks put a hand on her head. Felt the blank space on top of her coarse mop of graying hair. Vern was reaching for them.

"Vern, no," she said. Then louder, "Stop!"

❄

Fizzy.

The boy stood in the middle of the street with that gross hat pulled down to his eyes and a dopey grin on his dopey face. Like a cat waiting for the mouse to poke her head out. The crowns looped around his arms and dangled at his elbows. Vern's little crowns were bunched on his left arm. Rinks's crown (the only one that mattered) was on his right. The only reason Fritz wasn't holding them like horseshoes was because his hands were already full. A cloaked figure stood on each side of him, holding his hands.

The king and queen.

Rinks could smell her sister in the dark cowl. The fragrance she wore in high school. The sweat after skating. She could feel the condescending stare behind the wisps of frosty breath.

"Hey, buddy," Vern said. "Remember good old Uncle Vernon? Yeah, it's me. Real quick, those are mine. Thanks for findin' them for me. I'll just—"

"Don't get any closer, Vern."

The general squeaked agreement from Rinks's shoulder. Vern froze with a hungry hand out and fourteen hungry eyes. "He got our crowns, Rinks," he sang.

"Mine!" another head shouted.

"It's a trap," Rinks said. She could feel it. It was her sister holding Fritz's right hand. She couldn't trust her, never could.

"But the crowns, Rinks."

"No, it's bait. They want you to step closer. Ain't that right? You want us to get in there and blind us with a memory, which is a lie, after all."

"Why would they want that?" Vern said.

"Because it's her! It's what she does. She's usin' poor little Fizzy as bait, don't you get it? It's disgustin', treatin' your own boy that way. I ain't fallin' for it again."

"But." Vern pointed at the other cloaked figure. "It's his dad. He says—"

"Shut up, Vern! All of yous. I know what I'm talkin' about here. You don't think I know what she wants? Fool me once, shame on me. Fool me twice, it's her fault."

Pink snow was streaming faster down the street. It stuck to her face, even stung a little, before it melted. She could feel the wind pulling them now. Somewhere in the opposite direction the snow was flying, Marie screamed in the distance.

"Where's that sandman of yours?" she asked Fritz. "Bet they took him away, didn't they? That's what your mom does. I'm sorry to say that, but it's the truth."

Rinks really put some sting on that, but he kept on smiling. Maybe he'd gone deaf, too.

She knew that wasn't her sister in that cloak. Not really. It smelled like her, it felt like her, but her sister was gone. Then again, Vern had seven heads. So there was a chance.

"I took your kids. You could start with a thank you. I didn't even want them." She said it right into that black hole inside the hood, glanced at Fritz after she said it. *Still smiling.* "Vern and me were perfectly happy before you and the hub packed it in. Now you guys are just goin' to, what, just come back and take it all away from us? That's just like you. You can have the kids back. I want my crown."

"Don't say that," Vern said.

"You don't want your crowns?"

"About the kids. Fritz is good. So's Marie."

"Phht. What planet you on? He don't talk, and she don't listen." There was a long distant moan. It was hard to tell if it was human or animal. Either way, it made the hairs stiffen on her back. "Besides, who you kiddin', Vern? You know her." Rinks took half a step and pointed. "She couldn't stand we had the castle. Could you? It was eatin' you up so bad you came back just to take it. It ain't fair, you know. I finally get somethin', and you can't stand it. You don't know what it's like to work for it. You don't. It all came sooo easy for you. Just wake up and someone givin' you awards and presents and all that. Family and money. Let me tell you somethin', sister. Money can't buy happiness."

Rinks felt the twist of hypocrisy in her stomach.

She grabbed Vern's arm. He was creeping closer to the crowns looped around Fritz's arm. The snow was starting to sting her eyes. The Candyland weirdos felt it, too. They were walking down the street in the same direction it was flying. Even the hussars retreated with them. Not her mice, though. They hid in the snowdrifts.

In the direction Marie had disappeared came a long, lonesome wail. Someone was crying. It wasn't an animal.

"Hear that?" Rinks said to her sister. "Hurts a little, don't it? Your angry daughter sad like that. Your son, all he does is smile."

"*Rinks—*"

"Hush it, Vern. She's got to hear this. How's that make you feel, sis? Me and Vern pickin' up your pieces. Who's the big mistake now? It ain't me. I'm the good one now. Bet that feels a little ugly, don't it? I know."

The hussars were marching in lines. The war was over. Good. They could all go on their way and leave her mice alone. Rinks held up her hand to block the snow. It was coming off the ground now and stuck to them. Her sister's cloak was dusted on one side like pink frosting.

"So you done havin' all your fun? Your nutcrackin' daughter done wrecked everythin' and went runnin' off. Fizzy here, you can have him. You think I give a hoot?"

Rinks dropped her hand. It was starting to tremble. Her voice cracked. She could taste the biting venom in her words. She thought it would feel good shouting at her sister. The words she deserved.

"You're not the queen!" Rinks pumped her fist. "I got news, you're just ordinary. That's all you are. And me, I deserve better. I deserve more! It's Christmas, and this is what I get?"

The last of the Candyland weirdos hustled with the wind. Some were caught up in the current and tumbled like beachballs in a sandstorm. Rinks was knocked off balance. Vern kept her from falling. She sniffed, then turned her head. Wiped her eyes so her sister wouldn't see the water starting to pool in them.

Fritz let go of their hands. The crowns rang on his arms. He held them out to them. That stupid little smile still on his face. The venom hadn't affected him in the least. *He is deaf.*

"What?" Rinks said. "You just going to give them to us? I ain't fallin' for it."

"We got a choice," Vern said.

"Choice for what?"

"We can stay here. That's what he said." He pointed at Fritz's dad, who hadn't moved an inch. Vern, evidently, understood the creepy silence inside that hood. "Everythin' goes back to normal, just like before. Like none of this happened. We keep the toy store and the kids. It's our choice." All of Vern's heads cocked their ears. In unison, they nodded. "If we stay, he said, you can get help."

"Help? Help for what?" He didn't say. Rinks knew what he meant. Help for what hurt deep inside her. "What's the other choice?"

"We take the crowns."

Fritz held them up. Vern looked in the direction the snow and the toys were going. The wind wasn't blowing them down the street. The snow was being sucked into the open door of the toy store like an industrial vacuum was running on all cylinders. Dwarves and hussars and a few mice and dancers and little army men and teddy bears and robots rolling inside it as well. The walls of the toy store were billowing inward. One of the windows shattered.

Candyland is callin'.

"What about her?" Rinks said, nodding at her sister. Vern shook his head.

Rinks twitched. The scar felt cold and heavy. Her heart felt the same. The air was thinning. It was difficult to breathe. She looked at the sky. Stars were strewn across a dark blanket. Somewhere something howled long and soulful. This time she knew it was an animal. Its call quivered inside her.

She looked at her husband. Her freaky, ugly husband and his

seven heads. She wasn't much different. She was darker than him on the inside, perhaps. The choice was a no-brainer. But the longer she stood there, the harder the decision became. Vern felt her struggle and removed the few crowns he still possessed off his heads. He held them to his chest.

He knelt before her.

She took a deep breath, then another. *Heavy is the crown,* she thought. And she wasn't wearing one. Did she want to?

The roof of the toy store collapsed. The walls fell over. Bricks tumbled into the street. Candyland was about to close up shop. She looked at her husband. The heads on his neck were beginning to shrink. *Everythin' goes back to the way it was.*

She chuckled and wiped her eyes. Sighed and looked down at her nephew still making his offering. "It's not what you *want*, ain't that what the fat man said, Fizzy?"

He didn't answer. Only smiled.

36

The town bell chimed.

Lights twinkled dimly. They were too numerous to be fire trucks, unless the entire state had been called. Exhausted, she approached them. All that running and she hadn't gotten far at all.

The great Christmas tree appeared.

The star on top of it shone like a lighthouse on a rocky shore. She had not one more step left in her. The sword fell from her aching hand. She dropped to her knees, hands sinking in the snow. The inferno that drove her had died to a tiny flame. She panted and shook, arms quivering. Legs weak. Her mind filled with the static that runs on a dead channel. Something was there. She just couldn't tune it.

The town bell signaled its last chime and faded into silence.

The snow continued to fall.

It piled on her back. Melted down her cheeks. She had nowhere else to go. No matter how fast or how far she ran, she would always be exactly where she didn't want to be.

Here.

Christmas was out there, somewhere. She could feel it reaching for her. It was a low hum that vibrated in the haze. It rose and fell as delicately as snow. Soft and comforting. Promising. The hum turned into a melody rising from closed lips and open throats. From the blizzard, shapes emerged. She had no strength left to grip the sword. No will to raise it. She let whoever had come for her come.

She could run no more.

The figures came out of the winter blur, tall and short. Some bearded, some not. They surrounded her just out of reach and cloaked in winter's veil. Their song humming. Their song comforting. They surrounded her, holding hands. She wished not to know who they were or what they wanted. Only to be left alone. To rest in the empty static.

Someone came forward. Beneath the blinking lights of the Christmas tree, she stood with her head bowed in a white cloak of fine silk, the cuffs trimmed with red. The hem bunched in the snow. Her hands no longer shriveled and dry, but tender and soft.

Princess Pirlipat reached up to pull back the hood.

The misshapen head was no more. The mouth no longer a slit, nor the eyes bulging. Marie looked up to a glowing princess. She reached for the nutcracker on her knees. The princess sifted her fingers through the coarse black hair on the soldier before her. A soldier who fought long and hard for longer than she realized. A warrior who battled to keep her enemies locked in a black box. A soldier exhausted from the conflict, collapsed before her. Totally exposed.

Marie looked upon the face of the princess.

Tears leaked from her wooden face. A trickle, at first. They ran down her hardened cheeks. They gave way to a stream. The black box that once was clotted with fiery rage now gushed with sparkling light. It surged forward as a tsunami, engulfing every bit of her. Her sobs came out in long cries that stole her breath. She collapsed under the weight of it, curling up in a bed of pink snow. Each wave racked her harder than the one before it. A briny flow of emotions extinguished anger and rage as it flooded through her. It beamed with light as bright as the star on top of the tree.

The princess knelt beside her.

The humming grew louder. It wrapped its song around her, sank inside her. They drew closer, hands locked together. Through a wash of tears, she couldn't see them. But she felt them. The love and support. Their presence and song embraced her. It held her while she let go of what she'd tried so hard to ignore. The thing that would destroy her if she faced it. Grief spilled from bottomless depths that she feared would drown her.

The princess leaned over, and in her ear she spoke in a voice Marie very much recognized. The princess said, "I miss them so very much."

Marie's wooden body splintered. Her wails of sorrow shook the star atop the Christmas tree. The armor crumbled off her, leaving her wounded and raw. She wept for her brother. She wept for her parents. For the first time, she dared to admit, to even allow herself to think what she held so dear in her heart. For if she did, she would not survive. She wept for herself.

I miss them so much.

The dark night continued. If the grief would consume her, she was helpless to stop it. Unlike Rose Lake, she did not fight it. She did not kick it away or flail in its depth. She allowed it to take her. She made space for the pain. All the feelings she'd stuffed inside the black box flowed into the current.

The circle around her parted, but their presence was still there. Through closed eyes, she felt a great shadow move over her. The musky smell of fur was in her nostrils. Large nostrils, wet and quivering, snorted the length of her. A big black eye looked deep inside her. The reindeer lifted his head. To the world, he opened his throat. Through thick, rubbery lips, he cried out long and loud enough to be heard all the way to the North Pole.

Ronin wept.

Marie curled up beneath him. His four legs planted around her, never moving. Nothing would ever hurt her while he stood over her.

She breathed in sadness and floated downstream with it, let it carry her away. Adrift in the long night of grief that lasted a lifetime.

Under a watchful eye, surrounded by the loving hum of song, she dissolved into slumber. On the edge of consciousness that still quivered and sobbed, she heard bells draw near. Ronin shuffled away, but not far. He stood beside her, watching carefully as someone approached.

Strong arms picked her up.

She tucked her hands under her chin, felt the tender lump in her throat. A nutcracker no more.

37

It was a long, winding river of night. Through the stars it flowed. In the small corners, it puddled. The journey swept her far and wide until she floated toward the sound of a crackling fire.

Her eyes were puffy and sore. Orange sparks flitted in the dark. *Christmas fairies off to deliver wishes,* she thought.

She was wrapped snugly in a swaddling, purple blanket. A fire danced in a round pit. On the other side of it were two empty Adirondack chairs, exactly like the one she was sitting in. On the armrest of one of the chairs, the nutcracker stood. He was a foot tall, mouth open. As stiff as a tree limb. The dragon and teddy, the ones she had found in the backyard, were below him. On the other armrest was a glass of milk and a plate of unwrapped protein bars.

Marie looked around.

Her head was heavy and filled with sand. Memories were elusive. She'd fallen asleep by the fire, she reasoned. Although reason was a flimsy card in her fizzy state. *Fizzy,* she thought. And then thought of Aunt Rinks with long whiskers and a pointed nose. *Fritz brought out the milk and protein bars. Didn't he?* The light was on inside the kitchen. A shadow went past the window. *Fritz?*

Her stomach ached, and her ribs were sore. She tried to remember, but everything was tangled and frayed. Memories were bits of flotsam on a salty tide of sleep. Waves of sorrow still washed up inside her, only now they slid over her instead of thundering down and churning her in a riptide.

It was a dream. She laid her head back and stared at the stars. *An awful dream.*

The air was cool. She sat at the edge of the fire's warmth, a thud in her stomach and knot in her throat. The lure of sleep cast over her eyes when an ash escaped the thermal rise above the fire. It fluttered in a random pattern. Marie watched it slowly drift toward her and noticed it wasn't gray. It landed on the purple blanket over her lap and began to melt.

It was pink.

Warm exhaust blew the hair on top of her head. She tried to sit up but was too disoriented to do much more than duck. Tree branches swung over her. A long, furry muzzle reached for the ground in front of her. Rubber lips snatched up slices of carrot strewn on the ground. A black eye turned toward her.

Marie leaned away, the armrest creaking. The reindeer lifted his enormous head, the antlers catching some of the overhead branches, then knocked over one of the empty chairs. She didn't move as he sniffed her arm. His nostrils tickled her cheek. Humid breath exhausting on her face.

The back door opened.

Someone came down the steps with a sigh. Backlit by the kitchen light, she couldn't see who it was, only knew he was much too big and round to be her brother. He stepped into the fire's glow, wearing a white T-shirt with black suspenders. His baggy pants were burgundy. His boots heavy and black.

"Watch your head," he said with a deep voice.

He wasn't talking to Marie. The reindeer snorted as the man picked up the chair that had been knocked over. He sat down with a groan (more like fell into the chair) and pushed wire-rimmed glasses up his pudgy nose. He looked over the fire at Marie. A smile hidden in his gray beard.

"Godfather?" she croaked. Her voice sounded like it came through a cheap speaker.

"Rest, dear. It's been a very long night."

The reindeer stretched his neck and barked agreement. He went back to snatching carrots off the ground, noisily grinding them between his teeth. Godfather watched Marie melt back into her chair. Kindness radiated from his eyes. He watched the reindeer search the weeds for lost carrots.

"It's been a long night," Godfather said. "I wanted to send him back with the others, but he wouldn't leave you."

Marie watched Godfather sip from the glass of milk. He licked his lips and picked up a protein bar, examined it in the firelight. On second thought, he put it back on the plate and took another swallow of milk.

This time of year is very busy, Marie recalled Godfather saying.

Marie shook her head, but it no more cleared it than if she shook a snow globe. A thousand questions rattled like bingo balls in a tumbler. Each one screamed for attention, begged to make sense from this dreamy scene. She swam in an ocean of unknowns. Only one question fell out of the chute. Depending on the answer to it, the other questions wouldn't matter.

"Is this real?"

"You are here," was all he said. "As am I."

She looked at the building. "Where's my brother?"

"He's home, Marie."

Home? A part of her wished that meant the impossible. That he was curled up in the bed he grew up in, and she was in the room next to him. And this *was* just a dream. *That* was home. The toy store was just a building.

"We wanted to be with you before you go back. After a difficult journey, I thought this prudent."

He put the glass of milk down and examined the nutcracker, turning him over to pull the lever. Watching the mouth open and close where nuts would surrender their treasure. Even ones impossibly hard. With a sigh, he looked at her again. His eyes so relaxed and open. She could swim in their kindness.

She pulled the purple cocoon around her tighter.

"I remember when your father was a boy." He tipped his head back and smiled. "When he was Fritz's age, he would make bows out of saplings. Fashioned arrows from tree branches. He and his friends would run through the woods behind his house like they lived in the wild. They cut vines and drank the water that dripped out, which made his parents quite concerned when they found out. But they liked his bond with nature and sent him to Earth Camp in the summer, where he camped and fished and carved bowls from wood. He went a week without changing his underwear. He also cut his hand and went to the hospital for stitches."

He dragged his finger over the fleshy base of his thumb. Right where her father had a white scar. Godfather chuckled deeply. His eyes twinkled with firelight.

"He was six years old when he got his first skateboard. When he wasn't running through the woods, he was practicing kick-flips. He and his friends..." He shook his head, chuckling. Looked up at her. "Those kids can do magic on four wheels. I don't understand it. And I've seen reindeer fly."

Godfather laughed heartily.

"He was scared of robots, your father. His parents would find him curled up at the foot of their bed. He got over that, given the things he would eventually build for me. He still buttoned his shirts wrong, though, and never cared. An artist's heart, he had. An imagination with wheels. He was kinder and funnier than most. He was a beautiful boy, Marie. And a great man."

He let that thought hover between them. It landed on the soft part of her mind like seeds blown onto black dirt. They gave rise to vivid memories of what he was like. Memories she'd stuffed down at the bottom of that emotional black box. Buried beneath the hurt.

Memories she could now see.

"And your mother." Godfather grumbled with laughter. "Not like your father. Nothing got in her way. Not even when she was a toddler. A will as strong as steel. When she put her mind to something, it yielded to her wishes. From the time she was born, she moved with intense grace and fierce elegance. She was on the naughty list, your mother."

He held up four fingers. *Four times.*

"Oh, yes. Your father was an explorer, but she was a pioneer. Testing boundaries was her hobby. She got good grades and all, but do you know how many times she was suspended?"

Marie knew that answer. Her mother had told her when Marie was suspended for fighting a girl in gym class who stole her phone from her locker. Marie got it back, but not before they ended up on the ground. Her mother took her out for lunch and a long talk. *There's good trouble and bad trouble,* she had said. Marie didn't exactly know what that meant at the time.

"Your mother had her regrets, Marie. She damaged relationships she couldn't repair. She was human."

He shared more stories. The awards her mother had won. The hours of practice it took to win them. The way she fought with her parents and her sister with a head as hard as concrete. Marie sank into the chair, felt like she was dripping between the seat slats. There was space for her to hold these memories now. Before, she could only think about them from a distance, then slam the lid shut. Before other feelings escaped. The memories Teri, her therapist, wanted her to explore.

Joy and grief can coexist, Teri had said.

"When your mother and father met, it changed her. It changed them both. They shined together. I knew them better than most people. She grounded your father, instilled him with risk to find his endless potential. He softened her, made her feel the world more deeply, to not try to bend it to her will. Together, they were beautiful. And so are their children."

He didn't take his eyes from her. She didn't look away. They sat that way for a very long minute. The air between them warm and swirling. This moment perfect in its brokenness.

"They're gone, aren't they?" she said distantly. "They're not coming back."

"My dear," he said softly. He touched his heart. "They never left."

He reached into his pocket and pulled out the gift. Still wrapped in red and white paper with a green bow. He put it on the armrest of the chair between them. He stood the nutcracker next to it.

She leaned forward in the chair, swaying as she did so. Ronin grunted, put his head down to keep her away from the fire. She grabbed the bony ridge above his nose and stood up. The blanket fell away.

She didn't notice what she was wearing or the bandage around her left arm. She was too focused on the wrapping paper that had torn from the side of the gift. She shuffled a step, hanging onto Ronin, and reached for the gift. The wrapping paper ripped off the sides and fell into the fire. The dying flame brightened. The box was simple. It was black.

Christmas is what you need.

The back gate squealed. The trees around her rustled. A song rose up from those who were coming into the ring of fire. Marie looked down to see the white cloak of fine silk she was wearing. It bunched on the ground around her feet. Red trim along the hem and cuffs. The clothing she'd seen someone wearing at the top of the castle. And at the great Christmas tree when she had knelt next to Marie and whispered in a voice that sounded, to Marie, very much like her own voice.

"You found yourself," Godfather said.

Ms. Clara approached from the back gate with Ms. Trutchen by her side. Garl waddled out from the trees. The mechanical elves came down the narrow path with their crude wooden tools in hand. Pate the hussar came bouncing out of the dark with both arms raised. The hussars from the market were with him. The teddy bear and the dragon she found in the trees leaped up. The gummy worms crawled in the dirt. The Counselor with his gray skin and long, flowing overcoat stood to the right of Godfather. And a snowman made of sand was on his left.

Marie felt her legs wobble. She leaned against Ronin. Ms. Clara was the first one to hug her.

She wrapped Marie in her tender, strong arms. Ms. Trutchen put her arms around her, too. Garl was at her thighs. The soldiers' stiff arms around her shins. More and more they came, all humming the song she'd heard at the Christmas tree. The song that had lifted her through the dark night and carried her to the other side so that she could see the joy.

The Christmas spirit that was always there. That had never left.

The greatest gift of all.

38

Stars floated on a black tapestry like bright little bugs, randomly shifting about and blinking. A slow-moving dance. Hypnotic. Marie swam with them, weaving a dance of her own. Free to move, no longer confined by the hard shell of a body. It was timeless and lovely. A dreamless sleep that embraced and nurtured. She had no thoughts of where she was, no thoughts of here or there. Of waking or sleeping.

Then, slowly, ever so, space turned gray. She didn't know to call it that—*gray*—but sensed things had changed. As the transition continued, she felt the weight of the world wrap around her, and opened her eyes.

Morning light sparkled on a textured ceiling.

The bed was bigger than the one she'd slept in as a child. It was king-sized. A soft comforter was on top. The sheets smooth; the pillowcase smelled like fabric softener. Fresh paint was in the room. The walls bright yellow.

A chair was in front of a dresser. On the nightstand next to the chair, several wrappers were piled up. Chocolate smeared on the insides of them. A cup with a dried ring of orange juice at the bottom.

Even in the elegant comfort of the king-size mattress, aches and pains poked her arms and legs. She felt like a stone that had tumbled down the mountain, the sharp edges rounded and smooth. Bruised and beaten. She sat up on one elbow, winced at the tender pain in her arm.

A bandage was wrapped from wrist to elbow.

Memories were details in a fog, poking their heads out and laughing when she looked for them. A fragment escaped, and she saw a shiny object that had cut her arm: the long red line, the sticky crimson drips on her elbow. And the thing that threw it. A thing with seven heads.

How awful dreams could be.

A shelf was on the wall. A single object on it, looking back at her with spreading wings and a clock in its belly. Menacing eyes unblinking. It read ten o'clock. The clock her aunt hated. Said it made her stomach hurt.

This is her room.

It smelled different, though. No mold or dust; no spiderwebs on the ceiling. No dirt balls. A complete and total makeover that was as bright and clean as the sunlight coming through the window.

Slippers were by the side of the bed. She slid her feet into them. Exhaustion clung to her like a winter coat. She was a sponge squeezed of every drop and left to dry on the windowsill. She shuffled to the window, her rusty joints beginning to loosen. Across the street, two-story buildings of brick and glass stood. No snow on the awnings. *And something else*, she thought. *Something more ridiculous than snow. No cake icing. Or gingerbread walls. How odd.*

Outside the bedroom, the kitchen looked familiar. A new table and chairs, new cabinets and floor. Marie peeked in the other bedroom. The air mattress was gone. In its place was a bed (not as wide as the one Marie woke up in, but new). Red string lights were on the wall. A dresser was in the corner, the drawers half open. Above it, in the corner, was a hole where a camera used to be.

It was all so strange, like she'd accidentally awakened in a different reality, one that seemed familiar. It had that new-house smell with a hint of bacon and eggs. *Where was I?* she wondered.

There was a faint memory of sitting at a fire with a big dog eating carrots off the ground. And Santa Claus drinking milk. *I'm still dreaming.*

Then she saw a hat on the dresser. Beat up with a white rind of salt. The bill frayed. It smelled like a tackle box. The adjustable strap was tightened as far as it would go. Her stomach twisted a little. Fritz never went anywhere without that hat, not since they moved in with Aunt Rinks. Last time Marie saw it, someone else was wearing it. That someone was hiding in the mists of memory. *Someone in a cloak.*

But she dreamed that, too. She dreamed Fritz holding the stranger's hand at the end of a long, narrow hallway. The hat on the stranger's head. And light beyond.

It wasn't a stranger, she thought.

The workbench was sanded and coated with a layer of polyurethane. The owl clock that had sat on the top shelf was gone. *I took it with me.* Before she could tell herself that was a dream, too—that she hadn't dragged that strange clock into a box where a land of candy awaited—she saw the soldier standing guard at the checkered wall.

She felt weak and woozy.

The blocks on the wall looked new. The one with the X—the one she had removed first before solving the puzzle—was different. She picked up the nutcracker. The legs stiff, the coat starched. Memories swirled from dusty corners of what it felt like to be strong and unyielding. Smoldering with power. She pulled the lever on his back. The square jaw opened and closed.

We found her. We found Princess Pirlipat. I cracked the nut to break the spell. She rubbed her front teeth. Her gums were tender. *Fritz gave me the nut. Only it wasn't a nut, and I cracked it open and gave it to her. I closed my eyes and counted my steps. And then...*

The seven-headed Mouseking. The Mousequeen. The castle came apart. Everything broke open. Including her.

Did it happen? Did we really reach into a gift and go to Candyland?

Nussknacker had never come with them. Sandy had always said

he was there, but she never saw him. Because Sandy knew. He knew all this time.

"I was you," she whispered. "I was always you."

Memories came loose and crammed into her head like an attic full of keepsakes shoved into a suitcase. Her head hurt worse than her arm. She remembered it all.

The journey didn't end. It escaped into the real world. The buildings became gingerbread. Toys ran in the streets. The mouse army in formation. The hussars riding. I was on fire. There was only one thing I wanted, one question that I had to answer. And it tore me apart when I did.

❄

Voices came from the storefront.

The nutcracker creaked in her hand. She put her ear to the door. They were muffled voices. Barking laughter. She put her hand on the door, closed her eyes. Her heart swelled. She hugged the nutcracker under her chin. Her eyes felt drained of tears, but a slick of moisture appeared as she listened.

"Thank you," she whispered to the nutcracker.

He said nothing, of course. Just stared back with an open mouth.

She opened the door. The shelves were filled with toys. The windows were clean and new. The front door was not damaged; the doorframe not torn open. On the small stage in Storyteller Corner, the rocking chair had been pushed aside. A chessboard was on a circular rug. On one side, a young boy was reaching for his bishop.

"Sure you want to do that?" said his opponent. Scratching his round chin with a stick. Sand appeared to crumble on the board.

Fritz turned his head.

Marie threw the door open. Her brother was barely off the floor when she grabbed him. There was little chance he could breathe given that her embrace would frighten a grizzly bear. She never wanted to let go. Out of that dry well, one more tear found its way to the surface. It tracked warmly down her cheek.

Sandy threw his sticks around them. He wasn't real. But he was back. Her brother was safe, and Sandy was back. Maybe it was a dream. Some of it.

"Good morning, Ms. Marie."

She put her arms out and shoved Fritz behind her. He was smiling, though. Happy. The stranger had come from the other side of the storefront, wearing a long cloak. Marie felt faint as he reached for the hood.

His face filled with sunny color.

※

MARIE SAT at the kitchen table.

The Counselor cracked two eggs in a skillet. Bacon sizzled in another. He cooked with efficiency. Not a wasted movement. Total focus. It was easy to forget he was a machine. So natural the way he moved.

"Checkmate?" Sandy shouted from the storefront. "I think you're getting ahead of yourself, kid."

The Counselor poured a glass of milk. Put it on the table. "Take a few sips," he said. "You have not eaten in quite some time."

He went back to the stove, flipped the eggs. Toast popped out. He put it on a plate with the bacon and plied it with butter. There was an appetite somewhere in Marie. She hadn't found it yet. She took a sip of milk to soothe her throat. She put the glass back on the table and said: "Where is it? The gift."

"It is safe."

"What's that mean?"

His gears or something were whirring. "Godfather felt it was better in his possession now that the game has ended."

Game. That's a kind way of putting it. Great-Uncle Corker might have had something to do with Candyland (he was a game maker), but that wasn't a game.

"Do you know what happened to us?" she said. "To my brother and me."

"You completed your journey. I know that much. You have been asleep for nearly twenty-four hours. You are exhausted and quite sore, I understand. Your journey was not easy." He wiped grease from the counter. "One of that nature rarely is."

"Does he remember what happened?" Marie said. "Fritz."

"Of course. It was his journey, too."

She looked at the door leading to the storefront. "Is he... is he okay?"

"He is quite well."

"I thought I lost him." She struggled to remember the details. But the feelings were crystal clear. "Everything got so confusing, and... I couldn't find him and thought he..." She shook her head.

"He is exactly where he needs to be, Ms. Marie. As are you."

The Counselor's voice was soothing. The kind of voice that could hypnotize. That was by design, she figured. But liked it just the same. Marie let go of the glass of milk. Her fingers trembled. All the tension, the weight strapped on her shoulders, floated away. She leaned her elbows on the table before she slid out of the chair. Her cheeks were chafed and dry. Like she'd been walking into a winter storm too long.

"Are you hungry?" the Counselor asked.

Marie shrugged. She felt full and empty at the same time. Light and free. She rested in this moment, tired and confused. He put the plate in front of her. The bacon woke her taste buds up. She grabbed a slice, heavy and oily, and took a bite. It crumbled on her tongue. She chewed slowly, eyes closed. Wondering if food always tasted this good.

"Let us have a look at that, shall we?"

The Counselor took a knee next to her. He cradled her arm in his warm hands, began to unwind the bandage around her forearm. Her fingers greasy with bacon fat, she ate with her free hand. A rosy line ran from her elbow to her wrist. It was already healing. No stitches needed. The Counselor's faceplate sparkled as he inspected it. His hands were soft. He fetched cotton balls and a bottle of ethanol to clean outside of the wound.

Marie continued eating, staring at it like it wasn't her arm he was caring for. The cut was real. It was tender and sore. It stung when he dabbed the cotton ball too close to the wound. There could be an explanation for how she hurt herself. Maybe she scraped it on the back gate or cut it on a branch when she was working in the backyard. That was possible, but not true. She knew exactly how she cut her arm.

It was wearing seven crowns.

"Was Candyland real?" she asked. "Or did I dream it?"

"What do you think?"

That was what her parents said when she asked if Santa was real. They let her decide. And when she answered, they winked.

"The snow was pink, just like the sky. The buildings became gingerbread, and toys were out there on the street. The mouse army and hussars. How did it go back to normal if it wasn't a dream?"

"Perception is not reality," he said.

"Then it wasn't real."

He touched the bandage on her arm. "It was *very* real."

She didn't understand how that could be. How she was injured, but everything went back to normal. A blending of real and unreal. Was it all in her mind? The cut on her arm hurt. And sorrow was in her belly. The howl of Ronin standing over her.

"I was him." She turned toward the nutcracker standing on the table. He was watching the Counselor wrap a new bandage around her arm. "I was so... so rigid. And big. And..."

Angry. And scared. All this time, all these feelings were inside the black box. Teri was right. But I didn't have time to look inside it until it was full. That's not true, though. I didn't want *to look inside it. Because if I did, I would have to admit the truth. I'd have to let go of the wish I clung to with my fingernails—that one morning I would wake up in my bedroom, Mom would be downstairs, Dad would be outside. What happened was all a bad dream.*

"The nutcracker story you told," she said. "She was cursed and needed to be found. You knew, didn't you?" She waited for him to answer, then added: "You knew she was *me*."

The Counselor looked up, tilted his head. His face blossomed blues and violets and greens. He held her hand between both of his hands. So kind and understanding. She dropped the last bite of bacon and wiped her nose. The courage to say the next words out loud wavered in her throat. They came out on a quivering breath.

"I miss them." She wiped her puffy eyes with the back of her hand. "I miss them so much."

She fell into his waiting arms, engulfed in his warm embrace, and wept into his soft shoulder. A new well of tears was found. He held her firmly, rocked her gently.

"I know," he whispered.

Marie sobbed as quietly as she could. It wasn't very quiet. It came from a deep place she'd locked in a box and sealed shut. A box capped with resentment and bitterness for what the world had taken from her. Now it was open. She could feel it all. The grief. The sadness. The longing and sorrow. And the joy of remembering. *Where are they?*

"They are here." The Counselor held her tighter. "They are here."

※

"I'm not going to say I got robbed," Sandy shouted from the storefront. "But I got robbed."

Marie looked away from the table, wiped her cheeks with the heels of her hands. Her eyes were tender and pink. She pushed her hair back. On second thought, she decided not to face whoever came through that door. She was so soft and vulnerable. Held together with sticks and twine. *Alive.*

"Who's next?" Sandy said when Fritz opened the door. "F-Dog is a cheater."

"In a minute," the Counselor said. "Marie just started breakfast."

Fritz went to the refrigerator. Sandy's bottom scratched across the floor. He stopped near her. "I don't think she likes your cooking, Big C."

Marie sniffed and tried a smile on. Before she found the courage to face them, a hand was on her shoulder. Fritz peeked at her with big eyes and a crimped frown that dimpled his chin. She managed half a smile.

"I'm okay," she said.

He knew exactly what she meant and took her hand. His fingers were cold. She warmed them against her cheek. Now would be a perfect time for him to talk. That would come in time.

"Perhaps you can fetch the Christmas present," the Counselor said. "It is under the tree."

Marie nodded again. This time she smiled and meant it. Sandy followed her brother back to the storefront, begging for another game of chess if he didn't cheat this time. She stared at the door, waiting for him to return. Her leg started shaking. She considered going after him.

"You do not have to protect him," the Counselor said.

"I'm not." When his faceplate spattered a collage of yellows and oranges, her voice sharpened. "He's little for his age. Sometimes they pick on him. And I'm all he's got."

She shook her head and wouldn't stop; tried to shake off emerging memories. Seeing him after he was pulled from school, when a social worker delivered the news to them about their parents. The way his innocence shattered. It sounded like an expensive vase tipping over. Marie was the opposite. That day was the day she shoved her feelings in the box and welded the top closed.

The day I became the nutcracker.

"May I say something?" He was kind and generous. Genuine. Waited for her to nod. "Be there for him. If you put your heart back in the box, he will not have a sister. He can feel it. Your love is big enough for both of you. You are here now. That is what he needs."

To be here. That's where she thought she was. Here, protecting him from bullies, from Aunt Rinks. From his feelings. She hadn't been here, though. Not all of her. The journey brought her back.

Christmas isn't about what you want.

The Counselor cocked his head. The colors morphed through the spectrum.

"You knew what was going to happen, didn't you?" she said.

"That's why you told the story."

"I know a lot of things."

"You knew I was the nutcracker?"

"I knew you would find your way. Fritz, too. Of those things, I was certain."

She looked down and picked at the bandage. She thought of the empty thrones. The king and queen in their cloaks at the market, walking through the castle. She knew who they were. She asked anyway: "Was it them?"

The Counselor took her hand as if he sensed the emotions softening in her stomach. He didn't say anything, let her experience the swirling tenderness. Allowing her the space to finish her thought.

"Were they my *parents*?" she said.

"What do you think?"

She nodded and sort of laughed. She didn't want to see if he was winking. Because it wasn't them, not really. Candyland was real, but not really. But real enough for her to feel it. Real enough that Fritz had recognized the presence of their dad when he took him to find the princess. Let him wear the old cruddy, fishing hat one last time.

Real enough to say goodbye.

"What do we do now?" she said.

"You do what life requires. Sleep when you are tired." He nudged the plate. "Eat when you are hungry."

"What about Aunt Rinks?"

"She does not live here anymore."

"What?"

"Godfather has made arrangements that are in your best interest. Your aunt and uncle were poor guardians."

"They're not coming back?"

"At some point, they will. When they are done."

"Where are they?"

He stood up and squared his shoulders. He didn't answer. But she could tell by the colors on his face they were somewhere they needed to be. And they would come back. *When they are done.*

"In the meantime," he said, when he saw she understood, "I will stay with you. Is that okay?"

Living with a kind robot and a smarmy sandman? She smiled with her whole face. "I would like that."

"Then it would be my privilege, Ms. Marie. I am here to help."

❄

THE DOOR to the storefront opened. Fritz was holding a brand-new skateboard in one hand. In the other hand was a small, gift-wrapped box. This one flat and rectangular. Sandy skritched in behind him, singing merry Christmas to the "Happy Birthday" song. Fritz put her gift next to the nutcracker. Marie considered not opening it. She'd already gotten what she needed for Christmas.

"From Santa?" she said.

"Yeah, Santa," Sandy said. "Fritz and I didn't get you anything. We were all a little busy."

"What'd you get?" she asked.

Fritz held up the skateboard. It was all he'd wanted ever since their dad had done an ollie in the driveway. Santa must've known. Marie leaned in and whispered, "I heard that board is magic." He laughed through his nose and spun one of the wheels.

"What did I get?" Sandy barked. Marie held up her hand, but that didn't stop him. "I got underwear."

Tighty-whities appeared on his bottom half, which he slowly shook in a circle, throwing his sticks up in the air. The dance was silly, but it made Fritz laugh. Fritz got two things for Christmas. One was a tubby ghost made of pretend sand.

"Good to have you back," she said.

"Where'd I go?"

Maybe he didn't remember Rose Lake. Marie started to open her gift before he asked any more questions. She peeled one end. "You know, I met Santa Claus last night."

"You were asleep," Sandy said. He pretended to elbow Fritz. "She was asleep."

Marie shrugged. "One of the reindeer was there, too. The big one."

"Ronin? Yeah, right."

She opened the other end of the gift, ran her fingernail under the tape to break it. She took her time folding the paper, peeking at the Counselor. He was focused on the gift.

"Mar Mar," Sandy said, "let's go before next Christmas."

"I was just thinking about what Santa told me."

Sandy slumped in resignation. "What?"

"Christmas isn't about what you want. It's about what you need."

"Yeah, that's great. Godfather said it, so…" He rolled his branches to hurry her along.

The Counselor looked up when she said it. His face blossomed like a rose. And for a brief moment, a silver light winked. Marie smiled and winked back.

Finally, she opened the gift. Inside was a long, white ribbon. The one she'd given away to get the cookie cutter. Pate had used it as a sling for his injured arm. It seemed like so long ago. The emotions began welling up again. They would do that for a while to come and when she least expected it. Just when she thought she was empty of tears, more would flood her eyes. She was laughing and crying as Fritz tied the ribbon around her head to hold her hair back.

"You *really* like ribbons," Sandy said.

She hugged Fritz, and he hugged her back. Her heart was big enough for both of them. Their parents were here, right now. Hugging in the kitchen.

"Would it be all right if the Counselor lived with us?" she asked.

Fritz nodded. She had hoped he would talk, but that day would come. He could take all the time he wanted. When he was ready, he would cross that candy-covered bridge. The Counselor bent over to hug them. The three of them with their arms wrapped tightly around each other.

"Can I get in on this?"

Sandy squeezed in the middle. The Counselor's faceplate beamed merry color down on them. Fritz laughed, and Marie cried.

That was the day the building became a home.

39

Candy Meadow sparkled with sugary dew.

The Almond and Raisin Gate was still standing. The bridge over the chocolate creek, though, had fallen. The posts were splintered. Beyond it in the faraway valley, the castle stood beneath the blushing sky. No longer a tall mudpie. The spires glittered, and walls sparkled. Even from that distance (a week on foot, maybe two), Rinks recognized what had been beneath those dull chocolatey layers.

It was in Godfather's dumb basement.

It was the model they'd sat around when he gave her the owl clock for Christmas. The market was filled with people, not fabricated weirdos, but still... she should've known. In Candyland, the castle now showed its true self.

Vern scrambled through the grass like a dog off the leash, licking the sweet dew from his fingers, zigzagging in one direction, then another as each head won an argument of where to go next. He ended up at the Almond and Raisin Gate with his face buried in the creek. Surrounded by her army of mice, Rinks watched her ecstatic husband dip handfuls of grass into the flowing chocolate like chips in a bowl of queso.

She was not tempted in the least to lick her fingers. They were long and knobby with hair on the knuckles. No chance to find a razor. At least she didn't have a tail.

She inhaled the minty air and straightened the crown on her head. This was where she belonged. Hairy knuckles and all. This was her choice. Her sister had nothing to do with it. She would tell herself that for years to come. These were her people (or mice). They belonged to her.

I'm the Mousequeen, she thought. Then decided another name would be more fitting. A new start deserved a new name.

"Come on, Rinks." Vern looked up. Every head covered in chocolate. "The stream ain't that deep. We can wade over."

"I don't think so."

"Well, we can rebuild that bridge. It won't take much. The mice can chew down a few trees. I'll have it up in no time. We'll be at the castle before night." He looked at the sky. "Does it get dark?"

She didn't know if there was a sun or a moon. There was a lot about this new world she didn't know. She was fixing to change that.

"The castle's not ours, Vern."

"What?"

She shook her head. "We're not goin' over there."

"Where we goin'?"

General Rat whispered in Rinks's ear. She looked over her shoulder. A narrow trail went between the red-striped trees. Rinks looked at the unblemished sky. A canvas of watermelon with puffy clouds of cotton. Not a black square in sight.

This is home.

"You deserve a name," she said to the rat on her shoulder. "How does… how does Harlequin sound?" The general winced. "Too romantic. Harry? Too obvious with the, you know…" She ran a finger down the general's back. He purred like a cat. "I've got it."

She snapped her fingers and whispered to her loyal rat. His chest ballooned. He lifted his pointy nose and flung his tail around her neck.

"Well, then, shall we?" she said. "General *Harley*?"

He squeaked his approval of the name and direction. They started for the dark path that cut through Christmas Wood into uncharted territory. The mice funneled onto the trail before her. Vern came running up behind her. Lips smacking and teeth chattering.

"Where we goin', Rinks?"

"To make our own kingdom, Vern," she said. "And my name's not Rinks anymore."

He stopped short of the tree line, unsure of what that meant. That was all he'd ever called her. She turned around with cool shade covering her face. Only her long and pointed nose was in the light.

"My name is Mouserinks."

EPILOGUE

It had been almost thirty years since Sean had been home.

There was no reason to come back. His mom had remarried and moved across the country with her second husband and three stepsons whose names he couldn't always remember. His brother had joined the service out of high school, got kicked out a year later. He was on his third marriage now, living in a log cabin somewhere where it rained a lot. Sean hadn't seen him in ten years. His brother probably didn't know Sean was a granddad. If he did, he wouldn't care.

His granddaughter was riding on his shoulders with sticky fingers in his hair, steering him like a donkey across the street, bucking him to go faster. When he reared up and whinnied, she laughed so hard she tooted.

He'd played horsy for four blocks. This time of year, parking was impossible. He'd parked in a neighborhood four blocks away. They'd walked past the big fountain. The Christmas tree was decorated, and a line of people waited for Santa to come out of his trailer. Old Uncle Dan had done that job when Sean was little. He would hide in Santa's trailer until someone came for him. When the time came, he'd climb the ladder to Santa's throne and let strangers sit on his lap. He did that for five years. But then he started riding his motorcycle around town in the Santa costume. Parents didn't like that much. It ruined the magic. They canned him and took the costume away. Sean heard he sometimes came down with his own costume and got in fights.

Sean checked the time.

The sidewalks were filled with shoppers, but most of the kids were crowded on the corner. Sean remembered the first time he'd taken his daughter to this event. He'd never gone to the toy store when he was a kid. It had just reopened, and the toys were stupid. When he was married, his wife at the time had made him take his daughter. The next year, he volunteered to do it. And the year after that. He'd even gone once by himself. Stood in the corner with other adults who didn't have little kids anymore.

Now here he was, thirty years later with his granddaughter pulling his hair and farting down his back.

Twin girls had their hands cupped to the window. Inside, three mechanical elves swung wooden tools in super-slow motion. They stood in a bed of cotton with a Christmas tree covered in red lights. Hard to believe those things still worked. He remembered when he was little. They had been somewhere else, though.

An elf was handing candy out on the sidewalk. Nancy Fluss wore curly-toed shoes and a green, velvety outfit. A bell rang on her floppy hat when she turned her head. She used to sit in front of Sean in English class, and he'd cheat off her spelling quizzes. Now she taught third grade and colored her hair sandy blond. Sean didn't have much hair to dye.

"Merry, merry," Nancy sang. "And who do we have here?"

"This is Leslie Sue. Can you say hi to Santa's elf?" Sean lifted his granddaughter off his shoulders. She hid behind his leg. "It's her first time."

"First time?" Nancy knelt on the sidewalk. "Your grandfather brought you to a very special place, did you know that? I'm so happy you're here. Do you have your elf ticket?"

Grandfather. Hearing that word out loud made him wince. He put a golden ticket in his granddaughter's hand. They hadn't been selling tickets when Sean's daughter was little. Now you had to reserve a spot. Leslie Sue waved the ticket at Nancy Fluss the Elf.

"Thank you!" Nancy scared the little girl with great exaggeration. "Go on inside. That elf right there will show you to your seat. Have a wonderful ride, darling."

Nancy didn't recognize Sean. He didn't bother reminding her he was a terrible speller. He walked into the building and was greeted by old smells and loud conversation. Leslie Sue put her hands over her ears. Sean hiked her onto his hip. He was dizzy with memories. The place hadn't changed. There were toys on the shelves and stars on the ceiling. Boxes in the corners and presents being wrapped. There was a herd of helpers at the checkout. A line of customers waited for an elf to ring up their totals.

Sean saw the elf Nancy had pointed out. He was having a serious conversation with a bearded man wearing wire-framed glasses.

"Here." Sean raised Leslie Sue's hand. "Wave it over your head so he can see us."

He held her up, and she nearly touched the ceiling. From that vantage point, she would be able to see across the store. She put her thumb in her mouth.

"Wave, Leslie Sue. Wave it."

She waved the golden ticket like a little flag. The bearded man with the wire-framed glasses saw her. The elf turned his head, excused himself, and worked his way through the crowd. Sean put Leslie Sue down, who promptly hid behind his leg. The elf approached slowly. His graying hair curled from beneath his floppy green hat. He nodded at Sean, then took a knee.

"Can I tell you a secret?" he said. When she peeked out with a thumb in her mouth, he said, "You've come to a magical place. Can you feel it?" When she went back into hiding, the elf stood up and extended his hand. "Sean, how are you?"

"Good. It's been a minute."

"A few."

"This place hasn't changed."

"Unlike us, right?"

"Right." After an awkward pause, Sean added, "You still skating?"

"Skating?" The elf laughed. "No. Bones break easy now. You?"

Sean shook his head. He hadn't been on a board since high school. He was never much good at it. Not like the elf was. The bearded man was watching them.

"How's your brother?" the elf said.

"Still alive, I think. Who's the fat man?"

He turned around. The bearded man didn't look away. "Just an old friend."

"Do I know him?"

"Sort of."

Sean didn't know what to make of that. The fat man didn't look that old, so he hadn't been a high school teacher when Sean was growing up. He did seem familiar, though.

Bells began to chime.

"Better get to your seat. Let me show you."

Sean followed him down an aisle. They worked their way around a group of kids. The elf pointed to an empty spot on the floor.

"Enjoy."

"Hey, what about your one friend?" Sean said. "Is he, uh, going to make an appearance?"

Sean remembered how the *friend* had stolen the show when he took his daughter long ago. It was hard to believe. He seemed so real. And funny. Sort of mean, too. Nice to the kids but roasted some of the adults. It took the elf a second to process whom Sean was asking about. Then he reached into his pocket and held something in his hand. Leslie Sue stared at what looked like a metal walnut with stripes.

"He'll come out at the end."

Sean hoped he'd say that and couldn't wait for his granddaughter to see it. *Now that's magic.*

"Good to see you, Sean," the elf said.

"You too, Fritz."

※

SEAN STEPPED over people sitting cross-legged on the floor. He walked onto the small stage in the corner of the store and squeezed between a skinny lady wearing a sleeveless gym shirt and a sweaty man with tattooed arms. They both had a kid sitting on their laps. The one was poking at the man's tattoos like they were buttons.

There was barely enough room to cross his legs. Thank God Leslie Sue weighed as much as a puppy.

They had a good view of the woman in a rocking chair. She wore a purple blanket over her shoulders. Hands folded on her lap; she kept her eyes closed. People were talking like she was a decoration. She looked asleep, she sat so still. She looked younger than her age. Not a sprig of gray in that hair bound in a white ribbon. Smooth, rosy cheeks and toned arms. And she was older than Sean by ten years.

"See her?" He wrapped his arms around Leslie Sue. "She beat up your great-uncle Bobby."

Leslie Sue had never met her great-uncle Bobby. And didn't care who beat him up.

Bobby never admitted it. Always said he slipped on the grass, and she jumped on his back. That he didn't want to hit a girl. Sean had seen the whole thing. His brother deserved it. Sean wasn't innocent. And there was the thing that started it all. It was standing on a small table next to the rocking chair. Looked as new and young as the woman did. It couldn't be the same soldier, but it looked just like it. Sharp jacket, tall hat and bushy eyebrows.

Sean remembered taking it from Fritz that day. And how it bit his brother's finger. He deserved that, too.

Something about the room suddenly changed. Like the humidity rose or the temperature dropped. A hush fell over the crowd. In minutes, the store was silent. Except for the *screech, screech, screech* of the rocking chair. Leslie Sue's thumb fell out of her mouth. The tension had them leaning forward, ears turned.

A grin grew on the storyteller's lips. It spread to her eyes. The chair stopped rocking. It was so still even cars stopped driving past the building. Or at least Sean didn't hear them. He hugged his granddaughter. When the tension reached a breaking point, the storyteller's eyes opened.

"Once upon a time..."

AFTERWORD

I started writing book II in the Claus Universe in November of 2022. Like most stories, I had a broad story arc in mind. I hadn't planned on loss and grief being the crux of this adventure, but that's where the story went.

Six months later, I was nearing the end of the rough draft. I had just finished an emotional chapter where the main character faces the loss of her parents and the grief that consumes her. I finished that chapter on April 27, 2023.

On April 30, my son, Ben, ended his life. He was twenty-eight years old.

The only people I had lost in my life are grandparents. They were late in life when they passed. I am fifty-six years old. I have never faced loss on this level. It is a tsunami that washes everything away.

There was no sleeping that first night. After that, the shockwaves began to settle. It would take weeks for life to come back together. It's not the same. Never will be. Even today, there's a small part of me waiting to wake up from this dream.

I began writing stories over twenty years ago. It began when I wrote a story for Ben. That became the Socket Greeny trilogy. I wanted to express the difficulties of life in story form. The twentysomethings is a very difficult time. It is that jagged terrain between childhood and adulthood. For some, the journey is long and treacherous. I have always envied those who seemed to cross over without breaking a sweat. Many of us, though, become exhausted with no guarantees we will complete the journey.

I was fortunate to have met teachers during that time in my life—therapists, meditation practitioners, mentors—who buoyed me during storms, taught me how to grow up, to find purpose. It was long and arduous. For my son, it felt impossible.

Ben was funny. Entertaining.

He was creative and thoughtful. You could count on him in a pinch.

He was memorable. Never did he leave without bringing a smile.

His hugs were meaningful. His handshake solid.

He danced like a wild man when the spirit was right.

He was kind and generous. Loving and sweet. He cried easily.

Ben was a son, a brother. A boyfriend and a skater. He was not immune to struggle.

He was loved by many. Will be missed by all.

YOU DONATED TO A WORTHY CAUSE!

By purchasing this book, you have donated 10% of the profits to **Ben's Friends.**

A few months after our son, Ben, had died, we were talking about his struggles with substance abuse (as we often did). The core of his struggles was beneath the addiction, but it was impossible to address without getting clean.

He'd been skateboarding since he was six years old. Skaters were his people. His community. His family outside his family. But there just wasn't support to be sober.

By total chance, we saw a flier for a support group. It was started by two people in the Charleston area and has since gone nationwide. They began the program after a friend who struggled with addiction had passed. His name was Ben.

Ben's Friends is a community of chefs, bartenders, line cooks, servers, sommeliers, host and hostesses, GMs and owners who have found or are seeking sobriety.

Their mission is to offer community, hope and a path forward for those struggling with substance abuse and addiction. While this wasn't the skateboard community, it checked all the boxes for what we want to support.

You Donated To A Worthy Cause!

And it's called Ben's Friends.

https://www.bensfriendshope.com/

THE CLAUS UNIVERSE

Don't stop now. The rest of the Claus Universe is waiting.

https://bertauski.com/claus/

Printed in Great Britain
by Amazon